Praise for the Christi:

The Wond

"Book five in the Christiansen Family series is as compelling and delightful as its predecessors. . . . Faith, family, and all the complexities of life's roller-coaster ride can be found in this engaging romance."

BOOKREPORTER.COM

"The contemporary romances in the Christiansen Family series are swoonworthy, but they have a subtle, edgy realness that adds depth, too. . . . This story was impossible to put down. . . . Get this book for yourself and see why!"

SERENA CHASE, *USA TODAY*

"Warren is truly gifted with her characterization and her ability to write a spiritual message that is organic to the story."

ROMANTIC TIMES

"This novel confronts the importance of honesty and trust in relationships, the devastation that secrets can wreak, and the hope that forgiveness brings. Readers will delight in the continued antics of the Christiansens and revel in the devotion to family, community, and faith that underpins this series."

RELZ REVIEWZ

Always on My Mind

"The fourth book in Warren's Christiansen Family series shows this writer's gift for creating flawed yet redeemable characters. . . . As always, the spiritual message shines and is an integral, purposeful part of the story."

ROMANTIC TIMES

"Readers will . . . delight in the romance that unfolds in spite of Casper's and Raina's intentions."

BOOKLIST

"*Always on My Mind* is a beautiful story filled with hope and faith that is captivating and powerful from page 1 to the very end."

FRESH FICTION

When I Fall in Love

"[*When I Fall in Love* is] an exquisite romance. Profoundly touching on the topic of facing fears, this book is a true gem."

ROMANTIC TIMES

"Readers who are already enamored of the sprawling Christiansen clan will feel even more connected, while those new to Warren will be brought right into the fold."

BOOKLIST

"Warren has a knack for creating captivating and relatable characters that pull the reader deep into the story."

RADIANT LIT

It Had to Be You

"*It Had to Be You* is a sigh-worthy, coming-into-her-own romance highlighting the importance of family, the necessity of faith, and how losing yourself for the right reasons can open your heart to something beautiful."

SERENA CHASE, *USA TODAY*

"This character-driven tale with a beautiful love story . . . gives excellent spiritual insight and a gorgeously written look at what it means to surrender and let go."

ROMANTIC TIMES

"Susan May Warren delivers another beautiful, hope-filled story of faith that makes the reader fall further in love with this captivating and intriguing family. . . . Powerful storytelling gripped me from beginning to end . . . [and] lovable characters ensure that the reader becomes invested in their lives."

RADIANT LIT

"A gem of a story, threaded with truth and hope, laughter and romance. Susan May Warren brings the Christiansen family to life, as if they might be my family or yours, with her smooth writing and engaging storytelling."

RACHEL HAUCK, BESTSELLING AUTHOR OF *THE WEDDING DRESS*

Take a Chance on Me

"Warren's new series launch has it all: romance, suspense, and intrigue. It is sure to please her many fans and win her new readers, especially those who enjoy Terri Blackstock."

LIBRARY JOURNAL

"Warren . . . has crafted an engaging tale of romance, rivalry, and the power of forgiveness."

PUBLISHERS WEEKLY

"Warren once again creates a compelling community full of vivid individuals whose anguish and dreams are so real and relatable, readers will long for every character to attain the freedom their hearts desire."

BOOKLIST

"A compelling story of forgiveness and redemption, *Take a Chance on Me* will have readers taking a chance on each beloved character!"

CBA RETAILERS + RESOURCES

"Warren's latest is a touching tale of love discovered and the meaning of family."

ROMANTIC TIMES

YOU'RE THE ONE THAT I WANT

You're the One

One

That

Want

a
Christiansen Family
novel

SUSAN MAY
WARREN

Christy Award–winning author

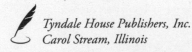
Tyndale House Publishers, Inc.
Carol Stream, Illinois

Visit Tyndale online at www.tyndale.com.

Visit Susan May Warren's website at www.susanmaywarren.com.

TYNDALE and Tyndale's quill logo are registered trademarks of Tyndale House Publishers, Inc.

You're the One That I Want

Designed by Jennifer Phelps

Edited by Sarah Mason Rische

Published in association with the literary agency of The Steve Laube Agency, 5025 N. Central Ave., #635, Phoenix, AZ 85012.

Scripture quotations are taken from the *Holy Bible*, New Living Translation, copyright © 1996, 2004, 2015 by Tyndale House Foundation. Used by permission of Tyndale House Publishers, Inc., Carol Stream, Illinois 60188. All rights reserved.

You're the One That I Want is a work of fiction. Where real people, events, establishments, organizations, or locales appear, they are used fictitiously. All other elements of the novel are drawn from the author's imagination.

Library of Congress Cataloging-in-Publication Data

Warren, Susan May, date.
 You're the one that I want : a Christiansen family novel / Susan May Warren.
  pages ; cm. — (Christiansen family)
  ISBN 978-1-4143-7846-6 (sc : alk. paper)
I. Title. II. Title: You are the one that I want.
  PS3623.A865Y685 2016
  813'.6—dc23   2015032258

Printed in the United States of America

22   21   20   19   18   17   16
7   6   5   4   3   2   1

For Your glory, Lord

ACKNOWLEDGMENTS

I JUST LOVE THIS SERIES. I love the characters, the plots, the themes . . . It's turned out better than I could have asked or imagined, and I have so many people to thank for their help! My deepest gratitude goes out to the following people:

Rachel Hauck, my writing partner, who pesters me with that ultimate question: But *why*?

David Warren, my in-house story crafter, who helped me get Owen and Casper's brotherly relationship right. "But, Mom, brothers love each other one second, and the next they want to throttle each other." Right. Got it. Thank you!

Karen Watson, fantastic editor and captain of the ship, who kept us going in the right direction. Thank you for the gift of partnering with me on this series!

Sarah Mason Rische, my line editor, who has the amazing ability to get inside the stories to pull out the best elements, smooth out my prose, and turn the story from raw-edged to sparkling. Wow.

Steve Laube, my agent, soft-spoken, wise, and the guy who believes in me. Thank you.

Sarah Erredge and Neil (her cute hubby), Peter Warren, and Noah Warren, who land on the pages with their antics more often than not. Thank you for helping me write what I know!

Andrew Warren. The guy who taught me what grace looks like in the flesh. Where you are, I am home.

And my amazing readers, who continually encourage me to dig deep, write stories of family and faith, and remind me that we are all in the journey together. Thank you for blessing me with your friendship and enthusiasm!

Finally, yes, the God of heaven, who, as I struggle through every scene, shows up to shower upon me truth and His words on the page. I am overwhelmed by the grace, responsibility, and joy of this calling. Thank You.

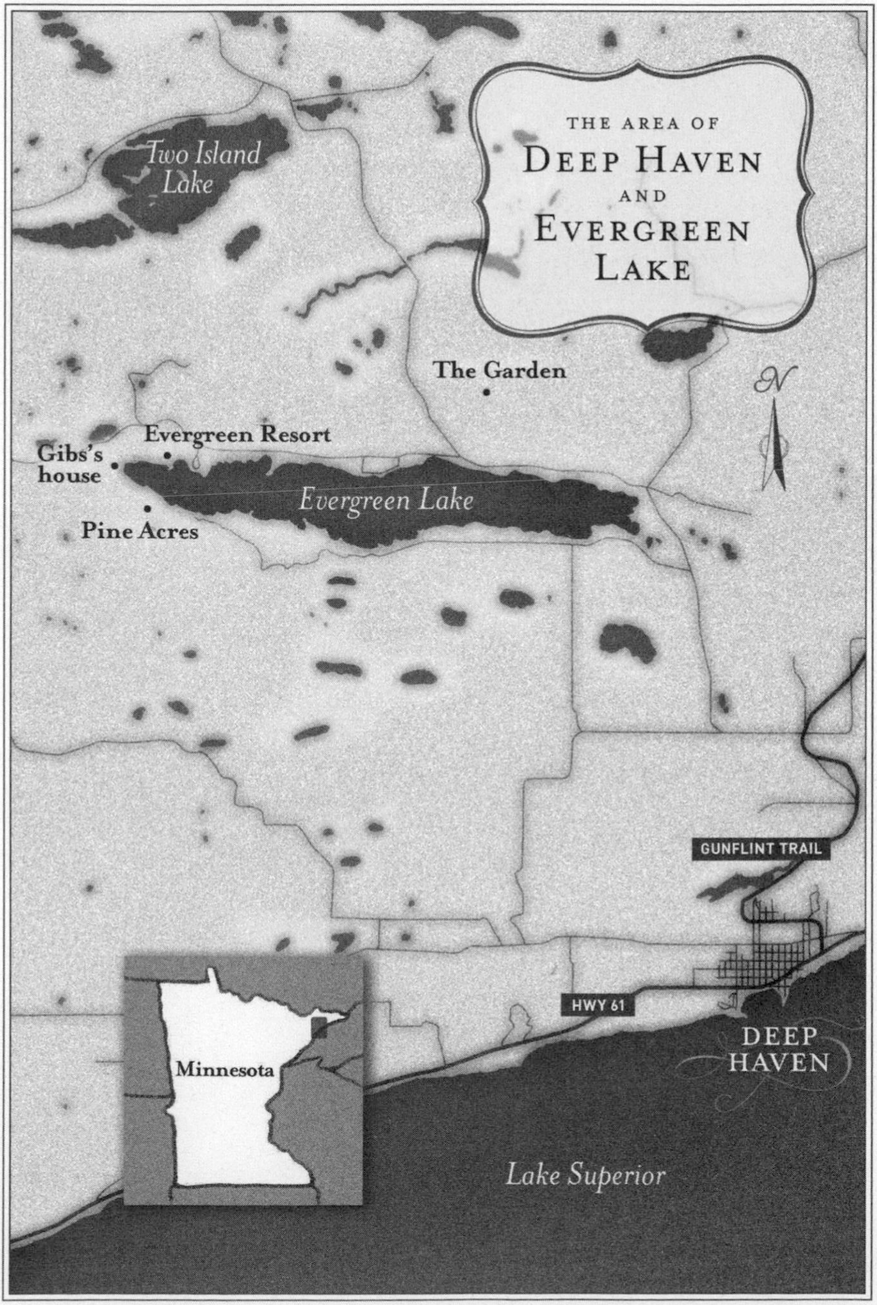

THE AREA OF
DEEP HAVEN
AND
EVERGREEN LAKE

Two Island Lake

The Garden

Evergreen Resort

Gibs's house

Pine Acres

Evergreen Lake

N

GUNFLINT TRAIL

HWY 61

DEEP HAVEN

Minnesota

Lake Superior

My dearest Owen,

From the moment I first held you in my arms, I knew you were destined to leave us and make your own mark on the world. Whether it was your curiosity, your desire to keep up with—and surpass—your brothers, or your insistence that you could do it "by myself," I knew that the moment I let go of your hand, you would follow your heart into adventure.

Armed with your charming smile and your desire to confront and conquer your challenges, you can become anyone you want to be. You are so much like your older brother Darek—bearing his determination, his focus. And also like Casper, with your thirst to discover something beyond the borders of Evergreen Resort. But unlike them, you also have a zealous, no-holds-barred passion for life. It's what will propel you into an amazing future, no matter what you do.

However, it will also litter mistakes in your wake. And, I fear, regret. Because a person doesn't plunge himself into life without the occasional misstep. Without wanting to reel back time and rethink, redo, relive.

It is a normal, expected part of life to make mistakes. But in order to live without the haunting voice of regret, you must learn to forgive yourself. To embrace mercy. To open your eyes and see God in your past and His grace in your future.

Your mistakes don't define you. Your past doesn't define

you. You are not the sum of your bad decisions. You are the decision you make right now. You are the decisions you will make tomorrow.

Most of all, you are an impulsive, valiant, giant-hearted child of God, deeply loved, created to be exactly the person you are.

God has a special place in His heart for messy, passionate, live-out-loud people. The young. The inexperienced. The blindly brave. The ones who dive in, not looking back, believing they can slay giants with a stone.

Because God loves faith. The wild belief that yes, everything will work out for our good, according to God's plan, if we simply remember we are safe in His hands.

And this, perhaps, is the gift you bring to us. A life of faith. Of believing big, hoping long, and swan diving into life.

Do not feel guilty for wanting to fly from the nest. You were created to soar.

And I, for one, can't wait to watch.

Your loving mother

CHAPTER I

No one died tonight, not if she could help it.

Except Scotty McFlynn could feel tragedy in her bones, just like she could feel the shift in the wind. Instincts—like the kind that directed her to a crab-filled pot o' gold on the bed of the Bering Sea. Or the kind that told her a storm hedged against the darkening horizon, the sky bruised and bloody as the sun surrendered to the gloomy, fractious night.

Yes, she could taste the doom hovering behind the sleet that hammered the deck of the F/V *Wilhelmina*, now crashing through the rising swells. Freezing waves soaked the 108-foot vessel, tossing frozen boulders across the deck like bowling balls and glazing the surface into a rink of black ice.

She couldn't shake the pervasive feeling in her gut that tonight someone was going overboard.

Pellets of ice pinged her face as the boat turned windward. She'd long ago lost the ability to close her fist in her rubberized gloves—a condition fishermen called the claw—and her feet clunked along like granite in her boots. But they had four more pots to drag from the sea, empty, sort, and reset before she could grab a minute of shut-eye, then relieve her father at the helm for the evening watch.

Old Red's last run, and she intended to make it his best. Forty-eight hours until their delivery deadline, and for the first time since his heart attack, they just might meet their quota.

"Where's my bait?" deck boss Juke Hansen bellowed, over the thunder of the waves and the clanging of the crab pot against the hydraulic lift, to the eighteen-year-old greenhorn hauling the bait from the chopper.

Greenie—she'd forgotten his real name—dragged the herring bag and two fat cod on a bait line over to the open pot, climbed inside, and hooked the line to the middle.

Once he climbed out, two more deckhands, Carpie and Owen, closed the trap door, and the lift levered the pot up and over the edge of the boat, dropping it into the sea with an epic splash.

Juke threw in the shot line, the rope uncoiling into the frothy darkness as the trap descended six hundred feet to the seabed. Carpie followed with the toss of a buoy, marking the pot set.

The crew sank back, hiding against the wheelhouse, holding on as Old Red motored the boat into a trough and up the next wave, toward the next buoy along this seven-mile line of pots.

Scotty shot a glance at Owen, the other greenhorn, although he'd run "opies," opilio snow crab, with her father back in January, while she'd been stuck in Homer. He'd stayed at the rail, ready to catch the next pot they reeled in, his bearded face hard against the brutal spray.

If she had a say, she might have kicked him off the boat on day one, when he'd assumed she was their cook.

"A crab boat's no place for a girl." Yeah, she'd walked into that comment dropped to the ship's engineer, Ned Carpenter—Carpie—while they repaired pots on the loading dock.

"First mate, relief skipper, or 'Yes, sir,' will do," Scotty had snapped at Owen.

She'd caught snippets of Carpie's explanation as she stalked toward the wheelhouse. *Part owner. Captain's daughter. Tough as nails.*

You betcha.

But after three weeks of working side by side, watching Owen clean the deck every morning, going at the accumulated ice with a sledge to clear off the ropes as the lethal ocean splintered around him, she'd decided maybe he could stick around.

He worked like a man with something to prove.

And prove himself he had. He looked every inch the crusty crabber with his thick beard, rich with russet highlights to match his curly golden locks that hung nearly to his shoulders, usually tamed by a hand-knit stocking cap. Despite the eye patch that earned him an occasional "Aye, aye, matey," she could admit he didn't exactly send her running when he peeled off his cold-weather gear down to sweatpants, suspenders, and a T-shirt that did just fine outlining all the hard work he put in hauling in eight-hundred-pound pots.

However, hiding behind his yes-sir attitude and that reserved sort of chuckle that held him a step back from the rest of the crew, she recognized a lingering darkness.

She'd bet her badge that he had a story to tell. But she had no desire to resume her detective role quite yet. She'd live and let live, as long as he didn't stir up any trouble.

Like the kind that ignited, deep inside, when she caught his dark-blue gaze trailing her. In all her years working the crab seasons with her father, never once had she found herself wishing she didn't garb herself as one of the guys. Wearing orange bib overalls, a stained Homer PD gimme cap, no makeup, her dark hair pulled back and unwashed for days, she could pass for a wiry but tough eighteen-year-old boy.

But Old Red wouldn't allow it any other way. Which meant that as one of the guys, she couldn't in the least smile back at Owen, linger in the galley as he read one of her father's worn novels, or even play a game of rummy as the boat pitched around them, weathering a gale.

And after their scheduled delivery only forty-eight hours from now, Owen would walk off the pier, thirty grand in his pocket, and out of her life.

Not that she cared.

Caring only meant she'd eventually get hurt.

"Pot comin' in!" Owen threw out the grappling hook, snagged the buoy line, and dragged it in, water washing over the deck. She guessed the swells were at twenty-plus feet now and hazarded a glance at the wheelhouse, where she knew her father would be fighting to keep the boat righted and directed into the waves.

Owen affixed the shot line to the winch, and Juke began to hoist the pot from the depths. Trailing seagulls cried in the darkness—an omen, maybe—and Scotty shivered as the spray hit her face. Heavy yellow sodium lights from the wheelhouse sent puddles into the inky ocean.

The winch groaned as Carpie and Owen lined up to grab the swinging pot and direct it onto the hydraulic bed.

To survive out here, you gotta have instincts. You gotta know where the crane is, anticipate which way the pot's going to swing. It's gotta come from inside, in your bones, if you wanna be a crab fisherman.

Old Red's words rang in her ears, remembered from nearly ten years ago when he'd agreed to let her work her first season. She'd broken two fingers, nearly washed overboard, frostbitten her fingertips, and collapsed with fatigue, while Old Red had just stood by, a gleam of challenge in his weathered eyes.

Now she knew why.

Because accidents happened after a long grind, when exhaustion blurred vision, froze reflexes, and she had to hone her instincts if she wanted, someday, to captain her own fishing vessel.

The pot came up dripping, snow crab hanging from the webbing, jammed half-full with pancakes—flat, huge male crab.

Owen grabbed one edge of the pot, guiding it in.

"Yee-haw!" This from Greenie, who had been counting his fortunes like he'd never heard of Kenny Rogers. "Must be more than two hundred crab in there!" He edged the table toward the hydraulic lift as the pot swung in.

"Greenie! Watch out!" Scotty screamed above the roar of the sea, lunging at the kid.

Owen was faster. He kicked the kid hard enough to send him sprawling into Scotty's arms, just as the pot slammed against the table.

An inch from the ghost of Greenie's head.

The kid swore at Owen, untangling himself from Scotty on the icy deck.

Owen ignored him, fighting the pot, the choppy sea, the pitch of the boat. The swell lifted them, slammed them hard into the trough, and the pot unseated, jerked by the winch.

"Owen!"

"I got it!"

Only he didn't, not with the wave forming behind him, the foamy sea gathering to knock them over. Owen couldn't see it—not with his patched eye. It took instinct and peripheral vision to spot the wave breaking.

The green water would wash him overboard. Four minutes, tops, and he'd perish.

Scotty kicked Greenie away, scrambled to her feet. "Owen, look out!"

He was built like a tree, but she tackled him like a linebacker, breaking his hold on the pot as it jerked up with the swell of the wave.

The pot swung up, then out over the ocean.

Owen slammed against the railing, one arm around Scotty as the freezing water crashed over them. She closed her eyes and hung on. To Owen, to the railing. Anything to get purchase as the boat shuddered, water streaming off the deck. It stole her breath, left her numb, weak. Shaking.

Too aware of Owen's arm tightening around her.

She blinked the water from her eyes as his voice rose over the rush of the waves.

"You okay?"

"I think so. Are you hurt?"

"That pot would have knocked me overboard."

"Maybe," she said, pushing away from him.

He grabbed at the pot, now swinging back over the boat, snagged it, and set it on the lift, working fast to secure it, to unhook it from the winch.

Scotty gestured to Greenie, and he shoved the sorting table under the pot as the trap door opened. Fat, flat crab poured onto the table, writhing, pincers snapping. Greenie and Carpie leaned over, began sorting the larger from the smaller, ineligible crab.

She moved to help but felt a hand on her arm.

"Scotty—" Owen turned her to face him. "Not *maybe*. I *would* be dead right now."

His blue-eyed gaze had the power to steal her words out from under her. Yes, the man screamed trouble, right here, on the high seas.

She managed a cool shrug. "That's what shipmates do. Watch each other's back."

And she meant it. Because no one died tonight.

That's what shipmates do.

Scotty's voice ticked through Owen's head, a background rhythm as he replayed every second of the way she'd jerked him away from the swinging pot. Saved his miserable life.

And it all funneled down to one raw, unedited truth.

He didn't want to be just her shipmate. No way, nohow. Because *she* might see herself as one of the crew—or rather the relief skipper, "yes, sir"—but he'd been watching.

Scotty McFlynn had a smile that could light up the darkest Arctic night and a laugh that, rare though it might be, could find his raw places and make him forget his sins, believe in a better tomorrow. She stood just below his chin but somehow seemed taller when she slid into the captain's chair or emerged on deck to fill in as a deckhand.

He'd probably fallen in love with her that first day, when she'd put him to rights and he realized that he'd finally met a girl who didn't see him for his past or for the magnetic, trouble-on-a-motorcycle aura he'd worn since fleeing the world of professional hockey.

She only saw a drifter, a hard worker, a guy trying to make sense of the cards life dealt him.

For the first time since losing everything, he felt the old ignition inside him, the adrenaline he'd taste before a game, the challenge of going one-on-one against a goalie, and the sense that victory might be right there for the taking, if he reached.

If he named it, he'd call it hope.

But he didn't exactly know what that hope would look like after they got off the ship. A date? Right, he'd ask Scotty McFlynn out for what—dinner? Dancing?

More like big-game hunting.

Or perhaps that's just what she wanted Carpie, Greenie, and Juke to think. Maybe she wore her tough-girl attitude as armor. After all, it couldn't be easy to spend a month with grimy sea dogs desperate for the company of the ladies they left behind.

As if he'd conjured her up, Scotty made her way down the stairs from the wheelhouse into the galley, where the guys sat around the table, tucked onto benches, nursing a bracing sludge Carpie called coffee.

"We've got roughly two hours of sack time before we round back up to the head of the line. We have some weather coming in, and no time to spare, so I suggest you each crawl into your bunk and find your happy place."

She'd probably been up with the skipper—her old man, Red—charting the lines, reading the weather.

Owen watched as Greenie flexed his hands. "I can't close them all the way," the kid said, looking wan and ragged.

An old memory surfaced about practicing so long he could no

longer hold his hockey stick. But Owen took a sip of coffee, shaking the story away. No one knew about his life before he signed on to the F/V *Wilhelmina*, and he meant to keep it that way.

Scotty had shucked off her jacket, wore a sweatshirt and a baseball hat, her long black ponytail trailing out the back. Now she opened the fridge, stared long into it, then finally closed it and headed into her private bunk area, the one concession to having a female on board.

"I can't wait to get home," Carpie said, getting up. A polar bear of a man, he wore his white hair long, his beard in a thick white goatee.

Home. The word settled over the crew, and an ache swept through Owen.

"My mom's already ordered my ticket. Eight hundred bucks, straight from Anchorage to Des Moines," Greenie said, sounding puny, not at all like the cocky redneck he pretended to be.

Des Moines, just a few hours south of Minnesota. Where Owen should probably go after they docked.

Or maybe he should keep moving. It wasn't like anyone really missed him after what he'd done.

Juke and Greenie got up, headed to their bunks. Owen dumped the coffee sludge into the sink, then rinsed his cup and set it on the sideboard.

He had turned toward the bunk area when he heard a moan behind him, coming from beyond Scotty's curtain.

Owen paused, his heart thumping. But he heard it again, short, low, but enough that, without thinking, he swept open the curtain.

Scotty looked up, her eyes wide, frozen in the act of taking off her sweatshirt. She'd pulled her hat off, freeing her thick sable hair to cascade over her shoulder. "What are you doing here?"

"You're . . . moaning." That sounded awkward, and now he wanted to back away before anyone got hurt.

Or maybe not, because he saw the tiniest hint of pain around her eyes. He'd been an athlete long enough to know when someone was hiding an injury.

"I'm fine."

"You're not fine." He stepped into the room. "Shut up and let me help."

Her mouth tightened into a knot of annoyance, but she let him take the arm of her sweatshirt and pull as she eased out of it.

One of her eyes closed in a wince and she cradled her arm to her body.

Dropping the sweatshirt on the bunk behind her, Owen was aware suddenly of how her T-shirt clung to the curves she hid beneath her bulky layers. "Let me see."

"I'm fine."

"You're not fine, so quit saying that and let me see." He gave the overhead light a tug and illumination splashed over them. He gently took her arm, seeing now where an ugly bruise knotted in her upper arm.

"This happened when we slammed against the rail, didn't it?"

"It's no biggie." She made to pull her arm away, but he pressed his hand over the injury. Her arm radiated heat; his cool hand acted like an ice pack.

"You probably bruised the muscle, maybe even the bone the way the blood is pooling here. You could use some ice and some rest."

"We have work to do. My father is exhausted, and I told him I'd spell him." But she didn't pull her arm away, just let his hand cradle it, cooling the muscle.

She had such soft, smooth skin. And the way she caught her bottom lip in her teeth . . .

Yeah, maybe he should leave because her bunk room seemed to have shrunk around them. In fact, if the boat lurched the wrong direction—

A creak and Owen found himself off-balance as the *Wilhelmina* betrayed him, keeling over with the chop of the ocean. He braced himself on her upper bunk before he pitched into Scotty.

But she'd grabbed ahold of his shirt to keep herself from falling back. His hand left her arm, curled around her waist, caught her up to him.

And in that second, he caught a whiff of her skin, some sweet scent that slammed into him like a sharp check into the boards. Good grief, how long had it been since he'd held a woman in his arms?

He knew exactly how long. Remembered every sordid, regrettable detail. But this was different. *He* was different—or trying to be.

Then the boat rocked back and Scotty fell against him. Owen caught her wrist, helping her right herself. The pulse there thundered, matching his own.

A smile slid up his face. Well, well. So perhaps he should plan dinner . . . maybe even dancing?

Clearly his thoughts showed on his face because she yanked her wrist away. "Get out."

"Scotty—"

"'Yes, sir,' is the right answer."

He didn't know what to name the emotion that shot through him. Frustration? Tenderness? Maybe a combination of both as he tamped down the hot flare of desire. "C'mon, Scotty . . ."

She untangled herself from his grasp, not looking at him. "Go. Before anyone starts getting ideas."

His lips tightened. "Yes, *sir*."

She shot him a look, and he instantly regretted his tone. Owen softened his voice. "At least go easy on that arm. Get some ice on it."

He might need some himself, actually.

"I'm fine. You just take care of yourself."

He knew how to do that real well and, frankly, was tired of it.

Owen let the curtain fall behind him, his heart still hammering, pretty sure he should turn around, barge his way back in, and figure out what might be out there for them, if either of them had the guts to reach for it.

But the memory of being that guy before, cajoling his way into a woman's life, leaving her heart in shambles, tasted raw and sour.

So he stumbled back to his bunk, climbed in, and fought the ever-lingering memory of his brother, his best friend, connecting with a right hook to his face.

A right hook he'd deserved, even if it had taken him nearly a year to admit it.

Owen pulled his sleeping bag over him and huddled in the chill, praying for sleep. Because there, in his dreams, he could make everything right.

He could go home.

"Red, it's my watch. Give me the helm before you land in the hospital again."

Scotty stood in the doorway to the wheelhouse, thick with smoke from her father's flattened pack of Winstons, fatigue a blurry memory after tossing in her bunk for an hour.

Thank you oh so much, Owen Christiansen, for stirring up feelings forbidden on a crab boat, feelings she'd spent a decade learning how to avoid.

Mr. Eye Patch wasn't the first good-looking, muscle-built drifter they'd hired aboard the *Wilhelmina*. Just the first one with manners. And a smile that did crazy things to her pulse.

The way he'd held her arm, soft, like a caress . . . "Pop, really—"

"Not *Pop*, not here." Red tamped out the cigarette in his ashtray, overflowing now. Evidence of the weather rolling in. Two computer screens lit up the room with Doppler, and over the radio, other crab boats called in positions and updates.

Right. Not *Pop*. She knew better. "You haven't slept in thirty-six hours. Let me skipper, just for an hour."

It felt like arguing with a grizzly, and she treaded around the edges, not wanting to provoke him. He possessed the ability to take her—and any of his crew—down with a string of salty words that could curdle a pirate's blood. And in a raspy, deep-throated voice that sounded like the motor on his low-riding Harley Fat Bob.

"We're heading into a mess. Everything changes when you get weather—I need to stay put. You get some shut-eye—"

"I'm fine, and I've skippered this boat through worse, if you remember."

He shot her a look, and she didn't care that she'd dredged up the past, made him take a look at his pride, his fears. Someone had to keep them both alive. Still, even in that glance, the old man looked haggard, lines drawn down his face, his brown eyes bagged with fatigue. He'd gained weight despite the doctor's orders, a result of Scotty taking over his hands-on duties, maybe, or his onshore diet that consisted too often of the special down at the Moosehead Tavern—wings, chips, and the double-decker jalapeño burger.

But what did she expect? Red McFlynn had the skin of an old snow crab, tough and impenetrable. He ran his boat with a steel hand, demanding as much from himself as he did his crew.

In fact, he spent more time on deck, hauling in pots, throwing in line, chopping bait, than any skipper she knew, an old-school captain who abided by his rule to know every inch of his boat, the shortcuts of his crew.

Scotty had learned everything she knew about fishing from Old Red. Everything about life, really.

Shoot straight. Pay your debts. Expect no compromise.

Trust few.

And most importantly, no crying.

She had, however, also learned how to wrestle the helm away from his steel-clawed grip.

"We'll need you later, when the wind's blowing forty-five and we have thirty-five-foot swells. I can't hold the boat in that weather."

A lie because she knew exactly how to sail the *Willie*. Knew exactly how to pilot the single-screw into four-story swells, the delicate dance of throttle and jog stick that feathered a fishing boat into a wave. Knew how to judge the weight, whether the boat was heavy with crab or corky in the water. Knew how to make the waves work for her, instead of fighting them.

She knew not to take a wave on the starboard side, where her guys worked the pots and the lower rail meant a wave could wash them right over. But take too many waves on the port side and it would jerk them off course.

And she knew how to recognize "slack tank," or partially filled crab tanks, and the dangerous rhythm of water sloshing inside the boat that could roll it over, send it to the bottom.

In short, she understood the delicate physics it took to keep them alive, swell after swell, in fifty-knot winds, blinding sleet, and the unpredictable roll of the icy black water that had entombed so many of their friends.

She picked up his crumpled pack of Winstons, handed it to him. "I can't sleep anyway, and they'll need me down there if you're right about the weather, so get in your rack and get some sleep. Just an hour. Please."

She added a softness at the end of her sentence, let it linger long enough for Red to sigh.

"Just an hour. Wake me when we reach the tip of the string." He slid off the chair, lumbered into the nearby captain's room, and shut the door. She heard a groan, followed by the creak of the bunk as he settled into it.

One hour to make sure they stayed on course, to batten down the ship in case the gale turned lethal. Scotty took the captain's chair, already checking the weather, the maps. They were moving at 10.3 knots, 1600 RPM, and the radar showed three other ships in their vicinity and moving south, toward port.

Which maybe they should be doing.

She throttled back as the *Wilhelmina* dipped into a trough, not wanting to ram the bow into the crest of the next wave. Or bury the bow in the trough, raising the propeller out of the water.

In her worst nightmares, the boat yawed to one side and breached or even pitchpoled, flipping end over end.

She'd seen it happen once, or rather, been on the rescue end of trying to locate survivors.

She throttled back even more, glancing at Red's cabin. Right now, they'd be safer slowing down to bare steerage and cutting through the waves at forty-five degrees, riding the swells as they tacked their way north. Sure, it might slow their trip, but they'd live.

Red had already set their course, plugged it into the VMS, and she kept her eyes on the radar, the navigation, a green hue washing the wooden cabin.

"I figured you were at the helm." Carpie edged into the wheelhouse. "The ship slowed, and I don't feel quite so ill."

"I thought you were sleeping."

"Naw. Praying, mostly."

Carpie, always the religious one. Maybe that's why Red kept him on, twenty years now, a fixture on the *Willie*. The connection to whoever might be up there.

"Whatever floats your boat, Carp."

A wave splashed over the bow, jarring the boat, and Scotty wrestled to slow their speed into the trough.

"It's what keeps us all afloat, Scotty. God's with us, always."

"Right. Why don't you get some sleep—"

"Not yet. I got this itch, honey, that says something's going to happen tonight, and I can't let it go down without talking to you."

Ah, no. Their yearly "Jesus loves you" talk. "I'm too old, seen too much to believe in the great Santa Claus in the sky. Save your breath, Carp. Better yet, go preach to Greenie. Or maybe Owen. He seems like he might be carrying around some baggage."

"Something in his eyes, isn't it? Like he's looking over his shoulder." Carpie reached over to grab the ashtray, emptied it in the trash. "There's something okay about that boy, though. I feel it."

The swells seemed to be speeding up, and Scotty checked her instruments. "Waves are at thirty feet."

"I wish we hadn't thrown that last line."

She blew out a breath. "I know Red hasn't said anything, but it's his last run. We need to reach our limit."

Carpie stilled, and she felt his old eyes on her as she continued, "The boat's in hock after Red's heart attack. If he doesn't pull in a decent catch, he'll never climb out of debt."

"And you—you're taking over the *Willie*, right?"

She adjusted the throttle, her gaze on the gauge. "No. I . . . I don't know." What could she say, really? She didn't have the cash to buy the old man out but—

"Please tell me you're not going back on the job."

"I know you don't believe this, but I actually like being a cop."

"No, you don't. Not anymore. The shooting changed you."

"It didn't change me. Just flushed the glamour from my eyes. Besides, being a cop is all I got. The job and this boat, and I can't have the boat, so . . ."

"Being a cop nearly killed you, Scotty!"

She glanced at him, past him, toward the galley, where his voice surely echoed. "Take it down a notch, Carp. I just didn't handle it well."

"And how could you? You saw your best friend killed in front of your eyes. You had to shoot a family member."

"Distant cousin. I hardly knew Evan."

"You knew him well enough to let it shake you. And I get it. Nobody heals from seeing their best friend murdered. Not without God."

"Again with the religion. I know you mean well, Carp, but I don't need God's help. Yeah, I will admit it was rough, that I went down some dark places, but I'm okay. And I don't need help from a God who hasn't bothered to show up in my life, like . . . *ever*. So thanks. I'm just fine without God's help."

He sighed and she knew it was coming. Braced herself as his low words began.

"Remind me, but that was you I hauled out of the Moosehead six months ago, hiding the fact that you could barely walk, right?"

"It was just that one time—"

"I know. But in Alaska, once can get you dead. Listen, I know you think you're fine alone, and yes, you've picked yourself up, been cleared to go back to work. But I can't help but worry, Scotty. You can't live holding people at arm's length. We need people."

"Alone seemed to work okay for Red."

"Really? You think it's okay that he can count the sum total of his friends on his closed fist?"

"Enough. You know what being Red's daughter has taught me? That there is no room for crying. Life happens. People die. There're no fairy tales or happy endings. It's the way it is, and if I want to survive, I can't let people get close enough to hurt me. So yeah, I have a job waiting for me in Anchorage after this run, and I plan on taking it. Now if you'll excuse me, my job tonight is keeping you and everyone else on this ship alive."

The boat crested another wave, and this time she throttled down across the back side to beat the next crest.

By the time she topped it, turned the boat to tack her way across the next wave, Carpie had disappeared.

Probably to go pray for her lost soul.

The nudge broke Owen free of the darkness, and he blinked awake.

"Time to work," Juke said.

Owen glanced at the clock: 8 p.m. It felt like he'd dropped off seconds ago; how had two hours passed? Kicking out of his sleeping bag, he ran his hands over his face, scrubbing away the exhaustion.

He'd been on this ride before—a thirty-six-hour grind hauling in the last of the pots before heading back to Dutch Harbor.

Nothing compared to it—not hours of practice in the juniors, not a heavy workout in the weight room, not even the grimy, sweaty hours he'd spent fighting wildland fires with the Jude County Hotshots.

Carpie handed him a cup of coffee as Owen leaned against the galley doorframe, trying to hold his eyes open.

"I know," Carpie said. "I just got to the good part in my dream. Going home, seeing the wife. One last stretch and I'm kissing dry land."

The waves unseated Owen, and he grabbed the doorframe as his coffee spilled onto his shirt. He bit back a word, made a face. Setting the coffee down, he dragged his T-shirt over his head and unfortunately stood bare-chested as Scotty came down the stairs.

She glanced at him, lingering a moment before she addressed the crew, still wiping sleep from their eyes.

Owen grabbed another shirt from the tangle of clothes in his duffel, this one cold and a little smelly, and pulled it on as she spoke.

"Okay, guys, it's blowing forty-five, sleeting, and getting gnarly out there. The swells are really starting to stack up, and I've decided we're not taking any chances." She carried what looked like a modified survival suit and tossed it at Juke. "Happy birthday, everyone gets a pretty orange suit."

"I'm not wearing this," Juke said. "It's too thick and hard to work in. Can't we just wear our life jackets?"

"It's made to work in. It's just like a dry suit the military wears. Made of neoprene, and it'll keep you dry and warm if you should go in. And it acts as a flotation device. It should keep you above water long enough to be rescued. Red special ordered them—"

"No, *you* special ordered them," Carpie said. "And we thank you for it."

"Speak for yourself," Juke said.

"I promise you can work in this. Maybe not as fast, but better safe than sorry."

"I'm already sorry," Juke said.

"Stuff it, Juke. You go over, you have about thirty seconds before the waves take you out of reach of the boat. Another four minutes and you're dead. This suit could save your life—at least long enough for us to find you and pull you in. So the right answer is 'Yes, sir.'"

Owen raised an eyebrow as Scotty picked up another suit and tossed it at him. He caught it. "Yes, sir."

She didn't spare him a look. "Listen, we've only had two over-boards on the *Wilhelmina* in twenty years. Both were from rough weather and deckhands taking chances. Not today."

Greenie took his suit without argument. Carpie had already begun to work his on.

"Let's not kid ourselves. No one is getting rescued if they go in the drink," Juke said. "You go in, you die."

Greenie looked up, eyes wide.

"No one is going over," Owen said and glanced at Scotty with a frown.

She drew in a breath. "No one is going over."

"I have kids at home, and I plan on not only living through this, but getting paid," Carpie said as he zipped up the suit. He shoved his feet into his boots, pulled the hood over his gimme cap. "It's time to fish."

Owen zipped his suit and headed outside, noticing how Scotty had vanished into her bunk to squeeze into her suit. Probably so he wouldn't hear her moan in pain, which only fueled a small knot of frustration inside him.

Two hours of sleep hadn't erased the memory of her fitting, ever so perfectly, in his arms.

If only she weren't so stubborn. Impossible. Bossy.

He emerged to a world of chaos on the deck, the boat tossed in a frothy sea with forty-foot waves. The sorting table jerked against its lashings, the riggings white with ice. The boat pitched into a trough, then crested to the top and splashed down again, the water sheeting over the bow onto them.

"We're supposed to fish in this?" Greenie yelled above the gale wind.

"Let's just get it done!" Juke said and climbed up to man the crane as they pulled the pots in.

Scotty joined them topside, dressed in head-to-toe orange. She signaled to the wheelhouse, and Old Red's voice boomed from the speaker. "Last string. Let's get these pots in and go home!"

As Owen grabbed the grappling hook and swung it out to snag the buoy line, the word hung in his mind.

Home.

He caught the rope, hauled in the line, and attached it to the winch, his face against the spitting ocean spray, a surge of adrenaline firing through him.

Yeah, home. To see if he could face his mistakes, repair the damage of his impulsive actions.

The pot emerged, dripping, bulging with crab. The winch lifted it and Owen reached out with Carpie to pull it in.

They worked it onto the lift, and Owen unhooked the winch as Carpie opened the trap.

A hundred opies, as big as Frisbees, spilled onto the sorting table. "Woo-hoo!" Greenie shouted just as the boat dipped into another trough.

Owen grabbed the rail to keep from ramming into it.

"Let's get these in the well!" Scotty said, the wind taking her voice. She leaned over the table.

The next wave hit the boat like a hammer, crashing down, the vessel shuddering as icy water engulfed the deck. Shards of foamy ice fell like an avalanche, the wave scooping up everything in its path.

The force of this one slammed Owen against the railing, raking pain across his chest. Then the crest sucked him under, dragging him across the deck, rolling him like the ice chunks spilling over the edge.

He flailed, fighting for purchase, and found it on the edge of the lift, one hand on the pot. He worked his hand into the netting and held on against the surge.

Then, suddenly, the pot broke free and started sliding back toward the ocean.

Dragging Owen over the lift, his hand entangled in the netting. *No! Not like this!* He writhed, bracing his legs on the lift, shaking his hand, straining to stop the rush—

His hand broke free and he tumbled back hard as the pot slid into the sea. He gulped icy breaths, hearing only the thunder of his heartbeat, the roar of the waves.

The bitter edge of regret cut through him. He shouldn't be here. Not anymore. Time to think about his life, his future.

"Help!"

The voice jerked Owen up. He rolled over, and his gaze landed on Greenie, wedged against the hopper and the live well.

Carpie lay on his back under the table, blood dripping from his chin.

"Juke!" Owen yelled.

"Over here!" He clung to the drag anchor.

Owen pulled himself up, began to scramble toward Greenie. That's when he heard the words, riding the wind—from Juke or Carpie, he didn't know, but they turned him cold.

"I think I saw Scotty go over!"

No. A quick scan of the deck—Carp, Greenie, Juke. No Scotty.

"Scotty!" Owen ran to the rail and held on, shaking away the spray in his face.

He scanned the turbulent water, the frothy darkness, and then—"There!" He made out her neoprene orange suit bobbing just inside the puddle of light. "Scotty! Hang on!"

"Is everyone all right?" Red called from the wheelhouse through the PA system.

"Alarm! Man overboard!" Juke's voice. "Throw out a life raft!"

Owen didn't wait. He had a leg over the edge when Carpie shouted, "Owen!"

But he didn't listen, launching himself overboard and into the sea.

CHAPTER 2

GROWING UP IN MINNESOTA, just thirty miles from the Canadian border, and then later, spending every day on the ice during his hockey career, Owen knew cold. He knew how it turned every movement to shards of pain slicing through a man's body, and the terrifying welcome of numbness, the effortless fall into fatigue.

He knew how easily the cold could entice a body to surrender, pulling it to the bottom of a lake. Or as the case might be, the ocean.

No amount of neoprene could stave off the breathtaking grip of the Bering Sea. Worse, frigid water seeped into his collar, inside his suit, turning his body to ice. The waves tossed him, turning him around, crashing over him.

Drowning him.

"Scotty!" He fought the choppy sea and his own blinding panic to search for her in the darkness. "Scotty!"

He found her twenty feet away and drifting fast from the light. The waves bounced her like a buoy. "I'm coming!"

Owen lay on his back, paddling with his hands and feet, calling her name and trying not to ingest seawater. Behind him, the emergency horn sounding man overboard blared into the night. Growing dimmer.

"Scotty!" How she might hear him over the chop of the sea, he didn't know, but she turned, treading water.

"Owen!"

Thatagirl. "Swim to me!" He rowed his body harder through the water, long strokes from his years growing up on the lake. He looked over his shoulder. "Swim!"

She flailed toward him as if afraid to take her eyes off him. It took too long, but he finally reached her. His hand found her suit and he fisted it.

She was breathing hard, her face drawn, white. "You . . . idiot." Huh?

For a moment, it seemed she might crumble. Then she gritted her jaw, her eyes fierce. "Now . . . we're both . . . going to . . . die."

There it was, her determination not to cry in front of him. Too tough for her own good. Still, he grabbed her arms. "No, we're not. Listen. The horn."

It continued to blare, a hum over the choppy sea. But the waves had sent them out of the splash of light.

"They can't see us!"

He held on to her, cumbersome as it was. "We have to paddle back. Take a breath, Scotty. We can do this."

Her eyes had gone so wide with fear that he thought he'd lost her. But in a moment, she returned to herself, shaking the seawater from her face. "Right. Yes. We can do this!"

The boat dipped on the horizon, and Owen refused to acknowledge that it seemed to be drifting farther away. Or that he'd taken in too much water, and it swam in the bottom of his suit. Or that he seemed to be ingesting the sea with every breath.

He lay back. "Swim." Already the weight of the water at his feet tugged at him, urged him to the bottom. Next to him, Scotty struggled as she pawed the water.

"Scotty. Remember your training. Lie back."

She rolled onto her back, and he grabbed her shoulder, yanking her forward, kicking through the water.

Only then did he realize the searing pain in his chest, deepening, squeezing his ribs with every kick.

"We're not moving!"

He grabbed her just as another wave crashed toward them. "Hold on!" He turned then, kicking along the angle, riding the wave up, over the crest.

"We're just going farther away. We're not going to survive out here!"

Owen righted himself, confirming her words as he watched the light from the boat vanishing in the swells.

"They're never going to find us. We have about two hours before we die, even in these suits." Scotty's voice shook.

And that was just . . . it.

"Stop, Scotty. You don't give up, you hear me?" He found her eyes in the fading light. "We're not dead till we're dead, got it? We're going to lie on our backs and link up." He turned her in the water.

"Don't let me go!"

"I got you. Just lie back. Link your arms around my legs. We're going to paddle together."

He gripped her around the waist with his feet and began to paddle, fighting through the waves. "Kick, Scotty. You have to kick for us. We're going to ride these waves all the way to the *Willie*."

Owen angled them into the waves, which lifted them, settled them back into the trough, pushed them forward again. He blinked back water, but it no longer crashed into his face, no longer spewed down his gullet.

Please, God, let this work. Let us find the ship.

But he'd lost the feeling in his feet, his body shivering uncontrollably.

"Turn your light on, Scotty," he said. The survival suit came with a beacon, and she flipped it on, a pulsing flash against the darkness.

Numbness spread over Owen, his body becoming a boulder in the water.

Sinking.

Even Scotty seemed to have settled down in the quiet rhythm of her kicking.

Not dead till we're dead. Not dead—

In a pulse of light, he spied it. An orange floatable, something large and enclosed—

"A life raft!" Scotty sat up in the water. "They threw out the life raft!"

She roused new strength as she surged toward it, wild in the water, catching the dragging line and pulling it to herself, hand over hand.

Owen caught up to her, grabbed the raft—inflated, tented. Thank you, Carpie. Or Juke. Or maybe even Greenie.

28

Or God, probably, giving him a sliver of the grace he knew he didn't deserve. He didn't second-guess, just gripped the line with one hand, Scotty with the other. "I'm going to push you in."

She put her hands over the edge of the raft's doorway as he grabbed her around the middle. Then with everything inside him, he threw her over the lip and into the raft.

But Owen had hurt himself—really torn something—because suddenly he couldn't breathe. Jagged edges knifed his insides. He didn't even possess enough air to scream.

He doubled over in the water, moaning, writhing. Oh—

"Owen! What is it?" Scotty gripped his suit, pulling him against the raft. "Get in!"

The raft bumped him, pushed him away, would have crested right over him had she not held him up against it. "Owen!"

He panted, "I . . . can't . . . breathe."

"Oh no you don't! You're not dying on me. Not yet. We're not dead till we're dead!" She got a better grip on his suit, and suddenly he found himself dragged up, crying out as the pain seared through him.

But he kicked hard, surging through the agony to grab the edge of the raft. And just when he started to fall back into the ocean, Scotty grabbed him around the waist. Hauled him in to safety.

He landed hard in the belly of the raft and rolled onto his back, wanting to howl.

One breath, then another, and the band cutting off his breathing loosened. But his torso burned, and he'd endured enough past injuries to know the truth. "I think I broke a rib. Or two. I think I'm bleeding internally."

"Okay. Okay. Just . . . okay." Scotty pulled off her hood, worked off her gloves, her hands trembling. "I'm going to shoot a flare."

Right. A flare. Good thinking. Owen tried not to let the pain consume him as he watched her fumble with the supply box, find the flares, fit the flare into the pistol. She hung on to the raft as she leaned out the door and pulled the trigger.

The flare illuminated the night in a spray of bloodred light. He watched it fall, turning the sky from red to pink before returning to black.

Then Scotty velcroed the door shut. "They'll find us," she said. She ran her hand down her face, wiping it. "Red won't give up."

"Mmm-hmm," Owen said. He hadn't realized how much water his suit had trapped, and now it settled around his legs, his back. And he'd started to shake harder.

Shock.

He closed his eyes, trying to ride the waves, to calm his heart.

Trying not to wish he'd called his mother, at least once, before stepping foot on the *Wilhelmina*. Or further back, that he hadn't been the guy who so neatly eviscerated everything he'd stood for. Faith. Family.

Mostly, as he stared at the ceiling in a pitching black sea, he tried not to regret nearly every moment of the past two years.

Please, God, save us—I promise to fix it if You just save us.

Scotty hovered above him, her light illuminating the orange of the tent, her beautiful gray-green eyes so fierce, her expression so resolute, that he thought she might have read his miserable mind.

She pulled off his glove, and he felt her hand grip his, warm, solid. "You're not going to die, Owen Christiansen."

He opened his mouth to disagree, but she put her other hand over it, silencing him. "No one dies tonight."

He closed his eyes. "You're so bossy."

"A 'Yes, sir,' will do."

~~~~~~

Don't panic. Keep your head in the game. Breathe.

"Are you talking to me?"

At the sound of Owen's voice, Scotty lifted her face from where she'd buried it in her up-drawn knees, waiting. Listening to time tick away hope as the waves buffeted the raft. After an hour, someone should have found them, right?

She flicked on the flashlight, scrounged from the supply box, and let it shine over Owen. In a raft built for twelve, they had plenty of room, but he huddled near the middle, curled nearly in the fetal position. He had his hand lashed to a safety rope on the inside of the raft, holding on for dear life as the waves threw them from one trough to the next.

She'd never felt so sick.

And he looked worse. He'd already thrown up once, probably from the pain, although how he'd managed to crawl to the door to empty his gut, she didn't know. With every minute he seemed to turn more pale.

I think I broke a rib. Or two. I think I'm bleeding internally.

Yeah, she'd heard him, but she wished she hadn't. Because now she had to think about the fact that if the Coast Guard—and surely Red would have called for help—didn't find them soon, she'd be all alone in this boat.

Which felt so utterly selfish when she thought of the fact that she wouldn't even be in the boat if it weren't for Owen Christiansen diving into the ocean like a fool to save her sorry life.

That pushed another wedge into her throat, daring her to cry.

No. Because if they lived through this, she'd never live that down.

Still, the urge to weep, to shake, to hold on to Owen like he might be her lifeline swept through her, and she shuddered with the longing to . . .

No.

"Scotty, are you okay?" Even with his own suffering—she'd heard more than one moan escape in the darkness—his voice emerged gentle, caring.

Just like it had in her bunk room.

It didn't take much imagination to remember the way he looked at her on the boat, a softness—even, perhaps, desire—in his expression. Followed ever so fast by a smile, one she didn't want to interpret.

Stupid girl, letting her emotions trickle out like that. Holding on to his shirt like she needed him.

But now she had her emotions safely tucked back into place, had managed to keep her voice calm, her wits about her as she struggled to hang on in the turbulent waves.

"I'm fine."

"I'm glad one of us is because I'm not. I'm totally freaked out here." Then, crazily, Owen grinned at her through the light.

"If you're trying to be funny—"

"Oh, c'mon, Scotty, calm down. We're going to be fine. Red and the crew are searching for us right now. Have a little faith."

Seriously? "I have faith. I have faith in the fact that we are out here alone, in the pitch darkness, and not a soul knows where we are. Red is probably frantic. We're too far from St. Paul Island for the Coast Guard to just send a chopper, which means they'll have to send the cutter out first, and that could take hours. How are they going to find us in thousands of miles of ocean? You're bleeding, probably to death, if hypothermia doesn't kill you first, and I'm not much better. My arm is killing me, my head aches, and . . ."

She hadn't noticed, but he'd moved over toward her and now pressed his hand on her arm. "You forget, Scotty."

"What have I forgotten?"

"You're with me." He smiled, white teeth, a sparkle in his eye, and the entire thing felt so absurd that she had to laugh.

And laugh.

In fact, something of delirium must have caught her because as she looked at him, sitting there grinning in the wan light as if they were out on a catamaran instead of in the icy ocean on their way to perishing, the entire thing felt ridiculous.

She of all people, Ms. Safety, thrown overboard. And rescued by some version of Jack Sparrow.

How could she be laughing? "Forgive me. I didn't realize you had this all under control."

"Under control? I planned this, baby. How else do you think I was going to get you all to myself?"

Her breath caught. His smile faded.

Oh, brother. "You can't seriously be hitting on me in the middle of the North Pacific, in the last hours of our lives," she said.

The world decided to conspire with him then because another wave lifted them, threw them across the raft.

Landing her right in his arms. Or almost, because she braced herself on the rubbery edge and he pulled her to the side, away from his injury, even as he tightened his arm to protect himself.

But he groaned, and with it, she winced.

They rode the wave out; then Scotty pushed herself up, looking down at Owen. "Did I hurt you?"

"Deeply."

She stilled.

"Right here in my broken heart." He pointed to his chest, a half grin sliding up his face.

"Listen, Casanova, I don't know what you're thinking, but I just want to live through this."

Owen grimaced. "Me too." His breath came out choppy. "I was just trying to . . . Well, the thing is, Scotty, you're so pretty that I totally forgot we were about to die."

She didn't even know how to react to that, to sort out humor from his solemn words, laced with the finest edge of agony. He drew in another pained breath. "I could just stare at you all day long. You have this funny little way of curling your nose up and sneezing when the sun comes out. And yeah, maybe my timing's off, but I've been wanting to ask you out ever since that first day when you made me call you *sir*."

"Which is exactly why I could never go out with you! I'm your skipper—"

"Relief skipper."

"Boss."

"Fellow life rafter."

"Captain."

"Aye, aye." He winked.

"Owen—"

"See, now you're mad. Not scared. And you haven't thought of dying once in the last thirty seconds."

Darn it, he was right. Jerk.

"That's not funny, Owen."

"I'm not joking."

"Really? You really want to go out with a girl who knows more about fishing crab than flirting?"

"You flirt just fine."

"I don't flirt!"

"Ha. Like when you showed me how to throw out a buoy—which I already knew. You wiggled your hips and stuck out your chin—"

"You're kidding me, right?"

He grinned, closed his eye again. "I liked it."

"Just . . . you . . . sit there and bleed to death, will you?"

"Maybe." He gritted his teeth, sucking wind through them.

Oh. "I didn't mean that."

"I know." He opened his eye, sighing. "But I'm getting tired, you know? And cold. I got a lot of water in my suit."

"You did? Maybe we should get you out of it, empty it—hey, stop looking at me like that. I'm not that kind of girl."

"Calm down, toots; neither am I. Anymore."

"Toots?"

"Would you rather *bunny*? Or how about *sugarplum*?"

"Scotty's fine."

"Not *sir*?"

Oh. Right. "*Sir*'s better."

"Too late."

Wow, she wanted to smack him, although that couldn't help with his injury. And suddenly she did sort of wonder what it might be like to be off this raft and on a real date, somewhere with music playing and candlelight . . .

Another wave hit and rolled him away.

She had the urge to grab his hand, keep him from rolling too far. Which probably accounted for why her mouth decided to betray her. "We live through this and I'll go on that date with you."

Silence. The wave righted them.

"Really?" Owen moved his hand to touch hers.

Now she felt stupid, her face heating. "Maybe."

"Too late."

He smiled, and she felt it again, that crazy stirring inside.

This time, when the wave hit, she braced herself and reached out, holding him as they tumbled around the raft. She didn't miss the way he groaned.

"I'm sorry I went overboard," she said as the wave settled them back against the side.

"You should be. I had a lot of crab to catch and one of Carpie's omelets waiting for me."

"Can I ask you something?"

"Make it snappy. I have places to be."

"What's with the eye patch?"

His smile fading, Owen licked his lips as if thinking through his response.

"You don't have to tell me—"

"I hurt my eye in a fight."

Oh. "A bar fight?"

He shook his head, then pushed off the patch. A spiderweb of scar tissue issued out from his left eye, now cloudy around the blue iris. "A hockey fight."

"You played hockey?" Scotty asked.

"I played for a team in Minnesota. NHL. The St. Paul Blue Ox."

"You played in the NHL? I'm a huge Aces fan."

"Aces?"

"They're a minor league team out of Anchorage. But we watch the Flames and the Canucks. I'm surprised I didn't recognize you."

"I know, great disguise, huh? I only had to lose an eye to pull it off."

"I can't believe you're joking about this."

His expression turned solemn. "Listen, a guy with one good eye can't afford to spend any time looking over his shoulder. I laugh about it or I cry, and laughing feels better." He reached up and touched her cheek. "Right?"

Then he smiled, winding his hand behind her neck.

"Are you trying to kiss me?"

"Why? Do you want to kiss me?"

"I'm not going to kiss you! What is wrong with you? We're lost at sea."

"And dying. Don't forget I'm dying."

"You're not dying!"

"I could be. This is all very tragic—sort of a Nicholas Sparks movie." He sighed.

"Oh, for pete's sake. Do you take anything seriously?"

He dropped his hand. "Yeah. Actually." But he didn't continue, and she regretted not letting him pull her closer.

There it was again, the story lurking behind his eyes. Or eye. "Does it hurt?"

"No."

"Can you see?"

"It's fuzzy around the edges, and it's more distracting than helpful. So I wear the patch."

"How very Rooster Cogburn of you."

"Rooster—?"

"It's Red's favorite movie. The John Wayne version."

Owen frowned as he pulled the patch back down.

"*True Grit*?" Scotty said. "Oh, please, it's a classic."

"I spent my childhood at hockey rinks and playing my Game Boy on long trips."

"Tragic."

"Sometimes." He didn't appear to be kidding.

"Don't talk to me about tragic until you've been snowed in with the complete John Wayne collection on VHS. I can recite *The Cowboys* on cue." She sat back, cleared her throat. "'Now I don't hold jail against you, but I hate a liar.'"

"Wow."

"Or 'It's not how you're buried; it's how you're remembered.' And Red's personal favorite: 'I'm thirty years older than you are. I had my back broke once, and my hip twice. And on my worst day I could beat the *bleep* out of you.'"

"Bleep?"

"That was my aunt Rosemary's idea. I lived with her and my uncle Gil when Red was out fishing. She wouldn't allow profanity in the house, so she made my pop bleep all the good parts. Life lessons from Red, courtesy of John Wayne."

"I gotta ask, Scotty—why do you call him Red?"

She let that question settle for a moment, sifting through the easy answers to the truth. "For the same reason he calls me Scotty instead of my given name. My mom named me Elise, but Red thought it sounded weak, too dainty for our life. At least, that's my guess. He's been calling me Scotty for as long as I can remember, and he became Red the minute I started sailing with him. That way we don't get tangled up in the messy father-daughter relationship or admit something absurd, like the fact that we might care about each other."

"But you do, don't you."

"He's my father. Of course I care. But it's easier for him to keep that all neatly tucked away and forgotten."

He frowned, touched her hand, and for a second, she wanted

to yank it away. But then he met her eyes. "He's an idiot. If I had a daughter, I'd never want to forget her. She would be everything to me."

He also possessed this crazy way of making everything all right.

"Yeah, well, I grew up like one of the boys, and you see my world—there's not much room for a woman on a fishing boat."

"I'm sorry I said that."

She shrugged. "Any other boat, any other woman, I might agree. But—"

"You belong at the helm, Scotty. You know how to fish, how to captain."

"Actually, I'm a cop."

"Really?" He stared at her.

It had been a test, sort of, because she wanted to see his reaction. A flinch, maybe a scowl, anything to tease out that hint of story.

But no, instead she netted a wide, embracing grin. "Sea captain and police officer. I definitely think I'm in safe hands. Carry on."

"With what?"

"Rescuing me."

If that curl of warmth hadn't already built to a flame, now it burst into a full-out blaze. She laughed. "Please don't be a criminal. I would hate to have to arrest you."

"Do you arrest a lot of people you know?"

He didn't know how his words nicked her heart. But her face must have betrayed it.

Then, because she felt ridiculously safe despite the fact that they were trapped in the middle of the Bering Sea in the middle of the night . . . "I left the Homer Police Department about six months ago because I had to shoot someone I knew."

His smile, his humor, died. Oh no, why had she—?

"Scotty, I'm so sorry."

The softness in his voice raised more stupid, sudden tears. She blinked them back, managed to sound casual. "It's fine. I mean, I'm fine. It happened on the job, justified, but . . . I'd never shot anyone before. And never want to again."

"You can't be fine," Owen said. "That leaves scars. And I'm sorry."

She lifted a shoulder, wishing she hadn't given in to the emotional nudge to open up her past because now the silence dragged out between them.

That frustrating Owen Christiansen and his ability to make her stop thinking, start wrenching open forbidden places.

"Okay, fine. I promise to behave," Owen said.

Huh? She looked up.

He winked at her.

And just like that, the tension washed away. She found a tentative smile. "That includes not dying on me, Eye Patch."

He grinned. "I'll do my best, honey. But we've already established who the hero is here."

Had they?

"Maybe we should send off another flare." She opened the box, found the flare, fitted it into the gun. "There's one left after this."

Scotty ripped open the Velcro door and leaned out. Night still shrouded the sky, not a hint of sunrise to the east. Spray from the waves sliced at her face. Just for a second, she searched the horizon for any sign of the ship, yet even the stars refused to shine.

Lost at sea indeed.

She held the gun out.

The raft rocked, pitching forward, and Scotty screamed as her weight fell against the edge, tumbling her toward the blackness.

"Scotty!"

She grabbed for the edge of the raft even as she felt Owen's hand on her suit, yanking her back. She landed hard inside the raft as the wave crashed through the door. It filled the bottom of the tent with foamy, frigid water.

Owen had already struggled to his knees, was wrestling the flap closed, running his hand over the Velcro.

Scotty grabbed the flap and helped steady it as he finished sealing it.

Then, as water sloshed around them, Owen fell back. Pain straining his face, he went back to the shallow, panicked breathing.

They were going to die.

"I'm so sorry—"

"It's okay." But his voice emerged as if pushed through a sieve.

"How bad is it?"

He forced a smile through gritted teeth. "I'll be okay."

Right. She curled up next to him. Didn't even protest when he took her hand, wove his fingers through hers, chilly though they were.

For a long while, the waves stirred them. She held on to his hand, trying not to notice how he moaned.

Finally, quietly, she said, "I dropped the flare gun in the ocean."

He held her hand in silence until she finally flicked off the light.

Don't panic. Keep your head in the game. Breathe.

Casper Christiansen would need a miracle if he hoped to locate his kid brother.

"I don't know where else to look, Raina," he yelled into the phone. "I swear, he's dropped off the planet."

"I can barely hear you!" Raina shouted back.

Casper could barely hear himself over the ruckus of the Seattle Seahawks' on-the-road win over the 49ers. Why he'd picked this bar and grill to grab a late-night burger, drown his sorrows with a little chocolate milk and a basket of seasoned curly fries, he wasn't sure. Something about the massive flat screens showing not only the Seahawks, but also a late-season game of the Mariners and highlights of the last Washington Huskies game, made this seem like the right place to hide, maybe forget the past four-plus months of failure.

The joint smelled of cheeseburgers and fries, and with the gleaming wooden bars, the signed NFL jerseys and NHL sweaters in frames, and the familiar comfort food menu, it felt easy. Maybe Casper simply craved the loud, boisterous Thursday night football game, the cheering he was missing back home in Deep Haven, surrounded by his brother Darek, his father, and even his little nephew, Tiger. Boys' night, although Ivy, Darek's wife, knew the teams as well as he did.

But even Ivy might have been intimidated by a crowded restaurant filled with jersey-clad, face-painted Hawks during the last two minutes of the tied game.

He'd sat at the bar, watching the win and eating his fries, his mind wandering through the pit stops over the past four months since he'd left Deep Haven in the apparently fruitless quest to find his prodigal brother.

Yeah, sure, he probably should have gone home. But a big part of him knew that if he stepped foot back in Deep Haven, back into Raina's arms, he wouldn't leave again.

The longing for her had stirred up the desire to call home, even if he rousted her out of bed. He just had to hear her voice.

"I said, he's dropped off the planet!"

Of course, that's when the bartender flipped the channel to the late-night news, much to the chagrin of the cadre of fans still hanging on to their well-imbibed celebration.

The bartender—nameplate, Jim—gestured to Casper's empty glass. Casper nodded, even as he cupped his hand over the phone to shield his voice. "Maybe it's time to call it quits."

"What I've been saying for weeks. You've done the best you could—it's time to come home, Casper. You won't even recognize Layla. She's crawling now."

He clasped his finger and thumb to the bridge of his nose, trying to massage away the pulse of a headache just starting to form. Every picture Raina texted him of the eight-month-old, with her curly black hair, those huge blue eyes, the lopsided smile, and every gurgling coo from the other side of the phone made him ache. His daughter—oh, he wanted to claim her as his own. Had, really, in his heart.

But he couldn't fully become her daddy until he got the okay from the biological father—aka his stupid, reckless, arrogant, broken kid brother.

"She's also cutting teeth, and I wouldn't be sad if you were here to mop up some of the drool. I've never met a soggier kid."

He could imagine Raina sitting on the sofa in a flannel shirt, pajama pants, her long black hair down over her shoulders, one finger twirling it absently. It always had a hypnotic power over him, made him willing to hand her his heart all over again.

He could feel her in his arms, smell her—lavender or baby powder—and lost himself for a moment. "Wow, I miss you. I can't wait until we're married."

Which meant he couldn't give up the search. "I can't come

home yet. I'll never feel right about marrying you if Owen doesn't know he's a father—I'd feel like . . ."

Well, like he'd stolen her. And worse, like he was hiding a terrible secret, always looking over his shoulder. How could he be a proper father to Layla if he thought he had no right to be there?

"It's just important to me; that's all."

"Are you still in Seattle?" Raina said, her voice soft, probably a reaction to hearing him sigh.

"Yeah. I spent another day on the docks, flashing Owen's picture around like I'm a PI or something."

"You are, sort of."

"I'd be a broke one if I was doing this for a living. I thought after I finally tracked down Jed with the Jude County Hotshots, I wasn't far behind, but I think it's going to take something close to divine intervention to find him."

After discovering Owen had quit the Hotshots and traveled with a friend to Spokane, Casper had found the man's family and learned that Owen had left after a few weeks, then headed to Seattle.

"I found an address here in Seattle where he lived. Talked to the landlord this morning. She remembered him—hard to miss a guy with an eye patch, I guess."

"He's still wearing that?"

"Apparently. She thought he might work down at the docks but hadn't seen him since his buddy moved out last January."

The bartender set another glass of chocolate milk in front of him. Casper held on to his plate of curly fries. In desperation, he'd even shown Owen's picture to the crowd here, the bartender, a few waitstaff. But Owen would have had to be painted navy and green, maybe play wide receiver, to get a second look here.

Behind him, the crowd dispersed, just a few loud fans remaining to talk smack about next week's matchup against the Rams.

"This afternoon I tracked down someone who recognized him from the Pike Place Fish Market. Said he was a monger for a while."

"What's a monger?"

"A fish tosser. Apparently he had great reflexes. The monger who remembered Owen said that he thought he hooked up with some guys headed out on a fishing boat. But that was eight months ago."

"You'll find him, Casper. If anyone can, it's you."

He'd like to believe that, but lately he'd been thinking that his luck might have run dry after landing the treasure-hunting find of his life earlier this year—the fortune of a steel baron, lost in the north woods of Minnesota. The finders' fee had given him enough to prop up the family resort, infuse it with new life, make his engagement to Raina official with a ring, and maybe someday buy a house . . . if he could locate Owen and garner his blessing.

Or maybe his forgiveness. Because even more than moving forward with Raina, Casper wanted to set the past right. It haunted him—their fight, the way he'd tackled his brother, slammed his fist into his face, and in that moment, hated him.

Hated. That's what burned in him the most. He couldn't shake the regret, the awareness that he'd wanted to hurt Owen, *really* hurt him.

The fury that had taken over scared him. That day Casper had just wanted to make Owen pay for what he did to Raina. And to him. Because they'd never escape the specter of Owen in their life. Not with Layla there to remind them. As much as Casper loved Layla, he feared he'd never look in her eyes and truly see his reflection. What if Owen would always be staring—smirking—back?

Still, Casper couldn't live with the gash he'd cut in the family. In his own heart.

He longed to forgive. And be forgiven. But he couldn't deny how his hope of that waned with each empty lead.

"I can't think of anywhere else to look. But I can't . . ." He picked up a curly fry, tossed it through the ketchup. "I can't come home yet, either."

The fry was cold, turning sour in his mouth. He washed it down with the milk, then pushed the plate away, glancing up at the news. Weather, then sports. Oh, joy, more Seahawks.

"Amelia left for Africa today," Raina said. "The whole tribe went to the airport. I know they missed you."

"I missed them. How's her ankle?" He still couldn't believe the story Raina had told him about his kid sister nearly dying of injuries and exposure in the north woods of Minnesota.

"She's good. Limping a little, but healed up. I think she's going to love Africa."

"And you—how are you?"

"I'm missing you. Your mom and Grace have been watching Layla during my shifts at the antique shop, but I think I need to find day care and increase my hours. I can't keep living on the dole."

He knew she meant it as funny, but he didn't laugh. "If we were married, it would be our money, not mine. You could stay at home and take care of Layla—"

"I doubt that, Casper. I've never been the kind of girl to just sit around. I'd probably work at the resort, helping out. Maybe clean cabins."

"Don't you dare mention that to Darek. He'll take you up on it."

She laughed. "I am glad to help out, Casper. It . . . Well, it's my family resort too, in a way."

"In every way." Oh, he could barely take it, the need to reach through the phone, weave his hands into her silky hair, pull her into his arms. "That's it. I'm coming home."

"Casper—"

"No, I'm serious, Raina. Forget Owen. He clearly forgot us. He's wiped his feet, shaken off the dirt, and left us behind. I don't know why I'm trying so hard to find someone who doesn't want to be found. And it's not like his blessing has any bearing on our future. I'd marry you if I had to knock him over to get down the aisle. He doesn't have a shadow of a hope of getting back in your life—or Layla's. I'm her daddy, not Owen, and maybe I need to come home and start acting like it."

Silence; then he heard an intake of breath. "If . . . I mean, yeah, that's—of course, that's what I want. But are you sure—?"

"More than sure." Casper slid off the stool and cradled the phone as he reached into his pocket for his wallet. "I can't believe I was such an idiot to leave you and Layla for this long. I should be there instead of chasing my ghost brother across the world. He's probably laughing on some beach in Hawaii right now." He gestured to the bartender, covering the phone. "Check?"

The barkeep nodded even as he glanced at the television. Casper followed his gaze, his eye catching on some news story.

"If that's what you want, Casper, I understand. Yeah, I think Owen should know he has a daughter, but it doesn't change anything between us. I love you—I want you, and Owen is out of my life for good."

Casper dug through his wallet for his debit card.

"Hey, bud," the bartender said, turning toward him. Casper handed him the card, but Jim shook his head, pointed to the television. "Isn't that the guy you're looking for?"

Casper froze, his gaze on the pictures of a bearded Owen and a woman with long, dark hair—reminded him a little of Raina, in fact.

And below their mug shots, a caption. *Swept overboard.*

Jim turned up the volume as the reporter finished her segment.

"The Coast Guard has suspended the search for tonight, the winds too high to attempt a rescue. Searchers say they will resume their hunt in the morning." She tossed it back to her anchor, her expression grim as they finished the segment.

Casper couldn't move, couldn't breathe.

"Casper, are you there?"

Swept overboard.

"Casper!" Raina's voice cut through the disbelief, the fog, yanking him back to reality.

"Oh . . . my." No, please—

"What's the matter? Are you okay?"

"I . . . Raina, I think I found him." He stepped up to the bar, tried to press his voice through what felt like a crushing hand on his chest. "Oh no, no . . ."

"You're scaring me now."

Yeah, well, he was scaring himself. He stared at the barkeep, who took his debit card, something of apology on his face.

It couldn't end. Not like this. "It's Owen, Raina. He's . . . he's lost at sea."

CHAPTER 3

A COUNTRY SONG PLAYED through Owen's mind, something that stirred from the depths of his memory.

Twangy. Mellow. The music issued from an old transistor, the knobs slathered with white-and-green paint, the speaker overlaid in coarse green fiber. The song blared out from the workbench where his father bent, sharpening his skates.

"I pretend to hold you to my breast and find that you're waiting from the back roads . . ."

Owen allowed himself to sink into the past, to smell his mother's cookies seasoning the autumn air, to hear Casper and Darek raking the yard and arguing. He heard the crunch of leaves at his feet, felt their curly fingers at his face and down his shirt as he leaped into the pile, scattering them again to the wind.

He let the song find his lips, added the tune. "'By the rivers of my memories, ever smilin', ever gentle on my mind.'"

"Are you singing?"

Scotty's voice urged him to rejoin her in the raft. She knelt near the entrance, where she'd opened the Velcro just enough to let the water from the pump hose dribble back into the sea. Two hours of pumping and she'd just about managed to drain the frigid puddle.

While he lay in the back of the raft, letting her be the hero. She'd become even more breathtaking as night lifted, her eyes big against the pale hue of her face in the graying light. Her dark hair had dried and now lay in long, midnight curls.

"Don't stop," she said. "It's nice." She closed the Velcro, then came over to kneel next to him.

"I don't remember all the words. It's an old song tucked away in my memory."

The waves still rocked them back and forth, but he no longer feared they would flip over, drown under the weight of the raft. The calming of the water tempered the jostling, the agony.

And with the daylight might also come rescue.

Owen reached up to touch Scotty's hair, letting it fall between his fingers, and he didn't care that the gesture seemed intimate. He'd been wanting to touch her hair, twirl a long lock around his finger, for three weeks. And shoot, he was dying. What did he have to lose?

He could feel the life ebb from his body. The fatigue pressing him into the numbing water, the way he just wanted to return, sweetly, to the memory of Evergreen Resort.

"My dad likes to listen to country," he said, his voice thinner than he'd like. "Mom hates country, so she makes him listen to it in the garage. Or used to. Maybe not anymore, I dunno."

So much he didn't know anymore. His fault—he knew that.

"Where does your family live?"

"On a resort in northern Minnesota called Evergreen Lodge Outfitter and Cabin Rentals. Beautiful place—twelve cabins, all perched along the lakeside. It's been in the family for four generations. Except it burned down two years ago."

"Oh, that's terrible."

"My brother Darek is rebuilding. He's got this cute little boy named Tiger and got remarried last summer. His first wife died when Tiger was a toddler."

"Sad."

"He's happy now, I think. I dunno."

"That's a lot of dunnos."

Hmm. "My mom makes the most incredible chocolate chip cookies. She puts peanut butter chips in them, and I swear, right now I can taste them."

She smiled. "You're just hungry."

Funny, he wasn't quite as ravenous as he had been earlier. "Have you ever had a s'more made with two chocolate chip cookies? During the summer, we had a cookout every weekend, and Mom would drag out her cookies . . ." He sighed, and now he started to feel pressure in his gut, building. Hot pressure against his ribs, his lungs, his heart.

"It sounds fantastic," she said.

"My sister Grace is this amazing cook too. She has a recipe for hamburgers—I don't know what she puts in them, but I've never eaten a burger that could make you cry. Except for Grace's."

"That's so sweet. I bet she misses you."

Do you take anything seriously? Scotty's words must've drilled into him, found a foothold, because he'd spent most of the night listening to them. Yeah, actually, he did take some things seriously. Like his regrets.

"I haven't talked to my family in over a year. I have three sisters and two brothers, and I haven't talked to any of them since my eldest sister's wedding." He made a face. "Meet the family prodigal, the official black sheep of the Christiansen family. The one most likely to screw up something good."

He met her eyes then, so filled with a concern that looked a lot like friendship. Or more.

He would have liked to live long enough to discover the *or more.*

"I don't believe that."

"Yeah, well, everyone has a story, right? And mine is simple. I was stupid and impulsive and because of it, I lost part of my sight, my career. I drove away and didn't look back."

"Why not?"

There it was, the Great Question. The prodigal's shame—why didn't he turn around or even call just once?

So many ways to answer that.

Because I was a jerk and slept with the girl my brother ended up falling in love with.

Yeah, uh, no.

Because I got in a fistfight with said brother at my sister's wedding. Which of course would lead back to reason number one.

Again, no.

And the biggest reason: because he couldn't bear to see the accusation, the hurt in his family's eyes, starting with his mother all the way to his kid sister, Amelia, who he knew looked up to him more than he deserved.

There had to be an answer, and he found the one that summed it up. "Because, really, I left them long before I got injured. I was all about hockey back then, driven by the headlines. I always dreamed of a life beyond Deep Haven, beyond the resort, even in the early days, when Casper and Darek dragged me out on the ice. Casper was better than me back then, but he was always pushing me to get better and I caught up fast. I thought we might play together on some NHL team. Then I joined the juniors and everything started happening, and by the time I caught my breath, I realized I didn't belong anymore. I was on the outside looking in, and I couldn't figure out how to make my way back or even if I wanted to." He gave a wry chuckle that contained nothing of humor. "And now it might be too late."

He didn't exactly know why he said that, but suddenly the past year rushed over him—the fight with Casper, the months on the road living so far beyond the person he ever thought he'd be.

"Owen, are you okay? You're scaring me a little bit."

He forced a smile, tried for something light, teasing. "You could hold my hand."

Her frown deepened. "I am holding your hand." She lifted it and he realized that he could no longer feel his own grip.

"Right. Just testing."

She put a hand to his forehead. "You're really cold."

"Yeah, well—"

"No smart remarks about my trying to keep you warm."

"So selfish." He tried another smile, but she had started to unzip his suit. "What are you doing?"

"I'm trying to figure out how to warm you up. You're—oh no." She had his suit unzipped down his chest. "Your stomach is distended." She pressed around his abdomen, and it felt like she'd dropped an anvil on his body.

He groaned, too loud, but the pain turned him weak.

"I'm sorry."

"I'll be okay," he gasped.

"We gotta get you out of this suit."

"Please."

"Be serious."

He looked away. "How about this for serious? Open the port-hole. I want to see the sunrise."

"What?"

"And I can't seem to move my arm, so could you take off my eye patch too?"

She made a funny noise but pulled the patch from his eye. He could see—barely, right in the center, but everything else looked blurry, watery. His vision might have improved, just like the doctor said, if he'd given it a chance to heal, tried to use it. Instead he'd dug into his grief, covered his eye up in darkness, and let it atrophy.

Scotty stood and uncovered the porthole on the top of the life raft. "I don't know if we're facing the right—"

"It's amazing. C'mere. You have to see this."

She settled next to him again. The sky after the storm had turned a light, glorious pink, with streaks of crimson and gold.

"In the summertime, Darek and Casper and I would camp out on the dock. We'd wake up to loons calling across the lake and a sunrise just like this. Once, my sister Amelia camped outside, and we all were so worried about her that we each snuck out to protect her. My brothers and I got in this terrific wrestling match. Grace fell in the lake—and we all made such a commotion, the neighbors across the lake called the cops."

She laughed, and it made him want to live.

"Your family sounds amazing. I would have given anything for a sibling."

"I loved summers at Evergreen. It was the only time I felt like I was a part of the family."

"You should go home." She pushed up on one elbow. "When we get rescued, the first thing you do is hop a plane. I don't care how stupid you feel or if you think they can't forgive you. You go home." She traced her finger down his face. "You don't really know what it's like not to have family, Owen. Don't find out."

His eye started to blur further, perhaps with the disuse, and probably she would think he was crying.

"Nah. I . . . My brother and I had a fight—like a real fistfight. It was ugly and . . ." He grimaced. How did he get here, to the wretched truth? "I keep reliving it. Yeah, I should call my mom, but Casper—he doesn't want to have anything to do with me." He could hear his voice as if far away now, and he fought to pull it back.

"What was the fight about?"

"Me. Being a jerk." He swallowed, not wanting to tell her but feeling a strange catharsis in just blurting it out, like releasing a poison too long eating his insides. "I had a one-night stand."

He met her eyes but saw no censure in them. She lifted a shoulder. "And—?"

"Just so you know, I wasn't the same guy back then. After I got hurt, I was all about proving I still had it all or that it didn't matter that I'd lost it. But I've changed—"

"It's okay. Are you kidding me? The first thing every deckhand does after he leaves the boat is visit the Dutch Harbor Saloon."

"That's not me. I mean, I wouldn't . . ."

Except he had been that guy.

"Calm down, Owen. I didn't expect you to. I'm just saying, you can't surprise me."

"Maybe not, but you should know that . . . six months ago, not long after I got paid from the opie haul, I woke up in a hotel room, hungover and robbed."

She took this in without a blink of shock. Right, a cop.

"By the woman you brought home that night?"

He nodded. "But that wasn't the worst of it. I looked at myself, once I dragged myself out of bed, and could see that I'd been in some kind of fight I couldn't remember. As I stared in the mirror, I didn't know that guy. Or I didn't want to. I was sick of myself. But I didn't know how to escape him."

"You don't have to tell me this."

"I thought of my parents and what they'd say—probably tell me to go to church. But right, like I could step foot in church. So I went down to the docks, hoping I could sign on to a tuna boat, and who did I see there but Carpie."

She raised an eyebrow. Nodded. "Say no more."

"I'm no saint, Scotty. Far from it. But I am trying to figure out how to be a guy who deserves forgiveness instead of the reckless, angry, bitter ex–hockey player who took everything he had left and threw it away."

And now he'd never get it back.

Oh . . .

He couldn't die, not yet. Not when he had so much left unsaid. So much of his life he wanted to reach out and grab. Forgiveness, yeah. But . . . maybe also a fresh start.

Not this.

"Why did you and your brother fight?" Scotty asked, her voice soft.

"That's when things got complicated. My brother Casper apparently fell in love with the girl I'd . . . Her name was Raina.

56

He dated her after I left, and when he found out that we . . . well, he just went off. Completely unraveled. He decked me at my sister Eden's wedding. I didn't know what to do, so I hit him back, and it turned into a brawl." He shook his head. "I keep seeing my mother's expression and the way my dad looked at me like he didn't know me. Maybe I saw a piece of myself that I didn't recognize either. So . . ."

"You left."

"I left, yeah. And kept moving west, all the way to Seattle. Finally got hooked up with some guys headed to Alaska, just in time to sign on with your old man during opie season." He made the colossal effort to meet her eyes. "And hung on long enough for my luck to change."

She frowned.

"I met you."

Scotty bit her lip, her eyes darkening with concern. "Owen?"

He looked away, back to the sunrise, the pressure now a band around his chest. He'd noticed it for a little while, his breaths too difficult, turning shallow.

He just wanted to sleep. But he kept his gaze on the sky, the way the reds bled into the gold, dissipating into one orange glow.

He had no doubt that the Coast Guard would find them—or rather, Scotty—alive.

And that thought made him drill down, unearth the words, because really, it wouldn't matter. He turned to her, found her eyes shining, her face glowing in the dawn.

"If I go back, you have to come with me," he whispered.

"Huh?"

"Back to Deep Haven. You know . . . meet my family." He closed his eyes, the weight too much to hold them open. "You'd like them. They're loud, and yeah, we fight, but it's not unlike being on the boat with Juke and Carpie."

"Owen . . ."

The tremor in her voice caught him, and he held it in a quiet place, forcing his own tone to stay light, despite the cold hand of truth moving over him. "In fact, since we just spent the night together, I think you should probably do right by me—" he took a breath, then another, gathering his strength—"and marry me."

He opened his eyes just to catch a glimpse of her face, her gray-green eyes so beautiful as they widened in surprise.

Perfect.

He smiled. Now maybe she'd stop thinking about the fact that he was dying and start arguing with him again. Get worked up enough to hold on until she could get rescued.

Then blackness began to seep over him, blurring his vision, his thoughts.

"Owen!"

Mmm-hmm? "Is that a yes?"

And there went the song again, round and round as he faded into darkness.

"You're waiting from the back roads by the rivers of my memories, ever smilin', ever gentle on my mind."

"Owen?" Scotty ran her knuckles down his sternum. He barely responded with a grunt. "Owen!"

She leaned over, listened to his chest. His breathing sounded garbled at best, rattling. As if his lungs were drowning. In seawater or blood?

"No, you don't die on me!" She lifted his arm, took his pulse, found it erratic, light.

That's when she tugged up his T-shirt and discovered his belly and chest had turned purple. Whatever he'd hit had shredded his insides. And he'd been lying here, slowly bleeding to death.

She leaned over him, slapping his cheek. "Wake up."

But he didn't even groan, and that had her raising her voice. "Listen, fine. Yes. Yes, I'll marry you! Yes, do you hear me? But you have to live. You have to *stay alive*."

He didn't open his eyes.

He looked, in fact, peaceful, like he might be sleeping, the sun turning his beard to rose gold, his cheekbones high, his hair curly and long around his neck.

She pressed her hand to his chest, feeling it rise and fall. Then she closed her eyes, still, paralyzed.

Now, *right* now, she wished Carpie were here. Because he'd pull out his Bible and thump it a little, and then he'd pray, and if God was really listening, really cared, He'd do something.

Because Carpie believed.

Have a little faith.

Owen's words, and after hearing his story, it all clicked. She'd seen him hanging out with Carpie when he was reading his Bible, so maybe he'd meant *faith*.

As in the kind that came with looking into the sunrise and knowing that it was created by Someone. And believing that Someone cared. Watched over. Intervened.

Scotty sat beside Owen, wishing her hand could warm his body, wishing he hadn't told her about his life because she could see it—his devastated mother, wondering why he'd never called, and his siblings, white-faced. His brother Casper regretting a stupid fight over a woman.

Have a little faith.

"How could you have a family and not . . ." She shook her head. "You're right, Owen. You're a jerk. First you save me; then you flirt with me; then you make me hungry—I'd love a chocolate chip cookie right now, thank you so much. And then you, what—propose? Of course you do. Because you know you're dying, and it won't matter. Well, listen up, bub: you're not getting out of that proposal so easy. You'd better live because I say *yes*." She leaned over him, her voice in his ear, so close she could kiss him. "Do you hear me? Yes."

Oh, she wanted to kiss him. The crazy urge just about made her touch her lips to his. She didn't know how he'd managed to crawl under her defenses so quickly—except it hadn't exactly been quick, had it? Because she'd watched him with a keen eye since that first day.

Had wondered, yes, what it might be like to be in his arms.

And for a moment last night—only hours ago—she'd discovered herself there in his embrace, feeling all those solid planes of his body, muscles wrought from hard work and hours at sea. If she'd been a smart girl instead of a proud girl, she might have wrapped her arms around his neck, held on. Given the pirate a chance before life threw them overboard.

She checked his breathing again. Slight, ragged.

Slowing.

Scotty sat back, wiped her hand across her face. "You better not die on me because I want a wedding. Flowers and a dress." Not really—what would that look like? While she deserved to wear white, she hadn't worn a dress, well, ever. Because she wasn't the kind of girl who believed in dating or true love or happy endings.

Have a little faith.

She took his hand, folded it between both of her own. Clutched it to her chest. "Do not leave me, Owen. Do not leave me in this boat by myself."

His hand tightened. Or maybe just a spasm, but she searched his face for life.

Please. Oh . . .

She didn't care that her eyes filled or that she'd begun to shake.

Have a little—

"Fine! Please, God. If You exist, if You're up there at all . . . if You see us, if You care in the tiniest bit, keep him breathing. Just keep him breathing."

Owen's hand spasmed again, and she held it to her face, her voice cut thin, bare. "Just keep him breathing."

The ocean had calmed and Scotty rode the gentle waves, watching the sunrise bleed out into perfect blue skies. Owen refused to rouse, but his chest kept moving. Up, down, up—

And then she heard it. A humming, a *whap-whap-whap*, then a horn.

A helicopter. Searching the sea. She leaped up, stood under the porthole, waving her arms outside.

She saw nothing, but she could hear the rotary blades chopping the air.

A flare. Except without the gun . . .

She ducked back inside, found the supply case, and opened it, taking out the last stick flare inside.

She stood up again, aiming the flare through the porthole.

Please work. *Please.*

She broke the flare and it lit, a shiny, bright signal. It burned in her hand, and she waved it, hoping to catch a mirror or binoculars or whatever they might be using.

"Help! Help!" Probably expending her breath wasn't wise, but it seemed the right accompaniment to her frenetic waving.

The stick burned, and as she threw it in the water, she listened for the chopper.

Gone. No hammering of the air, no drone of an engine.

She sank back inside, listening to her heartbeat rage in her chest. Then she crept over to Owen. "It's going to be okay. They'll find us."

She settled her hand back on his chest.

It was still. "No . . . Owen, no!" She jammed two fingers against his carotid artery. Nothing. She cupped her hand over his mouth. No breathing.

Silence.

"Owen!" She rose above him, began to pump his chest. One, two . . . all the way to thirty, just like she'd been trained.

C'mon, Owen . . .

She leaned in, listening for breath sounds. Gave two strong breaths, then more chest compressions. Her stomach clenched with the exertion but—

Outside, again she heard the chopper.

Breaths.

Compressions.

It seemed louder as if the chopper might have looped back. She braced herself so the waves wouldn't dislodge her.

Breaths. She stared at Owen's face. He looked pinker, maybe.

The helicopter sound droned louder still.

Please, God. Please. She might have even started begging aloud.

Compressions.

The rotors chopped the air, the raft walls beginning to ripple.

Breaths.

Then a voice. "Hello, the life raft. If you're in there, please acknowledge." The rotors chopped the air.

Compressions. "Owen!"

She stared at him, saw his color had definitely improved, but he stayed still, no life.

"I'm sorry—I'm so sorry." She jumped up and stuck her head through the porthole. "I'm here! We're in here! Help! I need help!"

Above her, a beautiful black-nosed, white-and-orange MH-60 Jayhawk chopper hovered over the water. She wanted to weep with the sight of it but turned away, back to Owen, as a rescue diver clad all in orange dropped into the sea.

Breaths.

Compressions.

Hurry.

She heard the Velcro door separating, then the diver opening the hatch. "Hello?"

Breaths.

He climbed inside.

Scotty moved back to compressions, her face wet. "Help me. Please help me."

"Ma'am, I need to evacuate you—"

"Not without Owen."

"Ma'am, we'll take over."

"Listen, he saved my life, and I'm not leaving until you have oxygen on him and his heart is pumping, so either help me or get out!"

The diver radioed the chopper.

"Breathe, Owen. Please." She added breaths.

The diver moved alongside her, started compressions.

Another diver appeared, this time with a medical kit. He climbed inside the raft. "We got this, ma'am."

Breaths. "I'm not stopping!"

The medic opened his kit, pulled out a rebreather, cupped it over Owen's face. "We've got him."

"He's been bleeding for hours. Into his gut, but maybe into his lungs too."

The medic checked Owen's pulse, then pulled out a stethoscope. "It looks like a hemothorax. Get her in the basket. I need to relieve the pressure and maybe we can get his heart beating again."

"Ma'am—" The first diver took her arm.

She yanked it away. "I'm not leaving him."

"The sooner we get you in the chopper, the sooner we can send down the basket for your friend."

The medic doused Owen's bare chest with antiseptic and pulled out a large-bore needle.

"Ma'am, let's go now." The diver stood at the door, gripping the edge of a basket lowered next to the raft. He grabbed her suit.

She couldn't take her eyes off Owen. "He has to live, do you hear me? Owen, you have to live!"

"We're doing our best."

The medic had inserted the needle, and dark, thick blood began to drain into a bag. He glanced at Scotty. "Please. The faster we get him on board the Coast Guard cutter, the better his chances."

She climbed into the basket. Held on as the chopper winched her aloft.

Another diver strapped her into the chopper and she watched, not breathing herself, as they finally loaded Owen into the basket, pulling him up. He wore the oxygen mask, two black patches on his chest where they'd probably shocked his heart.

Once Owen was loaded in beside Scotty, the medic closed the door. "His heart's beating, for now."

Then probably hers could too.

As the chopper headed away from the raft, she peered down at it, their nest in the middle of the inky-blue ocean.

Then she reached down and clasped Owen's hand. Looking again at the medic, she shouted over the noise of the chopper, "You can't let him die because I'm going to marry him!"

CHAPTER 4

SCOTTY KNEW OWEN couldn't have been serious about the proposal. Nor, really, did she intend to marry him.

The lie just became so convenient as it grew, took on life, significance.

"Ma'am, if you'd like to go into the ICU, you can visit for a few minutes."

Scotty got up from where she'd stretched out on the sofa in the family waiting room of the Providence Alaska Medical Center in Anchorage. A chill still embedded her bones despite the hypothermia treatment. They'd warmed her with blankets, finally let her shower, given her scrubs to wear, then released her to pace the halls as Owen underwent surgery.

She'd gotten ahold of Red and the crew. Listened to her old man's tight voice. "Glad you made it in."

She told him to finish hauling in the pots, but with half their crew gone, she doubted they'd finish, at least not before their delivery deadline.

But she couldn't think about anything beyond Owen.

Her fiancé.

She'd thrown that word around like it belonged to her, and when she sat next to his bed in the ICU, the machines beeping, the oxygen hissing, she took his hand as if they might be high school sweethearts.

"Owen. Hon." She didn't even glance at the nurse, clad in friendly pink, examining his IV tube and taking his pulse. "You have to wake up. I'm so worried."

The nurse touched her shoulder. "He's in serious condition, but his blood pressure is holding strong. You're marrying a toughie."

She nodded and for a second could admit she longed for that outrageous, impossible happy ending.

Married to Owen Christiansen.

A man she barely knew. And she should get her head around that. Twelve hours in a raft didn't mean they were soul mates.

Crewmates. Survivors. Not engaged.

The nurse left, and Scotty pitched her voice low. "Listen, if you're freaking out about what I said in the boat, don't. I know you weren't serious about the proposal. You were trying to make me laugh or maybe stop me from thinking you were dying and going to abandon me on the high seas."

And he would have, too, if it hadn't been for . . . Well, she wouldn't call it God. Maybe fate. Luck.

She didn't know quite how to name it because now that she had land under her feet, she didn't want to think about faith. She just wanted to think about the fact that they'd lived.

"And don't worry; I haven't picked out a dress or anything, so you can wake up. Hear me? You can wake up, Owen."

He looked thinner, beat up, in the late-afternoon sun. Not like the man who'd jumped into a raging sea to save her. Or even the man who'd flirted with her, laughing, hiding his pain.

"You're such a jerk. Yeah, that's right, because guess what? You got me thinking about what it might be like to be married to you. And how annoying you'd be, all fun and games, not a serious bone in your body."

Except he had gotten serious—enough to tell her about his life. His family. His mistakes.

She blinked back the burn in her eyes. Stupid Eye Patch, almost making her cry.

"I mean, we don't know each other. Not really." Even if he was the kind of man a girl might want to marry—his wide shoulders, blond hair, the way he looked up occasionally to find her watching him, to flash her a smile.

How she loved that smile.

And to discover that it came with a laugh that made her feel seen, even pretty . . . If she was going to marry anyone, ever, it might have been Owen Christiansen.

For a moment, she let herself linger there. Married to Owen— what would that be like? To have a family. More, to have a man who didn't see her as a fellow deckhand or, worse, a boss. One of the guys.

They might build a life together, get a house, have children— little towheaded charmers like Owen and dark-haired spitfires like herself. Be a family.

Wow, that vision filled her, and she had to shake it away.

She had a life to get back to here in Alaska. And Owen . . . he just had to live.

She held his hand, ran her thumb over the IV. "So here's what I was thinking. You wake up—we start with that—and then maybe we don't get married, but we . . . we go to Deep Haven." She looked up, hoping for a response. "Don't be such a chicken. If your family is anything like what you described, they'll be overjoyed to see you. And if it helps, I can lie a little and tell them you were brave."

Please, Owen. She pressed her ear to his chest, listening to his heartbeat.

Even if he didn't wake up, she planned on bringing him home. He deserved that much.

"Ma'am, your visitation is over." The nurse, sneaking in behind her.

Scotty lifted her head, nodded, then leaned over and kissed Owen's forehead. "Wake up, honey. Wake up."

She walked out of the ICU, back to the waiting room. Settled on the sofa, closed her eyes.

"Coffee?"

The voice woke her and she opened her eyes, rubbed them. Carpie stood over her holding a steaming cup of joe from the cafeteria. He appeared wrung out, eyes bloodshot.

"Carp." She stood as he put the coffee down and pulled her into his arms. She hung on, breathing in the solid warmth of him. "Where's Red?"

"Aw, he's outside in the truck. Smoking. You scared him pretty good. Needs to get his legs under him."

"That's Red for you. Mr. Emotional. He'll be in when he knows everyone's in the clear. Probably yell at me for making you guys work shorthanded."

"Yeah, well, he seemed pretty emotional when he dropped the gear."

"What?"

"All the pots, the rest of the line—still sitting at the bottom of the Bering Sea. I think he's going to let the *Alaska King* pull it in, maybe give them half the take."

"We'll lose the boat!"

"We searched for you all night. He'd mobilized the fleet to find you, and when the Coast Guard radioed in that they'd grabbed you, he simply took off for Dutch Harbor at thirty knots. I swore we were going to die."

"Sorry."

"Took the first flight out of Dutch Harbor, left Juke and Greenie to unload, picked up his truck in Homer, and drove like a maniac only to sit in the parking lot for the last hour. I finally left him to stew."

"You did the right thing."

"I've never seen him so shaken up, Scotty."

"Serves him right for nearly making me watch him die."

Carpie made a face at the reminder of her helming the ship in a January storm as her father collapsed on the floor of the pilot-house. Maybe she didn't want to remember either.

She and Red might not be close, but they were all they had.

Carpie shook his head. "You two are cut from the same cloth. I remember you threatening all the way to harbor that if he died, you'd follow behind and kill him again."

She lifted the edge of her mouth, added a shrug.

"So how's Owen?" Carpie sat next to her on the sofa.

"He broke a couple ribs when the wave hit, and they caused internal bleeding. His heart finally stopped and he nearly drowned in his own blood, but they were able to save him."

"All I could do was pray. Just pray, for twelve hours." He took her hand, squeezed, his voice suddenly wrecked. "I love you like you were one of my girls, Scotty. Don't you do that to me again."

A surge of warmth crested over her at his words, and she leaned in, wrapped her hand around his arm. "Bossy."

"A 'Yes, sir,' will do."

She grinned.

"I still can't believe it happened," Carpie said, reaching up to run a thumb under his eye. "One second I'm gulping in seawater; the next I look up and there Owen is diving into the ocean like he might be a superhero. Juke yelled at us to throw out the life raft and Greenie grabbed it, opened it to inflate it as it lifted off the boat. We tried to keep our light on it, but it vanished, just like Owen." He cupped her hand on his arm. "Just like you."

"He found me. If it wasn't for Owen, I would be dead."

She let that sit there a moment.

The door opened and the nurse popped her head in. "Ma'am, your fiancé is starting to wake up. If you'd like to go in and see him, you may."

Next to her, Carp stilled.

"Thank you," Scotty said, affecting a smile.

The nurse left. Scotty found her feet. "Not a word, Carp. It's just—"

"You're engaged? After twelve hours on the raft?" He pulled off his cap, ran a hand over his head. "Engaged. Wait until Red—"

"Not a word to Red." She grabbed his arm. "It's just . . . pretend, okay? Yeah, he proposed, but he didn't mean it—"

"He proposed to you? And you said yes?"

Technically . . . She nodded.

"Have you lost your ever-lovin' mind? What happened in that raft?"

"Nothing!"

"Then you can't marry Owen Christiansen."

She stared at him. "Why not? You don't think I'm marriage material?"

His face said it. The way his lips tightened into a revealing knot. "You don't!"

"Scotty—"

"What, you think I'm too . . . tough? Not tender enough?"

"Of course not. It's just—Scotty, marriage isn't something you try out. It's for life. It's all in, committed. And you're . . ."

"You're saying I'm not the marrying type. Thanks. Thanks for that."

"I love you, Scotty. And by God's grace you survived what most people never would. I'm not saying that you weren't made for the sea, but you have to decide what life you want. Marriage, family? I'm all for that. But yesterday I was trying to talk you out of picking up your shield again. And now you're engaged? What's going on?"

She sucked in a breath, his words hitting her like a slap. "I don't know, okay?" She pressed a hand to her head. "You're right. I'm all messed up. Maybe I'm not marriage material." She sank back onto the sofa. "I admit I'm a little tired of arresting people I know. But we're clearly losing the boat, so what else do I have?"

Carpie shook his head. "I don't know, honey, but I don't think it includes marriage to a guy you hardly know."

"A girl would be lucky to be married to Owen Christiansen. I think."

Maybe that was simply hope talking, because yeah, Carpie was most definitely right. She'd lost her mind in a swirl of emotions that she squarely blamed on Owen "I-am-charming-even-when-dying" Christiansen. "But don't worry. I'm not going to marry him."

Carpie blew out a breath, his voice softening as if he were talking to his thirteen-year-old. "Good. Listen, you were dead set on returning to the force. If you want to do that, maybe stop by the Anchorage police station, see if you can start early. I know you're not due to report for a couple weeks, but maybe they have a position available now. Will you do that before you run off to Vegas?"

She let a smile leak out. "Calm down. I bet he can't even remember proposing."

"Of course he remembers." Carpie winked. "A guy never forgets proposing to a pretty girl."

Sweet.

"I gotta go. I don't want him to wake up without me."

But as she stood, Carpie took her arm. "Scotty. Are you in love with him?"

She stiffened. Frowned. Stepped away. "No. Of course not."

His expression fell. "Oh no."

"What?"

"Just . . . don't let him break your heart."

She made a noise of dismissal, chased it with a laugh. "I'm one of the guys, Carpie. And a crab fisherman. I got a tough hide. Just like Old Red." Bending down, she popped a kiss on his weathered cheek. "Go home and say hi to the girls for me."

She chewed over his words as she headed toward Owen's room. *Are you in love with him?*

Maybe a little, if love felt like the pounding of her heart when he looked at her and the sense of panic thinking he might die.

If she let her emotions speak for her, then maybe her *yes* had really meant . . . *yes.*

She took a breath, pushed open the door to his room.

A man stood at Owen's bedside, dressed in a leather jacket,

flannel shirt, and jeans, his dark-brown hair curling just behind his ears. He folded his arms across his chest, his jaw tight.

Maybe he was a surgeon, checking in one last time before he headed home.

Owen, for his part, did seem to be stirring. Scotty glanced at the man, then walked over and took Owen's hand. "It's time to wake up . . . honey." Just in case the doctor started to flex his visitation-rules muscles.

Owen's eyes moved under his lids. She put her hand on his cheek. "That's right. C'mon. Come back to me."

"Excuse me," the doctor said, his voice quiet. "Who are you?"

See, this was why she had clung to the lie, why she'd stepped into it, embraced it. For moments like this, when Owen was returning from the dead and some overzealous doctor wanted to kick her out of the room. Family only.

Right now she was all the family he had. She glanced at the doctor, affecting her skipper's voice. "Me? I'm sorry; we haven't met yet." She held out her hand across the bed. "I'm his fiancée."

The man took her hand, one eyebrow raised.

And then she heard it—Owen's voice, muffled under the oxygen mask. She leaned over. "Sweetheart, I'm here."

His gaze landed on her a moment, and questions filled his expression. Then suddenly warmth entered his blue eyes as, hopefully, it all rushed back to him.

She smiled. "You're back."

He nodded, but his gaze ranged past her, to the doctor.

And everything darkened. His eyes, his expression. It broke in a moment to a frown, confusion.

He reached up as if to grab his mask, but she caught his hand. "What is it?"

He spoke, but she couldn't make it out, so she moved his mask aside. "What's the matter, Owen?"

His focus stayed on the doctor, still unmoving beside the bed. "What are you doing here?"

"Swept overboard." The man shook his head. "How epic." He lifted his hand as if shaping the headline. "'Former Hockey Player Lost at Sea.' You could have *died*, Owen, and no one would have known. Mom would spend the rest of her years wondering— hoping you'd call. Waiting for *nothing*. Is that how you wanted to play this? Punish us all forever?"

Huh?

Owen swallowed, then looked at Scotty, such confusion on his face that she wanted to lean over him in a full-out body block and order this jerk from the room.

In fact . . . "Listen, mister, I don't know who you are, but he's been through enough. Don't let the door hit you on the way out."

The man turned his gaze on her.

Wait. *Mom*, he had said. And in truth, if she put the two men side by side, they had the same high cheekbones, chiseled lips, a tightness to the jawline that could only be a genetic arrogance.

And then, as if Owen had the ability to crawl inside her thoughts and had been slightly conscious during all her visitation sessions, he stirred from his stillness, back to reality, and played along with their charade. "Honey, I want you to meet my brother, everyone's sweetheart, Casper Christiansen."

A guy just returning from the dead should have a few seconds to catch up. To ask questions.

Like . . . they'd lived? Apparently yes, based on the deep ache in Owen's chest, the hiss of oxygen under his nose, his dry-as-ice mouth, and the way his heart monitor reminded him, with each beep, to hit his knees in gratitude.

He hadn't died. And it got better because surely God had heard his prayers if he'd not only come out alive but had beautiful Scotty McFlynn sitting beside his bed, holding his hand, looking at him like she might cry?

In fact, he might have convinced himself he was still sleeping if it weren't for the shocking sight of Casper, in all his glory, rocking him back to the sins he couldn't escape.

Which led to . . . what was Casper doing here?

"Everyone's sweetheart. That's rich, coming from the guy who's most likely left a trail of broken hearts from one end of the country to the other," Casper said.

Broken hearts? Owen glanced at Scotty, back to Casper, wanting to shut him up fast. Not that he'd hidden his past from Scotty, but he didn't exactly want to hash out his torrid months of trying to work the grief out of his system.

"How'd you find me?" Owen said, his voice sounding as if he'd done hard time as a two-packs-a-day smoker. He cleared his throat.

"Why? Hoping to stay lost?" Casper said.

"Maybe." He wished for a little more oomph, something that didn't make him sound like a man on his deathbed. "But if I remember correctly, I wasn't the only one who left without a forwarding address, so don't get righteous on me." Owen's voice faded and he licked his lips.

Scotty glanced at him, frowning. And in her glance he saw the quiet, hardworking guy he'd cultivated over the past months dissolve into the angry has-been athlete he'd been trying to outrun.

Shoot.

Casper's other eyebrow rose. "If I'd stayed, it would have ended badly."

"For you maybe." Aw, he wanted to wince at his own words. What was it about his brother—?

Scotty had grabbed his water. Now she angled the straw toward him and leaned close. "Your brother is here. *Right here.* And you nearly died. Be nice."

Yes. Of course. But he couldn't shake away the sense of being dressed down.

Casper shifted as if debating his words. "I came back. On my own. No one had to hunt me down."

"Are you looking for some kind of thank-you? I don't need my big brother to drag me by the ear back home."

"Prove it."

There it was, the condescension, the sense of competition between them that simmered right below the surface. The sense that Casper was always egging him on to be better, stronger.

Well, he had been, thank you. Who was the one who'd played professional hockey while the other brother talked about hoboing around the world hunting for lost treasure?

And apparently Owen was his greatest find. Casper certainly appeared smug, standing beside the bed. Same old Casper . . . except maybe taller than Owen remembered, wider shoulders, and something about him that seemed more confident. Less brash.

It didn't mean Casper wouldn't finish what he'd started once Owen got back on his feet.

"Mom and Dad sent you to find me?"

"In a way." He looked away, his mouth forming a grim line as if holding back some errant emotion. What—was big bro actually worried about him dying?

That ignited all kinds of untamed emotions that Owen funneled into one. "Casper, I can take care of myself. I don't need you chasing me down, trying to talk some sense into me, or whatever they want you to do."

"They just want to know . . ." Casper shook his head. "You're a jerk."

"Right back at ya."

And then, strangely, Casper looked at the floor and let out a sigh. "This is not how I wanted this to go."

That left Owen just a little undone. Especially when Casper ran one hand, quick, sharp, under his eye.

No. He couldn't really be—okay, so maybe Owen was a jerk, being too hard on his brother. After all, they had been close once upon a time.

Once upon a very, very long time. Before Owen destroyed it all. "Casper—"

His brother turned away. "Leave it. It's just good you're not dead."

Scotty put Owen's water down. "Wow, you two are brothers. Sheesh, now I remember why I'm glad to be an only." She turned to Owen. "This is the same Casper you couldn't stop talking about? The one who taught you to play hockey—"

"He didn't teach me—"

"Totally taught him everything he knows."

Owen glanced at Scotty, tried to put words into his gaze. *Stop. Please stop talking, Scotty.* Because he didn't want Casper knowing how much he regretted just about everything that had happened between them.

How he'd longed, as his life passed into the shadows, to go home.

Not yet. Not until he figured out—"Really. How did you find me?"

Casper had composed himself, and now he shrugged. "You made the news. In Seattle."

He wanted to chase that with another question—namely, what was Casper doing in Seattle?—but Scotty plunged in again.

"There were reporters here this afternoon. I told them to get lost."

See, she was his kind of girl. Last thing he needed was an overzealous reporter getting wind of his identity and replaying his short, sad NHL career. If they hadn't already . . .

"Although—" she gave him a lopsided smile—"I would have liked to tell them how you dove into the ocean after me."

"Scotty. Shh. Let it be over," Owen said quietly. "Please."

She met his eyes, and he took a moment to soak it in.

They'd *lived*.

But there was more, something swimming around the back of his mind. He fished back to the past, tried to push through the shadows and darkness to find solid ground.

Sunshine. Heat on his face and golden light over the horizon.

Voices and the whisper of her lips on his? "You saved me," he said to Scotty. "Right?"

"No more than you saved me," she said. But he wanted to call her a liar because he knew he'd been dying, knew his body had filled with blood.

"How did we—?"

"The Coast Guard picked us up just in time. You had surgery for your punctured lung." She angled a glance at Casper. "Thanks to your broken ribs. That you got when you *saved my life*."

"I think the ribs were from the wave. On the ship—"

"And made worse when you pushed me into the raft, again *saving my life*."

Casper held up a hand. "Okay. I got it. He saved your life.

80

Which, yes, I'm utterly glad for. That might make him your Prince Charming, but it doesn't erase anything he's done."

"Wow. Forgive much?" Owen said.

Casper raised an eyebrow. "Apologize much?"

"For your information, he's no Prince Charming, but he is a gentleman—"

"Seriously, how well do you know him?"

"Well enough," Scotty snapped, and in the back of his head, Owen heard, *A "Yes, sir," will do.*

He grinned as she glanced at him with a frown. "What are you laughing at, Eye Patch?"

This got a chuckle out of Casper.

And there it was, that stirring inside that told Owen he was going to live. Definitely, absolutely live, at least long enough to get out of this bed and chase Scotty right into his arms.

In fact, now that they'd lived, he planned on never letting her go. Which brought him up short. He'd forgotten something else.

"Wait—is everything okay with Mom and Dad? They're fine, right?" It hadn't occurred to him that maybe—"No one is sick?"

This seemed to shake Casper a little, and his posture relaxed. "Breathe, Bro. They're fine. Amelia is on her way to Africa—mission trip."

"Wow."

"Yeah, and oh . . . Butter died." Casper shoved his hands into his pockets.

Owen winced, fighting a rush of emotion. He hadn't expected that—never gave the old golden retriever more than a passing thought. But they'd had Butterscotch since he was a kid, and of course, he hadn't expected the old dog to live forever. Still, his throat thickened with the news.

"Mom took it pretty hard, but she's okay now." Casper paused a minute as if pondering what he was going to say.

"What aren't you . . . ? There's something you're not telling me. Are you sure everyone is okay? How's Jace, Eden—?"

"Jace is coaching for the Blue Ox now. Darek and Ivy had a baby girl."

"No, really?"

"Mmm-hmm. Baby Joy. And Grace and Max eloped and are now adopting this cute little girl from Ukraine."

Grace and Max, married. The man who'd caused his accident, in the family forever.

But maybe he could leave that behind too—the anger that could choke him in the dark hours of the night.

"I don't know the details—Raina just told me."

And there it was, Owen's sin, named. He'd spent more than a year trying to forget her—had, in fact, put her so far out of his mind that just hearing her name again felt like a slap.

He kept his voice light. "Raina? So . . . you're still . . ."

Didn't that sound awkward? He glanced at Scotty, who now just looked from Owen to Casper and back, the slightest frown on her face.

This right here was why a prodigal with his rap sheet had no business chasing a girl like Scotty.

"Yeah," Casper said quietly. He sighed, his eyes finding Owen's, holding them almost in challenge. "Raina and I are still together."

"Super. Awesome. That's great."

Only, something about the way Casper looked at him . . . With every word he uttered, it seemed Casper wanted to drive a stake through Owen's heart.

Scotty was listening to the family summary with an enigmatic expression.

"Wow. I can't believe I missed . . . so much."

"Yep," Casper said. Then he shook his head, his voice becoming strangely distant. "I don't even know where to start with all you missed."

Owen glanced at Scotty again, turning their conversation from the raft over in his head. He remembered more now. He had been talking about his family and then . . . yes, about going home. And bringing her with him.

You should go home. She seemed to read his thoughts—and nodded.

"I think it's time for me to go home," he said in quiet echo of their conversation.

She smiled, and it healed the wounds of his confession. Yes. Go home. With Scotty, he could—

Scotty turned to Casper. "It's all he talked about before . . . in the raft."

The raft. He was missing something, but with everything in him he wanted to reach up and wrap his hand around her neck and kiss her—really kiss her—because he'd been thinking about that for what seemed like an eternity. Pretty much the only thing that kept him alive—the thought of pulling her into his arms and kissing her.

He had to figure out a way to make her come with him.

He turned back to Casper, hanging on to the moment. "I'm sorry I didn't call Mom."

"That's the first smart thing you've said."

"For the record, I didn't plan on nearly dying."

"I did mention he dove into the water to save my life." Scotty looked at Casper. "Crazy. Idiot. Jerk." She was smiling, though.

Owen laughed, then moaned.

"Stop it," she said; then she laughed too. And Owen was right back in the raft, teasing her, watching her eyes shine. Wow, she could take his breath away.

Casper wasn't as easily charmed. "Who are you, exactly? Are you really his fiancée?"

Owen froze at the word. Then a beat, a pulse, and the rest of his memory rounded out.

He'd . . . *proposed.* On a whisper of breath, his last breath. He remembered the sunrise, the feel of her curled beside him, the sense of life peeling back, leaving behind only his regrets, his what-ifs, and in that moment, he'd let the voice inside run away with him.

In fact, since we just spent the night together, I think you should probably do right by me . . . and marry me.

A joke, perhaps, yet by the looks of things . . .

He glanced at Casper, sorting through a response. *She's my fiancée.* Ha, right, because she hadn't, wouldn't . . . not for a second . . . really have taken him seriously.

Right?

Who'd agree to marry him? A vagabond with one good eye, a deckhand with a motorcycle and a backpack to his name. What kind of life could he give her?

Except Scotty didn't seem the type to need a man to give her a life. They could give each other one, couldn't they? Start out simple here in Alaska. Build what they wanted together. He'd buy a fishing boat—or work for her father, maybe—and they'd get their own place. And he would marry her because he suddenly hungered for the life that had formed in his mind in the first light of morning.

His reason for living was right here.

Holding his hand.

Gray-green eyes in his. Long, silky black hair tumbling down over her green scrub top. Her face washed clean, the slightest smile catching her lips.

So he said it. Let the words just tumble out like a wave crashing over them. Testing them. "She's . . . Yes, Scotty is my fiancée."

He expected something like he'd given Casper about Raina—a warm congratulations. A laugh, maybe. A "Way to go, Bro." But his eyes were on Scotty, gauging her reaction, so he didn't exactly notice Casper's quietness—or didn't care because yeah, he was shocked too.

Not Scotty. She smiled slowly, then looked away, shaking her head.

"Right?" Owen said. "You said yes, didn't you?"

She giggled.

He'd never heard that from her. A giggle. And if it was possible, she even blushed.

"I dunno . . . I guess, yeah," she said.

In Owen's book, that sounded like a goal that should have been accompanied by sirens and a thunderous crowd cheering his name.

Scotty McFlynn, marrying him.

"Don't make me think about this too hard," she said. "Because Carpie thinks I'm crazy, but . . . yeah. Maybe. What if, right? Maybe that's why we lived." She giggled again, and he just about found the strength to kick his brother out of the room, pull her alongside him.

He was suddenly feeling much, much better.

"Right," he said. "We're getting married—"

"Oh, that's a fantastic idea," Casper said, his voice low.

Huh?

"Why not? Out of all your available choices, we just have to find the most irresponsible, and that's what you'll do."

His words sliced through the ethereal, ebullient happiness sifting down from never-never land.

"You're absolutely determined to destroy lives."

"Sheesh, Bro—"

"If you care at all about this girl, you won't marry her," Casper said, and this time his words felt like a punch.

Owen schooled his voice. "For the love of pete, Casper, what's your problem?"

"My problem is that you don't think." Casper pointed to his head. "Everything is fun and games with you."

"I'm not kidding here—" Owen reached for the railing, held on.

"Sit tight there, bruiser," Scotty said, her hand on his chest.

"No, I don't think you are," Casper said, not rattled in the least by Scotty rising to her feet. "You're dead serious. And that's the problem. You don't think beyond what feels good right now. What's going to make Owen happy. How much does she really know about you, Owen?"

The darkness of Casper's words cut off his breathing.

"You're upsetting him!" Scotty said, and Owen grabbed her hand even as she started to round the bed as if intending to push Casper from the room.

"Well, good. Maybe he needs to start thinking past his own enjoyment to the destruction his choices leave behind."

"I fail to see how marrying me—"

"Look, Scotty, I'm sure you're fantastic. And maybe marrying you is the best thing that could ever happen to Owen. But this really has nothing to do with you. You are just one more person

Owen can make fall in love with him before he runs away and leaves you brokenhearted."

"What did I ever do to you?" Owen said, now pulling himself up.

"Lie down!" Scotty barked.

"Really?" Casper said.

Owen heard the heart monitor begin to beep. "I know I made a few mistakes—"

"And now I have to hurt you." Casper turned away from him, blew out a breath.

Owen surrendered to Scotty's push on his shoulders, sinking back into the bed, nonplussed.

His brother braced his hands on the windowsill. "Owen, I actually don't care if you marry Scotty. In fact, yay, you. But you're coming home first."

Owen frowned, trying to get a grip on the ferocity of Casper's response. "No problem? I was . . . We were going to do that anyway, weren't we, hon?"

He kept his voice light, fighting the urge to let it end with a sharp edge.

Next to him, Scotty still stood, holding his hand. She managed a slow nod.

Then Casper rounded on them. He pushed his hand through his hair. "Yeah. Uh, I'm not so sure that's a good idea. . . ."

"Why not? Scotty needs to meet our family."

Casper's mouth tightened. "Fine. I was just thinking that you might want to sort a few things out before you decide to let her meet the fam."

"Like what?"

"Like—nothing." Casper ran his hand down his face. "I've

completely mucked this up. I'm sorry." He moved toward the door. "I'll come back later, when—"

"Like what, Casper? Just tell me! Like apologizing to Mom and Dad? Done. Making peace with Max? Fine. Done. What other penance do I need to do to be forgiven by the beloved and perfect Casper Christiansen?"

Casper stopped at the door. Then he turned, his eyes reddened. "How about figuring out how to be a father? Huh? How about that?"

Time stopped. Along with Owen's heartbeat. His breath.

And then Scotty's hand slid out of his.

Owen wanted to reach for it, pull it back, but she clasped her arms around her middle, a frown dissecting her forehead, eyes just a little wounded.

"Scotty . . ." He turned to Casper. "What are you talking about?"

Casper had that dark expression—the one he'd worn at Eden's wedding—and for a wild second Owen wanted to push the call button, maybe get some security in here.

Then Casper breathed out as if he had everything under control. He walked over to the bed. Swallowed. "I wanted to say it in a way that . . . was better. Like I didn't want to rip out your throat every time I thought about it. Apparently that's not going to happen. There's no good way to say it. The fact that you got a girl pregnant and then deserted her? Yeah, I didn't know how to sugarcoat that."

"What. Are. You. Talking. About?" Owen said as the word started to settle in. *Father?*

"You have a daughter, Owen. A beautiful, black-haired, blue-eyed daughter."

Silence.

"Who—?"

"Sheesh, Owen. I realize it's probably hard for you to sift back through the list of hundreds of girls you've bedded but try real hard to remember the one—"

"Hey!" Owen started, but then he stopped, thought for one second. He had been selfish. Reckless. Stupid. Arrogant. He swallowed hard. "I admit I made mistakes, but I haven't been that guy for a long time."

"You only have to be that guy once."

He drew in a breath. "Do we have to do this in front of Scotty?"

"Don't mind me," she said in a voice he didn't recognize.

And he was once again in the raft, losing his grip on the sunshine.

"Scotty—wait." He turned to Casper. "I'm not trying to be obtuse here, but *what girl*?"

Casper closed his eyes.

Then it all made sense. Why Casper had decked him at the wedding. How his brother had turned into a person he didn't recognize. Furious. Owen would feel the same way if Casper or Darek had been with Scotty and left her pregnant.

"Oh . . . It's Raina. Raina had my baby," Owen said quietly, not looking at Scotty. The words sank through him like inky darkness.

Casper's jaw tightened. "Yep. In January. Her name is Layla."

That's when Owen heard the footsteps.

He looked over just in time to see the door closing behind Scotty.

"Scotty, come back!"

Owen's voice trailed her into the hallway, squeezing through the door before it shut behind her. Scotty stopped just outside, her heart banging in her chest.

For a long time she stood, listening to the sounds from the nurses' station down the hall, smelling the clean antiseptic scent of the hospital, and tasting her own stupidity.

Owen had a child.

A child.

And he didn't even know it.

That fact made her run her hands over her face, lean against the wall, relishing the coolness after the sudden heat in the room.

She groaned. A child. With Casper's girlfriend.

Which, of course, accounted for Casper's furious behavior toward his almost-dead brother.

More, it seemed that Casper had come to tell Owen to man up, take care of his responsibilities. Which meant what? That Owen wasn't free to marry Scotty because he had to marry Raina?

But if she read the conversation correctly, Casper was with Raina.

Talk about family drama. It certainly added fuel to the fire between the Christiansen brothers.

It didn't matter anyway. The whole fantasy of meeting Owen's family had begun to disintegrate as she listened to them argue. Casper was probably right. Owen had acted on impulse when he proposed. She got that. Because she'd just as impulsively said yes. Which, of course, was Owen's superpower—making her break her own rules.

They should both be thanking Casper for his razor-edged candor.

Scotty stalked down the corridor. Stupid, idiotic, foolish girl, falling for a drifter. She knew better. She knew *better*.

In her gut, she'd known that the man had secrets, and she should have listened to her hunches.

She was just about to break into a jog when she heard her name again. "Scotty!"

The voice was lower but still familiar, and it made her turn. Casper strode down the hallway after her. "Scotty, stop!"

Curiosity glued her in place as Casper caught up.

He blew out a breath, ran his hands through his curly black hair. He had the rugged Christiansen appeal, she'd give him that. He wore the lumberjack look well, and yes, he possessed the same work-wrought muscles, that sense of strength that made Owen immovable in a storm. But Owen was hard-edged and heartbreaking, and a girl lost her mind a little when he held her with that intense gaze.

She needed to get out of this hospital and back to her life, fast.

"Listen. I didn't mean for all that baggage to come out quite like that. I just want to . . . apologize. I've been stressed out and angry and searching for him for four months. And he didn't exactly leave a trail behind, so no one knew where he was. Mom was frantic, and I guess I'm still too angry at him."

"For having a baby he didn't even know about?"

"Yeah . . . okay. Well said. But you know a different Owen than I do. The Owen I knew was angry and selfish and deserved a little 'come to Jesus.'"

"What he deserved was a brother glad to see him."

"I *am* glad to see him—more than you can know. I was nearly sick with relief when I got here and found out you'd been rescued."

"I could tell by the crying. Someone get me a hankie."

Casper's mouth tightened around the edges. "I guess I deserved that."

"I get being so upset you can't think straight. My old man is sitting outside in his pickup—has been for the past two hours— because he can't face the fact that he nearly lost me. So he's finishing off his second pack of Winstons, trying to figure out how to tell me he loves me, which he'll never be able to do. I get relationships tangled up in love and anger until something spills out that you regret. But the guy you just yelled at isn't the guy who got your girl pregnant."

He started to say something, but she held up her hand. "Save it. Instead, let me tell you about the Owen I know. Hardworking. Humble. Kind. Sacrificing. Funny. Self-deprecating. The kind of guy you want on your side. And if you dig back into your past, maybe you'll find that you know that Owen. Or maybe not. Maybe this is a new Owen. All I know is that the man lying in there is not the man who would shirk his promises. That's a man who dove into an ocean to save someone he barely knew."

"So that he could propose to her," Casper said. "Sounds like he knew you better than *barely*."

Oh, she wanted to hit him.

"No. He proposed to me as he lay dying. Because he thought it would help me not despair. Because if he proposed, maybe he could stop me from thinking about the fact that I might die too. So no, he wasn't trying to have another one-night stand, if that's what you were insinuating. He was trying to keep me alive."

Casper closed his mouth and had the decency to look chagrined. "Sorry. That was uncalled for."

"You bet it was, bro."

"I just don't want you to get hurt. Owen's left a lot of girls behind."

"What are you trying to do? Shock me? Let's meet again, shall we?" She stuck out her hand. "Scotty McFlynn. Relief skipper, first mate, and the only woman in the entire Bering Sea working full-time on a crab boat. I started when I was sixteen. Me and a crew of guys, working round the clock for a month. Do you think

I don't know what they were thinking? What they did the moment the ship docked? I'm not stupid. And in case you think I'm just nice, I'm also a cop. One who, only six months ago, killed a man who happened to be related to me. He'd beaten his wife and kid and was holding them hostage. High on meth—and I had to shoot him. I've been alone and not a little out of whack since then, and you might start considering the fact that Owen was the best thing that happened to *me*."

He stared at her, not moving.

"By the way, Owen told me about your girlfriend, the fight, and the fact that he regrets it more than you will ever know."

That seemed to knock him off his stance.

"He told me a lot of things. About you and your family. About how he wanted to go home. And I told him to be brave, to look beyond his mistakes—that maybe you'd all welcome him back. Apparently I was wrong about that. You seem set on hurting Owen as much as you seem to think he tried to hurt you."

Casper looked away and actually winced.

"Why are you here, anyway? I mean, sure, your parents are worried. I get that you wanted to find him for your family. But people go for years without talking to their relatives. But not you—you have to track him down. What's with that? He would have eventually gone home."

His family had a lot of secrets, judging by the way they floated across his face. Then he sighed. "I'm in love with Raina, and I want to marry her and be Layla's dad, but I need Owen's blessing."

After a beat, she let out a laugh, harsh, high. "You want his blessing after the way you treated him in there? Made him feel small, like a thirteen-year-old kid? I wouldn't be surprised if he never talked to you again."

Casper closed his mouth. Had the decency to look sorry.

And then as if a light flashed in her head, Scotty got it. Oh, she got it. "There's more, isn't there? You don't just want his blessing—you want him to *give up* his daughter to you, don't you? That's what that was all about—driving home to Owen how horribly irresponsible he is. What did you say—'learn to be a father'? You don't want him to do that; *you want him to admit he can't.*"

Casper met her eyes. "He hasn't the first clue how to be a dad to her."

"And you're willing to steal his kid away from him? Just like that—write him out of her life?"

"No. I wasn't—"

"So he could be, what, the special uncle? Nice, Casper. That's brotherly of you—"

"Please stop acting like you know anything about this situation. I understand you think you know Owen, but spending a month with him only scratches the surface."

"And spending a year away from him has made you blind to the person he really is. Hurting, yeah. But a guy who follows his heart, which, for you, might just backfire."

Casper blinked at her.

"A word of advice. I suggest you go back in there and try again. Make friends. Tell him the truth. It doesn't have to be you or him in this little girl's life. And frankly, maybe he'll be an amazing dad. Or could be if someone believed in him."

"Someone like you?"

"Have a little faith," she snapped, surprised by her own words but latching on because they seemed to make sense.

Casper considered her. "I'm starting to think Owen's proposal wasn't just a game. And apparently he thinks you said yes. Did you say yes?" He raised an eyebrow, and for a second, she could completely understand why Owen would launch himself at his arrogant brother, take a swipe at him.

He had the innate ability to get under someone's skin. Maybe the entire family was like this. She should recognize the warning flares.

Scotty said nothing.

"Answer the question."

She turned, but he grabbed her arm. She yanked it away. "Keep your hands off me."

"I'm sorry." He held up his hands in surrender. "I just want to know. Do you want to marry my brother or not?"

She glanced back, remembering the way Owen's face crumpled, the pain on it when he discovered he had a child he didn't know about. The embarrassment, the shame.

Right then she'd known. He was going back to Minnesota. Back to his family.

Back to Raina.

Maybe not to marry her because Casper clearly would tackle him before he reached the altar. But Owen planned on being in his daughter's life. Hadn't he said that very thing on the boat?

If I had a daughter, I'd never want to forget her. She would be everything to me.

Now that he'd discovered he was indeed a father, his life was in Minnesota.

And Scotty's? Well, she didn't quite know, but it certainly wasn't in the Lower 48. To follow on the heels of her man like some dutiful wife? Maybe Carpie was right—she wasn't made to get married. Ever.

This entire thing had been a joke. Or at least convenient. Until now.

So Scotty looked at Casper and said, "No." She let the word strengthen, empower. "No. I don't want to marry him."

Casper's eyes widened.

"Nice to meet you, Casper. Maybe be nicer to him when you bring him home. After all, to some, he is still a hero."

Then she turned and walked straight ahead, trying to swallow the burn in her throat before it moved to her eyes, glazed them over. She got on the elevator, rode it down to the first floor. Please, let Red still be sitting in his truck.

She strode through the lobby to the parking lot and paused at the edge of the sidewalk, scanning the lot. Snow began to fall from the smoky sky, turning gray along the pavement. Plows thundered by, peeling back black slush. The air bore the gloom of something bigger, hovering, something to flee before it settled upon them.

She finally spotted the old red beat-up Mazda pickup with the topper on the back, deer horns mounted on the front, and her father in the cab, smoking. Tucking her head, she charged across the parking lot.

When she opened the door and slid in, Red looked at her.

For a second he just stared, miserable, his cigarette burning long. Then he ran his hand under his nose, followed it with his sleeve. Flicked his cigarette out the window. "So," he said. "Where to?"

Scotty looked out her window. Swallowed the burn in her throat.

No crying.

She reached for her seat belt. "Buckle up, Red. The fairy tale is over. It's time to get back to my real life."

CHAPTER 5

"I'LL GIVE YOU A HUNDRED DOLLARS if you go out and get me a pizza." Owen sat on the bed, eyeing the green Jell-O wiggling in the pink plastic bowl on his dinner tray.

A sure sign of his brother getting better—the desire for pizza. "Stop whining and eat your supper, or they'll never discharge you." Casper grabbed the Bluetooth hookup and pulled a chair up to the TV. "Are you sure you want to watch the game? It's still preseason."

"Two hundred. Cash. And yes. I haven't seen a Blue Ox game in . . . Okay, never since I walked away. Maybe it's time to start." Owen pushed the Jell-O farther away. "The doctor says he might spring me by tomorrow. Oh, and by the way, your battery is low."

He dug out the phone and tossed it to Casper, who caught it with one hand and shoved it in his back pocket before returning to the array of plug-in choices. He could call up the game on his smartphone with his NHL app, but putting it on the big screen had taken two trips to the electronics store with detailed pictures of the television to show the pimply-faced teenager behind the Geek Squad desk.

"Did you get ahold of Scotty?"

Silence. Casper glanced at Owen. He was stirring his spoon through a pile of what looked like mashed potatoes.

Apparently that was a no.

"Sorry, Bro."

After four days holed up at the hospital, Owen looked more like a grumpy trucker than a patient who'd recently had his chest cracked. A scraggly beard, long stringy hair, and an odor that suggested he required more than a sponge bath. That hospital gown seemed flimsy at best as Owen shifted in bed, trying to find a decent position. Off oxygen and free of the other tubes monitoring his heart rate, O_2 level, and pulse, only an IV still attached to his arm where the doctors administered antibiotics against infection.

If his griping was any indication, Owen might be right about heading toward a morning discharge.

Which meant they would be on a plane to Deep Haven.

Namely, to Layla and Raina.

Casper had called Raina with the good news but had opted to keep his parents in the dark. Just in case Owen turned on him and ran for the hills again.

Casper didn't know why, but sometimes his mouth got up and sprinted out in front of his brain. Cutting off all common sense. He wanted to reel back time to four days ago, start over, this time with relief and a little humility. To cut Owen some slack. He'd just not known where to put all his emotion—relief, yes, and then frustration, maybe leftover fury and a significant amount of disbelief.

Thankfully, they'd found a tentative peace.

"Scotty's clearly done." His brother shrugged. "I don't blame her. She didn't sign on for a guy with this kind of baggage. Besides, were we really serious? Probably we would have both cut and run before we made it down the aisle. I mean, it's me, right?" Owen looked up at Casper, made a face. "Since when have I stuck around?"

Casper had the urge to open his mouth and protest. Repeat a smidgen of what Scotty had leveled at him. *Hardworking. Humble. Kind. Sacrificing. Funny. Self-deprecating. The kind of guy you want on your side.*

If any of it were true, Casper might be in big trouble.

Because if Owen were any of these things, then maybe he wouldn't dismantle Layla's life. Maybe Casper didn't have a right to step between father and daughter.

He found the HDMI port, plugged in the device, then stepped off the chair and reached for his phone. "Wow, you left me a whopping 14 percent." He grabbed his charger, searched for a socket.

"Layla has my eyes," Owen said quietly.

Casper glanced at him.

"Sorry, but I couldn't help it. I checked out your photos. She's so pretty with that dark hair. And Raina—she looks good too. I kind of forgot how beautiful she is."

"I didn't," Casper said, thumbing through the NHL listings on his phone. "I never do." He kept his voice light, biting back the strangest spurt of panic.

He found the right game and tapped on it to bring up the feed.

Then from Owen: "I don't get it. If you think I'm such a bum, why do you want me in her life?"

And there it was. Casper didn't want him in her life. Not really.

Scotty's words resounded through his head. *And you're willing to steal his kid away from him? Just like that—write him out of her life? . . . He could be, what, the special uncle?*

Maybe he'd thought that—hoped that Owen would admit the entire thing was over his head and thank Casper for stepping in.

Casper shook the pinpricks of guilt away. "I want your blessing, okay?"

"My . . . blessing? Seriously? My blessing to marry a girl I barely know?"

"You knew her well enough to make a baby with her."

"Here we go again. What do you want me to say, Casper? I can't take it back at this point. There's no erasing my colossal stupidity. But it happened, and Layla is breathtaking, so we're moving on. Yeah, okay, I'm a dad. That doesn't mean I'm getting in the way of you and Raina. You don't need my blessing."

Uh, yeah, he did. Except maybe he wouldn't call it a blessing, but . . . what was he going to say? *Actually, I need more than that. I need your permission. . . . I want you to surrender your rights to Layla.*

Maybe not. "Okay then. Come home, meet Layla, and if you're cool with it, Raina and I get married. You take off; we're all good."

That's when he'd have that ever-so-awkward conversation. The one about supporting a child long-distance and how Casper would be glad to take over, fill in, let Owen off the hook.

In fact, he was still desperately counting on it.

Owen lay back, closing his eyes. "When I was out there on that raft, all I could think about was Dad playing that transistor radio, some old country song on it. Mom's cookies. I would have given my right leg for some of her cookies. I kept seeing us in the yard, raking leaves, and . . ." He looked at Casper. "I really want to go home."

"Then it's settled."

"No, I want to go home to stay."

Casper stilled. "Stay? As in . . . get a job? In Deep Haven?"

"Sure. Buy a house, coach junior hockey, maybe start a business. I have a little fishing experience—"

"Owen, what are you talking about? Staying is . . . a big commitment."

"I'm a dad now. You even said it—I have to learn how to be a father. I think that means getting to know Layla and Raina. Being a real dad."

A real dad . . .

More of Scotty's words rang in Casper's ears. *Frankly, maybe he'll be an amazing dad. Or could be if someone believed in him.*

Now, looking at Owen in the bed, Casper saw that his kid brother had the makings of exactly that. His patch was off, the scar crinkled around his eye. And yeah, he sported a few bandages, but he'd filled out, his arms thick, his chest sculpted under that hospital gown. He didn't look like an overgrown kid with a big paycheck and a cocky smile anymore, the kind to seduce a woman into a one-night stand, but a grown man who'd made decisions and survived on the high seas.

Casper hadn't exactly thought about the possibility of Owen *staying*.

Or that Raina might be glad Casper brought him home. A father for her daughter—Layla's *real* father.

No, Casper hadn't thought about that at all.

"What about Alaska and Scotty?" Casper said. He found the

right input and the Blue Ox fight against the Denver Blades appeared in high def, without sound.

Owen sighed. "I don't know. You saw her walk out of here. And I called Carpie, who hasn't seen her since I have. Her father isn't answering, and I'm not sure who else to call. My phone is probably back in my rack on the *Willie*, and hers might be at the bottom of the Bering Sea for all I know, so I'm at a loss. I hope she's not back in Homer but . . ."

"Did you seriously propose?"

"Yeah, I proposed." Owen made a face. "But you were right; I wasn't really thinking about what would happen if she said yes. I was trying to get her to hope, to hang on until we were found." He went quiet for a long time, just breathing, running his fingers over the top of the covers. "But . . . here's the thing. I've really made a mess of things. Getting injured, ending my career, the scene at Eden and Jace's wedding—"

"No, that was me. If you recall, I tackled you. You just hit me back."

"Maybe you should have played football instead of hockey."

"Maybe you should have learned how to throw a punch," Casper said.

Owen looked up, sharp.

"Don't get your shorts in a wad. I'm kidding."

Owen glanced at the screen, not smiling. "I'll never forget the look on Mom's face. Or Dad's. I felt twelve again. I thought they were going to separate us and make us say ten nice things to each other."

"You aren't completely ugly," Casper said.

"You don't smell like socks." A grin appeared on Owen's face, the first one Casper had seen since Scotty fled out the door. Then it fell away. "I miss them. I miss everyone. I didn't want it to be that way. It's just . . . I couldn't face myself and the life I had lost. And now . . . Well, you try floating around for a day on the ocean and see how you feel. Everything starts to snap into place."

Casper went back to fiddling with the TV connections, suddenly not wanting to think about his brother nearly frozen in the middle of the ocean.

"Yeah, I made mistakes—a lot of them. But I got a good look at the guy I didn't want to be anymore, and I've been trying to put it back together. I've even been . . . reading my Bible. Praying. Trying to figure out if there is any reason why God might want to save my wretched hide."

Casper glanced at him, not expecting that.

"I want to be someone who can go home and fix what I messed up. But I don't know how. I have this sort of sick feeling when I think about starting over. Like I'm going to bomb, big. Again. Make a mess of everything. The family screwup."

Casper stared at the screen again, not sure what to say.

"Truth is, I don't know if Deep Haven is really home anymore."

This made Casper look away from the game, at Owen. "What are you talking about?"

"I didn't leave home when I was eighteen or even twenty. I left when I was sixteen, and before that I spent every weekend on the road. I barely know you guys. I knew Eden because she lived close by and hovered over me for years. But the fact is, I'm not really a part of the family. . . ."

"Of course you are."

"Think about it. I barely know Amelia, and I haven't been on one meaningful vacation with the family since I was thirteen. I've always been standing on the outside, looking in. And the last two years didn't help. I'm not . . . I don't really belong."

Casper had nothing. Because while four days ago he might have agreed, seeing Owen hurt and defenseless had him feeling like the king of all jerks.

And Owen had pegged it. Casper *didn't* want him to stick around Deep Haven, make a mess of the happy picture Casper had painted in his brain. One that gave him full legal custody of Layla and erased Owen's biological claim on her. And yeah, relegated him to distant uncle.

Still, Casper's mouth opened on its own. Again, running out ahead of his brain. "You belong, Owen. We all missed you. And I know I came off a little, well, hot, when I found you, but it's just because I was so stupidly relieved that I didn't have to go home and tell Mom you died at sea."

"You're going to make me cry."

"Then I was sitting on the mother of all land mines, and here you were, all happy and engaged and . . ."

"Stop before I reach for my hankie. Fine. I'll go home already."

Perfect. Casper wanted to bang his head against the wall.

The sounds of the game came over the screen. Casper stepped back, searching for Max on the ice.

"He's in the penalty box," Owen said quietly, his face changing. And in a moment, Casper saw the brother he'd known. Passionate, giving his all to his sport. He went after what he wanted with everything inside him. Like hockey. And saving the woman he loved—or thought he loved—from drowning. And living through a punctured lung.

Yeah, Owen had the uncanny ability to go after the goal and score. Every time.

Casper sank down in the chair, his stomach clenching. He noticed that Owen's jaw had tensed and asked, "Should I turn it off?"

"No. Jace should tell them to defend against the spread and look out for a backdoor crease pass—ah! Like that one!"

The siren sounded the Denver goal.

"Maybe when I get home, I'll give the Blue Ox a call, see if they need a trainer. That way I'll have a job while I stick around and get to know my daughter. Maybe I can get some tickets—take her to a few games. Do you think Raina would let me?"

"She's not even a year old yet, Owen. Give her a chance to walk, maybe talk, understand what she's looking at."

"I started skating when I was four. I once saw skates for two-year-olds." Owen leaned back, pulled up the covers. "C'mon, Casper. Three hundred dollars for a pepperoni and mushroom. You know you want it."

Shoot, but he did.

Less than a week since her life nearly ended, Scotty found herself saying good-bye again. This time it was on purpose.

"C'mon, Red, it's getting late." She stood in the door to the wheelhouse of the *Willie*, watching her old man take the helm one last time. He peered out over the dark, frothy waters of Dutch Harbor as if about to face his final gale.

"Did you clean the galley?" he asked without looking at her.

"Aye, Captain. Uncle Gil is outside in the truck. We have a low ceiling coming in and I need to get back to Anchorage."

Shake off her past once again. Start over.

Forget.

She'd spent the last four days cleaning the nooks and crannies of the *Wilhelmina*, hosing down the crab tanks, repairing the sorting table, helping Juke weld the hoist back into place, and finishing the minor repairs that would make the old floater salable.

In fact, her father had already listed the 108-foot single screw, and she hoped offers would pour in. She'd tell him to accept the first one, take the money, and flee.

They just might break clear with twenty cold ones for his retirement, what little of it there would be if he didn't hold off on the cheeseburgers.

"I can't believe it's over," Red said now, quietly. He held one hand on the jog stick, the other on the engine throttle, as if he were about to ease her out of port into the icy crab fields.

It doesn't have to be. The words tiptoed across Scotty's lips, but she swallowed them. What choice did they have? With the less-than-quota crab haul this season and his mountainous medical bills . . . "You don't have to shut her down. You could let me take over payments—"

"No." He turned away from the helm, his gaze landing hard on her. "Crab fishing is no place for—"

"A girl, I know."

He gave her that no-comment sound that might be agreement or could simply be his desire to kill the conversation.

A retort was forming on her lips when—

"I can't spend every minute worrying about you getting yourself thrown overboard." Then he brushed by her, down the stairs.

Huh.

Scotty scrambled after him, pausing to scoop up her duffel bag and her last meager possessions from her quarters.

She'd found Owen's bunk and rolled up his sleeping bag with his toiletries kit and, oddly, a Bible she found under the prison-striped pillow. Maybe he'd meant his words about faith after all.

She'd also found two pictures lodged in the springs of the bunk above his. She recognized Casper in one shot and guessed the rest of the crew in the picture might be the family Christiansen. The other picture was of a very young Owen on skates, arm around the neck of a barely older Casper.

No wonder they'd nearly come to blows. People who loved each other that much knew how to wound the deepest.

She planned on dropping the kit off, along with his pay, at the hospital later when she landed in Anchorage. Just a quick stop-in.

No trouble, no emotion. All business.

She caught up with Red just as he reached the truck and stopped him before he wrangled his girth into the backseat of the extended cab. "Sorry, but not this time. You have shotgun." She dumped both duffels into the back. "Hey, Uncle Gil."

"Elise," the police chief said.

She let the use of her real name pass—his way of trying to turn her into the daughter he'd never had. Her father's best friend, "Uncle" Gil was everything Old Red wasn't—warm, bighearted, loud, tall, and strong, with hands that could tear an apple in half, and more of a father than Old Red had ever attempted to be. But that's what happened when you had a wife, two sons—a real family.

Gil put the truck in gear and pulled away from the dock, leaving the *Wilhelmina* tied up, the deck empty, the crane looming and rusty against the steel-gray sky. They'd unloaded the two hundred pots into their storage area, ready for new ownership.

Scotty didn't look back but noticed with a twinge in her chest the way her father's hand tightened on the door handle, fighting a final look at the boat he'd named after his wife.

"You sure you don't want to stop in and see Rosie? She'll make dinner," Gil said. "There's no real rush, is there?"

"I'm meeting someone for dinner." Not exactly a lie. She would meet up with Angie after she picked up some takeout. Probably. After all, that's what happened when you bunked with an old friend.

Gil glanced at Red. "Does he have a name?"

"Angie and I went to police academy together; don't get excited." She hid a smile when his fell.

"She has a fella," Red offered, pulling out his Winstons. "The guy she went overboard with."

"Red! He is not my fella."

He lit the cigarette, smoke tunneling from his nose. "According to Carpie, he proposed."

"Really?" This from Uncle Gil, who glanced at her. "Marriage?"

"No. He proposed we go skydiving. Yeah, marriage."

From the silence, apparently all the men in her life agreed with Carpie. Not marriage material. Perfect.

"He wasn't serious. And neither was I. It was . . . something we did to stay alive."

More silence.

"Really. It's over."

Except it didn't feel over. Not with the news that Owen had been trying to track her down. First through Carpie, then her father's missed calls—four of them on his cell phone that she discovered while cleaning up the wheelhouse.

As if Owen might still be thinking of her too. . . .

She shook her head as her uncle drove them along the bay to the tiny one-runway Dutch Harbor FBO. A snowstorm simmered along the western horizon, just above the mountains that edged the bay. They needed to get in the air soon if they wanted to beat the descending ceiling.

Uncle Gil pulled up to the hangar, and Scotty climbed out after her father, dragging her duffel over her shoulder.

Gil's pretty Cessna 172, a white albatross with a red racing stripe, sat gassed up, preflight checked, and ready for the trip back to Homer, then on to Anchorage.

Taxi service, Alaska style.

Scotty retrieved Owen's duffel, cast it over her other shoulder, then loaded them both onto the plane. Her father buckled in behind the pilot as she hopped into the cockpit.

Uncle Gil finished his walk-around, then climbed in and started his preflight rundown. She helped him, and in a moment they were ready for taxi.

"Last chance for a homemade meal."

Giving no response, Scotty slipped on her headphones.

Something about drifting above the ocean, as opposed to in it, gave new resonance to the fact that she and Owen had survived. Up here, the Bering Sea appeared dark and vast. How the Coast Guard had managed to spot one tiny flare . . .

Have a little faith.

She banished Owen from her head and instead listened to the radio chatter, settling herself into her decision.

The Anchorage police seemed eager to have her, especially with Gil's recommendation. One chief to another. And though she'd have to start out on patrol, Chief Elmore assured her of a detective job within six months.

She'd be solving cases by this time next year.

They touched down in Homer and her father got out, headed toward his truck. "Water my Christmas cactus!" she yelled after him, and he raised a hand. "And take your shoes off when you walk on the carpet—"

"He's a crusty old sea dog. Do you really think he's going to tiptoe around your cute little house in stocking feet?" Uncle Gil shook his head as she shut the door.

"He might."

"I'll check in on him, make sure he's behaving."

"Just make sure he doesn't have another heart attack. I'm not ready for him to die on me."

Uncle Gil patted her hand.

They took off again and made the short hop to the Anchorage airport. The early afternoon sun hung low in the sky, waxing Lake Hood a brilliant umber.

Uncle Gil finished his postflight check and tied down the plane; then Scotty followed him to the terminal. As he stopped in at the office to file his return flight plan, she wandered into the north terminal. Her stomach growled as she stood peering out through the two stories of glass toward Lake Hood, the snow now falling lightly, like the finest dusting of ash as it hit the ground. A cadre of orange plows lined up along the far edge of the parking garage, ready to free travelers from the tangle of weather.

Alaska wasn't for the weak. Which was why Scotty thrived here. And probably why she'd never make anyone a good wife. She simply wasn't . . . well, girlie.

She was Alaskan. She thrived on the challenge, the brittle cold that could steal her breath from her chest, hold it in midair for her to consider. The endless layers of snow, determined to bury her. The millions of miles of wildland that could spin a person around, leave her wandering. Here, she meted out justice to any foolhardy criminal who escaped north to hide, only to be rooted out by those who knew their tricks.

So maybe she didn't need the boat, her fishing life. She could make a place here, finally find her footing. Even set down roots.

"Your shield is still in my top drawer," Uncle Gil said as he came out to stand next to her.

"I know. But I can't . . . I thought I could go back to Homer after this season, but the memories are too fresh. Every time I drive by Cindy's house, I'm going to see her with two shots to her head, dead in her living room. And I'm going to know it's my fault."

"Elise—"

"No. It's Scotty, Uncle Gil. Here, it's Scotty. I've never been Elise to anyone but you. It's time for me to move on. I need to do this."

He said nothing as they headed toward the transportation area. "I called ahead. Chief Elmore said he'd send a guy." He gestured toward a cop headed in their direction, shorter, a thatch of light-brown hair, and young as if fresh out of the academy. "Dillon."

"Sorry, Chief. I had to call for another ride for you," he said, saluting Uncle Gil. "We got a call in from TSA. They have a couple of yahoos here trying to board a plane with BOLOs on them. I'm picking them up."

"No problem; we can wait."

"I have a ride just two minutes out." He glanced at Scotty. "Ma'am."

Sir. It was on her lips, but she bit it back and gave him a nod as he hustled away.

They walked outside to wait. She wore a down jacket and a pair of Sorel work boots, but she tasted the edge of winter in the snow pelleting her face.

Not fair. It shouldn't be snowing on October 4.

The cruiser pulled up and Uncle Gil knew this recruit too. But that's what came from his summer stint at the academy, probably.

Gil took the front and she climbed in the backseat, pulling Owen's duffel in beside her.

"I need to stop by the hospital," she said as they left the airport. A light snow fell from the steel-gray sky. Anchorage always felt so different from the rest of Alaska, connected somehow to the Lower 48 with its shopping malls and Walmarts and sleek downtown.

She tried not to rethink her conversation with Uncle Gil. No. She needed a fresh start, especially now. Maybe she could find a cozy remote cabin in the woods, once she had her legs under her with the new job.

They cut over to Providence Drive. The officer pulled up to the front.

"I'll just run in," Scotty said quickly.

She caught her breath, hating how her heartbeat thundered in her neck as she strode down the hall, Owen's duffel bag bouncing against her hip.

Oh, hey, Owen. Yeah, I was just . . . You left this on the boat and . . . What am I doing here?

She stood outside his room. Drew a breath.

Hello, Owen. How are you feeling? I was in the neighborhood and wanted to drop this off. Have a good life.

Yep, that's all she wanted. Then she could walk away, forget him.

She knocked, then pushed the door open.

Stuttered to a stop.

Empty?

She walked over to the bed, touched the covers, tasting her heartbeat. Certainly they hadn't discharged him already. She'd called nearly every day since leaving, just to check on him, still using her identifier as his fiancée.

Wasn't he getting better? She slipped her hand to her mouth. No—this couldn't be right—

"Can I help you?" A nurse, and she looked familiar.

"Do you remember the man who was here? Owen Christiansen?"

"Oh yes. You're his fiancée."

She let the lie stay for now. "I think I must have . . . Well, do you—?" Wow, she hoped suddenly that this nurse didn't have to deliver dismal news to Owen's beloved. "Where is he?"

The RN frowned. "He was discharged this morning."

"Right! No wonder he called. I had to go down to Homer and I missed a few of his calls." Not a lie on either account.

"Aren't you going back to Minnesota with him? I think their flight left today."

Scotty tried not to let those words wallop her. "Yeah. Of course. Except I'm not going out for another week or so—too much wedding planning to do here."

The nurse nodded, her gaze falling to Scotty's bare ring finger. Oops.

"Thank you," she said, too quickly, and pushed past the nurse to the door.

The woman's words fell around her as she stood in the elevator. *Aren't you going back to Minnesota with him?*

Apparently not.

She didn't care, not in the least, that he hadn't said good-bye. After all, she'd marched out of his life.

He'd saved her from looking even more foolish.

Still, her eyes burned as she stepped back out into the cold.

She threw the duffel on the cruiser floor, climbed in after it. "He's gone," she said to her uncle.

"Did he . . . ? He didn't pass away, did he?"

See, people made assumptions. She wasn't crazy. "He went back to Minnesota with his brother." Where he belonged.

In fact, they were both exactly where they belonged.

They pulled up to the police headquarters, just down the road, a two-story gray-and-brown municipal building, the Alaskan and American flags flittering in the snowy breeze.

Scotty got out and followed her uncle inside, dragging the duffels behind her and killing the oh-so-tempting urge to drop one of them in the nearby Dumpster.

She trailed Gil through the lobby to the administrative offices. Chief Elmore met him across the room with a handshake.

Balding, with a tough-guy smile, the man could be a poster boy for the local SWAT team, with his crushing handshake, not to mention the way he'd done a thorough assessment of her at first glance.

"Great to have you join us, Scotty. Your uncle spent an hour begging me not to give you a job."

"Thanks for that, Uncle Gil."

"If she weren't our best detective, I might not have fought so hard. Because did I mention she's also stubborn?"

Elmore nodded. "That's how we like 'em. Unfortunately, like I mentioned when we talked, the position isn't open for another three weeks. We have a patrolman retiring then, and I'll scoot you into his slot until the new recruits are ready. I have no doubt we'll have you working major crimes by spring."

Three weeks to wait, letting memories churn around in her

heart while she bided her time. Scotty tried not to make a face. "Sounds perfect, sir."

"There's nothing she can work on until then? Cold cases, maybe? She just, well . . ."

Scotty glanced at Gil, nonplussed.

"She needs to stay focused on something," he finished.

Oh, thank you so much, Uncle Gil. Broadcast my broken heart to the entire world—

"I don't know if you heard, but she got pulled out of the Bering Sea last week, and I think she needs to get back to work, if you catch me," Gil continued.

Clearly not thinking about her broken heart.

In fact, she might be the only one. And maybe she should stop labeling it as a broken heart.

She'd never see Owen again, and yes, she could live with that. Cheer, even.

"Well, maybe I have something," Elmore said. "We just brought in a couple travelers from the airport who fit a BOLO description. If their IDs are confirmed, we'll have to send them back to the Lower 48. With an escort." He turned to Scotty. "How about a mini vacation?"

Babysitting?

Her uncle grinned like he'd just handed her tickets to Hawaii.

It was true that she didn't exactly relish the thought of the pullout at Angie's. Besides, how long could it take? A flight down, a day for processing, a flight back. Two days, tops, and she could dig in and hunt for an apartment. Take a couple weeks to settle into her new life.

"I guess so."

"Great. You can stow your gear in the locker room. I'll have you issued a key. Gil, are you sticking around for a beer?"

Her uncle begged off, gave Scotty a hug.

She picked up the duffel bags, feeling like a vagabond.

"Follow me," said a female officer, and they headed down the hallway, past the holding rooms to the locker area.

"I'm telling you, we're not criminals!"

The voice rebounded from an anteroom the opposite direction.

Scotty stopped. Glanced at the officer. "Who's that?"

"I don't know, ma'am. I think it's those two Brian just brought in from the airport. One of them is wanted for questioning in connection to a murder in Minnesota."

Murder. In *Minnesota*? No, it couldn't be . . . "What's his name?"

"I don't know. I just heard Brian talking."

Banging shuddered the door. "Shouldn't we be getting a phone call or a lawyer or something? For cryin' in the sink, we're not fugitives!"

Murder. Scotty dropped the duffels, dragged them down the corridor toward the voices.

"Ma'am?" The officer followed after her. "You can't go in there—"

Scotty stopped. "Actually, yes, I can. I'm babysitting." Then she pushed open the door.

Both occupants froze when they looked up at her.

"Pipe down," Scotty said as she shut the door. "You want to end up in handcuffs?"

Casper backed away from the door, holding his shoe in his hand, his hair mussed, his shirt untucked.

"Put the shoe down, Casper," she said quietly.

Then she turned to Owen, who was sitting on a chair, one arm tucked around his chest. He'd trimmed his beard to a thin copper thatch, and with his eye patch, his blond hair neatly capped with a black tuque, and Casper's worn leather jacket, he looked mysterious, if not dangerous.

What in the world had Owen gotten himself into? But even as she let the thought drift through her, she shook her head.

No. She'd seen his drawn face, heard his voice as he confessed his regrets. He'd made mistakes, sure, but he would not murder anyone.

"Scotty," he whispered, a smile skimming up his face. "You came back."

She let out a noise that sounded a lot like the churning inside her chest, half chuckle, half disbelief, lots of I-really-can't-believe-you-two.

Thankfully, she had his duffel. She thumped it on the table in front of him. "Yeah, well, you forgot something."

And shoot, if he didn't let that grin rip, Mr. Eye Patch, trouble in a leather jacket. "Indeed I did."

CHAPTER 6

"I think you should arrest us."

"What?"

Scotty had left them after dropping off the duffel bag, not returning for so long that Owen vowed if she did come back, he would suggest something—anything—to make her stick around.

Even handcuffs.

Because he knew deep in his heart that this was his last chance. If she left him again, that would be it. She wouldn't come marching back into his life, and everything he'd conjured in his mind would be over.

He still couldn't believe he'd let her go, almost without a fight.

That killed him the most. The fact that he hadn't chased after her. Why not? Stupid man.

And yeah, he'd been strapped to his bed with an IV and oxygen cannula. But five days later, he could have wrestled himself from bed, found his clothes, trekked out of Providence hospital, and headed back to Dutch Harbor.

Instead, he'd stupidly let Casper talk him into getting on a plane.

Unbelievably, God still had his back. He'd led Scotty right back to Owen. It was a sign. A happily-ever-after sign that maybe God wasn't done with him yet.

In fact, God might be all about answering his prayers, helping him fix his mistakes. He didn't know exactly how to thank Casper for showing up on his doorstep, caring enough to let him walk back into Raina's life and meet his daughter. Maybe the guy wasn't so bad after all. Even if he had the subtlety of a snowplow.

"If we're criminals, you probably need to make sure we don't escape. Maybe you should handcuff me to you, at least," Owen said.

Scotty frowned at him. "What? No. Listen, you shouldn't have caused such a ruckus at the airport. Yes, there was a BOLO out on you, but you didn't have to threaten a TSA official, Casper."

Casper pursed his lips, looked away.

"But now that you're here, we just need to ask you a few questions. You're not *under arrest.*"

She closed the door to the holding room and sat on the edge of the table. Before she'd left, she'd brought in another chair for Casper, who had somewhat managed to put himself together after the altercation at the airport. He still looked flummoxed, pacing the room.

"Sit down, Casper," Scotty said, her voice on the lee edge of impatient, and Owen missed the sweet sarcasm from when she'd dropped his duffel on the table. *You forgot something.*

Boy howdy, had he. In fact, he'd nearly leaped across the table, wanting to take her into his arms, scroll back to that moment when Casper had dropped the bomb about Layla. Tell her to just breathe, that they could figure this thing out.

He'd spent the better part of a week forming a sketchy plan. He'd go back to Deep Haven, hit his knees, and beg his father for a job. Or maybe get on the horn to Jace, see if he could work as a trainer for the Blue Ox. Most of all, he'd prove to Raina, one day at a time, that he could be trusted to be a father—a real father who stuck around and protected her and Layla both.

And somewhere in there, he'd also prove to Scotty that they weren't done.

"Casper, I mean it. I'll tell you what I know, but I'm not going to do it until you stop pacing like a monkey in a cage."

"I feel like a monkey!" Casper rounded on Scotty. "You have no idea what it felt like to be going through security, finally headed home after months on the road, and wham—there's cops everywhere, jumping me, pulling me into another room. I felt like any second they'd throw me to the floor and frisk me. I thought I might get Tasered."

"None of that happened," Owen said, shaking his head as he glanced at Casper. "They simply asked us to step into another room, where we waited until the police showed up."

"My shirt was rumpled."

"That's because you got up and demanded to know what was going on—and I grabbed it to keep you from doing something stupid. And then you started threatening people. No wonder the cops put you in cuffs. Sit down, Casper." Owen turned to Scotty. "Ignore him; talk to me. What do you know?"

"Well, to be honest—Casper, take a deep breath—you're wanted for questioning in connection to a homicide in Minnesota." She said it calmly, like, *Casper, you have a parking ticket.* Or, *Casper, you jaywalked.*

Owen looked at him, trying to tamp down the smallest stir of vindication. "See, I'm not the villain in this story—you are. I've always known it, and now it's time for the rest of your fans to catch up. Me: not the bad guy, just terribly misunderstood. You: bad guy. I can't believe you pointed at me in the airport and said, 'This is all on you, Bro.' Good try. Who did you kill?"

Owen meant it as a joke, because, c'mon, Casper? Kill someone? Crazy. But he still enjoyed the teasing.

Casper didn't laugh, didn't smile. He looked pointedly at Scotty. "Who's dead?"

"I placed a call to the Deep Haven Sheriff's Department . . ." She looked at the file she'd returned with. "The victim's name is Monte Riggs. That mean anything to you, Casper?"

As Owen watched, the blood drained from Casper's face.

An icy hand slid down Owen's spine. "Casper," he said, suddenly solemn. "I was kidding. But I have the feeling you know him. Who is this guy? Is there something you're not telling us?"

"No. I have nothing . . . I didn't . . . He was Raina's old boyfriend."

Raina's old . . . "What, before she met you? Wait, is this the same Monte Riggs whose family owns the antique shop?"

"Yeah."

"I don't get it. I thought she was new to town when I met her."

"She was but . . . Well, it's a long story."

"Apparently we have time."

Casper's mouth tightened into a grim line. "Fine. After I found out she was pregnant, I sort of freaked out and pushed her away. So she dated Monte Riggs."

Silence.

Then Owen said, "I'm glad to know I'm not the only one who makes impulsively stupid decisions."

"Which part of this was impulsively stupid? The part where I freaked out because the woman I loved was—"

"How about the part where the police think you killed her boyfriend? What did you do—beat him up too?"

"He was abusive with her."

Owen stilled. Then he turned to Scotty. "I think we need a lawyer."

"No! We don't need a lawyer. I admit I thought about it—and yes, we got into a fight, but I would not—never—" Casper looked beseechingly at Scotty. "I did not kill Monte Riggs. There's been a mistake."

"Actually, Casper, the report just has you wanted for questioning—that's what the BOLO is about. Go home, tell the truth, and I'm sure this will get cleared right up."

That took the steam out of Casper. He sank back in his chair. "Fine. Of course I'll go home. I was on my way—"

"Unfortunately, because you've been gone for nearly five months, even though the BOLO was filed a week ago, you've been listed as high risk. You need to be accompanied."

Owen crossed his hands over his chest. "I love it. I'm the baby-sitter; you're the high-risk fugitive. I knew it would come to this someday. Finally the world figuring out that Casper Christiansen isn't a saint. What I've been saying since that time you buried all my trucks in the sandbox."

"That was Darek."

"A sweeter day has never arrived. Casper, the family criminal—"

"Hey!" Casper said.

"You're not the babysitter," Scotty said, hiding what looked like a smirk. "He has to be accompanied by a law enforcement agent."

"Even sweeter."

"What?"

"Aw, c'mon, Scotty. You know there's more between us—and this is perfect. You can be his escort, come to Minnesota, meet my family . . . let me show you that this doesn't have to be as complicated as you think."

"Owen, I can't just—"

"Yes, you can."

"I don't need anyone to accompany me," Casper said. "I'm not going to run. I'm not the outlaw Josey Wales."

"Don't listen to him, Scotty. He's a renegade. He's got runner written all over him. Look at his eyes. He's got Richard Kimble crazy eyes," Owen said, leaning forward. He hid a wince as the bandages tightened around his chest.

Scotty was smiling now, and it brought him back to the raft, to her eyes shining in his. Yes, this was better than handcuffs—a real reason for her to come home with him, where he could charm her with his small town, romance her by the lake, awaken her to everything that could be between them. He glanced at Casper. "Cuff him."

"What—?" Casper half rose from his chair.

"Down, boys." Scotty shook her head. "This is a monumentally bad idea; spending more time refereeing you two could kill me. Maybe I should send Dillon the rookie."

"Dillon? Are you kidding me? Casper has two inches and fifty pounds on the guy. He's no match for—"

"I'm not going to run away!"

"Besides, what if this is real and Casper did do something wrong?"

"Seriously?" Casper shook his head.

"Fine. What if he is accused of something? We'll need someone on our side to help us untangle him."

"I'm innocent. They don't send innocent men to jail," Casper said.

Even Scotty's expression held something of incredulity.

Casper sat back, again turning a little white.

"What if he gets blamed? Scotty, we need you." Owen paused, lowered his voice. "I might need you."

That got her attention. She looked at him, frowned.

So he met her eyes and let his words escape slowly as if continuing the conversation they'd started on the raft so many days ago. "I . . . really . . . might need you."

She made a face. "Owen, knock it off. I know I just walked out on you. You deserved better, and I regretted it the second I left. You deserved more explanation from me, like the fact that I *did* consider marrying you. My *yes* was real then. But when the light of day hit and everything shook out, I realized that I had been too impulsive, and so had you, and maybe we should just be happy with living through what we lived through and—"

"No, Scotty." Owen stood and issued a groan because, wow, his pain meds were wearing off.

He sat back down.

"Are you all right?"

He covered his chest with his hand. "I was trying to do something gallant and make a grand gesture, but sadly, I'm still reduced to lying on the bottom of the raft, hoping you'll save my life."

"Please don't hurt yourself."

"I'm already hurt. My entire body hurts not being with you. See, the more I got thinking about this daughter I have, the more

I realized, *I want Scotty to meet her.* Because I don't know the first thing about being a dad, but you somehow make me believe that I could be one and . . ." He glanced at Casper, who stared at him with a sort of horror as if he'd grown a foot out of the top of his head. "Uh, this is a private conversation, Casper."

"Well, what do you want me to do? Go sit in a corner, plug my ears, and hum?"

"Fine. Scotty, the point is, please come to Deep Haven with me, and we can see what happens from there. But please, come with me. If I remember correctly, you promised on the raft."

"I didn't promise." She angled the folder on her lap, thumbing the pages as if thinking. "I don't know. I'm pretty busy. I have a couch to sleep on, a take-out order waiting—"

"Scotty!"

A smile broke out on her face and it loosened the claws in Owen's chest.

"Here's what I got. Two days. I'll fly you down, bring Casper in, find out what's going on, make sure he's treated fairly, and then I gotta get back. Two days, max. That's all I can do. Take it or leave it."

Two days. Owen sighed as if disappointed. But boo-*yah*, he could work with two days. It had taken him only twelve hours on the boat to get her to say yes to his proposal. Why, two days and he'd have them hitched and on a honeymoon in Cancún.

"I think I can make two days work." He reached out and took her hand.

She yanked it away. "Not two days of romance, Owen. Two days of me working. And you getting it through your head that what we had was a quick and easy fling—"

"A fling? A fling includes a lot more—"

"Still here, still listening," Casper said. "And you might want to consider your audience."

"I just meant that we didn't have a fling, Scotty. What we had—have—is more. Deeper. Better."

Just for a second, he saw the slightest glimmer of her guard falling, like it had those first few hours on the raft when he'd managed to get her smiling.

But, "I'm only going to make sure Kimble here doesn't run for the border."

"I'm not a fugitive!" Casper said, pressing a hand to his head.

"Pipe down," Owen said.

"Stop calling me a criminal."

"Owen, I'm serious: no funny business. Don't try to charm me with your sweet talk. I'm not falling for it. Whatever we were, we're over. It was a fun little fantasy, but our lives are vastly different. I belong here, in Alaska, and you need to go home." She got up. "I'll get us booked on the next flight out. In the meantime, you want something to eat?"

"Oh yes, pizza. Please, a pizza—pepperoni and mushroom."

"I'll see what I can rustle up." She walked to the door.

When it closed behind her, Casper turned to Owen. "Did I hear you right? Did you just finagle a date out of my misfortune?"

Owen grinned. "Hush up, prisoner 24601."

Clearly Owen hadn't listened to a word she'd said about keeping their next two days professional.

Not with the way he slept, looking so heartbreakingly sweet, those long lashes brushing his cheeks, his tousled curls tempting her to twirl them around a finger, then run her hand over that spicy red-gold beard. He curled up in the window seat like a two-year-old, the stress of the past five hours creeping up on him, turning him once again into the wounded man who'd nearly died on her watch.

She was bringing him home, just like she'd promised.

Next to her in the aisle seat, Casper shoved the in-flight magazine into the pocket of his seat and leaned back. "You had to get the last row? These seats don't recline."

"Not only were these the last three seats on this packed flight, but you should be glad you're not handcuffed," she said under her breath. "I'm doing you a favor."

Casper grimaced. "I know. I'm sorry. I just can't believe they think I might have killed Monte Riggs. I didn't—"

"Shh. Keep your voice down. People don't like murderers on the plane with them."

"I didn't—" Then he saw the grin she flashed him. "Oh."

"He seems to enjoy the idea that you're in trouble," Scotty said. "I couldn't help it."

Casper glanced at his sleeping brother. "Yeah, well, I used to be the official troublemaker in the family. For a long time, I thought maybe it was my fault—that I'd somehow set a bad example."

She considered that. "He told me that he felt you were always pushing him to be better. It might have had something to do with feeling like he let you down."

Casper said nothing. Sighed.

"For the record, I don't know you, Casper, so I don't know if you're the kind of man who could kill someone. But let's all remember it's just questioning. Even if Owen seems to be turning the knife a bit, you should know that while the Anchorage police processed you out, he spent a good amount of energy trying to convince me to stick around and make sure you didn't get pinned for a crime you didn't commit."

"That has more to do with you than me." He raised his eyebrow, a twinkle in his eyes. "'If you give a mouse a cookie . . .' And you managed to hand over the entire Keebler package to him with your two-day agreement."

"I'm not getting involved. Deep Haven has a sheriff's department, and I have no doubt they know what they're doing. Hence my round-trip ticket. Trust me, I'm going to drop you off and drive away." Return to her new life in Anchorage. No entanglements, no broken heart. And no arguments. "So Owen told me all about his family on the boat, but remind me . . ."

For a moment, it appeared Casper wanted to chase down her words about not getting involved. Then, "Right. Okay. Uh, my parents, John and Ingrid, run the Evergreen Resort. Actually, that's not true—my older brother, Darek, took over. He has a son, Tiger, who's seven, and a baby girl, Joy. His wife, Ivy, is our assistant county attorney."

"That could get interesting."

"You're the one who said it was just questioning."

"Sorry."

"I'm sure he told you about Jace and Max—"

"Not really. Jace is the one who married your sister Eden on the day of the big fight, right?"

Casper made a face. "He told you about that, huh?"

"It's his biggest regret—of course he did. But I don't know details." She glanced at Owen, lowered her voice. "What happened, exactly?"

Casper looked away at the family sleeping opposite them. The sun had fallen, their red-eye flight the last out of Anchorage. But to the east, the slightest edging of gray lipped the horizon. In two hours, the sun would light up the sky with brilliance, just in time for them to land.

"I'm not sure how far back you want to go."

"You know an Owen I've never met. Start there. Because he thinks he doesn't really have the right to go home. That he doesn't belong. And I don't think it started with the fight."

"We were his biggest fans."

"Even you?"

Casper shrugged. "Maybe I was a little jealous. Hockey came so easy to him. He was playing varsity in eighth grade, left home at sixteen to start playing in the juniors. Got drafted at eighteen with the Wild, then traded to the Blue Ox—a regular hometown hero. They gave him a 3.1-million-dollar contract."

"Wow."

"Yeah. Then, one night after a game, he mixed it up with a few players in a pond game and got into a brawl. I think he'd been drinking, although I got that part from Max, my sister Grace's husband."

"How did Max know—was he there?"

"He was the one who accidentally shoved his hockey stick into Owen's eye, broke the orbit, and ended his career."

She made a silent, round O. "That's . . . some interesting family dynamics."

"Max was—is—sick about it. Especially since he still plays for the Blue Ox. And Jace coaches for them. He used to be captain, back when Owen was playing. Owen and Eden were pretty close in those days—she sort of took care of him while he was starting out in the majors. She took it pretty hard when he left town."

"After the wedding?"

"No, he left before then, shortly after his injury. Just . . . gave her the keys to his apartment and his car and took off. Next time we saw him, when he showed up for Darek and Ivy's wedding, he was wearing the eye patch, angry, broken, and hungry for something."

"And that's when he met . . . uh, your—"

"That's when he hooked up with Raina, yeah. There's nothing to forgive—she didn't know me then—but I can admit, it hurts to think about it. Owen had changed by then. He wasn't the guy I'd watched in the juniors. But Eden said that he'd changed before his injury. She said that the money, the fame, had gone to his too-young head. Whatever it was, he wasn't the brother I knew, and I keep telling myself that. He left town again after Darek's wedding, and that's when I met and fell in love with Raina. I knew she'd met Owen but had no idea they had a past. I started to figure it out over the summer, and especially when he walked into Jace and Eden's wedding a few months later. Raina had discovered she was pregnant and was avoiding me, and I blamed Owen, the way he treated her, and . . . well, that's when the fight happened."

The flight attendant had finally reached their seats. Casper asked for water, drank it down in one gulp.

Scotty opened her pretzels. "Owen said you left first?"

"Yeah, I was so angry, I went down to Roatán, a small island off Honduras. But I couldn't get Raina off my mind, so I finally went home, and that's when I discovered that she was pregnant. With Owen's kid."

"More family drama."

"It doesn't have to be. Maybe Owen will turn out to be a great guy, even see things my way."

"As in, letting you adopt this little girl."

He drew in a breath. "I know I owe you an apology. You were

right—from the outside, it does feel like I'm trying to steal Layla. But that's not true. I do want Owen to know her. I just . . . I just think it would be better for her to have one dad."

"You."

He lifted a shoulder in a shrug. "Sorry, but yeah. My fear is that I've ignited a custody battle—"

She put her hand on his arm. "Your brother loves you."

Casper glanced at her. Swallowed. Then looked away. "No wonder he wants you to stick around. You really do believe in him."

Oh. She hadn't expected that strange vote of confidence, and now her throat tightened. "I can admit that being around Owen makes me—briefly—wonder what it might be like to be in a big family . . . but it's not a good idea."

Casper held up his cup for more water as the flight attendant went by again. "Our family isn't all drama. Actually, we get along pretty well. My parents are bighearted. They love Raina, despite the strangeness of the situation."

"My mother had a big family. Cousins everywhere. My dad sent me down to live with them in Seattle one summer. Two big sisters, two kid brothers—they loved large and loud. But . . . big families mean messy, tangled relationships, and I've been on the dark end of family drama. I can't get caught up in that again." She folded the airplane pretzel bag into tiny squares.

She hadn't really wanted to revisit their conversation in the hallway, but maybe he needed more information, and she needed an ally. "One of those cousins came up to Alaska and lived with us for a while. I didn't realize he was running from a drug conviction in Seattle until after he married one of my best friends." She held up the pretzel litter to the flight attendant, dropped it in the garbage bag as she passed.

"He was making meth in his house and, when he was high, abusing Cindy and their little boy. I suspected something, but I was . . . Well, he was family. We knew each other, and I didn't want to believe . . . Anyway, it all went south, and he was killed." She shook her head, the images fresh, bruising. "Their son went to a good family. I still see him sometimes." She looked out the window, wishing for the dawn, but darkness covered the plane. "It's the curse of a small-town cop—you know everyone, and eventually you have to arrest someone you love."

"You mentioned it threw you out of whack. What did you mean?"

She glanced at him.

"You told me. In the hallway, remember?"

"Yeah. I quit the police force for a while. But . . . I'm okay, or getting there. I'm back on the police force in Anchorage, and everything is sorted out. I just don't . . . I can't have any more family drama, okay?"

Scotty probably carried a bit too much emotion in her eyes when she said, "Please be telling me the truth about Monte Riggs, Casper, because I don't want to arrest anyone I care about."

This time he pressed his hand over hers. Squeezed.

Owen shifted again, then turned in his seat. Scotty froze when he settled his head on her shoulder.

Casper grinned. "I think he likes you."

She smiled, inhaling the smell of Owen, flannelly and masculine. "And I like him."

Casper's smile fell. "Just not his loud, messy family."

"Or his complications. He has a lot to sort out with you, Raina, and his baby girl, and I've been in the middle of one too many domestics. I just need to keep this professional, not get involved until I can get back on a plane for Alaska. Owen and I can't ever be anything more than shipmates."

Scotty looked away as the airplane hurtled toward Deep Haven, Owen's head warm on her shoulder.

She must have fallen asleep because the change in air pressure jostled her awake as they made their descent into Minneapolis. Casper had also nodded off and now raised his head, sat up.

Next to her, Owen hadn't stirred, his head still resting on her shoulder. She nudged him. "Owen."

Nothing. She nudged him again. "Owen?"

And when he didn't respond, for a blinding, ragged moment, she was right back in the raft, trying to keep him alive, begging him, begging God to intervene—

He drew in a long breath, lifted his head, and her world righted, leaving only her heart to thump wildly in her chest.

Shoot. She'd need to break free of his effect on her if she hoped to walk away unscathed. Or maybe it was enough to be able to walk away.

Just shipmates.

Owen sat up, stretched.

"Are you going to live?" she asked as he scrubbed his hands down his face.

"I don't know." He leaned back and groaned. "Casper, do you have my meds?"

Maybe she'd relaxed too soon.

In fact, her worry for him grew as they disembarked, then found their next gate for the commuter hop to Duluth, still two hours from his hometown. At the gate, Owen sank down onto a chair, grimacing now and again.

"Maybe we need to get him back to the hospital?"

"I'm fine," Owen mumbled. "Just let the meds kick in."

"He has broken ribs, you know," Scotty said to Casper.

But she stopped talking when Owen took her hand. Solid, without hesitation, as if he needed her.

So maybe he needed to hang on for now. And she'd consider it part of her professional duty in getting him home.

She led him onto the plane, then opted to sit next to him instead of her fugitive for the fifty-minute flight to Duluth. By the time they landed, the meds had clearly kicked in, Owen's gaze brighter.

They retrieved their duffels from baggage claim—she had to admit some dismay that her only attire for this excursion would be her smelly crabbing clothes. She'd planned on doing laundry at Angie's.

Way to make a good impression.

Owen reached for his bag, but she grabbed it. "Good try."

Meanwhile, Casper rented a car at the desk, came back swinging the keys. "I would have called someone, but I wanted to surprise them."

"Oh, this will be a surprise all right," Owen said. "You in handcuffs. Surprise!"

Casper glared at him. "I meant the part where I found you. Finally."

"Let's go," Scotty said, stepping between them. Casper lifted Owen's duffel off her shoulder.

They found the Ford Escape in the lot, and Casper manned the wheel. Owen settled in back, leaning his head against the seat as if watching the scenery. Morning crested through the evergreen and birch trees, turning them golden, and at the bottom of a hill, the great Lake Superior stretched out, dark blue touching the horizon to the east, bordered on one side by a busy shipping harbor.

"Welcome to Duluth," Casper said. "The western port city of the Great Lakes chain."

"It's gorgeous."

"It's no Bering Sea," Owen said.

"And there's no mountains," Scotty said. "But it feels like Alaska."

"It's tamer," Casper said.

"This is why I belong in Alaska," Owen said quietly, shifting in his seat.

Scotty couldn't read his expression. Pensive? Or worried? She had the crazy urge to reach back, squeeze his hand, and for a long moment didn't regret traveling home with him at all.

"Breakfast, please," Owen said, and Casper pulled into a drive-through McDonald's.

They left the city and traveled northeast, the lake a rich indigo under the climbing sun, the evergreen trees a vibrant, lush emerald. On the hills opposite the lake, autumn bedazzled the trees in hues of amber, crimson, and magenta.

Scotty smelled woodsmoke hanging in the air when they got out to stretch at an overlook.

"I could forget I'm in Minnesota," she said to Owen, sitting with his door open, feet on the ground.

"I'd like to." He shook his head. "Truthfully, I didn't think it would be this hard. I feel nearly sick with the thought of . . . everything, I guess."

And there it was again, the wild urge to take his hand. Or maybe pull him into her arms. "It'll be okay."

His mouth flattened into a grim line of disagreement, and she could almost see the past scrolling over his face, the words he must have said, the very real face-to-face meeting he'd have with his mistakes. The apologies he'd have to utter.

Yeah, if only for the next thirty-six hours, she planned on being the friend to him that he was to her in that raft. Save his life right back.

Leaves kicked up, scampered across the overlook. She watched the waves comb the shore, water soaking the pebbled surface before washing away, leaving the glitter of the sun behind. Overhead, a seagull cried, echoing into the breeze.

"Let's get this over with," Owen said and climbed back into the car.

He said nothing more as they wound along the shore toward home.

Owen had described Deep Haven as a fishing town, and Scotty had expected a small port city like Dutch Harbor, with vessels at a dock, fishmongers peddling fresh trout or herring. Instead, as their rental topped the hill that overlooked the little town, she saw what she'd describe more as a postcard hamlet, with quaint shops and cafés bordering the shoreline and rocky harbor. A few sailboats rocked in the waves in the middle of the harbor, and a spiral of smoke curled from the smokehouse near the docks. A banner hung high from two tall poles, the entrance to Main Street: *Home of the Deep Haven Huskies.*

Owen sat up and wrapped his arms around his waist as he leaned forward between the two bucket seats. "World's Best Donuts, dead ahead. And over there—" he pointed to the lighthouse jutting from the end of a long cement pier—"we'd jump into the lake every Fourth of July."

"If you're wondering, the lake is about forty degrees by then," Casper said. "We have exactly two coffee shops, four hotels, seven restaurants, and twelve gift shops, including two fudge emporiums, a pizza joint named Pierre's, and a custard shop," he added.

"I thought you were a fishing town," Scotty said.

"We are," Owen said. "Except we do our fishing in the BWCA."

"The Boundary Waters Canoe Area," Casper said. "Although there are a few commercial outfits that go out on the big lake every day."

He turned just before Main Street and headed up the hill. "Ten miles to home."

Owen sat back, his breathing hard. Deep. Scotty noted the tight set of his jaw.

They passed the high school, the football stadium that overlooked the lake, then the hospital, with the helicopter on the pad. Then they climbed another hill, and she watched as the town dropped away into a bowl of charm. Victorians dotted the hills, tucked between evergreens and dogwoods and mountain ash.

"It's a Norman Rockwell painting," Scotty said.

Owen let out a long sigh, and it made her turn. "Owen, breathe," she said. But he looked so miserable, she couldn't take it. She unhooked her seat belt.

"What are you doing?" Casper said, touching his brakes.

"Keep driving. At this moment, it's not you who I'm worried will make a break for it." She climbed between the two seats. "Scoot over."

Owen made a face but obeyed, and she settled beside him. Then she gave in to the urge to take his face in her hands. Met his beautiful, troubled expression.

"Owen," she said softly. "We did it. Just like you wanted in the raft. You don't have to dream of your mother's cookies anymore— you'll get them. I'll even rake you a pile of leaves to jump in. I promise it's going to be fine."

He managed a half smile.

"I'm waiting for a 'Yes, sir.'"

What she didn't expect, however, was the way his smile fell, his gaze roaming her face just for a second, then falling to her lips.

Nor did she expect her heart to stall, right there in her chest, as he tugged on her jacket lapel and pulled her closer.

For him to kiss her, a whisper of longing in the touch of his lips.

She surprised herself with her surrender, letting him kiss her ever so sweetly, lingering as his fingers moved behind her neck to cup it, draw her closer.

Owen.

He tasted of coffee, and his beard scratched her chin, but right then, incredibly, everything dropped away. Casper, the tension of meeting Owen's family, even Scotty's resolve.

Especially her resolve.

Because Owen had a way of making her forget herself. Owen, the guy from the boat who'd followed her into her cabin because he'd thought she was hurt, the hero who'd followed her into a stormy sea. The incorrigible charmer who'd purposely made her angry so she'd fight to stay alive.

This Owen, she knew.

She found her hands on his wide, powerful shoulders and managed to steady herself, hold on.

And she couldn't deny the regret when he pulled away.

This Owen, she could have loved.

His thumb ran over her cheek. "I feel better, thanks." A slow smile crept up his face.

Scotty rolled her eyes, feeling her own smile. "I'll bet."

"Everybody's feeling just spiffy," Casper said.

"Just drive, Casp. The sooner I get this over with, the better."

Owen had her hand again, this time clasped with their fingers intertwined, clearly not intending on letting go.

She glanced toward Casper as he slowed, turned onto an access road. He met her eyes in the rearview mirror and shook his head as if in reprimand.

They followed the road through a jeweled forest, then past a sign: *Evergreen Lodge Outfitter and Cabin Rentals.*

Owen's grip tightened.

The road opened onto an expansive parking lot, and then, before Scotty, the resort came into view. Like a fairyland nestled inside a tall line of white pines. She made out tiny cedar-sided cabins, some with smoke curling from their chimneys. An SUV with a license plate from Wisconsin and a Honda from Canada filled two of the spaces.

Straight ahead, a two-story lodge cut off a direct view of the lake, but she spied it beyond the house, blue and inviting, rippling in the wind, with smaller cabins dotting its shoreline. The lodge, with its log siding and green roof, looked conjured right out of the land as if it had always belonged, since the dawn of time. It had two entrances, one labeled *Office*, the other sporting a pumpkin and a straw scarecrow, dressed in flannel and denim, perched on a rattan chair.

Casper parked next to a truck with the resort's name stenciled on the door. "Let the wild rumpus begin."

Owen stared out the window, unmoving.

"C'mon," Scotty said as Casper got out. Owen reached for the handle, then with a small moan—probably not entirely physical—pushed himself out of the car. She scrambled out behind him.

The air smelled of the loam of the forest, woodsmoke, and not a little evergreen from the trees edging the property. Beyond that stretched a wasteland of scrub brush.

"We had a forest fire a few years ago," Casper said. "Darek spent about fifty grand on trees to frame the property with evergreen."

"Where'd he get that kind of money?" Owen said.

Casper clamped him on the shoulder. "You'll find out."

Scotty still had Owen's hand and felt him jerk when the door to the lodge opened. She drew up beside him as a woman ran out, her long blonde hair in a ponytail. "Casper! You're back!"

She jumped into Casper's arms, and he twirled her around. Raina?

"That's Grace, my sister," Owen said, making no move toward the house. "She married Max."

Oh, the one who caused his accident.

Casper put his sister down. "Look who I found."

Scotty had only guessed at the impact of Owen's absence, had surmised that his family missed him, but she and Red went for months without talking, so she hadn't thought it earth-shattering. Until she saw Grace's face.

She stood in the middle of the driveway, her mouth open, her eyes glazing. "Owen?"

Scotty dropped his hand. Stepped back.

And Grace launched herself at her brother. "Owen!" He grunted as she put her arms around his neck, holding on, burying her face in his shoulder. "Oh, Owen."

"Easy there," Scotty said as she came up beside him. "He's still recovering."

But Owen had put his arms around his sister, apparently disregarding the pain.

Their sweet connection in the car vanished. Scotty could feel Owen detaching from her, sinking into the welcome of his sister.

But this was right—how it should be—and her heart almost burst with an odd bubble of joy for him.

Her words must have caught up to Grace because she lifted her head, put her hands on Owen's shoulders, disentangled herself from his embrace. "Why—what happened?"

The answer came easily. "He saved my life after I got washed overboard, and nearly died himself."

A gift to Owen, so easily surrendered, and it had exactly the impact she'd hoped. Tears cut down Grace's face, something of admiration in her expression. "That's my brother."

Scotty could nearly see the coiled darkness inside Owen unwind at his sister's words. The prodigal, freed, returning to the arms of his family.

The door opened again, and Scotty looked up to see an older man wearing a blue baseball cap, a flannel shirt, and jeans step out of the house. While he clamped his hand on Casper's shoulder in passing, he made directly for Owen.

Owen looked up. "Hey, Dad."

What Scotty would give to see that look on Red's face. Except maybe she had in the car—a fleeting look that said everything this one did.

"Son."

"Easy, Dad, he's hurt," Grace said as her father drew Owen into a hug.

Owen didn't seem to mind.

"Owen?"

The shaky voice came from the lodge, and Owen's father released him.

"Mom."

Scotty barely recognized Owen's soft, almost-broken voice.

Susan May Warren

So that's where he'd gotten his blond hair. Looking impossibly young to have six adult children, dressed in a flannel shirt and jeans, her blonde hair pushed back with a headband, Ingrid Christiansen came toward them already wiping her cheeks.

"You're home," she breathed, and then she had her arms around her son, holding on, weeping.

Owen tucked his head into her shoulder. His body shook, just a little, his lips moving quietly.

Scotty heard his words, even as she stepped back.

"I'm sorry, Mom. I'm so sorry."

She turned to stare at the blue of the lake, the sky, blinking against the sunlight.

Casper came alongside Scotty, slipped his arm over her shoulder. "Way to not get involved," he whispered.

"I'm not crying. I'm just tired—"

"I meant the kiss."

Oh.

Owen finally eased out of his mother's embrace, and Scotty's throat tightened when she saw his reddened eyes. He reached for her, took her hand.

Wait, uh—

"Mom, this is Scotty. She saved my life."

Not entirely true, except, well—

Ingrid reached out and crushed her in an embrace. "Thank you," she said in Scotty's ear. "Thank you for bringing my boys home."

Well, she hadn't exactly—

"You're a godsend to our family."

Huh.

CHAPTER 7

CASPER LEANED AGAINST THE WALL, watching the flurry of family activity. Clearly their prodigal son celebration needed more epic proportions. After all, no one had killed the fatted calf.

Although, with his mother whipping up a batch of her chocolate chip cookies, his father building a fire, Grace deciding to make Owen's favorite meal for dinner, and Darek taking a break from chopping firewood to get caught up on Owen's adventures, Casper certainly expected to be sent out to the barn with a butcher knife soon.

Did no one remember the trail of debris that Owen had left in his wake?

He wanted to raise his hand and point out the glaringly obvious but overlooked truth: Owen was the *villain* here.

Casper didn't expect a cake with his name on it, but shouldn't some nod be made to the fact that *he'd* tracked down said elusive brother? Another notch in his treasure hunter's belt that should, fairly, be acknowledged.

Apparently the rest of the family had moved on to Owen's harrowing heroics at sea.

"I can't believe you just dove into the water—what were you thinking?" Grace said from the kitchen, more admiration than admonition in her voice. "What if you died?"

"I wasn't thinking about dying, Gracie," Owen said. He took Scotty's hand.

Before Casper's incredulous eyes, she folded her fingers between his. Had he dreamed their conversation on the airplane, the one where she determined not to get involved?

He crossed his arms, checking his watch. He'd called Raina thirty minutes ago . . .

He couldn't wait to get this over with. The meeting between the child he loved and her biological father. He didn't relish the idea of watching his kid brother share a reunion—as awkward as it might be—with the woman Casper loved.

Worse, Casper hadn't given enough thought to the very uncomfortable reality that Raina and Owen had shared something Casper and Raina still waited for. And because of that, the child she'd had would never, not really, belong to him.

He shook himself. *Get a grip, Casper.* Once Layla dove into Casper's familiar arms, there would be no denying the fact that he could easily, and rightly, fill Owen's shoes as her father.

Casper shoved his hands in his pockets and walked into the kitchen. His mother stood at the mixer, scooping cookie dough onto a pan.

He stuck his finger in the bowl, pulled out fresh dough.

"Casper! Get your grimy fingers out of there!" His mother smacked his hand as he danced away with his loot.

He wasn't sorry. No doubt she'd be handing Owen the beater in a second here.

Grace was leaning over the counter, listening as Scotty told them about the raft, how Owen had thrown her to safety. "I couldn't see anything. It was pitch-black, the waves crashing into our raft, and I knew we were going to die."

An arm curled around Casper's waist, and he looked down to see his mother standing beside him. She held up the beater, grinned at him. "You are *my* hero."

Aw, Mom. He couldn't help his smile or the warmth that wove through him as she kissed his cheek.

"I might be too old for this," he said, taking the beater.

"Probably not." She winked, then turned and put the cookies in the oven, grabbed a towel to wipe her hands, and leaned against the sofa to listen, one hand on Owen's shoulder.

Maybe Casper shouldn't be so hard on everyone. Owen had turned into what seemed like an okay fella, the way Scotty told the tale.

Which, of course, was really what had Casper shaking, downright scared, deep in his core.

What if Raina agreed?

He banished the thought as he licked the beater and listened to Scotty's rendition of the rescue.

"Right after I heard the chopper, I realized Owen had stopped breathing."

Ingrid's hand touched her chest.

"I was so afraid they wouldn't find us that I stood up with a flare to signal them before I started CPR."

"And Owen was dying?" Grace said.

Darek had decided somewhere in the middle of the story to head back outside and now came in with another load of wood. Dropped it by the fireplace. "What did I miss?"

"Scotty saving Owen's life," Grace said.

Darek smacked the woodchips from his gloves. "I thought he saved *your* life," he said to Scotty.

"It was mutual," Scotty answered, and Casper couldn't help but notice the look exchanged between his parents.

Relief? Concern?

"I would have died if she hadn't kept up the CPR," Owen said.

"The Coast Guard team took over when they found us. He had a hemothorax, his lungs filling with blood. They were able to relieve the pressure and get his heart started."

Ingrid pressed a hand over her mouth. "God was with you."

Scotty glanced at her, saying nothing. But Owen nodded. "I suppose He wanted me to come home. . . ."

"We all did, Son," John said, nurturing the spark in the fireplace to life. A blaze lit the waxed pinecones, the tinder, and began to crackle.

Casper dropped the beater in the sink.

"So let me get this straight," Darek said. "You hooked up with the Jude County Hotshots, then went to Seattle, worked on the docks?"

"That's when I met a couple guys going to Alaska. I got a job on Red's boat—that's Scotty's dad—and started fishing crab. This summer, I worked on the tuna boats; then Red hired me back on this fall."

"So your dad has a fishing boat?" John asked Scotty.

"Had. He's selling it. The truth is, it's probably time for him to retire. He had a heart attack a couple years ago. I wanted to take it over, but I can't afford the payments. Besides, I have a job—"

"Scotty's a cop, Dad," Owen said.

And that's when, of course, Scotty's gaze swiveled to Casper, landed on him.

A beat passed as understanding settled over him. "Not yet, Scotty," he said quietly.

She wore a grim look. "Casper. They'll come looking for you if you don't go in."

"Go in where?" Grace said.

John frowned. "This is about that phone call a few days ago, isn't it? About the Deep Haven police wanting to question you about Monte Riggs? They found the body this summer, but it took a while to identify him. Kyle said you were a suspect—"

"I had nothing to do with—"

John held up his hand. "Of course not. We all know that, and I told Kyle that too. But you'd better get this ironed out, Son."

Scotty got up. "I told the Deep Haven police I'd bring you straight there."

"I'm not leaving until Raina gets here!"

Thankfully, he didn't have to protest further because the door in the entryway opened.

Casper turned, his breath gusting out of him as the woman he loved walked in, her dark hair shorter than he remembered, her brown eyes finding his, expectant, twinkling. "Hey, you," she said.

Raina. His Raina, and she could still sweep every thought from his head. He had no words, just a smile as he strode toward her.

On her hip she propped a baby girl with tiny dark pigtails. She wore a fluffy turquoise jacket, cute pink UGGs, and stared at the group with wide blue eyes.

"She's huge," Casper said as he put his arms around them, pulled them close. "Oh, wow, I missed you." He closed his eyes, smelled Raina's skin, her hair, and felt the sense of what he'd left behind acute and full inside him. He'd forgotten this feeling of wholeness, of home.

Or maybe he'd just been trying to survive missing it.

Raina curled one arm around his waist, put her head on his shoulder. "I was so worried about you. Kyle came to the house looking for you, said you'd been arrested in Alaska."

He leaned back and caught her face with his hands. "Not arrested. Don't worry; we'll clear this up."

Then he didn't care who was watching or that the rest of the family might find it out of place—*this* was his family, his future wife, his daughter. He kissed Raina with a sort of possession that had him realizing just how much he feared losing her.

But it dropped away as her lips softened. She sank into his embrace, surrendering to his kiss, belonging only to him.

Oh, Raina. He shouldn't have worried. "You're even more beautiful than in my memories."

On Raina's hip, Layla began to squirm, to cry out.

"I'll take her," Casper said, setting Layla on his arm and unzipping her jacket. "Hey there, little girl. Remember me?"

Apparently not because she stared at him, then began to cry, wriggling in his arms, turning toward her mother.

Raina shucked off her jacket, hung it on a peg, and reached for Layla. "She just woke up," she said, but Casper couldn't deny the fist in his chest.

Of course she didn't remember him. After all, he'd been gone for over half her life. And before then . . .

He swallowed the bite of disappointment and stroked Layla's back as Raina quieted her. "Ready for this?" he asked.

She lifted her shoulder, her lip caught in her teeth. He touched her face, ran his thumb down her cheek. "It'll be okay," he whispered.

She managed a hint of a smile, then looked past him.

Casper drew in a breath and turned.

Owen had found his feet, Scotty standing behind him. Casper tried to imagine what Raina might see. Did she remember the night Owen had charmed her onto the back of his motorcycle? He didn't know the details, hadn't wanted to ask, but now he hoped her memory didn't play out the rest of the night. Or even the next day, when Owen had treated her like she meant nothing already to him.

What if she saw the man who'd sidled up to her at Eden and Jace's wedding and suggested, in his arrogant, sultry voice, that he might protect her from *Casper*.

Casper stuck his hands in his pockets, dismissing that memory before it grabbed him around the neck, propelled him into another fight.

But maybe she saw the different Owen, the broken aftermath, with the eye patch, the wiry beard, the long curly hair, the way he held his arm across his body. Wounded, even fragile.

"Hi, Raina," Owen said quietly.

"Owen."

Ingrid had gotten up and moved to stand by John. Behind them, the early afternoon light filled the house as if the heavens might be watching.

Grace pulled the cookies from the oven, apparently on their way to burning.

"This is . . . ," Owen started, then swallowed.

"This is Layla. Your daughter."

Owen seemed frozen, barely able to breathe. He swallowed again, then made to reach out. But he dropped his hand, shaking his head. "I don't know what to say."

"How about, 'Hi, Layla. I'm your daddy'?"

No! Casper nearly leaped forward to catch Raina's words before they could finish. Owen was *not* her daddy.

He must have taken in a sharp breath because Owen glanced at him. Casper tried to warn him with a look, but Owen turned back too quickly to Raina.

"Right. I . . ." Owen took a step forward. "She's so beautiful, Raina. She has your hair . . ."

"And your blue eyes. And sadly, your rather crabby disposition."

She probably meant it as a joke, but it fell flat. Casper saw it on the face of his mother, his father. Even Owen, who winced.

Casper was instantly at Raina's side, wanting to rescue her, but Owen beat him to it.

"I'm sorry about that. I'm sorry about everything. I . . ."

And if Casper's eyes worked, his brother seemed to be . . . tearing up? Oh no—

"Aw, Raina, if I had known I got you pregnant, I would have . . . I should have . . ."

Then as Casper watched—as everything turned to ice inside him—Owen reached out for the sofa and gingerly lowered himself to one knee. "I know it's a little late for this, but . . . do you want to marry me?"

"What. Are. You. *Doing?*" Casper's voice turned into a loco-motive, tunneling out from some dark place inside him, and he advanced on Owen, grabbed him by the shirt. "Have you lost your mind? She's marrying me—"

Owen stood up, bracing himself on Casper's arm. "What do you want me to do here? I screwed up, and I'm trying to fix it. Trying to make it right. I mean, that's what Darek did, right? When Felicity got pregnant with Tiger, he—"

"Please leave me out of this," Darek growled.

"Isn't that what I'm supposed—what *we're* supposed to do?" He gestured to Raina, to himself. "You're the one who told me to come back and be a father. That's what I'm trying to do."

Casper still had him by the shirt. "Not like this." Not *at all* like this. "Excuse us," he snapped and jerked Owen toward the den.

"Don't hurt him!" This from Grace, and when he threw a glare over his shoulder, she added, "I'm just saying, remember he's wounded!"

"Not that wounded," Casper said, even as Owen gripped his wrist.

"Let go of me—"

Behind them, Casper heard Scotty say, "Don't worry—they'll be fine. I've seen this before."

"So have we," Grace said, and maybe she was right; they wouldn't be fine.

Casper shut the door behind him and rounded on Owen, barely resisting fisting his collar, slamming him up against the wall.

"Calm down—"

"What are you thinking?"

Owen held up his hands and sank onto the old sofa, family pictures on the wall reminding Casper to breathe as Owen rubbed his chest as if trying to restart his heart. He glared at Casper, looking ten years old, indignant, confused. "Stop shouting."

"I'll stop shouting when you stop opening your stupid mouth! Really? Proposing? That's your brilliant plan?"

A knock, and before he could bark, *Stay out*, Scotty came in. She took one look at Casper and closed the door. Leaned against it and folded her arms. "He's got a point, Owen. If I remember correctly, you proposed to me. What is this, your panic go-to?"

Owen looked appropriately stricken. "Sorry, Scotty. I—"

"Forget it. I'm glad I walked away from that in the nick of time."

"Hey! What do you expect from me? She had my baby," Owen said. "And she's standing there, and my brain just went blank—"

"So you *proposed*?" Casper turned, ran his hand over his head. "Might I remind you, she's already taken."

"Maybe I should say that to you." Owen pushed up from the sofa, landing hard on his feet. "I hate to say this, buddy, but if we're looking for proof as to who Raina fell for first, I think the answer's pretty clear."

Casper lunged for him.

Owen dodged, and there was Scotty, stepping in, using her elbow to land a jab in Casper's chest. "*Ho*-kay, that's probably enough."

Casper rubbed his chest. "I should have never brought you back—"

"That *is* a good question, Bro. Why did you bring me back if you didn't want me to do the right thing by her?"

"Because you've never done the right thing in your entire life! Why would you start now? I thought you'd take a look at the colossal responsibility it is to raise a daughter and run for the hills. Face it, Owen, you're not right for them." There, it was out. Or almost all of it. His voice pitched low. "The 'right thing' is for you to agree to sign away your parental rights so I can legally become her father."

Owen stared at him, his expression slowly morphing from shock into something Casper knew too well.

The same emotion he'd felt when he realized Owen had slept with Raina.

"Wow," Owen said, his voice lethal. "So this is what it feels like to be betrayed by your own brother."

Everything—the fury, the heartache, the pain of watching the woman he loved bear his brother's child—burrowed down, centered in one blinding core of heat. "Yeah, this is *exactly* how it feels to be betrayed by your own brother. Trust me, I should know."

Silence.

Scotty blew out a breath. "Casper, let's go to the sheriff's office."

She reached for him, but he jerked away from her. "Not on your life. I'm not leaving him here with Raina."

"What do you think I'm going to do, grab her by her hair and drag her to my cave?" Owen snapped.

Casper wanted to strangle him with his bare hands.

The door creaked open and John stood in the gap. He looked at Casper, then at Owen, his expression grim. "Kyle's here."

Kyle Hueston. The local deputy. Casper didn't move. "Why is he here? I haven't killed anyone. There's no need to drag me in like a criminal."

"Yet," Scotty said. "And let's keep it that way. C'mon."

"I'm not going in."

"Yeah, actually, you are," Scotty said, but she stayed put.

"He's not staying here with Raina."

Something sparked in Owen's expression. Then he sighed. "Get outta here and go clear your name. I promise not to make any sudden moves."

"Casper . . . ," Scotty said.

And then he was saved by Raina, who pushed the door open. She looked at Owen, then turned to Casper. Her hand landed on his chest, right over his thundering heart.

"Casper, take a breath here. I'm not going to marry Owen. Ever. I love *you*." She slipped her hand into his. "And I'm not going anywhere. Please go with Kyle."

It was the *please* that got him, along with her beautiful brown eyes, and the fact that the sooner he answered Kyle's questions, the sooner he could return and finish this.

It occurred to him, however, that *he* might be the one grabbing Raina and fleeing as far as he could from Owen and from the mess he'd made by dragging his younger brother back to Deep Haven. He let her lead him out of the room to where Kyle waited, eating a cookie. Ingrid held Layla, bouncing her on her hip. Casper walked over, picked up his daughter, and pulled her against himself, breathing in her sweet, powdery scent. She wiggled in his arms, but he didn't care.

He kissed her fat cheek, then handed her to Raina and smiled weakly. "It's going to be okay. I'll be right back."

"I'll go with you, Son," John said.

Casper just nodded. Then he let Kyle lead him away.

"Sorry about my boys." John drove the family truck on the tail of Kyle's cruiser, and now he glanced at Scotty.

He seemed like a nice man. Imposing, perhaps, but maybe that's where Owen and Casper—and even their brother, Darek—got it, along with the bravado, the confidence, the sense that life wouldn't knock them over, at least not for long. His eyes were kind, despite the look he'd given Casper as they left.

As if he might not be completely on board with Casper's vision of the future.

Family drama—she saw it simmering just below the surface. The sooner she dropped Casper off and escaped, the better.

And hopefully before Ingrid Christiansen offered her another chocolate chip cookie. Not that Scotty could be swayed into staying by the aroma of fresh-baked cookies or even the sweet reunion of Owen and his family, the overwhelming sense of belonging. But with Owen holding her hand, the unfamiliar feeling of family had woven right through her, and for a long second she'd forgotten that she didn't want the entanglement of people stepping into her life, worrying, caring. Forgotten that she didn't want Owen's thumb caressing her hand, holding on like he needed her. Wanted her there.

As if he'd meant that kiss in the car, nearly convincing her it might all be real.

Until . . .

Owen taking a knee in front of Raina was exactly what Scotty needed to snap her brain back to reality. To remember why she was really here.

"Believe me, Mr. Christiansen, this is nothing compared to the hospital when Owen woke up. I thought Casper was going to go for his throat, and for his part, Owen would have ripped out his IV defending himself. They really are brothers."

"It's been . . . Well, Owen hasn't made it easy for any of us. Especially Casper, who's taken this the hardest."

"And why not? He seems to love Raina and the baby, and Owen is about to mess everything up."

John's hands tightened on the wheel.

"But . . . I take it you think that Owen should marry her."

John offered what looked like a conciliatory smile. "Thank you for all you did for him. It certainly seems that he's smitten with you."

Smitten. "No, sir. I think that's just nervousness. He was a bit . . . concerned how you might all react when he came home."

"Hmm."

Coming back down the hill, the town of Deep Haven fanned out before them, the Victorians among rustic log cabins edging the dark-blue curve of the harbor. Evergreens dissected the autumn tumble of color as it fell into the bowl of the town, the sky overhead streaked with the barest hint of cirrus clouds. The sun had passed the apex now, starting to spill marmalade rays into the far horizon.

"It's beautiful here. Reminds me of Homer. Except there's already snow on the ground there."

"You're a cop there?"

"Detective. Or I will be soon. In Anchorage. Homer was too small for my own good."

Another *hmm* from John.

They followed Kyle's cruiser as it wound through a neighborhood of cabins until it pulled up to the sheriff's office, a nondescript brick building on a hill overlooking the lake. A couple more cruisers sat in the parking lot.

Scotty got out with John and followed Casper into the building. A few vinyl chairs anchored the small waiting room. A woman behind glass at the reception counter buzzed Kyle in through the locked door to the administrative offices. He gestured for Casper to go first.

"John, you need to stay here."

"Not on your life," John said.

Kyle raised his chin, and Scotty turned to John. "I'll go in. I'll make sure everything's okay. Sit tight."

It was like telling a moose to sit down and have tea. John looked at her, his face granite.

Then he sighed and lumbered over to the chairs. Picked up a magazine. Rolled it in his big hands and turned away from her to face the window.

Probably to hide the frustration she saw growing in his shoulders, the set of his jaw.

Kyle frowned but held the door open for her. He led Casper to an interrogation room, closed the door behind him, then faced Scotty with business in his eyes. "I know you did us the courtesy of bringing him back, but we don't need any help—"

"Listen. My own department isn't much bigger than this, and I know it helps to have fresh ears—and eyes. I barely know Casper, I'm unbiased, and frankly I think it'll keep everyone back at the ranch from freaking out. So what do you say you let me listen in?"

Kyle considered her a moment. A tall man, wide-shouldered, confident, he still seemed the type to listen first. Especially when he threw a glance at John, standing at the window in the waiting area as if contemplating a jailbreak.

Everyone just needed to calm down. She had no doubt they'd sort this out in fifteen minutes, and Casper would be back home in an hour, probably proposing to Raina. After all, it seemed to be the MO of the Christiansen men.

How fun to be one of the many victims.

"Fine. There's another room for viewing." Kyle opened the door beside the interrogation room. "Just don't get in the way."

She paused before entering the room. "Kyle, just between us, how good is he for this?"

For a blink, she saw behind the cop to the friend he must be. "Monte was found in a ravine not far from the Christiansens' house. They had two reports done on him. The first came back inconclusive, saying he might have died from exposure. That's what the paper printed. But then we had a second one done, and it suggested he died from a blow to the head, one they believe occurred before the fall—and that's when they opened the murder investigation. And he had two freshly broken ribs, although he might have gotten those when he fell into the ravine.

"But while the forensic evidence is lacking, there's plenty to connect Casper to his disappearance." He sighed. "I hate this part of my job—interrogating and arresting friends."

Scotty nodded as she closed the door behind her and stood at the window, watching Casper through the one-way glass. He had taken a seat, folded his hands on the table, but he apparently didn't realize anyone could observe him because he held an all-out internal dialogue with himself, shaking his head, looking at the ceiling, as if still at home with Owen.

Taking him apart, piece by piece.

She should have driven the rental to town; then she could leave as soon as Casper walked out the door, cleared. In fact, she should be on her way now—except for the slightest niggle of doubt.

Something about Casper's initial reaction to the news of Monte Riggs's death didn't sit right with her.

Kyle entered the interrogation room, tossed a file on the table, and sat down opposite Casper. "Hey, pal. Big day—bringing Owen home."

"Let's get this over with. I don't know anything about Monte Riggs's death."

"Just take a breath, Casper. Let's start from the top."

Kyle had his back to Scotty. Casper faced her, his lips tightened into a bud of frustration. To her, he looked tired, his shirt rumpled, wearing a layer of scruff on his chin that gave him, yes, a bit of a criminal hue. Maybe she should have suggested a shower, a shave.

She crossed her arms, searched, then settled herself on a cold folding chair.

Kyle had opened the file, reading the slew of documents. "Let's see, when was it that you and Monte had that fight in front of Liza's house?"

They'd had a fight? Yes, she remembered that. He'd mentioned that in Anchorage.

Casper leaned back. "You were there. I guess it was, what—March?"

"And the nature of the fight—"

"Did you not see Raina? Monte hit her—he was going to rape her. If I hadn't gotten there . . ."

Rape. Casper had said Monte was abusive but hadn't mentioned rape. That gave even more reason for vengeance . . . and even more motive for . . . She leaned in to listen even as Kyle held up his hand. "Right. I see your statement and hers."

Casper folded his arms over his chest, nodded.

"But then there's this, about six weeks later. A complaint taken out by the manager of the VFW, who says you and Monte had an altercation."

"It was nothing."

"It doesn't sound like nothing. According to witnesses, you and he had a fight outside the VFW. Tell me about it."

Casper lifted a shoulder. "It was . . . He started it. I was with Raina, and we just wanted a night out. I saw him and ignored him, but he made a point of leaving when Raina did, following her out of the building as I was paying the bill, and when I got outside, he had her cornered near my truck. She looked scared, and I told him to back off. He took a swing at me."

"And you what, ducked?"

Something dark entered Casper's expression. "Yeah, I ducked. And then I got between him and Raina."

"It says here that you tackled him, pushed him onto the sidewalk."

"He tripped."

Scotty shook her head.

"Listen, what would you do if someone hurt Emma? Wouldn't you want to send him a message?"

Oh, Casper, what did you do?

"What kind of message, Casper?" Kyle let the question sit there, and Scotty caught it up, hearing it in the thunder of her pulse.

Casper's mouth opened. "Not that kind. I took out a restraining order against him."

"It's not on file."

"Raina took it out. It's in her name."

Kyle made a note. "So you didn't get into a physical altercation that night? You didn't tackle him, didn't break a few ribs, didn't lose anything in the scuffle?"

"What? No. Yes, I mean, we tussled, but no, I didn't hit him hard enough to break anything."

"And this? Do you recognize this?" Kyle held something up and Scotty moved to see it over his shoulder. It looked like a coin on a leather thong. "Is this yours?"

"Yes—but no. It's mine, from Honduras, but I gave it away a while ago to Signe Netterlund."

"She works at the VFW, right?"

"Among other places. I'm not sure where."

"Why would you give this away? Were you two dating?"

"No. I—she wanted it. I didn't want to remember Honduras anymore, so—what does this have to do with anything?"

"It was found under Monte's remains, near Twin Pine Point."

"I certainly didn't put it—or him—there."

After a brief silence, Kyle asked, "When did you leave town exactly?"

"I left right after Mother's Day."

"So about a week before anyone reported Monte missing. Although, according to what we dug up, his fight with you was the last time anyone remembers seeing him."

Casper shrugged. "He had a business in Duluth. And he traveled a lot."

"Convenient."

"And true," Casper snapped.

Had he never seen an episode of *Law & Order*? Why hadn't Scotty insisted on a lawyer?

Because she'd believed him. Just like she'd believed Owen.

Kyle considered him a long moment. "Casper, we've known each other for a while, grew up together, and frankly I don't want you to look good for this."

"I didn't kill him, Kyle. I might have wanted to, but I swear, I didn't do it."

Shut up, Casper. She wanted to bump the glass, tell him to keep his trap closed.

"The problem is, not only do witnesses have you fighting with Monte at the VFW, but someone spotted you two by his truck in the municipal parking lot two hours later. You want to tell me about that?"

Scotty saw guilt or something akin to it flash in Casper's eyes.

Kyle would have to be blind not to see the way Casper's face drained of color.

He needed a lawyer in there, now.

His voice shook, just enough that she winced. "That was just . . . I wanted to tell him to stay away, something that I didn't want Raina to hear."

Scotty didn't have to be in the room to see Kyle's face, to know what he was thinking. She'd been there before and expected the next words out of Kyle's mouth.

"Or didn't want her to *see*? Like you taking a tire iron to his ribs?"

Casper jerked—from the memory or the brutality of the image? His outrage sounded real, however, when he said, "What? No. Yeah, I might have grabbed his jacket, but I didn't hurt him. We just talked."

"Like I saw you *talking* to Owen? I heard you, Casper. Five more minutes and—"

"No. Owen and I . . . That's different. It's personal, family business—"

"Sounds to me like when things get personal, you get violent."

Scotty looked at the door, considering how fast Kyle would throw her out if she barged in, shut this whole thing down.

"That's not true—I . . . Listen, I didn't hurt Monte. Except—he would have hurt Raina, so I wanted to remind him that she wasn't alone. Or helpless."

"No, she wasn't because she had you," Kyle said. "Like you said, he would have hurt Raina. And when it comes to Raina, you'd do anything."

Casper blinked, then slowly nodded.

Oh—stop! Casper!

Kyle slid a piece of paper toward Casper. "According to a hospital report filed after your fight in March, Monte walked away with two cracked ribs. It wouldn't have taken much to rebreak them in another altercation."

"I didn't know about any broken ribs. Kyle, we just talked. I told him that I was going to marry Raina and that he needed to let her go."

"Or?"

"Or . . ." Casper clenched his jaw, looked away.

There it was, the sound of prison bars slamming behind him. Scotty knew how quickly the legal system could close in. She'd handled interrogations exactly this way before.

This was why she shouldn't get involved, shouldn't care. Because now here she was, wanting to bang on the glass, haul Casper out by his ear, tell him to shut up and let her find a lawyer.

And figure out who really killed this Monte Riggs.

But that would mean sticking around, letting Owen wheedle his way further into her life. And what if she discovered Casper was guilty? Wouldn't that be a fun moment? Because she didn't care whose brother he was; if he did the crime, she'd have to do her job.

Kyle closed the folder. "No one blames you for wanting to protect Raina. But here's what I think. You dropped Raina off after the fight, went back, and got in Monte's face. Maybe it was an accident—Raina wouldn't be the first to file a restraining order against Monte. Maybe you didn't even realize that you'd killed him—just wanted to get him out of the way. So you loaded him in your truck and drove into the woods."

"No," Casper snapped.

"Isn't Twin Pine Point just a few miles from your house? Your mom likes to pick blueberries there."

"Everybody picks blueberries there."

"Her Evergreen Resort cookbook has a story about how she used to find you in the middle of a blueberry patch, covered in bug bites, happily eating off the bushes."

"You're reading my mother's *cookbook*? And that makes me a murderer?"

"You knew that area, knew the ravine was there. Maybe you thought no one would ever find him, that you'd disappear before anyone would notice he was missing. You'd be gone before anyone could point a finger in your direction."

"I went to find my brother!"

"And now we're back to this." Kyle held up the necklace, dropped it on the table. "I'll check into your story, but I'm thinking a treasure like this is one you wouldn't give away so easily."

"It's worth a few bucks, if even that much."

"I think you didn't want any other girl wearing it. Maybe that night you asked for it back and had it on you when you fought. And didn't realize it had fallen off when you shoved his body into the ravine."

"You're crazy. *This* is crazy. Kyle, you know me."

"I *do* know you, Casper." He sighed. "I do know you." Kyle got up, closed the file.

Scotty found herself with her hands on the glass, her heart in her throat. No—

"Casper, I'm sorry, but I have probable cause to arrest you for the murder of Monte Riggs. I'll hand the evidence over to the county prosecutor. She'll decide if she has enough to press charges. Please stand."

Casper stared at him, the blood draining from his face. "Kyle."

"Please. Stand up." Kyle had his handcuffs out. Casper hesitated only a second before he found his feet. Held out his hands.

Scotty left as Kyle began listing Casper's Miranda rights. She headed out into the lobby, stopping before John, who had finally decided to sit down. He closed his *Fishing Today* magazine and looked at her.

Her expression must have broadcasted the results because his eyes widened. "What?" he growled.

"We need to get Casper a lawyer right now."

"Believe me, if I knew what to say to fix this, I would say it." Owen sat on the floor of the den, holding a stuffed bunny, as Layla crawled around the room. He'd watched in silence as Raina changed his daughter's diaper and tickled her tummy so she squealed in delight.

His *daughter*. Watching her now pull herself up to the sofa, her bowed legs wobbly as she worked her way toward him in her fuzzy white sleeper, drool dripping from her cherub mouth, her long lashes framing beautiful eyes . . . it felt like his heart had been ripped out of his body and pinned to his chest.

He couldn't breathe with the immensity of the miracle.

He had a daughter. And she was perfect and—

"I should have never called you Layla's daddy. That was stupid."

Raina also sat on the floor next to the couch, ready to grab Layla should she fall back. The late-afternoon sun slung shadows into the den, the aroma of cookies and his sister's lasagna creeping in to season the room with memories. That, and the myriad of pictures on the wall chronicling his childhood.

The sights and smells of home, the chatter of his family as Scotty told them the story—it undid him. If it weren't for Scotty . . .

And then he had to go and propose to Raina. Oh, he wanted to bang his head against the wall, hard. A few times.

Panic set in and he'd done the first impulsive thing that came to his brain. Again.

Raina put her hand on Layla's back to steady her, even as the little girl wobbled and plopped down on her padded bottom. "I was angry and it came out wrong and . . . poor Casper. I should have thought what that would do to him."

"Why? I am her dad—"

Her sharp look brought his words to a halt. "Hardly. Just because we spent the night together doesn't mean we're a couple, in love, or even remotely parents together. I'd stop short of saying I wish it had never happened because then I wouldn't have Layla, but I so wish it had happened with Casper."

Ouch. Owen tried not to act slapped. "Casper's not the type to . . ." He ran his fingers through the soft fur of the stuffed bunny as his words slowed, sank in. "He's not me."

"If you're trying to find that one right thing to say, that's it. Casper is not you."

He tried not to let those words twist inside him, but he'd been fighting that battle since childhood. Casper preaching to him, telling him how to live his life. He was still trying to engineer Owen's future.

"Casper didn't desert me, even when he should have," Raina said.

He stared at her. "What are you talking about? He took off for Honduras. And then after he came home, he said he freaked out about the baby. You've got a funny definition of him not deserting you. Isn't that what this whole thing with Monte Riggs is about, you dating him after Casper bailed on you?"

"Casper didn't have anything to do with Monte going missing," she said, her voice low, even lethal. He hadn't remembered her quite this . . . angry. It occurred to Owen that he barely knew this woman. In almost every way that mattered, she was a stranger.

"And for the record, he didn't bail on me. He came back—on the very day I gave birth to Layla. You should have seen him. He didn't care that I was pregnant. He picked me up, carried me out to the car, all the while his heart must have been breaking."

"He didn't know you were pregnant when he left?"

"I didn't want him to know. I was . . . ashamed."

Ashamed. At what she'd—they'd—done.

Owen opened his mouth, closed it. Looked away. Took a breath. "Yeah. I guess that's fair."

He didn't know what to say, how to put into words the *why* of his actions. "When I showed up at Darek's wedding, I was trying to figure out how my life had derailed so badly. I saw my brother getting married and my sister with Jace—how they'd gone on—and everybody seemed to be fine with their lives while mine was dismantled, and . . . I wanted to stop feeling like the family tragedy."

He glanced at her, sitting in the orange halo of the fading sun. "You were there. You were pretty, and you didn't see the guy who'd destroyed his life." He watched as Layla crawled toward him, swatted at the bunny. "I guess I just wanted to feel better."

He handed the bunny to his daughter. She took it, sat back, and stuck it in her mouth.

"And I was lonely," Raina finally said quietly.

He looked up, met her eyes. He remembered them in the moonlight. Remembered, suddenly, the feel of her in his arms.

He shook it away, the heady realization of his mistakes washing over him. Casper had every right to want to clobber him. "Maybe I'm still trying to make myself feel better."

Raina smoothed a hand over Layla's curly, dark hair.

"How did Casper react when he found out the baby was mine?"

A sigh. "He was . . . upset. But then so sweet. He wanted to . . ." She swallowed. "He wanted to raise her with me."

Owen had no words, not at first. Then, "I don't get it. How did you end up dating Monte?"

She looked away, ran a hand across her cheek. "Casper didn't want anything to do with me after I decided to give up Layla for adoption."

Owen's breath stopped. "What did you say?"

"I was scared, Owen! I didn't know Casper would come back, and I didn't . . . Well, I didn't imagine that your family would forgive me—us—whatever. I looked ahead and saw only my past, my abysmal choices—"

His mind reeled, stopped on her words. *Abysmal choices.* "Like . . . me."

She nodded, sadness in her expression. "Yeah, like you. And I didn't want to screw up Layla's life. So I . . . I found adoptive parents for her."

He blinked at her, scrambling. "But I didn't know—I would have never known . . . How could you *do* that?"

Her eyes darkened. "How could I—are you kidding me? You were gone—"

"You didn't even *attempt* to tell me." Now his chest hurt, right at his incision, his heart thundering under it.

"How would I find you to tell you, Owen? Post it on the Internet? Facebook? C'mon, be real. You didn't want to know you had a baby with me. You wanted to be gone and wallow in your anger."

Owen leaned his head back. "Wow."

"Thankfully, the adoption fell through, and by that time I realized I wanted to raise Layla, alone if I had to. But I don't have to.

Because Casper loves her. He loves her so much that he didn't want
to risk losing her when you eventually came home and discovered
you had a daughter. He didn't want to rip either of your lives apart."

"He didn't have to tell me. I would have never known."

"Have you met your brother? He couldn't live with that. You
might consider that he really does care about you and the fact that
you're Layla's biological father. It's been more than a little hard
on him."

"He's always been the guy who fixes things."

"And he's always got your back, even if it doesn't look like it."
She pulled Layla onto her lap, held out her hands to play patty-
cake. "Casper is not trying to take Layla from you. He's trying to
be a good father to her. Think about it, Owen. What does this life
look like for her? What are you going to do? I love Casper and we
are getting married. That leaves you where? Doing what?"

Layla squirmed and Raina let her out of her grip as she said,
"What's your plan? That we trade her off every weekend? She goes
to your place and then back? And what happens when you decide
you want to get married? Now she has two mothers along with
two fathers? All because you and I made a bad choice? That's not
fair to her. Casper can give her a home. Stability."

Her words stung. Yes, maybe he hadn't thought it all the way
through, but stability? Casper? "I'm sorry; are we talking about the
same person? Do you mean my head-in-the-clouds brother who
is always talking about the next treasure hunt? The brother who is
even more of a drifter—more of a dreamer—than I am? Besides,
Casper doesn't have two pennies to rub together. If we're talking
about who can provide for Layla, I might look like I'm homeless,
but I guarantee—"

"Casper is a millionaire."

If she'd told him he'd just been promoted to Santa Claus, it would have stunned Owen less. "What?"

"He found a treasure, got the finder's fee, and like I said, he's a millionaire. But I'd marry him if we had to live in a box next to Pierre's Pizza. I don't care about the money. I care about the fact that he refused to marry me until he tracked you down and told you about your daughter. Until he could get your blessing— because, and I don't know why, he loves you that much. So, Owen, how much do you love Casper? Or Layla? Do you love them enough to do what is right? Because guess what? You dropping to your knee and proposing was exactly what you said—you trying to make yourself feel better. Another word might be *selfish*."

He rubbed his chest, pretty sure he had tread marks there.

But even as she spoke, even as he'd watched Layla crawl around the room, the sense of what Casper had—what he'd been trying to protect—settled over him. A family. A future.

The very thing Owen had seen on the raft with Scotty. That thing that made him want to live, the thing he'd held on to when he sat on the sofa, her hand in his.

A future he'd tasted when he'd kissed her in the car. The fact that she'd kissed him back, softened in his arms . . .

He wanted it and understood suddenly what had driven Casper to find him, to pose the audacious idea that Owen surrender his daughter.

Or maybe not *his* daughter, if he really faced the truth.

Except she could be.

That's when Layla decided that the fuzzy man sitting on the floor might be fun to climb on. She crawled into his lap, and Owen picked her up. She turned to him, rubbed her fingers in his beard.

His throat thickened.

Selfish. The word jagged through him even as Layla laughed, clapped her hands, made another dive for his beard.

He intercepted her with the bunny. She took it again, shoved it into her mouth.

The future hung there, in Raina's words. Her handing Layla off like a package at his door. His daughter's own tiny pink room in his, what—trailer? Apartment? Him trying to figure out what to feed her, how to soothe her when she cried, trying to keep up with her toys, diapers, needs.

Casper had held her like a natural. No awkward fumbling, no hesitation. Like a father might do with his child.

He so wasn't ready to be a father. Yet. And Casper knew that too.

Yeah, selfish. Because his plans weren't so much about falling in love with this amazing little girl as they were about holding on to the last decent thing in his life. The one good thing that had come from the mess he'd made of his past.

And worse . . . He glanced at Raina, seeing another wretched truth. He simply didn't want to lose. Not to Casper.

Not to the brother he'd spent his entire life trying to best.

He sighed, lifting his daughter so he could meet her eyes. "Casper is always trying to tell me what to do. And he gets mad when I don't do it his way."

He pressed a kiss to Layla's cheek before putting her down. "But in this case . . . I don't know. I will think about it."

Raina's expression softened. "Thank you, Owen. We would never want to keep the truth from Layla, but it would be less confusing for her, at least until she's old enough to understand."

He tried a half smile. "I know." He touched his chest again, where his wound had started to ache.

To his surprise, Raina reached out, took his hand. He squeezed hers back.

In the quiet, he heard the front door open, voices in the next room.

"They're back." Raina got up and Owen climbed off the floor, reaching for Layla.

He groaned, his wound turning to fire in his chest.

"Are you hurt?" Raina said as she picked up her daughter.

"I'll be okay," he said, bracing himself on the sofa. Please let Scotty have returned with them.

His hopes ignited when he came out of the den and spotted Scotty standing by the kitchen counter. Her gaze stopped only briefly on Raina before it landed on Owen, bearing a chill, something dark and pensive. He frowned.

Then his father appeared, walking right up to Ingrid, wrapping her in a hug. Everyone went quiet—his parents in the kitchen; Grace, who sat at the counter helping a little girl he'd never seen before with homework; Darek, who'd emerged from the adjacent Evergreen Resort office.

John released Ingrid, his hand finding hers. "We have a problem," he said. He glanced at Raina, then at Owen, holding his gaze.

"Casper's been arrested for the murder of Monte Riggs."

CHAPTER 8

SCOTTY DIDN'T KNOW how she'd ended up at the Christiansen dinner table, passing the garlic bread to Owen's sister Grace and embroiled in the family powwow about how to clear Casper's name.

The family wave had simply washed over her, like a ship at sea, the moment she exited the sheriff's office.

And now they looked at her as the resident expert in proving Casper's innocence.

"But what proof do they have?" This from Ingrid, Casper's mother, who sat at one end of the oval table, chopping her dinner into pieces but not really consuming it.

Next to her, and across from Scotty, Owen also seemed broody, with occasional glances at Raina, next to him, and at Grace's new daughter—a six-year-old named Yulia with braids and a tentative smile for Scotty when she'd returned home with John.

This seemed to be the family MO . . . adopting the lost. Because just like Yulia, they'd folded Scotty into the mix as if she belonged. Ingrid had roped her into setting the table, Grace had given her garlic bread–slicing duty, and all the while John had recounted the events at the police station, making it sound as though Scotty had been their secret weapon.

"It's circumstantial, at best," Scotty said, now passing the tossed salad. "Apparently he and Monte have a past—leading up to the fact that Casper might have been the last person to see Monte before he disappeared." She looked at Raina, who had turned deathly quiet, almost stunned with the news. She held Layla on her lap, feeding her baby food as she absorbed the conversation. Scotty kept her voice gentle. "Did you know he tracked Monte down after the fight at the VFW?"

Raina shook her head. "I told him to leave it be, that Monte didn't scare me, but . . ." She glanced at Layla. "I was scared, and he probably knew it."

Silence. Scotty stifled the urge to reach for her hand, to tell her that no one had the right to scare her. Casper's words during his interrogation rang in her head. *Monte hit her—he was going to rape her.*

Not dinner conversation, but definitely a reason for Casper to go after Monte. She glanced at Owen. "Kyle heard about the fight you two had, too, and used it to point out that Casper had the temper—and ability—to hurt someone enough . . ." She didn't want to continue, not with Yulia sitting right there.

"He does know how to hit," Owen said, and she hurt for him with that admission. "But he would never kill someone."

"Of course not. The entire thing is absurd." Ingrid pushed her plate away, pressed her hands over her eyes, and the table went quiet.

"Like I told John, you need to get a good lawyer to help sort this out. I'm not going to sugarcoat it—plenty of people have gone to jail on circumstantial evidence. The way Kyle painted the scene, along with Casper's own words, even I would have charged him."

"What did he say?" Raina asked, looking on the verge of tears.

Scotty didn't want to repeat it, to explain the venom in Casper's voice when he'd talked about protecting Raina. So she gentled her tone. "Just that he loves you very much."

Owen looked up, met Scotty's eyes.

Since she'd left with Casper, he'd changed and showered, trimmed his beard again to a tantalizing layer of golden-and-copper whiskers along his chin. He still wore his hair long but now held it back with a black headband, the curls drying in the air. He wore a turquoise T-shirt, something he'd probably found in Casper's clothes because the shirt read, *Dive Roatán.* The shirt only emphasized the difference between Casper's leaner but solid treasure-hunting physique and Owen's work-hardened chest, his biceps stretching the arms of the shirt from so many hours hauling in crab pots. He even smelled good, the scent of freshly showered male, a fragrance she'd caught when he joined her to help set the table.

Yet, for a moment when she saw him sit next to Raina, the image of them together in the past had hit Scotty hard, turning her dinner to acid in her throat.

No, this couldn't possibly be jealousy. She had made peace with Owen's escapades.

Or perhaps they'd only been theory until now.

It occurred to her then that she might be making things worse. After all, maybe Owen's cleanup act had everything to do with his wanting to fit into Raina's life.

The sooner Scotty escaped with her heart intact, the better.

"Excuse me," Raina said, pushing back from the table. She picked up Layla and headed upstairs.

Oddly, Owen didn't even rise when she left, just kept looking at Scotty.

Like she could make this all go away? Hardly.

"I called Max," Grace said beside her. "He's calling the lawyer we're using for Yulia's adoption, to see if he has a friend in the firm who can recommend a defense attorney."

"If there was ever a time for Casper to use his millions, it might be now," Owen said.

"Millions?" Scotty asked.

"Casper found a treasure that gave him a healthy savings account," John said simply. "But he invested a lot of it into the resort. Got us back on our feet and helped buy the trees around the property, add the Internet, make some improvements to the cabins."

"He's part owner of Evergreen Resort now," Ingrid said, picking up her plate and cup. "He and Darek are working together. Darek's the managing partner. Are you done, honey?"

Scotty nodded, and Ingrid took her plate too.

The phone rang in the quiet of that news. Ingrid went to answer.

Owen had returned to some attempt at eating but put his fork down when his mother greeted someone named Ivy.

Right, Darek's wife.

They all listened to the one-sided conversation, the *umm-hmm*s and "Oh no," which made Owen glance at his father, then push his own plate away. So much for his sister's welcome-home lasagna.

Finally Ingrid issued a calmer "I understand" and "Thank you, Ivy. Come by soon, if there's a good time for the kids. I know Owen would like to see baby Joy and Tiger."

Owen got up from the table as Ingrid hung up. She stood in the kitchen, cradling the phone. "Ivy said that the county prosecutor's office has decided to file a formal complaint against Casper. He'll have his initial appearance on Thursday, where they'll set bail. His evidentiary hearing is on Monday, and they'll decide whether to indict him for the crime." She looked at Scotty. "What does that mean?"

They all looked at Scotty, so she answered. "It means that we have until Monday to find evidence that Casper wasn't involved. If we don't, he will be held over for trial." *We.* Oops. But she couldn't go back and amend her words.

"Trial." Ingrid set the phone down. Turned away.

Owen walked over to his mother, putting his arms around her and pulling her to himself. "Mom, Casper is not going to jail. I promise. We're going to prove that he didn't do it, and everything's going to be fine."

And as if on cue, he added, "Have a little faith."

Owen's answer to everything, although it seemed to sink in. John looked at Grace, covering her hand with his. Owen's mom turned in his arms to pat his cheek, then leaned her head against his chest.

"I can't believe Ivy is prosecuting her own brother-in-law," Grace finally said, almost in a whisper.

"She recused herself, Grace," Ingrid said, untangling herself from Owen's grip. "And the county attorney opted to hand the case over to a prosecutor from Duluth."

"That's why this is happening," Grace said. "Because they don't know Casper. They don't know—"

"Exactly my point," Scotty said. "There's a lot of circumstantial evidence against him."

"Can I talk to you?" Owen had moved beside her, his voice low. Not that the entire table couldn't hear him, because they all went quiet.

Um, well, when he put it like that . . . Scotty nodded.

He headed toward the entryway, handed her jacket to her, then pulled what looked like an old letter jacket from the closet. Once he'd shrugged it on and buttoned it at the waist, he grabbed a box of matches from a shelf and held the door open for her.

"What are you doing?"

"You'll see," he said as he followed her outside.

The sun had finally dropped into the horizon, leaving only a deep magenta overhead, backdrop to the finest suggestion of a Milky Way evening. The smell of loam kicked up when the wind shivered the trees, tossing curly leaves over the pathway as Owen led her toward the lake. It glistened under the rising moon, frosting the waves and reminding her of the Bering Sea on a calm— unusually calm—night.

Scotty waited for him to reach for her hand, but he hadn't touched her since his impulsive proposal. Probably he'd figured out that a guy doesn't propose to another woman in front of his former fiancée.

Not that she could really call herself that. Still, it stung despite the absurdity of the situation.

Owen stopped at a cleared area, just before the beach. "Wow, they rebuilt the fire pit," he said.

She could barely make it out in the moonlight but got close enough to see five wooden benches, rough-hewn but polished, circling an inlaid-stone fire pit. She heard thumping as Owen retrieved logs, then watched as he bent to arrange them.

"Need help?"

"Grab some of that kindling from the tinderbox." He gestured to a tin box attached to the side of the log pile, where a cord or two of split logs lay stacked, ready to be consumed. Inside she found old newspaper, pinecones, and twigs. She retrieved a handful and squatted beside Owen, his assistant as he tucked the accelerant into the nooks and crannies of his Boy Scout tented fire mound.

She couldn't deny something deeply attractive about a man who knew how to build a perfect fire. He held the lit match to the paper, then leaned low and blew gently. The flame ate at the paper and nipped at a pinecone, which burst to life, igniting the kindling, charring the logs. The fire crackled, spitting sparks into the amaranthine hues of twilight.

Owen got up and scooted back to sit on a log, holding his hands to the fire. In the glow of the firelight, he appeared fierce, his jaw hard-edged.

"Are you okay?" Scotty asked.

He glanced up, and his expression eased. He even managed a small, tight smile. "Now that you're back? Yeah."

And right then, she returned to the car earlier today, the sense of being in his arms, that impossibly tender kiss, the way he'd hung on to her—

Oh, Owen. "You know I am only here another day."

"C'mere."

She took a step toward him, then hesitated. "Owen . . . we had rules, remember? No trying to charm me into staying."

His smile dimmed, and he tucked his hands between his knees. "Oh, you're talking about the kiss."

"And your proposal to Raina—"

"That was a mistake."

"But that's the point. You live by the moment, following your heart, and I . . . I can't do that. I have to consider all the ramifications, look ahead."

"Always the captain," he said, his mouth crooking up.

Well, yeah. She sat beside him, watching the flames.

"We need you, Scotty." He looked at his folded hands. "I need you. I can't let my brother go down for this. I know he's innocent."

She hesitated a moment. "Are you sure? Owen, you haven't been here. What if he's responsible . . . even unintentionally?"

He blew out a long breath as if yes, he'd considered that. "Then it was to protect Raina and Layla."

"If he did the crime, he needs to be brought to justice."

"No. See, that's my point. What justice is there in taking him away from his family when he was only trying to protect them?"

"You can't justify murdering someone—"

"I know. It's just . . ." He stared up at the stars. "Did you hear my parents? Casper used his fortune to rescue the resort. He's always doing that, rescuing people. Solving their problems. He didn't have to tell me Layla was mine, but he wanted to do what was right. That's essential Casper—always doing the right thing. That's why he shouldn't go to jail for this."

He sighed. "And that's why I'm thinking of giving my consent for him to adopt Layla."

Silence.

"I don't know, Scotty, but seeing them this afternoon . . . they're already a family, right? I feel like an intruder. No, worse. Like I'm repeating the past, about to destroy everything I wanted to fix." He sank his head into his hands. "I have to get this right."

This was the man she knew from the boat. Not the angry, impulsive, almost-desperate man she'd seen today, but the man no one else seemed to know. Sacrificial. Responsible. Honorable, even if he had left the litter of bad choices behind him.

Everything she'd felt in the raft and afterward at the hospital—all the images of growing old with this man, waking to his amazing smile every sunrise, building a life with him—suddenly rose inside her, turning her heart tender toward him.

Oh, the effect he had on her.

So what that he was impulsive? *Impulsive* had kissed her in the car, had talked her into coming to Minnesota. *Impulsive* had jumped into an ocean to save her life.

He might have read her thoughts because he took her hand, his gaze in hers. "I know that I blew it when I proposed to Raina—"

"It's no big deal. I get it, Owen." And please, if he'd stop looking at her like he had on the raft, a sweet hunger for her in his expression . . .

She made to pull her hand away, but he hung on.

"But I promise not to do anything stupid again if you help me figure out how to clear Casper. If he's free, then we can all figure out how to go on with our lives."

Oh. So maybe she'd read that wrong.

"I just need . . . I need your brains, Scotty. I'm a guy who does things the hard way. When I played hockey, I wasn't the player with finesse. I just worked harder than everybody else. I practiced longer, took more shots on goal, mixed it up and fought for every minute of ice time. But that's not going to cut it here. You're a detective—please help me figure this out."

And despite the fact that he wasn't exactly pleading for her heart, he was so earnest, so desperate in his petition, that she wanted to say yes.

Scotty pulled away, shoved her hands into her pockets. "I don't know what I can do. It's not like the Deep Haven sheriff's office is going to let me in on their investigation."

Owen fell silent beside her. A loon called, low, moaning over the lake. The trees cast their own offerings into the fire.

"You know why Casper and I fight so much?" he said, picking up a stick, poking it into the fire.

"Because you're brothers?"

"Because he's always right." Sparks scattered as a log fell. "My earliest memory is actually of him, right out here on the lake, bossing me around as I tried to handle a hockey puck. Even when I could skate circles around him, he egged me on, acted like he could outskate and outshoot me. I only recently realized that it was his way of making sure I was the best."

In memory she saw Casper standing above Owen's bed, his face so tight as if holding in an emotion he couldn't bear to free.

"I made a mess of everything because I was angry and bitter and, most of all, knew I couldn't be the guy Casper—or any of them—wanted me to be. I still can't believe they welcomed me back like . . ." He shook his head.

"Like they missed you? Like you're a part of the family?"

Her words elicited a sigh. "I don't deserve it; I know that. But I've been thinking that maybe God spared us in the ocean and then brought us both here because we're supposed to get Casper out of this mess. Ever since I met Carpie on the dock and started looking for a way back to the man I wanted to be, I prayed for a second chance. I knew I'd sinned—really sinned—and I feared that there was no going back for me. But here I am—here *we* are. Alive and yeah, with a second chance. I have to believe God heard my prayers. At least I want to."

A rueful smile twitched one side of his mouth. "Like I said, I'm not a detective, but I do have enough stupid grit to keep trying until we figure out who did it—or maybe just raise enough doubt about Casper's guilt."

His face became solemn then. "Please help me?"

Please. She had no defenses against *please.* Or against his voice, the softness in it, or the way he made to reach for her hand, then pulled back. "I promise not to propose or even . . . kiss you. Although—" a smile dragged up his face—"I did like kissing you."

She couldn't breathe past the boulder in her throat. "About that . . . why did you kiss me?"

"Because I didn't in the boat. And I should have. And . . . because you're so beautiful, I couldn't stop myself." He shrugged.

Then something mischievous, even sweetly dangerous, sparked in his gaze. Oh no. If she just leaned over or even let her eyes show what she was feeling, she knew in a blink he'd be kissing her again.

And she wouldn't have a bone inside her to stop him.

Wouldn't that be painful, come the inevitable moment when she extricated herself from his life? His family? This strange sense of happily ever after he kept dangling in front of her?

So she rushed into her words, clung to them. "No more breaking the rules. You can't kiss me, Owen. You can't hold my hand. It's over. What we had kept us alive. But it was impulsive and . . ." And why hadn't he figured out what seemed to be glaringly obvious to everyone else? "I'm not the marrying kind."

He frowned. "What are you talking about?"

She hated how he said it, the same way she had when Carpie implied it. But she'd seen the truth and so would he. She reached over to grab the stick he was holding and moved it into the fire, toppling one of the logs. "I'm not . . . I'm not soft and sweet . . ."

"Are you kidding me?"

185

"No!" She turned to him, more spark in her voice than she intended. "Did you see Raina? Or Grace? They love being mothers, taking care of their family. That's not me. I don't have the first clue how to take care of someone. I never had a mother. I had Red and a bunch of grimy-mouthed fishermen for brothers. I don't know the first thing about being in a real family."

She looked away from him toward the house, where light glowed out from the deck. "I guess I'm like Red. I'm no good with emotion. Or . . . faith. It doesn't make sense to me. Yeah, I got desperate on the boat when you were dying, might have done some praying, but that's not real faith."

"I disagree. Faith is reaching out, believing in what you can't see . . . But really? You prayed?"

"You were dying. What was I supposed to do?"

She didn't mean for it to come out quite so sharp. So she sighed, tempered her tone. "Homer had this little church bus, and sometimes they'd stop by and pick me up. I heard all the Sunday school stories, bought into the fairy tale of heaven. I liked to think of my mom up there with Jesus. But then I grew up and realized—what kind of God would separate a baby from her mother?"

"Aw, Scotty." He looked like he wanted to reach for her, but she held herself back.

"Or maybe God had nothing to do with my mom's death. Maybe that was just life. Life is cruel and harsh, and sometimes you survive, but sometimes you don't. Either way, you have to keep going. There is no happily ever after. There's only now, and trying not to get blown overboard, and doing your job."

She closed her eyes before the memories piled up, spilling out. Took a breath, hardened her voice as she stared again at the fire.

"Faith is . . . very messy and emotional. It's for people who can't face reality. Who want to believe that things are going to miraculously get better. But they don't. And I'm certainly not going to drop to my knees and start beseeching heaven for help. I don't owe God anything, and that works just fine for me."

Owen was silent beside her, his mouth a tight line.

"What?"

"It's just that . . . I used to think that way. In fact, when I first got hurt, I wanted nothing to do with God. Later, I couldn't face the colossal mess I'd made of my life. But then I realized I couldn't fix myself, that I needed help. When we got washed overboard— I'm sorry, Scotty, but God did step in and save us. He brought me—us—home. It's got me thinking that there's a chance I'm not a total screwup, or if I am, God can help me fix it."

His words settled upon her. "Owen, you're not a screwup."

He managed a smile. "When you say it like that, I almost believe you."

And that was just *enough*. "Fine. Okay. If only to prove to you that you're more than you see. Whether God brought us here to save Casper or it's simply circumstances, I don't care. I have three weeks until my job kicks in in Anchorage, so until then I'll do what I can. Which might not be anything. But if I can help you fix this, I will."

"Thank you." He nodded, glanced at her sideways, the rising moon turning his hair to gold. "There you go again, being my hero."

But when he met her gaze, she wasn't exactly sure who should be called the hero. Because he'd bared his soul in order to get her to stick around and help him save Casper.

That kind of family loyalty had her staring at the fire, a stirring, unfamiliar hum under her skin as the night descended. And as Owen sat beside her, dressed in that letterman's jacket, smelling of the woodland forest, dark and wild, she realized that she wouldn't have minded terribly if he'd pulled her, just for a second, into another impulsive, rule-breaking kiss.

Today was the day for second chances. Today Owen would track down Monte Riggs's killer and figure out how to woo Scotty back into his arms.

Today he'd steal pucks, score goals. Become a superstar again, if only in his own eyes.

Woken by the sun, he rose early in the quietness of his old bedroom, the three beds—two bunks and Darek's single—shoved into the attic. He'd always had the top bunk, and it had felt a little weird to choose Darek's bed last night.

Owen picked up his clothes, still smelling of the smoky fire, and stood at the window, staring out at the lake.

He should have kissed Scotty last night. Why did he make that stupid promise? She'd looked at him with those amazing gray-green eyes, and he'd wanted to call her a liar.

It's over. What we had kept us alive. But it was impulsive and . . . I'm not the marrying kind.

He didn't know what the marrying kind might be, but he didn't believe for a second that it was over. Not by a long shot.

Okay, fine. He wouldn't kiss her again, not until she knew—really knew—that it wasn't an impulsive, shot-in-the-dark kiss, but a kiss that he meant, a kiss that told her exactly how he felt.

Which, at the moment, he couldn't quite put his finger on. She'd thrown him with her words about God. *I don't owe God anything, and that works just fine for me.*

In his estimation, he owed God everything. And yes, he could agree that in the face of his sins, grace felt a bit too overwhelming. It almost seemed easier to live like Scotty—alone, unbeholden to God.

Because a God who dispensed grace was a God a person couldn't bargain with.

Except perhaps that was the point. God didn't want to bargain.

Owen watched the sun gild the lake. His entire life he'd wanted more than this view gave him. Hockey had given him that. And when he lost it, he'd run from the man he couldn't be.

So what man was he now?

He went down to the kitchen, feeling the strangest sense of déjà vu at the sight of his mother flipping French toast on the stove. Grace stood in the entryway, bundling up Yulia against a nor'easter wind that rattled the sliding-glass doors and tumbled leaves onto the deck.

"Coffee?" he asked and headed toward the cupboard. Opened it to find baking spices.

"I moved the mugs," his mother said, opening the opposite cupboard door and pulling one down. "But the creamer is still in the same drawer."

"We're off to school; then I'll come back and make some cookies for Casper. I'm going to go visit him today," Grace said as she left the house.

Owen poured himself a cup of coffee, made his way to a stool.

"Why is Grace living here, instead of down in the Cities with Max? I know the schedule is hectic—"

"The adoption hasn't been finalized, and your father and I are technically still Yulia's foster parents. In the meantime, Max sold his condo, and he and Grace are buying a house. Max is staying with Jace and Eden."

Because that's what teammates did. For a second an old jealousy flared. He noticed the door to the office open, so he went in and found Darek at his computer. He wore jeans and a green chamois shirt with the Evergreen Resort logo on the breast pocket. His brother seemed more serious than Owen remembered. Owen had often thought he was the blonder version of Darek, born with Darek's stubborn resolve to bully his way to an answer.

"Any reservations for this weekend?" Owen said.

"We're full," Darek said, looking at him. Were those lines around his eyes? Dude, he was getting old.

Or maybe they were all just growing up. Everyone but Owen.

Except he might be growing up too because he *hadn't* launched himself at Scotty like he wanted to when she said she'd stick around. When she told him that she'd help him fix this.

See, he didn't have to be completely impulsive. Always.

"Is this baby Joy?" Owen picked up a picture of Darek on the sofa, a dark-haired baby dressed in pink lying on his chest.

Darek smiled. "She's beautiful, isn't she?" He took the picture, letting his thumb linger over it. "I'm not sure how I got so lucky."

Owen wasn't either because he remembered the summer Darek got his girlfriend pregnant, how Darek had acted like his life was over. "Sorry about what I said yesterday, about you and Felicity."

Darek set the picture back on the desk. "Nah, I get it. I wasn't the best example."

Or maybe he was. Because here Darek sat, his life no longer in shambles. "How did you . . . how did you do this, Bro? Find the right girl, get married?"

Darek shook his head. "You're under the impression that I have this figured out." He turned to Owen. "Don't think I don't recognize the guilt that dogs you. I see your face, and I know what's

190

in your head. I was there, after Felicity. Even before she died, I couldn't escape it. The only difference between you and me is the fact that I've finally let God forgive me and stopped believing that He's got a perpetual frown pointed my direction. Believe me, I'm no saint. I'm just a little better at accepting grace."

The phone rang, and Darek moved to pick it up as Owen backed out of the room.

"French toast?" His mother slid a plate onto the counter.

Owen bellied up, grabbing the syrup. "These smell good."

"I have a new recipe for eggnog French toast. It's a little calorie naughty, but for you . . ." She winked, then reached over, touched his arm. When he caught her eyes, they glistened. "I'm so glad you're home."

Aw, Mom. "Me too."

And surprisingly, nothing of regret, no twinge of guilt, tempered his words.

"I'm going to figure out a way to clear Casper," he added.

His mother offered a weak smile. "I believe you will," she said, squeezing his arm.

He felt about sixteen, seeing his mother waving at him from the stands, hearing her cheer his name.

She leaned back to look over his shoulder. "Good morning, Scotty. Would you like French toast?"

Owen turned, and everything inside him became golden as Scotty came down the stairs, pulling her duffel bag behind her. She wore her hair down, long and lush, and a flannel shirt and jeans. "I need to find a Laundromat. I'm still dragging around my clothes from the boat."

"Me too. I had to raid Casper's stash." He gestured to the orange UMD Bulldogs T-shirt he wore.

"You're welcome to use our laundry facilities, Scotty," Ingrid said. "Get her set up, Owen. And if you bring your laundry down, I'll put yours in after hers."

"Really?"

"I know you're a grown man, but I remember you turning your hockey jersey purple." She looked at Scotty. "They were supposed to be blue and washed in cold. Coach made him wear it the entire year."

"I was in eighth grade, playing varsity, and it was humiliating." He slid off the stool and led Scotty to the basement. The smells of the past embedded the paneled walls—so many parties with the team, popcorn ground into the green shag carpet, endless games of Nintendo on the old Panasonic still sitting on the built-ins. He opened the door to the laundry room and found a new pair of high-efficiency front-loaders. "I remember the washer being a green top-loader," he said. "I'm not sure how to work this."

"Stand back. I like my clothes their original color." Scotty nudged him out of the way and dumped her duffel out on the floor. He averted his eyes.

"I don't need help. Go pour me a cup of coffee." She pushed him out of the room, and he refrained from grabbing her hands, pulling her to himself.

"Yes, sir."

She narrowed an eye, and he backed away, hands raised. Upstairs, he poured her a cup of coffee, set it next to him.

"I like her," his mother said, her back to him. When she turned, she held Scotty's plate of French toast. "She's a little dazzled by you."

"No, Mom, trust me. Not dazzled at all."

"Mmm-hmm." She set the plate next to the coffee as Scotty appeared from the basement.

Scotty climbed onto the stool, reached for the syrup. "These look amazing."

"Better than Carpie's burnt pancakes."

"Old shoes would be better than Carpie's pancakes." She dug in, making sounds of delight.

"My mother is a great cook. Grace inherited her abilities. A person could get fat living here—I mean, look at Darek." He made a face and glanced behind her at Darek emerging from the office, holding his cup of coffee.

"I can still take you. Anytime, anyplace." Darek set his cup in the sink and turned to Scotty. "He was scrawny until he was about seventeen. Used to score goals by skating under kids."

"Not true. It just seemed that way because I was so lightning fast."

Darek laughed. "Oh, that was it. Who was that kid on the team who hated you? Used to take your stuff, throw it out of your locker?"

"Rhino Johnson. A senior, about three times as big as me. He got it in his head that I took his spot—"

"You did. Hello, he was a starting wing before you skated in." Darek fired up the stove, reaching for the French toast fixings. "Owen could skate circles around him."

"And he made me pay. I would get to practice early, suit up, and be on the ice before anyone else. Then he'd get there, find my locker, and play hide Owen's clothes in one of the other lockers, or maybe put them in the shower or in a toilet stall. As an eighth grader it was a little daunting."

Owen soaked his toast in the syrup. "I would come home, sometimes in wet clothes, frozen and mad and frustrated." He washed a bite down with coffee. "Then one day I couldn't take it anymore. We were on the ice and I just . . . freaked out. I checked him as hard as I could, his helmet came off, and he broke his nose."

"Wow." Scotty stopped midbite.

"I know. I thought he was going to kill me. But he just avoided me after that. Maybe he realized I was tougher than he thought."

"Or maybe he waited for you after practice the next day, planning to take you out at the knees, and Casper jumped him." Darek flipped his French toast, turned to face Owen.

"He did?"

"Mmm-hmm. Told Rhino that if he went after you, he'd have to deal with Casper—and me."

Oh. Now Owen felt about fourteen again.

"Although I'm sure you made an impression on everyone else. Because if I remember correctly, you dominated the league in goals that season."

"Is that you on the fridge?" Scotty slid off her stool, going over to view the collection of articles stuck to the door. "This one is from when you signed with the Blue Ox."

"We were so proud of him," Ingrid said. "Owen worked so hard for that contract."

She left the rest unsaid—the part where he'd thrown it all away on an after-hours grudge match.

"Take it down, Mom," Owen said. "That part of my life is over."

"But it's still part of your life and something to be proud of. Just because life didn't turn out how you'd imagined doesn't mean you throw away the things you learned."

She pulled a picture off the fridge, handed it to Scotty. "This, however, is one of my favorites. It's the summer before Owen went to the juniors, and he decided to try out for a musical."

"Aw, Mom, you don't—"

"Doesn't he make the cutest Danny Zuko?"

Owen hopped off his stool, headed for the fridge, but Scotty had grabbed the photo and was dancing away with it.

And like a conspirator, Darek stepped in for the block.

"Give it!" Owen said.

But Scotty had backed against the wall, looking at the photo, and wore such a sweet smile.

"Fine. Yeah, I was Danny. I did it on a dare and got the lead."

"Oh, please, you ate up the attention," Darek said.

Scotty put the article behind her back. "I saw the movie once. How does it go? 'You're the one that I want, you are the one I want . . .'"

"'Ooh, ooh, ooh,'" Darek said.

Owen rolled his eyes. "Nice."

"I love it. Or how about this one. 'Summer lovin' happened so fast . . .'" Scotty's voice came out in song, and Owen couldn't help it.

"'I met a girl crazy for me . . .'" No singing, just words, and he trained his gaze on hers, stepping forward. *Okay, Scotty. You want to play this game, I'm all in.*

Her eyes widened, and it seemed the kitchen went quiet. "I . . . I don't know the rest," she said softly.

"Probably for the best. He didn't get great reviews," Darek said as Scotty ducked past Owen and handed Ingrid the picture.

Owen hid a smile. "People loved me. I was a hit. I nearly thought about throwing in my hockey career for Broadway."

"Owen was my most theatrical," Ingrid said as she replaced the picture. "Even on the ice, he had a flair about him—the camera loved him."

"Didn't you do a spread in *Hockey Today* magazine as one of the rookies?" Darek said.

"Can we change the subject back to how we're going to clear Casper's name?"

And that had the effect of a hammer on the mood. Scotty returned to her seat, stirring her food through the syrup. Ingrid turned to the stove. Darek leaned against the wall, holding his plate, eating.

"Sorry."

"No, you're right," Scotty said, flashing him a quick, business-like smile, and now he really hated himself. So they'd walked down memory lane . . . Maybe his mother was right. Not every remembrance had to be painful.

"Where do we start?" Owen asked.

Scotty picked up her empty plate, brought it to the sink. "First, we need to track down this Signe person and find out if she knows anything about the necklace found at the scene. Then we start making a list of people who didn't like Monte."

Grace walked in, pulling off her coat. "I just got off the phone with Max, who talked with a lawyer this morning. He'll be here for Casper's arraignment on Thursday. But Max pointed out that all we have to prove is reasonable doubt. We don't have to actually solve the crime. Just throw out enough questions so the judge won't hold him over for trial."

"Can we do that?" Ingrid said.

"Maybe not at the arraignment stage, but yes, it's a viable defense," Scotty said. "Just make the jury doubt; not only show the lack of evidence, but give them other, equally reasonable choices. It could work."

However, even as she said it, Scotty looked at Owen, her eyes dark.

And he remembered what she'd said. *If he did the crime, he needs to be brought to justice.*

He met her gaze. "Since Casper is innocent, this is a great idea."

She drew in a breath, and he held his own until she nodded. "So how do we track down Signe?"

"She works at the VFW," Grace said. "But they don't open for a while. Maybe you could start on that list. What about Monte's neighbors, Rhino and Kaleigh Johnson? A couple summers ago Kaleigh came into Pierre's upset because she said Monte killed their dog. Could be something?"

"Rhino Johnson. Why does that name sound familiar?" Scotty said, adding a tease to her voice.

Owen put his hand over his nose. Glanced at Darek.

"You're a big boy now. You got this." Darek winked. "Have fun storming the castle."

"Think it'll work?" Ingrid said.

"It'll take a miracle," Scotty finished and headed for the door.

"I really like her," Ingrid said as Owen followed Scotty out.

So did he.

CHAPTER 9

Now Scotty had the image of Owen as Danny Zuko stuck in her head. Dressed in a bad-boy leather jacket, his hair dyed dark and greased back, a dangerous curl in the middle of his forehead, wearing a yeah-I'm-trouble look on his face.

"You're the one that I want . . ."

She needed to purge him, and the song, from her brain. Because no, he wasn't. Especially since it seemed Owen had decided to obey her, for once, and keep his distance. No hand-holding, no opening the door for her, just lots of crisp fall air between them as they walked up to Rhino Johnson's ocher ranch house with fading white trim, located a couple streets from Main in Deep Haven.

Scotty spied a deflated kiddie pool in the front yard and a tricycle hiked into the bushes near a red potted chrysanthemum.

A pumpkin on the front step celebrated the month of October, and on the door, the wind blew the orange fabric bows attached to a straw wreath. The house sported all the embellishments of a young family.

Owen stood there for a long moment, eyeing the door.

"What?"

"I'm just . . . ah . . ."

"Oh, come on. I'll protect you." She hit the doorbell, moved in front of him.

Strangely, he let her.

The door opened, the storm door exhaling with it, and a pretty woman with long blonde hair who looked about Scotty's age appeared. "Can I help you?"

"Hey, Kaleigh. It's . . . me. Owen Christiansen."

A toddler peeked around her leg, a boy with equally blond hair, a fluff around his head. Kaleigh bent down and picked him up, propping the storm door open with her hip. "Owen Christiansen?" Her gaze warmed. She wore femininity in her loose hair, her pink T-shirt, the natural way she held her toddler. She'd probably been one of those cute girls in high school, the ones with a date every weekend.

That accounted for why she looked at Owen with such affection. "Wow. I haven't seen you since . . . what, tenth grade?" She took him in, and Scotty saw the appreciation in her eyes, let it ping against the irritating, burgeoning jealousy inside. "You look good. The eye patch is sexy."

He still wore the patch, but Scotty had long ago stopped seeing it. Or was trying to because Kaleigh was right.

"Thanks."

"What brings you back to Deep Haven? You're not playing hockey anymore, are you?"

That had to sting, but Owen seemed to let it bounce off him. He shrugged. "No. Actually, I'm in town doing some investigating into the death of Monte Riggs. This is Detective Scotty McFlynn."

He nudged Scotty like she should flash a badge or something. But she kept her hands in her pockets, smiled.

Couldn't he have introduced her as a friend? Even—call her crazy—his fiancée?

Of course not, but the thought poked at her.

"Sure, whatever." Kaleigh gestured with her head to the dingy brown house and overgrown lawn next door. "I don't know much—he wasn't home a lot."

"I hate to ask, ma'am, but we got a report of some kind of disturbance between you and Monte," Scotty said.

"He killed our dog, is what." The voice came from behind Kaleigh, and Scotty felt Owen bristle. A man appeared, and Scotty looked him over, surprised. From the story and the name Rhino, she had expected someone on par with Thor, the Viking god. Rhino was a big man, yes, but no bigger than Owen, and he had a girth around his middle. Still, he was good-looking, with dark-brown hair and whiskers over a strong jaw. Scotty noticed then the hint of a crook in his nose. He wore a rumpled T-shirt and sweatpants, his eyes bloodshot. "I just got up," he said as he took the toddler from Kaleigh.

"Rhino's a nurse at the care center," Kaleigh said. "He works the second shift."

His dark eyes skimmed over Scotty, then moved to Owen. "Owen Christiansen. I thought you were long gone. We were big fans when you played for the Wild; weren't we, hon?"

"Mmm-hmm. I was going to give Rhino a Fathead, but they didn't carry you in stock." Kaleigh still wore the warm smile, and

Scotty shook away the errant urge to step closer to Owen, maybe tuck her arm through his.

And hello, wouldn't that give him the wrong idea? Rules—she had them for a reason.

Rhino stuck out his hand. "Good to see you again. I always thought you'd turn out to be a big star."

Owen hesitated a moment, then took Rhino's hand. "Uh, thanks."

"That game right before you got hurt was a tough one. You had two fights, spent more time in the penalty—ow!"

He glanced at his wife, rubbed his ribs. "Sorry about your eye. You wanna come in?"

Scotty hooked her hand around Owen's elbow. "Yeah."

Owen seemed way too dazed to contribute to the conversation about Monte, the way he sat at the table, watching Rhino as Kaleigh made coffee and served fresh bran muffins.

"So Monte was a terrible neighbor," Scotty said, trying to keep everyone on track.

"He always had something of a temper, ever since high school when he took a bat to my truck for parking in front of him. He was a real peach to live next door to." Rhino regaled her with stories of an unkempt lawn, loud music, cars parked in their shared grass, and BBs shot at their dog. "Then one day he just dropped. Poisoned."

"Such a beautiful dog. Only a couple years old." Kaleigh handed her pictures from off the fridge. "We got her from a golden retriever breeder in Duluth. We would have gotten another one, but we had Dakota on the way."

"Sorry about your dog," Scotty said.

"You know, I think that was the same breeder you got your dog from, Owen. Remember that dog, Rhino? Mrs. Christiansen used to bring her to the hockey games—what is her name?"

"Butterscotch," Owen said quietly. "But she died recently."

"Aw, I'm so sorry." Kaleigh made a face.

Scotty glanced at him, feeling a tug of pain at how much he'd missed. Saying good-bye to the family pet, the addition of two nieces, Grace's wedding to Max. She pressed his hand under the table, but he didn't take hers, and after a moment, she drew it away.

Now who was being impulsive?

"Do you know anyone else who might have history with Monte?"

"Are you kidding me?" Rhino was bouncing his toddler on his lap. "Monte was the biggest cheat, liar, and bully in Deep Haven. Who didn't have history with him?"

"But maybe talk to Jackson Ripley," Kaleigh cut in. "He and Monte got into a fight—last winter, wasn't it, hon?"

"That's right. The annual Christmas bazaar. Monte had set up an antique booth, and Jackson said that some of the furniture he was selling belonged to his parents' estate. Said Monte cheated him."

Kaleigh turned to Owen. "You remember Jackson Ripley."

"No."

"Yeah, you do. He's married to Hannah Bockovich?"

Owen glanced at Scotty fast, then back. "Yeah. I know Hannah."

"Hey, wasn't she in that play—*Grease*? You were in that, right?" This from Rhino.

Scotty nodded for him. "He played Danny."

Rhino got up, handed Dakota to his wife. "That's right. And Hannah played Sandy."

"Oh yeah, I remember now," Kaleigh said slowly, smiling.

"That was a long time ago." Owen had risen. "Thanks, guys, for the info about Monte."

He was quiet as they climbed into the resort truck.

"So Hannah's an old girlfriend." She folded her arms. "One of Owen Christiansen's past flames."

"She was my first kiss."

There it was again, the low rumble of an unwanted beast inside. "Oh. Is there anyone in town you don't have some connection with? Nemesis, cheerleader, girlfriend?"

"It's a small town."

"And you were Owen Christiansen, local hero."

He lifted his shoulder in a shrug as he drove them to Main Street. "What are we doing?"

"The VFW is open. I thought we'd talk to Signe like you suggested. See if she can enlighten us about Casper's necklace."

Scotty had spent last evening telling the family, word by word, about the interview between Kyle and Casper, just so everyone had the facts, could refute them if possible. Only Darek had remembered the necklace, and just barely.

"In my gut, I have to believe she knows something," Scotty said.

Owen parked the car in the municipal parking lot across from the coffee shop. Scotty got out, stood for a moment. She'd only seen downtown Deep Haven as a quick drive-by—and truthfully, if she closed her eyes longer than a blink, she'd miss it. Two blocks of shops and cafés bordering the rocky harbor. Picturesque, a strange mix of New England and woodsy Montana—at least how she imagined those places.

The kind of town that belonged in storybooks with happily-ever-after endings.

The wind tossed the lake onto the beach, leaving a foamy

residue before it fell back to heave again. She smelled woodsmoke in the air, and gulls cheered from high above.

"The VFW has the best burgers in town, at least from what I remember," Owen said as Scotty followed him down the block and inside.

Images of soldiers and local football legends hung in picture frames on the brown paneled walls, a large pool table sat unused near the front stage, and an array of tables and pinball machines surrounded a long bar, where a handful of patrons dove into trays of crispy fries and double-stacked burgers.

Scotty half expected Red to be bellied up to the bar next to the assumed regulars in jeans, old sweatshirts, and work boots.

Owen pulled out a high-top chair dressed in faux black leather for Scotty, then climbed into the one next to it.

"As I live and breathe, it's Mr. Hockey, Owen Christiansen." A shapely blonde just a few years older than Owen, wearing a T-shirt and skinny jeans, came over with a smile. She eyed Owen with a look that made Scotty put her hand on the back of his chair.

Silly her. Still, if he noticed, he didn't let on.

"I can't believe it. You look good. Very high seas. I love the eye patch."

"Hey, Signe. Can you round up a couple cheeseburger trays with house fries?"

"For you? Of course." She left them with a wink.

"Is there anyone in town not in love with you?" Scotty asked. She meant it as a joke, but he didn't smile.

"Everyone here remembers me as this jock who hit it big in the NHL. They don't know the rest of the story."

And *she* did. Or some of it. But she wanted to know this story. *This* Owen.

He said nothing as Signe returned with waters, set them on napkins. "Would you like something a bit more grown-up? I don't even have to card you anymore."

"Nope," Owen said. "But maybe you can help me figure something out. My brother Casper gave you a necklace earlier this year. Do you remember it?"

Signe glanced at Scotty, then lifted her shoulder. "It wasn't anything. Just a copper penny on a piece of leather. He was acting weird about it—just gave it to me like he didn't care about it."

"You two weren't . . . I mean, was there any special reason . . . ?"

"Oh, honey, believe me, Casper has never had his eye on anyone but Raina Beaumont from the moment she joined his dragon boat crew last year."

Another story that Owen didn't know by the look on his face. "Right. So what happened to the necklace?"

"Nothing. I mean, I lost it." She leaned near Owen, giving him a little more to remember her by, and cut her voice low. "Don't tell him, okay? I had it, and then one night I realized I'd lost it." She leaned back. "I was showing it around the bar right about the time Casper made the papers for his big treasure find. And then, a couple days later, I went to put it on, and it was missing."

"Do you remember if Monte Riggs was around when you were talking about it?" Scotty asked.

At Scotty's words, Signe seemed to cool. "No."

"Are you sure? Maybe Monte took it from you?" This from Owen.

She glanced at Owen, frowned. "No, of course not. I barely know Monte. Why would he want my necklace?"

"It's just that the necklace might have some connection to, uh, what happened to him," Owen said, shooting a look at Scotty.

It did seem that Signe wasn't apprised on Monte's current status. "What are you talking about?"

"His death?" Scotty said, gauging a response.

She got one. Signe blinked, her expression slacking for a second. "He's . . . dead?"

Owen nodded.

Signe drew in a long breath, her mouth tightening. "That's too bad. But I can't say that I'm surprised. If he's dead, it's probably his own stupid fault."

Scotty stared at her, stupefied.

"I don't mean to be harsh, but Monte didn't exactly make friends in this town. He thought he was irresistible, but the guy never knew how to treat a woman right. If it wasn't a jilted woman, it was her boyfriend, mad that Monte had seduced his girl." She shot a look at Owen, raised a shoulder. "Probably beat him up and left him for dead in the woods, right?"

Owen had stilled.

Then Signe's eyes widened. "Oh. My. You don't think that Casper—"

"No," Owen snapped. "Never. We're just trying to track down the necklace."

"But I remember seeing Raina and Monte—"

"Can you call us if you remember anything about the necklace?" Scotty interjected before Owen completely unraveled.

Signe shot her a look, then touched Owen's arm. "It's good to see you again. And if you have any more questions, you can call my cell." She reached for a napkin, pulled out her pen, jotted her number down.

Scotty wanted to raise her hand and remind the woman that she was sitting right here.

Except Owen hadn't exactly introduced her, had he? In fact, despite her hand on his chair, he'd barely looked at her. Now he managed a smile for Signe, folded and pocketed the napkin.

Scotty dropped her possessive grip, realizing how ridiculous she must look. Especially when Signe winked at Owen again. "I'll go check on your food." She wiggled away.

"I'm not hungry," Scotty said and then wanted to retract it. Wow, she sounded like a thirteen-year-old. So much for being professional.

"What? Seriously, these are awesome burgers."

Oh, for—"Fine."

Signe returned with the burgers. "The Blue Monkeys are playing Friday night. Maybe you could stop by?"

Scotty waited for an *I'll be off at eight*, but Signe just smiled. "We really missed you around here."

Owen gave a wan smile. "We'll see."

And now Scotty just wanted to go home. *We'll see*? What about finding Monte's killer? Owen wanted to hang out in a bar and listen to music?

"Try your burger—they're awesome." He had cut his in half, was sopping his fries through the ketchup.

She stared at her uneaten meal. "Yeah. Sure." She took a bite, but it sat in her gut. She pushed the plate away, grabbed a napkin.

What was wrong with her? Of course Owen had friends—he grew up here. But suddenly it seemed like everyone knew an Owen she'd never met. A funny, Danny Zuko–type Owen, who charmed the ladies and made fans even of his enemies.

"What's the matter, Scotty?" He glanced at her discarded burger.

This was what she called not getting involved? She'd deserved every drip of Casper's sarcasm.

"When you said you were a hockey player, I don't know, I guess I didn't see it. Sure, I could imagine you playing hockey, but I didn't see your life, how much of a hometown hero you were— are, still." She looked up at him. "I don't know this man you were, and . . . I want to. I want to know the guy you won't talk about."

Owen stared at her without emotion as if her words had shut him down or simply stunned him.

Then he grabbed her hand, pulled her off the chair, and threw a twenty on the bar. Turning to Scotty, he said, "You want to see the guy I left behind? Fine. C'mon."

He pulled her out of the VFW, then dropped her hand when they reached the street, taking long strides to the pickup.

"Where are we going?"

"You'll see."

She climbed in beside him and had barely shut the door when he roared off, turning the corner, heading up the hill.

It wasn't until they passed the school and pulled into the community center parking lot that it clicked.

The ice arena.

Scotty scrambled out of the truck after Owen. The doors banged behind them as they entered the dark building, but he seemed to know exactly where the lights were, flicked them on and kept walking.

The lights illuminated a giant indoor rink behind glass, walled off from a carpeted warming/meeting area.

Owen walked down the ramp, opened the door, walked into the rink.

Scotty stood at the glass, watching as he stopped by a bin of skates—extras probably for free-skating times. He unearthed a pair of worn, ragged hockey skates, then sat on a bench, toed off his boots, and worked them on. He had big, confident movements as he laced up his skates, tightening them, wrapping the long laces around the top, knotting them.

When he stood, he seemed . . . bigger. Imposing. As if he'd grown five inches, his shoulders wider. She could imagine him in a uniform, extra padding under his hockey sweater, his curls hanging below his helmet, a chin strap against his trim beard.

A hockey champion.

Owen grabbed a stick from a box and kicked a nearby puck onto the rink.

Then he stepped out on the ice.

Suddenly the man she'd known on the boat vanished, and in his place appeared an athlete, graceful and strong. His body glided over the ice, his legs powerful as he circled, fast, then backward, looking over his shoulder, his strokes so utterly smooth he could steal her breath with the simple yet honed athleticism.

Owen kicked the puck around between his skates, turning like a figure skater, his partner the puck. He maneuvered it between his feet, then with his stick, flicking it around, one way, then the other. Deftly, the puck an extension of his movements.

He lined up on the opposite end of the rink and looked at Scotty. Only, no, not at her. At the net set up on her end of the rink.

His breath gathered in the brisk air of the arena—in, out, puffs of heat from his exertion.

And then he wound up and shot.

Scotty gasped as the puck flew toward her, all the way down the rink, and wanted to put her hand up to protect herself. Instead, she rested it on the glass, watching as the puck landed, bounced, then slid perfectly into the goal.

Before the shot cleared, Owen had already gone over to scoop more pucks onto the ice. He shot them where they landed, from every corner, like bullets across the ice.

Netted.

Netted.

Again, netted, the pucks landing one after another like pigeons behind the goal line.

Then he kicked a puck free and toyed with it up the ice between his feet and stick, graceful, so fast Scotty could barely keep her gaze on the puck.

He circled around the back of the net and dipped the puck in, backhanded.

Again and again he scooped up pucks, shot them into the net with finesse and deadly accuracy.

Scotty watched, seeing him now as they'd seen him, his fans. Their hometown hero. Their bright star. The one most likely to put Deep Haven on the map.

When the last shot landed, Owen drifted away, his stick across his knees. Just gliding. Silent, his breath streaming out behind him.

Then he crumpled to the ice, hung his head. Cupped his hand over his face. Was he . . . crying?

Oh, Owen. Scotty pushed out into the cool rink and stepped onto the ice, slipping her way toward him. His soft breaths echoed in the expanse of the arena, catching in the air. Her heart tore as she dropped to her knees, crawled over to him.

Not caring anymore about the stupid rules, Scotty put her arms around him, touching her head to his shoulder. "I'm sorry, Owen. I'm so sorry."

He shook his head, looked away from her. In a voice she could barely hear, he said, "I was somebody. I was going to be *somebody*."

"You still are."

He looked at her, his eyes reddened, and she sat back on the ice, pressing her hand to his cheek. "You still are."

"No, I'm not, Scotty. I can't even be a dad to my kid. I can't figure out how to get Casper out of jail. And the town is still living in the glory days. I should have never come back here."

"You've only been home for one day!"

"It's long enough to realize I'm not going to break free of this. I'll never be—do—anything. I'm half-blind. I can't play hockey. What am I going to do with my life?"

With a violent grunt, he pulled the eye patch off his face and flung it across the rink. "I'm so sick of wearing that. Trying to pretend it doesn't matter. But I can't escape it. Every time I look in the mirror, I see the fact that I screwed up my entire life."

He looked at her then, his eyes thick with unshed emotion. "You don't want to know the guy I was. That guy was arrogant and idiotic, and I'm not sure I can ever escape him. You were right to walk away from me. Casper's right. I'm only going to hurt you."

Scotty held his face in her hands, refusing to let him look away. "I wish you could see the guy I see. The guy who works harder than everyone else. The guy who wants to do the right thing. Your mom's right—the things you learned back when you were a superstar aren't wasted. That guy is still inside you. I saw him every day on the boat, and I saw him when he went into the water to save me—"

"That was me being stupidly impulsive again."

"You were being unstoppable. The guy I saw who made every shot, the guy who could probably make a hundred more—that guy is still in here. Still a superstar."

He closed his eyes, his jaw tight. "I want to believe you; I do—"

"Then believe me." She made a point of looking at both his

eyes, even touched his scars despite his wince. "Stop listening so hard to your failures. And to the echo of a future that will never be. Live right now, be the guy I know and—"

Love. She nearly said it, and in the silence, she thought she might hear it bounce off the walls.

No, not love. It had simply been an impulse, a passionate word on her lips. She cared for him, sure, but love was . . . messy. *This* could be messy. She swallowed, revised. "The guy I know. Which, by the way, is better than any Danny Zuko."

He stared at her so long she thought her heart stopped, lodged in her chest, waiting to beat again.

It did when a slow smile slid up his face. "I don't know . . . you never really heard me sing."

Sing? Talk about wooing her heart away from her body. "Maybe we should save that for another day. We have work to do."

But Owen didn't move. His gaze roamed over her, and a spark of mischief appeared in his eyes. "'Saaandy, can't you see I'm in misery?'" He started at almost a whisper, building into a tenor that echoed off the ice.

No, oh no. He had a nice voice, rich and sultry, and in the cavernous room it resounded like they were in an opera house, landing sweetly on the tender flesh of her heart.

Scotty found her voice, turned it hard. "Oh, for pete's sake. Get up." She grabbed him by the shoulder, intending to pull him up, but the ice betrayed her. She slipped, cried out, and tumbled back.

"Gotcha."

Indeed. He'd reached out, caught her, and she landed in his arms, solid, strong around her. He settled her on his lap, and she found her arms around his shoulders. His amazing, work-sculpted shoulders.

"You okay?" he said softly, pushing her hair from her face.

"Are *you* okay? Did I hurt you?"

He grinned. "'We made a start; now we're apart. There's nothin' left for me—'" Again with the singing, softly this time, sneaking in to unseat her.

Perfect. And when he added a waggle of his eyebrows, she nearly lost it. She pushed on his shoulders. "We're not apart. I'm right here."

He grabbed her hands, raised his voice. "'I sit and wonder why-y-y—'"

Scotty rolled her eyes, too aware of his hands holding hers. She pulled out of his grip. "Fine. You're a brilliant Danny Zuko. Can we go?"

Owen's smile dimmed, a serious edge appearing in his eyes that had the cool air heating around her, burning through her to her core.

His gaze fell to her lips.

Yes. She caught her lip between her teeth, keenly aware of him—his hand on her back, the other touching her arm. Her hand on his muscled, too-perfect chest. The smell of the exertion he'd shown on the ice mixing with the scent of the north shore— woodsmoke, autumn, the cotton of his flannel shirt.

Kiss me. She wanted to say it, just in case he thought she was hanging on to her rules, but the words only rang in her chest along with the thunder of her pulse.

Kiss me.

Abruptly Owen drew in a long, almost-frustrated breath, and in one sleek move he pushed Scotty to her feet.

She was still catching her balance when he popped up to his skates beside her. He put his arm around her waist before she could fall. "I got you."

Oh. Okay. She held on to his arm as he anchored her to himself, the hard plane of his body, his strong legs.

And she hoped too much that he was just getting a better angle to kiss her.

Instead, he helped her to the edge of the rink, then skated back to retrieve his eye patch before returning to the carpeted area and sinking down to untie his skates.

That was it?

Owen stood, dropping his skates in the bin. "C'mon. Casper needs us."

Right. Of course he did.

"It smells good in here, Mrs. Christiansen. What are you making?" Scotty said as she hung up her jacket.

Owen came in behind her. "It's banana bread. Oh, how I've missed that smell."

"It's Casper's favorite." Ingrid pulled the bread from the oven and set it on the cooling rack. "I'm going to wrap it up for him and bring it over to the jail later."

"The whole thing?" Owen leaned on the counter, inhaling the smell. "Mom, please. Just one piece. Casper can't eat the entire thing. Besides, Grace brought him cookies this morning—"

"How would you feel if you were sitting in jail, unjustly accused?" she said. "If we lived in a town with its own judicial service, he would have been out yesterday. It's not fair we have to wait for the circuit judge to arraign him before we can bail him out. And I can't believe I'm even saying that."

She picked up a towel. Sighed. "This whole thing stinks."

Now he felt like a bum. Owen slipped his arm around his

mother's shoulders. It seemed she'd gotten smaller since he'd left. "I know, Mom. You're right. Casper will love it—all of it. And he'll be home tomorrow."

"You can't really be hungry," Scotty said, sliding onto a kitchen stool. "The girls at the coffee shop gave him a free cookie with our lattes. It seems half the town had a crush on Owen. They greeted him like a war hero."

"Not exactly," Owen said, but he couldn't help but be surprised at the welcome he'd received. And not just from the handful of girls he could barely remember, but locals at Pierre's Pizza and a number of patrons at the Java Cup, where he'd bought Scotty a pumpkin latte.

"Exactly. Signe Netterlund practically threw herself into his lap when we questioned her."

"What—? No, she didn't." He shot Scotty a look.

She rolled her eyes. "Owen seems to be the town catch."

He stared at her, incredulous. Had she completely deleted the debacle on the ice rink from her memory?

He wasn't sure why they'd gone from sitting at the counter at the VFW, about to devour mouthwatering burgers, to her claiming she didn't know him. She did know him—she just didn't know how despicably far he'd fallen to get there.

You want to see the guy I left behind?

His impulses had simply taken over. He operated on a sort of furious autopilot as he drove to the ice rink, intending to show her the guy who'd had it all and lost it.

Then he'd hit the ice and everything clicked into place. He'd probably pushed himself too hard because his incision burned after so many shots on goal. But the cool breath of the rink slicking down his shirt, the delicious ache in his legs as he flew over the ice, the power in his shots . . . In those moments, he could hear the roar of the crowd and feel the sweet adrenaline that sluiced through him before a game.

As he skated, missing it had reached in and turned him inside out.

He hadn't expected the enormity of his loss to buckle him onto the ice, but the pain had crashed over him. The taste of getting what he'd worked so hard for had turned to ash in his mouth.

Shoot, he'd even cried. Like a child.

He hadn't heard Scotty approach until suddenly there she was, her arms around him, saving him again. Always saving him, not seeing the wreck before her, but believing in some guy he barely knew.

Stop listening so hard to your failures. And to the echo of a future that will never be. Live right now, be the guy I know and . . .

He'd let the curiosity of what hung on the end of that sentence niggle at him all day.

Care for? Saved?

Love?

He shook that last word away. But it could still undo him, along with the memory of her in his arms, fitting so perfectly, her long hair down and caressing his hands, her beautiful lips parting just a little like she hoped . . .

He'd nearly chucked the rules, pulled her to himself, and dived in, slaying the image of the guy in the middle of a hockey rink, his life in debris around him.

Except that's who he'd become, and no amount of belief or pep talking or even pretending she loved him could help him figure out how to put it back together.

Which had made him put her away from him and remind

himself that he had one shot at this second chance—rescuing Casper—and he couldn't blow it by breaking the rules.

"How was your sleuthing?" Ingrid asked, pulling out a Tupperware container.

"According to my notes, there were three restraining orders against Monte, including Raina's. Five people who say he stole estate money from them; Rhino and Kaleigh, who have a personal complaint; and a slew of people who say Monte Riggs should have been run out of town long before he disappeared." Scotty set the notebook she'd purchased to keep track of the names on the counter.

Ingrid moved over to peer at Scotty's list. "Do you think any of these people might have killed Monte?"

"Oh, I don't know. You have to have means and opportunity as well as motive. It will take a lot more digging."

From the office, the door opened and Owen's nephew, Tiger, barreled in. "Dad says he needs a cookie or he'll die right now!"

He stopped when he spotted Owen, his eyes wide. "Oh."

Owen squatted in front of him. Wow, kids grew fast. The Tiger he remembered had teeth missing, the chubby face of a kindergartner. This Tiger was taller, his big teeth coming in, his hair shorter. "I'm your uncle Owen. Remember me?"

Tiger nodded. "Dad has a picture of you on our refrigerator." Huh, really?

"Dad said you played hockey. I play hockey. I'm in the peewees."

"Dude, that's great."

Ingrid came over, holding a baggie of cookies. "Tell your dad that I'm onto his tricks. And yours, big guy."

"Thanks, Nana!" Tiger scooted back out and Owen watched him go.

"Darek's working on his house," Ingrid said. "I think he's painting with your father. Poor man, it's taking about four times as long as he'd hoped to finish it. Resort projects come first."

Owen glanced at Scotty. "You okay?"

She was searching through her notes, her finger caught in her cute mouth. She looked up. "What?"

"I'm going outside."

She had returned to the list before he closed the door behind him.

He hadn't walked through the resort since returning home. The recently planted evergreens towered between the resort, with its seeded grass and newly rebuilt cabins, and the wasteland of baby scrub brush to the north, scars from the wildland fire that had nearly decimated their livelihood.

Darek and Casper had managed to rebuild. They'd winterized the cedar-sided cabins, updated from their previous counterparts with Internet and cable television. Darek had planted chrysanthemums along the walkways to each cabin, blooming yellow, crimson, and ocher.

Beyond the cabins, the lake lapped at the shore. The fire had cleared the view, and Darek had built up the shoreline with boulders and woodchips. Adirondack chairs perched at the edge of the water, inviting guests to linger.

If possible, Evergreen Resort, like the pinecones and seedlings that survived the fire, had blossomed in the aftermath.

Owen wound his way through the resort and found himself at Darek's A-frame cabin. Freshly roofed with green tiles and covered in dark-red cedar siding, with a deck framing two sides and a hand-carved plaque on the door that said *Darek and Ivy*, probably to direct guests away from private quarters.

Tiger sat on the deck, his hand in the plastic bag, rooting for a cookie.

"I thought those were for your dad."

"They are. Dad said I could have one."

Owen tousled Tiger's hair as he headed inside and called, "Hello? Need some help?"

Darek perched on a ladder, screwing a bulb into the recessed lights of the arching, pine-paneled ceiling.

"Wow," Owen said as he stood taking in Darek's hard work. The front room ceiling soared two stories over an open floor plan that included a granite-countered kitchen with stainless steel appliances, a knotty pine hardwood floor, and a hand-built stone fireplace. A stairway led to a loft that overlooked the room, bordered by a railing with hand-hewn balusters.

It looked like a bathroom and two smaller bedrooms were tucked under the lofted area, and from one of these, his father emerged, holding a paint roller. "Great. We could use another hand. Take your coat off and grab a roller."

Owen followed the cardboard taped to the floor to a back room, where his father stood at one wall, covering it in pale blue. Plastic and cardboard protected the floor, blue painter's tape over the light sockets and window frames.

"I think this second coat will do it. We're nearly done."

Owen rolled up his sleeves, winced as he bent over to soak a roller in paint. But he hid it from his father—his own fault for showing off today in front of Scotty. "Tiger's room, I assume?"

"We're trying to get them in by Halloween. Darek's getting antsy in his rental. Had hoped to be in the house a month ago."

"I can't believe all the hard work he's done on the resort. It looks brand-new."

"It *is* brand-new. And upgraded. He talked me into the Internet in every cabin, although I'm not so sure—"

"Trust the next generation, Dad."

"I just don't want our guests to miss out on the purpose of Evergreen—to get away. To find a moment of peace outside the bustle of the city. People need silence to hear their own thoughts, even God's voice. That was my dad's thinking, at least. He said that sometimes people needed to even escape church. There was a quote he loved: 'God writes the gospel not in the Bible alone, but also on trees and in the flowers and clouds and stars.'"

Owen refilled his roller. "Sometimes we worked through the night on the boat, and I'd be awake when the sun came up. I'd watch the sunrise splashing over the water, turning the spray to crystals. It was like God was there, reminding me that He . . . well, maybe that He hadn't forgotten me."

His dad's voice was low, gentle. "He didn't, Owen. You were never lost to Him."

"I don't know, Dad. I . . . wasn't . . ." He couldn't finish because really, how did he tell his father how abysmally far he'd fallen from his own—or anyone's—expectations?

John rolled the blue paint on the wall. "'I can never escape from your Spirit! I can never get away from your presence! If I go up to heaven, you are there; if I go down to the grave, you are there. If I ride the wings of the morning, if I dwell by the farthest oceans, even there your hand will guide me, and your strength will support me.'" He dipped his roller in for a refill. "Psalm 139. No matter how far you run, you can't hide from God."

No. He got that finally. It was what to do with the grace he'd been given that had him stymied. Shaken.

"Dad, when I was out there on the raft, I . . . I wasn't afraid.

Not really. I mean, I didn't want to die, and I wanted to come home, but I wasn't afraid. I even told Scotty to have faith—me, the guy who can't seem to figure out how to do anything right. The guy who . . ." He stopped painting but couldn't look at his dad. "The guy who's been scared pretty much since I signed that Blue Ox deal."

Behind him, his dad painted in silence.

Which made it easier to just . . . talk. "Ever since I signed that contract with the Blue Ox, I've been afraid of screwing up. People were looking at me as if I could be the next Wayne Gretzky, and it freaked me out. I started listening to them and everything went south. But I'm still . . . Well, I have no idea what I'm supposed to do now. Other than trying to figure out how to clear Casper, I'm completely lost." And frankly, scared out of his head that he would somehow let Casper down, but he wasn't going to say that to his dad.

Especially with Darek in the next room. Darek, who had his life together, had managed to scrape new life from the Evergreen ashes and reseed the family legacy.

Even Casper had managed to land on his feet, despite his current circumstances—Owen still couldn't get the word *millionaire* through his head.

Apparently only one son had crashed and burned. Ironically, the one with the most potential.

He felt sick.

Finally John broke the silence. "God is not surprised by what happened to you, Owen. He didn't look down from heaven and think, *Uh-oh, now what?* There are no chance happenings with God. God does not stumble around, wondering what He's doing. He has everything under control, and you are always safe with

Him. Even when you're in the middle of the ocean . . . or coming home to face the child you didn't know you had."

Yeah. Just another of his colossal bumbles. "You have to know how much I . . . I wish I'd played that differently. I'd do anything not to have . . ." He shook the image from his head, hating that it would always reside there, that night with a woman who didn't belong to him. "I think I'm going to let Casper raise her."

His father stayed silent beside him.

"Casper and Raina are right—it would just be confusing for her to have me in the picture. And Casper loves her like a father." He hadn't expected his eyes to burn with the confession, but even as he said it, the words landed, settled, soaked through him. "It's the right thing to do."

Again, silence.

Owen looked at his father, who had turned, met his gaze, his own dark, unsettled. "You should know that I haven't exactly known what to say in this, Owen. She is your daughter. But Casper loves Raina. Still, I just need to ask . . . are you sure you don't want to marry Raina, try to make it work?"

"Dad. Seriously. Raina doesn't love me. And . . ."

"And you're in love with Scotty."

Owen stilled.

His father raised an eyebrow.

"No, I mean . . . yeah, but . . ."

"What do you mean, Son?"

"She's not making it easy."

"Didn't you propose?"

That again. Owen turned back to his wall. "Sort of. But . . . it was stupid. Impulsive. Which I guess is my worst flaw because now she's set up rules."

"Rules?"

"Like I'm not allowed to . . . well, propose."

He heard a chuckle from his father.

"Or kiss her. Or touch her in any way. She says we have to keep it professional because she's planning on leaving as soon as we can clear Casper."

"Smart girl, if she thinks you don't have a future."

Aggravating girl. "Except I could have sworn today that she . . ."

"She what?"

"I don't know. She seems to think she's not the marrying type. Her mom died when she was born. And she calls her father *Red*. They had a pretty rough life—lived in a cabin in the woods, except when he was fishing. On the boat she acts like one of the guys, so maybe she's right—I don't exactly see her in the kitchen baking cookies."

"Fresh-baked cookies do not make a successful marriage, Owen. It's knowing each other, valuing the same things, being what the other person can't be, making each other better people."

"She does make me want to be a better person; I know that. And it's not like I'm Billy Graham or anything, but when we were on the raft, I told her to have a little faith, and she did. She prayed for us. Which is a miracle. She's spent so much time alone, she has a hard time believing that God cares about her."

"You can't know how God is going to work in someone, Owen. But maybe you need to slow down, wait and see what He does."

Shoot, that's not what he wanted to hear.

"Scotty isn't the reason why I can't marry Raina. I'm sure I could love her eventually, and of course I want to be a father. But I know the truth, Dad. *Casper* is Layla's father. He loves her, and I don't even know her. Raina's right; I just showed up for . . . that part. But Casper's been there for the rest, and isn't that what being a dad is all about? Besides, there's no guarantee I wouldn't screw up the father thing too."

"That's about enough of that."

Owen frowned, turned.

His father had put down the roller and was wiping his hands. He looked up with solemn eyes. "So you made some bad choices. Some of God's best players were His imperfect, broken prodigals. In fact, iffy players are God's best picks. He specializes in short-tempered, reckless, flawed people to accomplish His plans. Consider Moses, the murderer; Rahab, the prostitute; Samson, the playboy; Paul, the terrorist; and Peter . . . the impulsive. God is constantly using broken, messy people to restore the world and bring glory to Himself. To touch other people, like you did with Scotty in the raft. And I'd bet they each thought God couldn't use them before His grace tracked them down, brought them back to His purposes. You can never outsin God's love, Owen. Or limit what He can do with you if you let Him. You're dripping paint onto the plastic."

Owen's chest tightened and he turned back to the wall, finished the final section. Swallowing hard.

His father's hand landed on his shoulder. Warm. Solid. "Son. You haven't outrun God's love. Or our love. I'm glad you're home."

That turned him. They just stood there a moment, Owen even more shaken by the tears in his father's eyes.

On impulse, like an old reflex, Owen leaned in and touched his forehead to his father's shoulder. "Me too, Dad. Me too."

In that moment, he wanted to be sixteen again and rewrite his life, starting with the day he left. The day he thought he didn't need home anymore.

"Hey, what's this slacking? I thought you were supposed to be painting." Darek stood in the doorway, grinning.

"We're done," John said, stepping away. Owen blinked away the glaze in his eyes and gave the wall a final swipe.

John left to clean his roller, and Owen moved to follow, but Darek stopped him at the door. "What he said about outsinning God's love and limiting Him . . . You asked how I got here? I dropped to my knees and begged God for a fresh start. Apparently He's into that sort of thing."

Owen said nothing as he pushed past Darek.

But he wanted the words to be true. All of them—Scotty's and his mother's, Darek's and his dad's.

Maybe he could step beyond the name of prodigal into something else.

Outside, he grabbed the hose, used it to clean his roller, then carried the trays and rollers to the garage, washed his hands, and headed inside the lodge.

John had already entered, his work coat hanging on a peg. And next to that, two more—the royal-blue team coats of the St. Paul Blue Ox.

Owen braced himself as he realized his brothers-in-law had arrived. Former enforcer Jace Jacobsen sat on the sofa, arm stretched across the back, watching as right wing Max Sharpe sat with his adoptive daughter, who unpacked her backpack, showing him her daily work.

The two men looked up as Owen came in the room. Jace leaned forward, started to get up. Max stiffened.

And in a second, Owen tasted the brisk air, heard the shouts of drunk men brawling, felt the dark adrenaline course through him as he threw a punch, connected.

Then the blinding, skull-cracking shot to his eye. Pain shattering him, buckling his knees.

On the other end of that hockey stick that destroyed his eye, his career, had been Max.

It all showed in Max's expression, too, even as he got up, held out his hand. "Owen. Hey. So glad to see you." Wary. Worried.

Jace had risen behind him, huge, and Owen didn't exactly know whose side he might be on.

But he didn't want sides. Not anymore. Owen stepped forward, met Max's hand. "Hey, Max. I heard congratulations are in order—on two accounts."

Max dropped a hand on his daughter's shoulder. "Thanks. I'm blessed; there's no doubt."

"How's the season going?" Owen said, trying to keep it light. No need to make everyone dodge the elephant in the room.

"We just played the Blades back-to-back," Jace said, holding out his hand. "We won both."

Owen shook his hand. "I saw one of those games. Max was in the penalty box, and they scored on a backdoor pass."

"We have a rookie who could use your go-to."

Nice of Jace to say that.

"Owen!" Eden came down the stairs.

Whoa, Eden looked about six months pregnant. "Wow, when—?"

"I'm due in February, but this *is* Jace's child. He'll probably be fifteen pounds." She reached the landing and pulled him into a hug, arms around his neck. "I missed you."

Out of all his siblings, Eden best knew the guy he'd been and could have been. She'd been his guardian through those stressful years in the juniors, even pulled him out of a couple bar fights when the money, the fame, went to his stupid head. And for that, he'd shown her annoyance, even rudeness.

He held her away from him, cataloging the changes. Her blonde hair was longer, her face fuller, and she looked . . . happy. "You still writing for the paper?"

"Chief editor of obituaries. And I have a book coming out this spring, reflections from working in the obits."

"Wow, you'll be a published author. I always knew you had a book in you."

She held his face in her hands. "I hear you have a few stories yourself. Like a high-seas rescue?"

"How—?"

"Scotty." She pointed beyond him to the kitchen, and he turned.

Words slicked right out of him at the sight of Scotty in . . . an apron? Holding a wooden spoon and grinning at him.

"What are you doing?"

Her smile fell.

"Owen!" This from Grace, who put a batch of cookies on the counter. "She's making cookies; what does it look like?"

"Yeah," Scotty said. "I'm making cookies." But her grin was wobbly, and shoot, he had the weirdest sense that he'd hurt her.

But . . . making . . . cookies? He scrambled to find the right response. "No complaints here. I do get the spoon, right?"

She handed it over, chagrin on her face. "I don't know what I'm doing anyway." Then she wiped her hands on the apron and reached for a hot cookie.

Driving him crazy, that's what she was doing.

CHAPTER 10

"Spill the beans, Scotty. Do you or do you not have the hots for my brother?" Eden sat cross-legged on a twin bed in the alcove of her old room, dressed in pajama pants and one of Jace's oversize T-shirts. "Has he kissed you yet?"

"Eden, leave her alone. That's none of our business." Grace had just created a bed for her daughter, Yulia, on the floor. Scotty had tried to protest kicking Yulia out of the third bed, but Grace wouldn't hear it.

"What's perfectly unjust is the fact that Jace and Max have to sleep in the boys' room when there's a pullout in the den. I haven't seen Max in nearly two weeks," Grace said as she pulled the quilt over Yulia. "If only we weren't full, I'd talk Darek into renting us a cabin."

"Jace isn't thrilled either, Grace. They just got back from three days on the road. But Mom seems to think that this is more fair—and with the entire family here, she's probably right that there will be some late-night game viewing in the den on the agenda."

Grace rolled her eyes. "I can't wait until we close on the house. I'm sure you'll be glad to get Max off the sofa in your living room."

"I *am* a little tired of going to bed alone, listening to them yell at the screen."

And as if on cue, a whoop ascended from the den downstairs, where the guys clustered around a Minnesota Wild game.

"Owen seems to be okay with having Max here," Eden said to Grace, then glanced at Scotty. "Max was the one who caused Owen's injury."

"It wasn't on purpose!" Grace said, shooting Eden a dark look before coming to sit next to Scotty on the bed. "They were in a fight and—"

"Owen told me," Scotty said. "And he's made peace with it." Well, after today on the ice, maybe she couldn't be sure of that, but none of his breakdown had included blaming Max. "He's just trying to figure out what the rest of his life looks like."

"Did he really dive into the ocean to save you?" Eden asked.

"Yep. And then, in the raft, he kept me alive by trying to get me to hope. Which is why he proposed. Your brother is a little—"

"Crazy?" Eden said.

"Passionate?" Grace suggested.

"Charming," Scotty said, feeling her face redden. "And no, he didn't kiss me on the raft."

"Oh, my inner investigative reporter is kicking in," Eden said. "You *did* kiss him. Just not on the raft."

More laughter from below, and Scotty thought she heard Owen

hooting as the Wild scored or perhaps simply stole the puck and made one of those breathtaking shots she'd seen from him.

Which only conjured up this afternoon and being caught in his arms. And wishing . . .

"Oh, you've got it bad," Grace said.

"Why not? Owen is a charmer," Eden said. "There's a reason *Hockey Today* named him one of the most eligible rookies."

"Wasn't Jace also listed as one of the most eligible bachelors?"

"Not anymore," Eden said. "But Owen—he has this way of getting under your skin. You can't stay angry at him, at least not usually. I can admit we had a pretty good run there over the past year. But now that he's back, I'm just so glad he's okay." Her eyes warmed. "Grace tells me we have you to thank for that. You gave him CPR? Kept him alive?"

Scotty nodded, dismissing the memory of her panic, the way she'd so completely crumbled and started begging heaven for help.

Apparently that's what Owen did—made her break her own rules.

"So that's when he proposed?" Grace said. "As he was dying?"

"I don't think we should take that too seriously. We both agreed that it was impulsive. I am not the marrying kind of girl." There, she said it, and maybe it would shut down the way these two were grinning at her.

"I didn't think Jace was the marrying kind, but he is an amazing husband."

"And Max said he never wanted to be a father, but he is putty around Yulia."

"Love changes things, Scotty," Eden said. "It's changed Owen. I see the way he looks at you. Like when he came in tonight and you were making cookies."

"He looked like he'd just walked onto the ice in his underwear in front of a hundred thousand fans. Totally flummoxed," Grace said.

Scotty had to grin at that. Yeah, the poor man had stared at her as if he didn't recognize her. For a while there, she hadn't recognized herself. Cooking with Grace, with Ingrid, who simply handed her hot pads and a spatula like she knew exactly what to do in a kitchen.

"I've never made cookies in my life."

"Really? You and your mother didn't do holiday baking together?" Grace picked up a bottle of nail polish, shaking it. She put her foot on the bed.

"My mother died. In childbirth."

Silence. See, that was why she didn't go around making that announcement. "But it's no big deal. My dad raised me. Red was . . . Well, I have to give him credit for trying. He didn't exactly know what to do with a girl."

She watched as Grace applied the polish, one red toe at a time. "Red is a fishing boat captain. Salty. Briny. He isn't much for emotions and girlie things. And we had to survive. So he taught me how to clean and fry fish, how to make a fire, how to tend wounds, and how to stay alive in the wilderness. When he would go out fishing, he'd leave me with his best friend, my uncle Gil, and his wife. They had two sons who thought it might be fun to teach me how to hunt and throw a punch, and mostly I grew up as a boy. If it weren't for my aunt Rosemary, I would have completely freaked out when I became a teenager and started looking like—and becoming—a woman. Even then, I thought like a guy. I started fishing with Red when I was nine, hanging out in the wheelhouse. I joined the crew, started working the deck when I was thirteen, although not the long shifts. By the time I was eighteen, I could captain a boat, throw line, reel in pots, sort crab—he made me his first mate."

Grace had finished one foot and moved on to the other. "You really know how to sail one of those big boats?"

"Mmm-hmm."

"But I thought Owen said you were a cop." This from Eden.

"That was because of Red too. He had a heart attack a few years ago and I had to take the boat back to port during a winter gale. It knocked him out good, and he missed two seasons. I wanted to get a job on another boat, but he sort of reminded me that the captain being my father protected me from . . . Let's just say that it's not a great idea to be the only girl on a boat full of young, hardworking men."

"I'll bet," Eden said.

"Uncle Gil is the Homer police chief, so Red talked him into hiring me. I attended officer training and started working for the Homer Police Department. Made detective last winter. By that time, the boat was in hock for his medical bills and Red was trying to regroup. He went out for the opie season—and that's when he hired Owen on. I took a sabbatical from the force this fall to help him put in a final catch but . . ." She found herself looking out the window as the night fell through the trees. "Red is selling the boat. He was already thinking of selling, and although he won't say it, I think it completely freaked him out when Owen and I went overboard." She shook her head. "I keep telling him I can take over—that I *should* take over, but he won't listen. I don't have the money, really, to buy the boat, but he won't even consider it."

"Almost losing someone you love can undo you," Eden said quietly.

"Which also accounts for why Owen went after you." Grace closed the nail polish, waved her hands over her toes.

"I don't think . . . I mean, Owen doesn't . . ."

"Love you? Huh."

"Here's a tip about guys, Scotty," Eden said, reaching for the bottle. "You gotta read between the words to the action. Diving into an icy sea? Yeah, that's true love." She unscrewed the top and began touching up her already-lacquered toenails.

"If that were true, he would have kissed me today when he had the chance."

In the silence that followed, Scotty glanced at Grace, who had stopped waving her hands. "He had a chance to kiss you and didn't?"

"Well, it wasn't . . . He was . . ." She stopped there, not wanting to betray Owen and the way life had suddenly seemed to man-handle him. "We have these rules."

"Rules?" Eden switched feet. "What kind of rules?"

"No kissing. Or holding my hand or impulsive overtures designed to make me fall for him."

"And Owen is *abiding* by those rules?"

"I guess so." She didn't mean for it to sound . . . appalling. "Which is good. The last thing I need is to get confused about why I'm here."

"Which is—"

"To clear your brother."

Eden handed the bottle back to Grace. "Listen. Casper is going to be fine. Max and Jace brought up a lawyer, and he's got this handled. According to Bryce, the evidence is circumstantial."

"I heard the evidence. Yeah, it's circumstantial, but with Casper's history with Monte Riggs . . ."

"Like Owen said to Mom. Have a little faith," Grace said. She handed the bottle to Scotty. "Your turn."

"Huh?"

"Get some polish on those naked toes." Grace pointed to Scotty's feet.

Scotty just held the bottle. "Um . . ."

"What?"

"I've never . . . I don't wear nail polish. Or makeup or . . ."

Grace's hand touched her shoulder. "Give me your toes."

Scotty frowned but put a foot up on the bed. Grace rolled up the cuffs of Scotty's jeans, glancing at Eden. "Get my makeup bag."

"What are you doing?"

"I get your rules, really. I mean, Owen has had some issues with self-control, but I think . . . well, I think you need to break your rules," Grace said, opening the bottle. She looked up, wrinkled her nose. "Sorry. But you do. You like my brother. He likes you. And enough of you thinking you're a boy. You're a woman, a gorgeous one, and you'll just have to convince Owen that you're worth breaking the rules for."

"How am I going to do that?" But she put her other foot on the bed, rolled the other cuff.

Grace grinned as she began to apply the polish. "We're Christiansens. We know what our brothers like."

Eden sat down beside them and began fishing through Grace's bag. "Where do I start?"

"Maybe just a little mascara. We don't want him to lose his ability to speak."

Eden stood, poised above Scotty with a mascara brush. "Look sultry."

"Look how?"

Grace laughed. "Look down your nose at me. And don't flinch."

With Eden tugging at her lashes, it seemed an impossible request.

"Your eyes just got ten times bigger." Eden stepped back to survey her work. "Wow, I'm good."

Grace had started on the other foot. "Lips. Just a little gloss, I think."

Eden fumbled through the bag again, and Scotty just stared at them. True Christiansens, they had decided to dive in and rescue her from herself. Whether she needed, or wanted, rescue.

Although, when Eden pulled out her iPod and scrolled to a song, it felt suddenly like one of those weird, girlie slumber parties she remembered from *Grease*.

And she was Sandy, getting dolled up for Danny Zuko.

Except she'd willingly submitted. Maybe even enjoyed it.

"'For all those times you stood by me. For all the truth that you made me see.'" Eden grabbed a hairbrush.

"Sing it, Celine!" Grace said, turning up the volume. Across the room, Yulia had sat up, grinning as her new mom joined in with Eden.

"'You're the one who held me up, never let me fall . . .'" Eden held out her hand. "C'mon, Scotty, let's hear it—"

"I don't know—"

"'You were my strength when I was weak . . .'" Grace pulled her from the bed.

Wait, maybe . . . yes, she knew this. Scotty found her voice and joined in. "'I'm everything I am because you loved me.'"

"That's right!" Grace said and gestured to Yulia, who bounced out of bed, catching her hand. Eden pumped up the music as she and Grace harmonized on the next verse, their voices rising to fill the room.

"Hit the high note, Grace!" Eden said.

Scotty laughed when Grace hit a wobbly "'I was blessed because I was loved by yooooou!'"

She caught onto the last chorus, and Eden launched into background embellishments, belting as if she were on a Vegas stage. "'Because you loved meeeeeee.'"

The music faded out and Yulia clapped her hands, laughing.

"Okay, it's back to bed for you, little miss," Grace said.

Eden dug into the makeup bag as another song came on. "Stick out that pouty lip," she said to Scotty.

Scotty obeyed, and Eden doctored her lips.

"So?" Scotty said, batting her eyes, a smile finding roost.

"Let's put your hair up. Turn around."

Eden pulled Scotty's long hair into a messy bun. She finger-curled a few errant strands around her face. Then she took Scotty's hand and led her over to the full-length mirror that stood in the corner. "You rule breaker, you."

To her own eyes, Scotty's neck suddenly seemed impossibly delicate, her eyes insanely huge, her lashes dark and long, her lips glistening with just a touch of pink.

Eden came back with a makeup brush. "Hold still," she said and blushed Scotty's cheeks. "Not that you'll need it when Owen takes a look at you but . . ." She winked.

Scotty just stared. "I can't believe . . ."

"That's you? It is, but if it's too much—" Grace suddenly wore chagrin on her face. "We didn't mean to take over."

"I like it," Scotty said. "I just have never . . . I never had a reason to wear makeup."

"What, you never went to prom or homecoming?"

"No. Red was . . . Well, I wasn't allowed to date. Ever." Scotty caught her lip in her teeth, turning away from the girl she didn't recognize in the mirror. The girl who seemed pretty, feminine even . . . maybe marriage material. "Besides, who wants to go out with a girl who smells like crab or spends more time learning how to hunt than flirt?"

"You don't need to flirt. Just be yourself. Because one thing Grace and I both forgot is that you—the fisherwoman, police officer version of you—are exactly the person Owen fell in love with. You don't need any of this to get his attention. This is . . . icing on the cake." Eden had gone to the closet. "How about a dress?"

"Ah, I think this will do," Scotty said before things got too far out of hand.

"Okay, listen, I'm going to go downstairs and distract Max. Eden, you do the same with Jace, and you'll have Owen to yourself," Grace said.

"And then what do I do?"

"Let Owen handle the rest."

Oh, boy.

Grace came up to her, turned her to face the mirror again. "Let's say tonight you throw out your rules."

"Within reason," Eden added. "This is Owen we're talking about."

Scotty shook her head. "Owen's changed. He's not . . . He's a gentleman. You should have seen him on the boat. He didn't swear, kept the other guys from talking crude around me. And when he had a chance to kiss me, he didn't. I didn't even think he liked me until . . . well, the raft. And that was just because he was freaked out. Pure emotion, and . . . that's not . . . real."

She sighed as she looked in the mirror. "Neither is this. I can't help but feel like I'm manipulating him."

"You are," Eden said. "That's the fun part about being a girl—

having your man look at you like you turn his world inside out. Have you never read Song of Solomon?"

"Song of what?"

"Ignore her," Grace said. "Listen, you're not manipulating anyone. And emotion is a good thing. Emotion gives meaning to your actions. Love, fear, duty—they're the power behind every sacrificial act, every grand gesture, the reason men go to war and women die for their children and yes, why Owen threw himself overboard. Don't be afraid of it, Scotty. No, you don't need any makeup to attract Owen—my guess is you already have his heart. You had it before he jumped into an ocean after you. But . . ." She reached over and grabbed a bottle of perfume. "It doesn't mean you can't wow him."

She raised an eyebrow and Scotty gave a nod, letting Grace mist the perfume onto her skin. Grace added it to her own wrists, then pulled up her hair, reached for the lip gloss, and spread it on with her pinkie finger, smacking her lips.

Across the room, Eden had pulled on a hockey sweater over her belly. "It's Jace's." She winked and reached for the perfume.

"Yulia, you go to sleep," Grace said, covering her daughter with the quilt, then kissing her forehead. "I'll be back later."

Then she hooked her arm through Scotty's. "C'mon. They've seen enough of that stupid hockey game anyway."

The Minnesota Wild were in the last fifteen seconds of a two-minute power play, trying to score against Arizona.

"That has to be over twenty shots on goal, and they still can't get it under the crossbar." Owen sat propped on the edge of the sofa, nearly on his feet. "*C'mon*, man."

"Smith is an amazing goalie," Jace said. He leaned forward in the recliner, his arms folded. "We'll need to learn to clean up on the rebound if we want to score against these guys."

The buzzer for the end of the second period sounded. Max threw his hands up, sat back at the other end of the sofa. "Not that I care about the Wild winning, but sheesh."

It felt easy, like old times, to be sitting with his teammates, watching the Wild—or any team, for that matter. Dissecting shots, deflections, checks, hits.

Owen could almost forget that his life had derailed.

That's about enough of that. His father's words hung in his brain. Yeah, he'd managed not to dredge up the past with Max. Had managed to talk hockey with Jace, his hero, like he hadn't nearly cost the guy his career the last time he was on the ice. Sometimes, the image of Jace taking the check for him, the one that would have destroyed his eye, the one that nearly killed Jace, still shook him.

In truth, maybe he *had* cost the guy his career. But both Max and Jace seemed to have moved on, and if his dad's words were right . . .

And I'd bet they each thought God couldn't use them before His grace tracked them down, brought them back to His purposes. You can never outsin God's love, Owen. Or limit what He can do with you if you let Him.

"I feel a little guilty sitting here watching the game with Casper in jail," Owen said.

Jace glanced at him. "We went by to see him on our way here. He's hanging in there but is pretty freaked out. Of course, your mother is keeping him well-fed, and I think Raina has just about camped out there, but yeah . . ." He clicked Mute on the remote. "This feels a little sacrilegious."

"Listen, we'll all be in court in the morning, and he knows we've got his back," Max said. "Trust me, I know about not wanting people's pity. The last thing Casper needs is us over here crying for him."

Owen frowned at him. Pity? "What are you talking about, Max?"

Max shot a look at Jace, then at Owen. "You don't know? Your parents didn't tell you?"

"Tell me what? You're still playing for the Blue Ox, right?"

"For now."

"You up for a new contract?"

Max shook his head. "Three years left. And I'm praying I can play all three."

"You're at the top of your game, Max. You're the last person I'd feel pity for, trust me." He gave a harsh laugh that seemed to echo against the silence in the room. Jace looked down, his jaw tight.

"What am I missing here?"

"I'm going to die, Owen. Sooner rather than later."

Owen froze, examining Max's face for the joke, the *Just pulling your leg, bro.* His voice fell. "What are you talking about?"

"I have the gene for Huntington's disease. It hasn't kicked in yet, but my brother is showing symptoms and I figure I have about six, maybe seven years before I start getting shaky, needing help walking. And then it's a long, downhill slide toward . . ." He looked at his hands. "I know I shouldn't have married your sister, but . . . I guess I'm weaker than I thought. I need her."

Oh. Owen felt the air empty from the room. "I'm sorry."

"Thanks. But we all have our handicaps. You made yours look pretty boss."

Owen reached up, touched the eye patch. "Grace never said anything."

"Grace is living in the now, hoping I never get sick. We'll just keep it that way, okay?"

The now. Talk about not wanting to look ahead. Owen might have decimated the future before him, but at least he still had one, even if he didn't exactly know what it would look like.

"I'm getting some of those cookies Grace and the girls were making today," Max said abruptly. "If I'm relegated to sleeping on a bunk bed tonight, I'm going to need cookies. By the way, I call dibs on the bottom."

"Oh, right, like I'd even fit on the top bunk? Not a chance, pal. I'm pulling rank," Jace said.

Max rolled his eyes. He turned to Owen. "Maybe you should sleep in the basement, let me and Grace have the den, and Jace and Eden have the boys' room."

"What, so she can sleep on the top bunk? No, we'll be fine here for the weekend," Jace said. "We're not here for . . . We're here to support Casper."

Max grumbled something and was getting up when he stopped, eyes on the door. "Oh, we're in trouble now," he said. "Are we being too loud?"

Grace came into the room, looking pretty, her blonde hair up. She put her arms around Max's neck. "Way too loud," she said and kissed him.

Owen averted his eyes, glancing at Jace, only to see Eden slide onto his lap, her arm around him.

"What's going on?" Jace said.

"I want to take a walk," Eden said.

Jace leaned around her to pick up the remote. "We have twelve minutes before the next period."

Owen smiled at that. It was always all about hockey with Jace.

Then Scotty entered the room, wearing her jeans rolled up and a pink T-shirt. She sat on the ottoman. "What's the score?"

Score? Words fled as he took in her long neck, her dark hair dripping down, thick and full, from a messy tangle at the back of her head. Her lips glistened as she smiled gently in his direction. Her eyes—something about them could pin him to the sofa.

He couldn't breathe.

She raised an eyebrow as if expecting something, and shoot, if she wasn't completely annihilating his resolve to follow her rules. Those stupid rules that held him hostage and kept him from doing something ridiculously impulsive like kicking Jace and Max from the room and pulling her into his arms.

He turned to the television. *Just don't look at her.* "The Wild are up, two to one. Uh, we netted a power-play goal in the first period, and then Parise got a wrist shot in just inside the left post, but Arizona came back with a quick goal. We're not getting the rebounds, and it's been pretty messy, so we'll have to pull ourselves together in the third period."

He looked up to find Eden smiling at him. "C'mon, Jace," she said, climbing off his lap.

"Where are we going?" He glanced at the television. "Okay, but we have ten minutes—"

"Shh." Eden took his hand, and Owen nearly laughed at the power his sister had over the six-foot-four former enforcer who could still make grown men cry with a growl. Eden cast a look at Scotty as she left.

"Max, how about a cookie?" Grace said, tugging him out of the room. Max caught her at the door, one hand going around her waist.

"Max doesn't want a cookie," he growled, pressing his lips to her neck, and she giggled as they left.

Awkward. Owen blew out a breath, ran his suddenly wet hands over his jeans. He shot another look at Scotty. She was barefoot and his gaze caught—too long—on the sight of her toes all dolled up with siren-red polish.

Huh.

"Sounds like a good game."

"Mmm-hmm." He tore his gaze away and focused back on the television, where the announcers were rounding up recaps of other games around the league.

He didn't even hear her move, just felt the sofa dip, the sense of her beside him. He stiffened, glanced at her, sitting so close to him that he could lean a little her direction—

Oh, man.

"Did you have fun with my sisters? We thought we heard you singing."

"Mmm-hmm," she said. She met his gaze, her mouth tipping up in a smile.

Lips. Pert, shiny lips.

He found his voice. "They're a little . . . Well, Eden has this tendency to never mind her own business. I lived with her for a while during my early years, and she's like the queen meddler."

"She's nice. I like her."

"And Grace is a dreamer. She seems to think that if she makes cookies, everyone will live happily ever after."

"Not a bad way to solve the world's problems."

"I think you'd really like Amelia. She's the most levelheaded, or well, she's . . . Actually, I don't know. Amelia was only fourteen when I took off for the juniors, and even then we didn't hang out that much."

"Owen, about today, on the rink—"

"Oh no, let's not talk about that, thanks. In fact, if you could go ahead and forget the entire thing . . . Just leave it, okay?"

She fell silent beside him.

Now he felt like a jerk. A jerk whose heart seemed to be lodged in his throat. "Not that I wasn't . . ." He cleared his throat, trying. "Glad, you know, that you were there. And . . . thanks for . . ." Wow, was she wearing perfume? It reached out to him, sweet and floral, and gave a little tug.

He couldn't take it. "Are you okay? There's something . . . Is there something different about you?"

Her jaw tightened, her smile vanishing. And it had the effect of the cold ocean washing over him.

He knew he should be scrambling here, for something, anything. "Scotty—"

"No. This is stupid. I *knew* this was stupid. I'm not like your sisters. I'm just not . . ." She got up.

What—?

"Wait, Scotty—wait!" He lunged for her, grabbing her arm. "What's going on? Are you upset?"

"No!" She shook out of his grip, wrinkled her face as if to rein in a rush of feelings. "I'm fine."

"You're wearing mascara?"

"No—yes—whatever." She turned away. "I'm so stupid."

Stupid? "What are you talking about?"

"Nothing." She headed for the door, but he wasn't about to let her get that far. He ducked past her, propped his hand over the doorway.

"Get out of my way."

"No." He put his hand under her chin to lift her face. "What's going on?"

She blew her nose, then wadded the tissue into her pocket. "I was trying to . . ." Shaking her head, she looked at the ceiling. "Flirt."

Flirt.

He couldn't help the laughter that burst out. "Flirt?"

"See, even you're laughing." She put her hand on his chest.

But he shackled her wrist and pulled it away, growing solemn. "Easy there, I'm still a little sore."

And now she looked stricken, trying to jerk her hand away. But he held it. "Scotty, tell me why you were trying to . . . flirt . . . with me."

Her expression betrayed defeat, her voice wavering. "I don't know. It's because of . . . this afternoon. You were looking at me like . . . I thought you were going to kiss me, and then you didn't and I thought maybe . . . And then your sisters put all this gunk on me and acted like your head would pop off—"

"My head is popping off," he said, a strange, wonderful warmth spreading through him. He reached up to run his thumb over the bones of her face, softly tracing them. "In fact, I haven't a thought left in my head except how utterly beautiful you are."

"I'm not. I probably have mascara running down my face—"

"You do. And it's very, very cute."

She bit her lip.

"You have gorgeous eyes. And your hair . . ." He reached up, loosened it, and it fell over her shoulders. He tangled his fingers into it. "You take my breath away, Scotty. You have since that first day on the boat, when you made me call you *sir*. And yeah, you're pretty amazing right now, but you've always been amazing. I don't care if you're dressed in overalls or a grimy thermal shirt, smelling of fish, or . . . well, I wouldn't exactly mind you in a dress."

Her eyes widened, her mouth opening.

And he didn't care one iota about her inane rules. "Scotty, your flirting *totally* works." He curled his hand around her waist. "In fact, I'm going to have to kiss you."

He'd imagined this, imagined kissing her—really kissing her—since that moment on the raft. Tasting the Scotty who'd saved his life and believed in him even when he couldn't believe in himself. And the kiss they'd shared in the car had only whetted his appetite.

Now he pulled her to himself, one arm around her waist, backing her against the wall. Then he braced a hand over her head, bent down, and met her eyes for a lingering second—one where he let her see his intentions—before he pressed his lips against hers. With nothing of hesitation, just so she knew he had no intention of holding back.

She tasted sweet, her lips soft under his, and if he wondered whether she really wanted to be kissed, she answered in the way she slipped her arms around his waist and molded her body to his, lighting every inch of him on fire. Yet her kiss was cautious, hesitant.

And that only made him love her more.

Love. The word crept into his brain, but once it got there, it spread through his entire body. Yeah, he loved her. He loved her bossiness and the way she refused to give up on him. Loved how she could flip from all business to holding his hand, caring, understanding. Around her, he forgot he was broken; he felt whole and as if he did have a future. A bright, brilliant future filled with the love of this beautiful woman.

The thought broke him away from her, and he stared at her, his breathing hard as he caught her eyes.

She blinked up at him. "Um . . ."

"Scotty. Please tell me that this isn't an impulse. That my sisters didn't talk you into doing something you didn't want to do. Because I'm so crazy about you I just might—"

"Propose?" Her mouth lifted up on one side.

She must have seen the panic on his face because she pressed her hand to his cheek. "Shh. Just . . . kiss me."

Right. Okay, yeah. Because even though he wasn't proposing, there he was, running ahead of himself, grabbing on to a future that he still didn't have a clear view of.

Except for her, right in the middle of it.

So he bent down and kissed her again, wrapping his other arm around her, losing himself in her sweet sounds, the way she became his with her surrender.

"Is it game time?" Jace's voice parted them. "Whoa—hey, sorry, dude!"

Owen glanced over to see Jace turning to block Eden's entrance.

At the sound of a giggle, he looked back at Scotty. He tucked her hair behind her ear. *I love you.* Wow, he wanted to say that, but it might be akin to *Will you marry me?* and he didn't want to freak her out.

"And that's how it's done," Eden said, pushing past Jace into the room. She patted Owen's shoulder, and he stared after her, bewildered.

Scotty ducked out from under Owen's arm, leaving him to lean against the wall, watching as she plunked down beside Eden, who handed her a bowl of fresh-popped popcorn.

"C'mon, Wild!" Scotty shouted.

Owen sat next to her, put his arm around her, and miraculously, she snuggled right in.

As if she'd always belonged.

Suddenly everything in his life seemed to fit exactly into place.

CHAPTER 11

CASPER HADN'T KILLED MONTE RIGGS, but he'd wanted to.

Or maybe he'd simply wanted Monte to exit his life, Raina's life, quickly, quietly. And he certainly didn't feel any grief over the news that Monte had ended up in a ditch somewhere.

Except, after sitting in the Deep Haven jail for the past two days, it seemed Monte had his revenge. And truth be told, if Monte were to show up today in the cell opposite Casper, he couldn't deny that he might do exactly what Kyle had accused him of.

"Remember, let me do the talking. It's just an initial appearance. They'll read your charges and set bail. You don't need to enter a plea or respond in any way. That's why I'm here." His attorney—a guy from Minneapolis he didn't know, procured by Max to appear with Casper in court today—paced the tiny holding room, preparing Casper for the next step.

The next step in his journey to prison if someone didn't start believing him. He could only say, *I did not kill Monte Riggs* so many times before he had to admit that no one was listening.

Casper sat at the table, his head in his hands, trying to hold in the fury that burned like an ember inside. "This can't be happening. I didn't kill Monte." He looked at the lawyer—Brian? Bruce? Clearly a man who had never spent a night in jail, with his slick wool suit, his manicured nails, his short, gelled hair. He even smelled good.

Casper smelled like old soap, two days of living in the same clothes, and the vibrant odor of increasing panic.

He hadn't been given a razor, but he'd cleaned up for today with a suit—one of Max's, maybe, because Casper didn't remember owning one—a white shirt, a tie. He looked like a lumberjack who'd gotten lost at some hoity-toity charity event.

"I don't want to know," the lawyer said. Bryce. That was his name. "I don't even care. What I care about is getting you out of here and home. We'll worry about your defense after that."

"We need to worry about it now! They can't just pick someone out of a crowd and accuse him of murder."

Bryce opened his briefcase, now on the table, and pulled out a folder. "They didn't pick you out of a crowd, Casper. They have a case that, from a jury's perspective, might seem open-and-shut. They're charging you with voluntary manslaughter, which means that even if you didn't plan on killing Monte Riggs, you had the ability, means, and opportunity to do so."

Casper shook his head, not really seeing Bryce, instead taking in the door with the reinforced window, the plastic table bolted to the floor, and the fact that in about ten minutes, Kyle would put cuffs on him and treat him like he belonged here.

A criminal.

"This isn't fair."

"It never is." Bryce closed the briefcase. "See you in court."

Casper looked away, not sure if he'd heard sarcasm or not. He waited in silence after Bryce departed, trying to find his breath despite the hand that seemed to push on his sternum.

Because Deep Haven shared a circuit judge, he'd spent two precious days watching reruns of game shows on an ancient television secured high on a wall and playing solitaire with a deck short three cards. And reading—a couple issues of *Popular Mechanics*, a *Reader's Digest* from the eighties. He'd even done a few push-ups because they burned off the energy that buzzed through him, kept him staring at the ceiling with what-ifs and how-comes and why-hims. Longest two days of his life.

He'd probably lost five pounds despite Grace's and his mother's food deliveries, his appetite having vanished the moment Kyle fingerprinted him.

If it weren't for Raina, he might have simply curled into a ball, refused to eat, but she'd been at the jail for every moment of visiting hours, reassuring him with her eyes, resting her hand against the glass to align with his own.

He longed to put his fist through the glass, to climb into her embrace.

To believe her words: *Everything will work out.*

The door opened, and Kyle came in. Casper glared at him, not a word to articulate the sense of betrayal.

"Get up and turn around, hands behind your back," Kyle said.

Casper obeyed, grinding his molars as the jangle of handcuffs echoed through the room. Then Kyle led him out through the jail, past the eyes of deputies Julie Applewood, who he'd sat next to in biology, and Marty Finch, who he had sold a pair of snowshoes to last winter.

They said nothing, and Casper refused to look anywhere but ahead.

Injustice burrowed through him as Kyle put a hand on his head and helped him into the cruiser parked outside. The slightest nip of winter touched his neck, the weather turning from autumn to early morning frost in the two days he'd been incarcerated.

What would happen if he had to spend weeks, even months, waiting in the Deep Haven jail for a trial?

He burned a hole in Kyle's head through the grate between seats as they drove the three blocks to the courthouse. Kyle pulled around back, next to another cruiser, and opened the door.

Casper managed not to yank out of his grip as Kyle grabbed his arm, directed him inside. "I know where to go," he grumbled, but that sounded guilty, so he shut his mouth.

Kyle brought him to an anteroom next to the courtroom, pointed to a chair by the wall. "Wait here."

Casper refused to sit, choosing to stare out the window at the lake, at the pewter-gray sky. Of everyone who should be in jail . . . well, it shouldn't be him. He did things right. Sure, he'd jumped Owen once upon a time, but frankly, he'd felt just a smidgen of righteousness over that act. Someone had to wake up his brother to his stupidity. And maybe it had worked because Owen seemed to have changed, at least a little.

Still, Casper had come home, swept up Owen's mess, fixed everything. And this was how life—how God—repaid him. Again, he wanted to say it—he wasn't the villain here. He leaned his forehead against the window, trying to breathe away the scream building inside.

Then the door opened and a bailiff came in. "It's time."

For what, execution? Because it certainly seemed like everyone had skipped over the innocent-or-guilty part and gone right to locking him up and throwing away the key.

Casper clenched his jaw and headed into the courtroom.

He stopped short at the sight of his family in the front two rows.

Raina he'd expected, and she gave him a smile, her brown eyes warm, reaching out to him with something probably meant to encourage him. She held Layla on her lap, his daughter—*his daughter*—working her pacifier. He'd also expected his parents, and yeah, they were here, his mother dressed in what looked like Sunday clothes: black pants, a white blouse, a scarf at her neck. His father had stuck to a green Evergreen Resort flannel shirt. They gave him a smile, his mother's expression one of pain.

But seated beside her, lined up like his own personal cheering squad, were Darek, holding Joy, and Ivy. Darek looked at Casper, gave a nod. Like *No worries, Bro.*

Beside them, Eden held Jace's hand, Jace looking solemn. Next to him sat Max, his arm around Grace's shoulder, managing a grim smile. Grace gave him a small wave.

Behind them, Scotty sat with her arms folded, her face stoic. He frowned at that—he'd expected her to be headed back to Alaska by now. But maybe Owen had something to do with that because he sat beside her, his hands in his pockets, his jaw tight, as if just barely holding himself back from launching over the gate that separated the court from the gallery. He gave a short nod to Casper.

His people, his crew. He felt like Braveheart before the English, his countrymen at his back, and took his place at the table.

"All rise," the bailiff said.

The judge entered and called the court to order.

They sat and Bryce leaned over. "I got you first on the docket. This shouldn't take too long."

Casper cast a look across the room, at the table for the prosecution, and wished Ivy were sitting there instead of the portly, middle-aged, balding assistant prosecutor from Duluth.

The prosecutor and defense attorney stood while the judge read the complaint.

"Casper Christiansen, you are charged with one count of voluntary manslaughter in the death of Monte Riggs, of Deep Haven, Minnesota."

Casper glanced at Bryce, who just . . . *stood* there.

This was not right. "I didn't do it!" Casper found his feet even as Bryce turned to him.

"Sit down," Bryce hissed. "This is not the time."

"But I'm innocent!"

In that moment, he heard himself. Angry, just like a defendant on *Law & Order*. The judge banged his gavel, but Casper missed his words as he stood there, helpless. Pitiful. Shackled.

He sank into his chair, feeling heat rise up his neck.

This wasn't right.

The county prosecutor began, "Your Honor, the state would like to ask for a no-bail hold on this defendant, as he's shown a propensity to flee the state."

What—? Casper nearly jumped to his feet again, but Bryce put a hand on his shoulder.

He wanted to drop his head down on the table. Instead, he impaled the judge with a look of disbelief.

"More, Your Honor, Casper Christiansen has recently come

into quite a bit of money, giving him the *means* to flee, should he decide to do so."

Oh, that. Casper closed his eyes. Hung his head.

He wished he could block out the next words. "This is a violent crime, Your Honor. The evidence points to a man with a history of violence against Mr. Riggs, not to mention members of his own family—"

Casper winced.

"—and also shows the motive to plan such an attack, namely Mr. Riggs's history with Mr. Christiansen's fiancée. Most of all, eyewitness accounts testify that Mr. Christiansen threatened Mr. Riggs's life on the day in question."

The one thing they actually got right. But he hadn't killed the man.

"Your Honor . . ." The prosecutor's voice took on a hometown flavor, like *C'mon, we all know this.* "Casper Christiansen grew up here. He knows how and where to hide a body, and by his own admission, he cannot account for his whereabouts on the night in question."

He'd gone for a drive to clear his head, finally arriving home late to a sleeping house. Which no one could verify, so apparently his alibi didn't count.

"For these reasons, the state humbly requests a no-bail hold until we have our preliminary hearing and decide whether to hold him over for trial." The prosecutor settled his girth back into his chair.

The words hollowed Casper out. Because he saw the case laid out before him. Him, angry—no, *furious* with Monte. Willing to do anything to protect Raina and Layla. The fight outside the VFW—had he broken ribs when he'd tackled Monte? Maybe.

Casper had certainly been angry enough—which led to the argument in the municipal parking lot later. And yeah, maybe he had grabbed Monte, shoving him against his truck, threatening him.

But he hadn't killed him.

However, honestly, he did have money—enough to disappear with Raina. The thought had crossed his mind more than once.

Except what kind of life would that be for her, for Layla? On the run? Always looking over their shoulders?

Bryce's turn. He talked about Casper's job at the trading post, his love for Raina and Layla, and how he had invested his money into the resort. "Your Honor, his family is here, right behind him, to support him."

And never had Casper been more aware of that fact as he felt their eyes on him. Sympathetic.

Even . . . ashamed? Because what kind of person built up enough of a reputation to be reasonably accused of murder? Looking at the fact sheet—his motive, his history—yeah, he would have arrested himself too.

Maybe he *was* the villain.

"I'm inclined to agree with the defense," the judge said. "As long as Mr. Christiansen agrees to stay in Deep Haven for the weekend, I'm not opposed to setting bail. But, Mr. Christiansen, if you so much as hint at leaving town, I'll revoke your bail and you'll wait for Monday's hearing in the Deep Haven jail."

He looked at Casper, who managed a terse, "Yes, Your Honor."

"Bail is set at one million dollars."

One *million* . . . Behind him, someone gasped, but he didn't look to see if it had been his mother.

Bryce returned to the table. "You'll only need to put up 10 percent of that, and you'll get it back, minus a fee, Monday morning when you show up for your preliminary hearing. By then we'll figure out how to plead."

"I'm pleading not guilty," Casper said as he rose. "And can you get these handcuffs taken off?"

"We need to get the bail order and terms set; then yeah, we'll get you out of here." Bryce was packing up his briefcase. "But as for your plea—we need to listen to the prosecutor's offer for a deal, if they have one."

"I'm not cutting a deal!"

He didn't mean for his voice to rise but—

Bryce took him by the arm, cut his voice low. "Let's not broadcast that, please. What you fail to understand is that if this thing goes to trial, the jury will only need to be convinced beyond a reasonable doubt to convict you. Do you doubt you did it, based on the evidence?"

"The evidence is . . ." Casper glanced at his crew, at his mother, who wound her arms around her waist, her face drawn. His father's hand dropped onto her shoulder. Grace looked at Casper with such pity that he couldn't bear it. And Owen's frustrated expression seemed just short of fury.

"What kind of deal?"

"I don't know, but if you let this thing go to court, and you're found guilty, you're looking at up to fifteen years—"

And that buckled Casper back into the chair. He bent forward, feeling light-headed.

"Buddy, breathe." Owen's voice, suddenly right there; then his brother was crouching before him. "That's not going to happen."

"Arrange bail, get him home, and give me a chance to take a look at the evidence, figure out a defense, talk to the prosecutor."

Casper looked up to see Bryce talking to Owen. Scotty stood beside him, nodding, her eyes fierce.

"I've got to get back to Minneapolis, but I'll call over the weekend with a preliminary response." Then Bryce turned away, in search of the prosecutor.

The bailiff came over, and Casper found his legs shaky as he was led to the anteroom, where Kyle waited. Then the tour back to the jail, where Casper sat alone, staring again at the walls, barely able to breathe.

Fifteen years.

He had gone numb, his brain shutting down over those words by the time Kyle came to collect him. "You made bail."

Not that it mattered. But seeing Owen and Scotty, Jace and Eden, Max and Grace, and his parents all clustered into the foyer of the police station burned pitiful tears into his eyes.

Raina met him at the door, still holding Layla, curling her arm around his neck. "It's going to be okay."

But it wasn't. Because he'd turned into a child as he burrowed his face in her shoulder, holding on.

He stood like that, feeling her strength against him. She always had that—a strength to help yank him out of his dark places—and he drank it in.

Finally he let her go, lifting his head.

"I made chili," his mother said, as if she could fix everything with a hot lunch.

Casper rode back to the resort with Raina, Layla in the backseat, sucking on her fist and staring out the window.

They'd convict him in record time if they listened to the evidence of the county prosecutor.

Fifteen years.

"I should leave," he said quietly as they turned onto the long drive to the house. "I should just . . . leave. I have enough money to get to Roatán or someplace where they have no extradition treaty with the US."

"What? Casper—no!"

"Raina, they're going to find me guilty for this—I would— and then I'm going to spend the next fifteen years in Stillwater. And worse, so are you. Because I know you. You'll do something stupid like move down there and come see me every weekend, and Layla will grow up with a father in jail, being ridiculed by the kids at school, and you'll have no one to . . ." His eyes filled and he shook his head, clenching his teeth to keep the despair from overwhelming him. "You'll be alone. And I can't take that. I'd rather live without you, having you married to someone else, than—"

"We'll go with you." She pulled over, shoved the car into park, and turned to him. "Right now, we'll leave. Start over." Her voice betrayed no doubt, no hesitation.

"No, see, I thought about that too. I thought about Layla and you always worried about me getting caught, or worse, someone tracking me down, and you getting hurt in the cross fire . . ." He took her hands, not caring that he blinked a tear down his cheek, that he looked desperate and weak. "I'll leave you money. All of it. It's already in both our names at the bank. You go today and take it out and put it in your own account. Divorce yourself from me. I can do this. I'll leave before they know it, and by Monday, I'll be gone. Just . . . away."

Now Raina was crying too, shaking her head. He pressed his lips to her hands. "Don't you see? This is for the best. I'm not a coward—I'm not afraid of jail. I'm afraid of what it would do to you. You can't live like that. You have to have a normal life. A normal family. Layla needs a father."

"You're her father—"

"I'm not! I always thought that I could fix everything—faithful Casper, swooping in to save the day—but I've only made this worse. If I'd stayed out of your life when you asked me to, maybe you would have been able to tell Owen when he came to Eden's wedding that you were pregnant. And he would have stuck around."

This was the hard part, the part that burned like a live coal in his chest. "He's a good guy, Raina. He is—down deep. And you would have brought out the best in him—you always do."

He wiped the tear from her cheek. "Please stop crying. You know it's true."

"I don't love him, Casper. I love you."

"But we both know that you can't. You shouldn't. Not anymore." He swallowed hard, forcing the words from his knotted chest. "Maybe I was supposed to find Owen, to bring him home . . . for you."

She was shaking her head almost violently now.

"Listen to me! You have to let me do this. And you have to marry Owen."

Her eyes widened. "Marry . . . Casper, no!"

"Yes. For me. Please, for me. You have to let him take care of you and Layla."

"I don't need anyone taking care of us—"

He took her face in his hands, leaned forward, touched her forehead with his own. "I know you don't, babe. But . . . I can't leave you knowing you'll be alone." He met her eyes. "Owen is a good man. He will be good to you and to Layla. I know he will."

She closed her eyes. "I want to hate you for this, but I—"

"Good. Hate me." He could barely get the words out, his voice shaking. "Because that way you won't go looking for me."

And then because the words had landed hard, because she looked at him with so much sadness, he couldn't help kissing her. Holding her face in his hands, pressing his lips hard against hers, fierce, desperate, willing life to be different or at least to leave in her heart the imprint of how she'd changed him, given him a future, a reason.

She put her hand around his neck, kissing him back, her tears salty on her lips.

Casper gathered her in his arms and held her. "Shh. Please don't cry, Raina."

But it seemed he couldn't obey his own words. He breathed her in, embedding the smell of her, the feel of her, in his memory. *I love you, Raina.*

She finally pushed away from him. "Don't leave yet. Please, let's talk to your family. See what they say. Maybe they'll have answers."

He gave her a weak smile, a slight nod, but he knew exactly the answer he needed. And he intended to get it from the brother who, surprisingly, seemed to be the hero they all needed.

"I just can't believe they think Casper would run." Owen's mother sat in the front seat, staring out the window, speaking almost to herself. "They don't know Casper."

"They think they do, Mrs. Christiansen. After all, he's got some pretty hefty evidence against him." Scotty didn't want to be the one to point it out but—"Frankly, I can't believe the judge granted him bail."

Next to her on the pickup's backseat, Owen glanced at her, frowned.

She shrugged. "What? I didn't say I thought he was guilty."

Owen touched her hand across the seat, his grip curling around her fingers. "I know."

She'd never experienced the solidarity of family that the Christiansens had shown in the courtroom, an immovable force of support that had no doubt influenced the judge toward granting Casper's bail request.

"We appreciate your insights, Scotty. And you're right—we all need to look at this more clearly," John said, turning at the Evergreen driveway. "Right now, though, we need to take a breath and have some lunch."

They pulled up to the resort and piled out, John and Ingrid, then Max, Grace, Jace, and Eden from their cars. Somewhere behind them should be Raina and Casper but—

No, Ingrid certainly was right. Casper, the guy who'd tracked his brother down to face up to his responsibilities, wouldn't hightail it to the hills and forsake his own.

And if he did, well . . .

Scotty put the thought out of her head. It wasn't her job to make sure he showed up in court.

Today she wasn't a cop. Today she was . . . Owen's girlfriend?

As if to reinforce that thought, Owen caught her hand again on their way toward the house. He pulled her aside as the door banged behind Jace.

"What are you doing?"

"Kissing you," Owen said. Leaning against the house, he slid his hand behind her neck, and his lips found hers. She clung to his lapels and pulled herself closer. He tasted of this morning's coffee and pancakes, smelled of the north woods, fresh soap, and the sense of coming home.

Oh, she could stay here. Right here. Caught in the middle of Owen's attention, the way he seemed to hunger for her. Need her.

He drew back to meet her gaze with his own, so devastatingly blue. "You're so beautiful."

She wanted to hold on to the woman he seemed to see, someone she didn't quite know but wanted to. A woman, pretty, strong, yet who belonged in his embrace.

He touched his forehead to hers. "I just wanted to make sure that I wasn't dreaming last night."

No more than she. Because she'd spent the rest of the night, after he'd walked her upstairs and pulled her into a quick, clandestine embrace, trying to figure out how she might fit into this family.

Which would, of course, mean *staying*. Right here, in Deep Haven.

Maybe she could get a job with the sheriff's department?

First, however, she'd have to figure out how they might prove his brother's innocence. Maybe John was right—lunch. Then a powwow, grilling Casper, and a game plan. A family game plan.

With Scotty a part of the family.

Behind them, she heard a car's tires against gravel, and Owen released her just as Casper and Raina parked.

Scotty could admit to a rush of silly relief.

Owen grabbed her hand and tugged her inside the house, to the tangy aroma of chili and a robust conversation about the court proceedings. Grace stood at the counter, buttering French bread, while Eden set out condiments—sour cream, cheese, green onions, jalapeños.

Scotty went over and grabbed bowls from the cupboard.

"Thank you, Scotty," Ingrid said, putting a handful of spoons on the table.

Scotty set the table, elongated to fit the entire clan.

The conversation died when Casper entered. Ingrid put down the salt and pepper and went to hug him.

His eyes seemed reddened, and he tucked his face into his mother's shoulder.

Not unlike Owen when he'd come home, needing something to hold on to. Their mother.

Scotty turned away, grabbed the salt and pepper, and added them to the table.

Raina came in, her eyes swollen. "I'm going to put Layla down in the den; is that okay?"

"Why don't you put her in the girls' room, Raina?" Ingrid said. "I put a porta-crib up there this morning. It just needs to be set up."

See, that's what mothers did—thought of everything. But maybe that kind of thinking wasn't beyond Scotty. Hadn't she made cookies yesterday?

"I'll help," she said to Raina and carried up the diaper bag.

Raina closed the door behind them and found the porta-crib in a zippered bag in the corner. While Scotty wrestled it open, Raina changed a cooing Layla, then set her on the floor to help with the crib.

"These things can get tricky," Raina said. "You have to pull up the sides, then push down the bottom." She had it snapped into place in a second.

"You're such a pro," Scotty said, adding the sheet to the crib.

"Hardly. I have no idea what I'm doing. If anyone is a pro,

it's Casper, having this huge family." She picked up Layla, rocking her against her shoulder. Layla stared at Scotty with big eyes, sucking on her pacifier. "I was completely freaked out at first. But now . . ." Raina bit her lip, turned away.

"Raina?"

"No, it's nothing." She swallowed, looked back at Scotty. "You know, I'm glad Owen found you. Or you found Owen. Whatever. Casper's right—he does seem changed. Not so dark and broken, maybe."

The jealousy monster died right there as Raina smiled. "We were never . . . Well, I was barely a moment to Owen. But you . . . you are everything to him."

She was?

Scotty's expression must have betrayed her because Raina laughed. "When Owen looks at you, it's like he's seeing a sunrise for the first time. Casper looks at me like that sometimes. Maybe it's a Christiansen men thing." Her eyes filled. "It's breathtaking to be at the center of that."

Yes. Yes, it was.

"I'm sorry," Raina said, wiping her cheeks. "I have to get Layla to bed."

Scotty nodded and headed back downstairs, where Owen, Max, and Jace were recounting last night's game to Casper. As if any of them really cared, but maybe it gave them a chance to do exactly what John had suggested. Take a breath.

She helped serve the chili in bowls; then Raina came downstairs and Scotty found herself seated beside Owen, across from Casper and Raina. On her other side were Max and Grace, who sat opposite Darek and Ivy.

Her spot there, smack in the middle of the family.

Ingrid held out her hands for prayer, and Scotty slipped hers into Owen's, then Max's, and with the rest of them, bowed her head.

She listened as John thanked God for family, food, home. Ordinary things that suddenly didn't feel at all ordinary.

They chorused an *amen* as if breaking for a play and began passing the condiments.

Not a word about the trial. Plenty about the resort and the upcoming town events, and chatter about the youngest, Amelia, off in Africa.

"We should Skype with her this weekend," Grace said. "She doesn't even know Owen is home yet. And she could meet Scotty."

No hint about her leaving. Scotty wasn't going to bring it up.

Across from her, Raina ate quietly, Casper, next to her, deeply silent.

The conversation around the table dimmed as if everyone, after trying so hard, hadn't the energy to continue.

John pushed up from his chair. Ingrid said his name, but he answered, "I'll be right back."

He walked to an end table near the sofa, then returned, holding a book.

A Bible.

He sat, opened it, and without preamble, began to read. "'I look up to the mountains—does my help come from there? My help comes from the Lord, who made heaven and earth! He will not let you stumble; the one who watches over you will not slumber. Indeed, he who watches over Israel never slumbers or sleeps.'"

He paused, looked up at his wife, and recited without reading, "'The Lord himself watches over you! The Lord stands beside you as your protective shade. The sun will not harm you by day, nor the moon at night.'"

Owen had found Scotty's hand, and across the table, Casper's arm went around Raina.

John looked at Casper then. "'The Lord keeps you from all harm and watches over your life.'"

Casper's jaw tightened, but he met his father's eyes.

"Casper, you need to remember that God has not looked away or fallen asleep on the job. You are a son of the Creator, and He holds your life in His hand. You will get through this. We all will."

John looked around the table. "Our God is one who brings the prodigals home, gives children to the barren, heals the sick, redeems the sinners, gives us purpose, and fills our world with family and love. This I know to be true, and we will not forget it in the days ahead."

The words seemed to reach into Scotty, settle through her.

Family. Love. And oh, she wanted it. Every morsel of Owen's messy, tangled, loud, even bossy family. Wanted to be counted at the table, to help with the dishes, to be on the football team in the backyard and tucked every night into Owen's arms.

Even if that meant staying in Deep Haven.

Maybe she was turning into marriage material.

"I made cookies," Ingrid said.

Casper erupted with an incredulous snort. "Mom, seriously?"

"I didn't know what else to do," Ingrid said. "Besides, cookies are good for the soul." She retrieved the cookie plate from the counter.

"Hear, hear," Max said.

Casper rose, glancing at Owen. "I'm going to bring in firewood."

To Scotty's surprise, Owen stood. "I'll help."

John had closed the Bible, was reaching for a cookie. Scotty watched as Owen pulled on his coat and followed Casper outside. She got up to carry her bowl to the sink.

Jace and Max began to discuss the case. "What did the prosecutor mean when he said Casper couldn't account for his whereabouts on the night in question?" Jace asked.

"He went for a drive, came back here late," Max said. "He told the lawyer everyone was sleeping."

"The prosecutor didn't even ask!" Ingrid said.

Jace mopped his chili with a piece of bread. "I suppose he will for the preliminary hearing."

"We need to retrace Casper's steps that night. If we can find someone—anyone—who can verify where he was when Monte went missing . . . ," Scotty said. "I'm going to find out what he remembers from that night."

She pulled on her boots and grabbed her jacket, peering out the window. She couldn't see Casper and Owen by the woodpile. Maybe they were chopping fresh wood.

She was just about to head out the door when she felt a touch on her arm. Scotty startled, then turned and startled again at the softness in Ingrid's eyes.

"Thank you, Scotty. I don't know what we'd do without you and your willingness to help us clear his name." Ingrid pulled her into a hug. A warm, motherly hug.

Scotty stiffened, but Ingrid didn't let go, so she let herself be hugged.

"You are exactly the kind of woman that I would have dreamed of for Owen," Ingrid said as she let Scotty go.

Scotty had no idea what to do with that. Except smile, something tentative. Ingrid winked, then headed back to the kitchen.

Huh.

Outside, the air had turned brisk, leaves escaping across the dirt parking lot. According to Owen, guests would start arriving tonight. By tomorrow night the resort would be full of tourists, here for the final colors of the season. His family would build a bonfire, hence the pile of chopped wood, and his mother would be in the kitchen—where else?—baking cinnamon rolls.

Scotty would line up for one of those.

"You don't have a choice, Owen. You have to marry her!"

Scotty froze halfway to the garage, in the gravel driveway, the voices lifting from the back, where it seemed Owen and Casper were having a discussion that had nothing at all to do with firewood.

"No, you're talking crazy."

"I'm not, and you know it. I can't stay. I've already talked to Raina, and she's agreed—"

She agreed? To what? Scotty held her breath.

"No, Casper, you can't leave. You're not guilty!"

"It doesn't matter. Plenty of innocent people go to jail, and you know it. This is best—for everyone."

"Not for Raina. Trust me on this—*you're* what's best for Raina."

"And you're Layla's father. Like it or not, Owen, you have a responsibility to her, to both of them. They have to forget about me—and you have to do the right thing."

Scotty's chest tightened, her breath webbing inside.

Owen's voice came again. "You can't go. You can't leave her."

"Do you think I want to? That it doesn't slay me to think of you . . . and her and . . ."

That was all Scotty could take. Because Owen simply fell silent. No *But I love Scotty* or even a more tepid *Scotty and I are together.* Just . . . nothing.

Really, what did she expect? Because Casper was right. Owen had a responsibility.

But he didn't have to marry Raina to accomplish it, did he?

By his silence, apparently he didn't agree.

Scotty backed up, turning toward the house before Owen could break her heart further.

And before she heard any more of Casper's plans. Because if he ran . . .

Well, someone in the family—or maybe *outside* the family—would have to bring the fugitive to justice.

And if she remembered correctly, that's exactly why she'd come to Deep Haven.

CHAPTER 12

OWEN HAD SPENT ALL DAY Friday and Saturday trying to figure out how he could confess to the murder of Monte Riggs. Because his brain simply couldn't conjure any other way to make sure Casper didn't do something stupid.

Like run.

As Owen stood in the pew of the morning service at Deep Haven Community Church on Sunday, he clung to the hope that his words to Casper had dug in, found fertile soil, and convinced his brother that his idea of running—and of Owen marrying Raina— could only end in heartbreak. Disaster. Prison for all of them, figuratively if not literally. Owen could easily follow Casper into jail for knowing and participating in his bail jumping. Most importantly, Raina would certainly pay the price. Casper had to see that.

He had to stop trying to fix things and just have, well, faith.

This morning, the entire Christiansen family had squeezed into two center pews. Owen stood sandwiched between Eden and Scotty, who gave him a wan smile as a hymn swelled through the sanctuary.

"'Blessed assurance, Jesus is mine! O what a foretaste of glory divine!'"

The sense of normalcy fostered in the sanctuary, along with the beautiful blue-skied morning, was exactly what his mother had decreed they all needed this weekend. She'd made them go out for burgers Friday night at the VFW, and he should have expected her announcement during the Saturday night game of Sorry! that she'd wake him for church.

It seemed, however, like the right answer.

He was thirsty for a life he'd seen taking shape over the weekend. A life that looked, if not exactly like, similar to what Eden and Grace and Darek and even Casper had.

His hand slipped into Scotty's, and he wove his fingers through hers. She held on but not enough.

In fact, ever since they brought Casper home, she'd seemed . . . distant. One second warm in his arms, then oddly . . . cooling. Maybe she'd simply come to her senses. But Friday night, as he'd drawn her onto the dance floor at the VFW while the Blue Monkeys played, she'd clung to him, her arms around his neck.

Later, as he'd kissed her good night in front of a blazing bonfire at the resort . . . No, definitely no cooling there. In fact, he'd had to reel back, remember that he wasn't the sum of his past but could be a different guy.

So maybe not cooling. Perhaps being dragged along with the family to church had unsettled her.

Except she had caught the tune of the hymn and raised her voice into the next verse.

"'Echoes of mercy, whispers of love.'"

Love. Yes. The enormity of that word, of his feelings for her, could sweep him under.

And if Casper felt for Raina what Owen felt for Scotty, only a raw desperation could have made Casper practically beg Owen to marry the woman he loved.

I'm leaving. I have to. They're going to find me guilty, and I'm going to jail for fifteen years, and that's going to kill us all. It's better if I just . . . disappear.

That's when the shouting had begun. Owen didn't remember the entire conversation, but somewhere in there, Casper had yelled his ludicrous suggestion. *You don't have a choice, Owen.*

That stopped him like a sucker punch that still had him gasping.

Because in his head, he had already formed a life with Scotty. Maybe in Deep Haven, maybe beyond, but . . . a life. Someday a family.

But if Casper left, Owen would have to stay. Maybe not marry Raina, but he had to own up to what they'd done.

He couldn't let go of Scotty's hand, not wanting to think beyond the wild hope that Casper might be coming to his senses right now.

"'This is my story, this is my song, praising my Savior all the day long.'"

Owen would like to rewrite *his* entire story. Figure out a way to make it end happily. Him with Scotty. Casper with Raina—and Layla because that was best for her too.

Instead he might just collapse, put his head in his arms, and weep for the mess he'd made. And for the fact that . . . he agreed with Casper. His brother should run.

After sitting in on the family powwow around breakfast Saturday morning, where they hashed out Casper's options via speakerphone with Casper's lawyer, the alternative solution on the table felt brutally raw, painfully reasonable. Bryce had bargained with the prosecutor for a guilty plea to involuntary manslaughter and suggested he'd get Casper no more than seven years, out in five.

Seven years.

"'Perfect submission, all is at rest . . .'"

As Casper had sat there, drained, his final *But I'm innocent* had fallen feebly between them.

Even his kid sister, Amelia, who'd joined them via Skype, listening to the evidence from her missionary base in Africa, put her hands over her face, crying.

Honestly, though he hadn't told Casper this, if Owen were facing those charges, without evidence to defend himself, he would have already disappeared into the night.

"'Watching and waiting, looking above . . .'"

But that was Owen, and they all knew it. Or maybe it was the *old* Owen. He wasn't going to run this time. Not when Casper needed him to stick around.

He closed his eyes, listening to the song rise, Scotty's sweet, surprisingly soprano voice singing something she probably didn't believe in the least. "'Filled with His goodness, lost in His love.'"

Lord, I don't even know where to start . . . but we need help.

The hymn reached its close, and Owen glanced at Casper, whose expression seemed drawn as he sat down, put his arm around Raina.

As if he sensed Owen's gaze on him, he glanced his way. Frowned. Gave a shake of his head.

And in his look, Owen got it. Casper *hadn't* changed his mind. In fact, if Owen knew his brother, Casper probably had a bag packed and would slip out today during the game, before anyone knew.

Before anyone could stop him.

Owen focused on the pastor as he came up for the sermon, trying not to be ill with the ruin of their lives.

Pastor Dan hadn't changed much over the past ten years—still fit, a full head of dark hair, with warm eyes for his congregation as he took the pulpit. "Today, I want to talk to you about the biggest rebel I know, a man named Jesus Christ."

Next to Owen, Scotty shifted in her seat.

"I know it's hard to imagine, but to the Jews, Jesus was a rule breaker. He hung out with tax collectors and prostitutes and Zealots, the dregs of society. He spurned the Pharisees and told people over and over that following God isn't about how many rules you obey, but rather about how you love Him and others."

Owen glanced again at Casper. At how he held Raina's hand, his thumb caressing hers.

"In short, Jesus was trying to show us how to have faith. But faith scares us. As A. W. Tozer points out, we want a manageable God. We want a God we can use, who shows up when we need Him—and not when we don't. Most of all, we want a God who follows the rules—*our* rules."

Scotty pulled her hand away, folded her arms across her lap.

"But the God who created the heavens and the seas will do what He wants. His plans will not be thwarted."

Was Scotty thinking of the raft, the way the sea had thrown them, helpless? Because suddenly Owen could smell the water, feel the darkness smothering him, taste the drowning sense of loss that had crept in as each hour passed.

"The trouble is that while we might believe God has a plan, we can't believe He is actually *for* us. How can He be? We so easily look at our lives and see our mistakes and realize what a fool He must be to choose us. To want us.

"But He does want us. For us, Jesus stood in front of death and said, 'No. You may not have them. They are what I came for, who I want.' He proved this by gathering all us wretched prodigals behind Him and spreading out His hands in our defense and paying for our sins." The pastor's voice softened. "And with those outstretched hands come victory. The laws that kept us from God are broken; the rules of death are demolished by Jesus, the rule breaker, the rebel."

Dan came around the pulpit. "If you're standing in a place today where you know you need more—healing, hope, a glimpse that there is a happy ending—it's time to become a rebel. To do something daring and wild and reach out for grace, even though it doesn't make sense. But I warn you, once you embrace Christ, you too become a rule breaker. Because a life committed to God requires us to live uncomfortably. Inconveniently. Accountably. Bravely. Transparently. Vulnerably. It requires us to love without rules. Welcome to grace."

Owen closed his eyes. *Welcome to grace.*

As the congregation stood to pray, Owen felt movement beside him and looked up just in time to see Scotty slip out of the pew and head for the vestibule.

He debated a moment, then followed her out. "Scotty?" he whispered.

She'd already grabbed her jacket off the hanger, was pushing through the double doors outside.

He scrambled after her. "Scotty?" Wait—"Are you crying?"

He touched her shoulder, and she rounded on him. "No, I'm not crying. But your pastor doesn't know anything, okay?"

She stalked away toward the Evergreen truck. Leaving him standing there.

Huh?

Owen followed. "Scotty—"

"I've spent long enough in this stupid town."

"What are you talking about? You can't leave." Even as he said it, a moan broke open inside. Maybe that's exactly what she should do.

Because if he'd read Casper's expression correctly . . .

But Owen couldn't let her go. Not yet. He caught Scotty by her arms. "What's going on?"

She looked at him, fierce. "That's easy for him to say. For all of you to say. You don't know what it's like to feel abandoned by God. To know that you did something awful . . ." She closed her eyes, turned from him.

He settled his hands on her shoulders, wanted to pull her against him, but she shook him away.

"I killed a man, Owen." Her voice had cut low, a bare whisper. "I killed a man I knew, and I still see it every day. I see the choices I made, and I know that I wouldn't want me, so why should God?"

Oh, Scotty. He reached out for her again, but she stepped away from him, her voice pitched low, almost talking to herself. "The whole thing is stupid. I was over this. I was fine—"

"You weren't fine, Scotty—"

She rounded on him. "I *am* fine. It was a part of the job. And I don't need forgiveness or healing or someone to tell me it's going to be all better. I don't need help!" She gritted her teeth as if folding her feelings back into herself. "I'm not weak, and the last thing

I need is to depend on a God who is just going to betray me when I need Him."

"What are you talking about?"

"Being a Christian makes you weak. Makes you . . . emotional. It makes you think there will be some happy ending waiting out there when really it's just . . ." She wiped her cheeks. "More ocean. More dark, freezing ocean."

Oh, Scotty. No wonder she couldn't have faith—she'd never had anyone but herself to believe in, and he knew from experience how that worked out, no matter who you were. He reached out to pull her into his arms, but she pushed against his chest.

"No." Then her voice softened. "You're such a good man, Owen. You don't even know it, but you are. And I *can* see God in your life. I saw that on the boat. God does see you, does save you. That's why it's so easy for you to have faith—because you've seen Him show up. And why not? You deserve it."

"Are you kidding me? It's not easy for me to have faith. It's the hardest thing I've ever done to come back here, revisit my mistakes. I don't deserve it—"

"Yeah, actually, you do. You might have gotten a bad draw out of life, but you're a kind, good person, Owen. You're brave, and the way you love your family . . ." She sighed. "You're the kind of person I could have loved. Even . . . married."

Could have?

A darkness formed in his chest, swirled through him. "Scotty . . ." He swallowed hard. "I love you. I'm so completely in love with you. You're smart and beautiful, and the way you argue with me—I'm not wounded in your eyes." He took a breath. "You may not want you, but I do."

Her expression grew so sad, he wanted to cry.

"What's the matter?"

"The thing is, I believe you," she said. "And . . . I want you too. But it's time for me to go home. We both know this will end badly. Let me leave before I can't. Before it gets really messy."

Messy? He searched her face. How could she—? No, she couldn't know about Casper. Or read his mind, right?

For a beat, he felt her words, let them settle. But he refused to believe it was over. That God had given him a fresh start only to let it walk out of his life. He took her hands. "Scotty, I know this is scary for you—all my family and the stuff with Casper. But please give us a chance to work this out. Have—"

"Faith?"

"Yeah. Have faith. Have faith in me and in us . . . and most of all, have faith in the fact that God brought us together."

"Is that what you believe, Owen? That *God* brought us together?"

Her words brought him up short. He *did* believe it, and the breadth of that swept through him, filled him. He believed exactly that.

"Scotty, I think God saved you for me. And me for you. That He was with us on that raft and every moment after. I think God is not just giving me a second chance but has something amazing out there for me—better than hockey or the millions I would have made. I don't know what it is—and right now, I can admit everything looks like it's going to fall apart. But I believe—" His throat tightened. "I believe God is on my side. And your side. And Casper's side. I believe that He stepped into my life to remind me that He didn't let me go. And that He's wildly in love with you too. We just have to hold on, wait, and yeah, have faith."

She had big eyes now, and he hadn't realized his voice had risen with emotion.

Or that his family had come out of the church, that Casper stood just a few feet away, his expression hollow.

Owen met his gaze for a long moment. "Right?"

Casper drew in a breath. Nodded.

"Good," Owen said softly. He turned back to Scotty, touched his forehead to hers. "So. Break some rules? Have a little faith?"

She gave him the smallest of smiles, her hands now on his. "I'll try."

Scotty sat in the den, on the end of the sofa next to Owen, his arm curled around her. Holding on.

She wished his embrace could stop the wild careening of despair in her heart. Oh, how she wanted to believe in Owen, in his words and in the way he'd looked at her when she suggested leaving. *You may not want you, but I do.*

So much in his words, his expression. As if he *wasn't* planning to help Casper run, wasn't going to marry Raina, the mother of his child.

Maybe she'd misunderstood, misheard, even let her emotions tangle her brains and make her overreact.

"Touchdown!" Next to her, Owen leaped to his feet, high-fiving his father as they watched the Bears and the Vikings tussle on the field. The Vikings had scored, to the whoops of the Christiansen men. She gave Owen a wan smile when he turned to her with a high five offering.

She smacked his hand, then shrugged. So much emotion for one silly game.

"We need this win, babe," Owen said, sitting down beside her again. "We Vikings fans have waited way too long for a decent quarterback. This might be our year to get into the play-offs!"

"There's still four minutes left in the game," Max said. "Time for the Vikings to blow a perfectly good lead."

"That's enough of that," John said, getting up during the commercial break to return the popcorn bowl to the kitchen. Jace sat in the recliner, Eden having gone to bed. Scotty could hear Grace and her mother chatting in the living room.

This was how it was supposed to be with a family. Watching football. Playing board games. Showing up in each other's lives. Loyalty—the Christiansens had it in spades.

Owen put his arm around her shoulders, tucking her close. As if it were all settled. But Owen didn't know God like she did.

The God she knew *couldn't* be trusted.

And life felt too fragile to believe in a God Scotty couldn't control.

She'd wanted to scream with every word the pastor uttered. *We want a God we can use, who shows up when we need Him— and not when we don't. Most of all, we want a God who follows the rules—our rules.*

Yeah, well, what was worse—trying to control God, having a few expectations of the Almighty, or just letting Him have His way with the world? It seemed He left all the hard stuff to people like her.

God would be so much easier to let into her life if He . . . if *Scotty* didn't have such high expectations. But the truth was, she knew the second she needed God, she'd only end up alone, her life in pieces in her hands.

I believe God is on my side. And your side. And Casper's side. I believe that He stepped into my life to remind me that He didn't let me go. And that He's wildly in love with you too.

Wildly in love with her? Hardly.

We just have to hold on, wait, and yeah, have faith.

Hold on. Wait. For what—Owen to break her heart?

And that's when she noticed it. "Where's Casper?"

She thought she felt Owen stiffen, but Jace looked over. "He went to take Raina home."

Right. She was jumping to conclusions . . . wasn't she?

Have faith.

Scotty got up, gave Owen a smile. "I'll root from the kitchen."

He offered a smile back. Was there a hint of guile? She didn't want to test it and instead wandered out into the living room.

Ingrid sat on the sofa, her glasses low on her nose, her sewing kit out, working on what looked like a felt stocking. Grace tinkered in the kitchen, the smell of something tangy brewing in the soup pot on the stove.

Scotty sat next to Ingrid and picked up a cutout of a boot.

"You can bead that if you want," Ingrid said, looking up from the pair of mittens she was stitching onto the stocking. "Use this little needle and sew the beads on where the dots are on the fabric." She indicated the beads, clear white, then a long, skinny needle already threaded with white floss.

"Who's the stocking for?"

"This one is for Jace. I figure, with a baby coming, it's probably time to make him an official member of the family." Ingrid winked and gestured to the pile of stockings in a nearby bag. Scotty went over to the bag and pulled them out one by one. A giant snowman for Darek, a reindeer for Ivy, an elf for Tiger. A teddy bear for Eden, a penguin for Grace, and a Santa for Casper. Owen got a puffy bear holding a sled. And finally, Amelia had a fuzzy kitty.

Laid out, the beading and sequins sparkled under the high lights of the cathedral ceiling. Scotty could imagine them hanging from the fireplace, limp, expectant.

See, this was why Owen so easily found his faith. Because she'd bet that he'd never, not once, woken to find his stocking empty by the hearth.

She put the stockings down, heard the cheering from the next room. "Sounds like the Vikings won."

"Miracles do happen," Grace said, tasting the soup.

Owen came out of the den. He could take her breath away by just appearing. His hair pulled back in a ponytail, his beard trimmed, he wore a flannel shirt folded past his elbows over a white T-shirt that stretched against his solid hockey frame. She saw it so easily—the man he would have become, the star athlete. Only she preferred this version—less arrogant, maybe, and sweet to the core, despite his pirate eye patch.

"Now that was a football game," he said, grinning.

With that grin he could win her all over again.

Yeah, maybe . . . *Have faith. Wait.* Perhaps God *was* on her side.

Owen stood for a moment, watching his mother sew.

Suddenly Ingrid looked up. Frowned. "Isn't Casper home yet?"

Grace answered her. "No, he's probably still at Raina's. They need some family time."

But Scotty's gaze fell on Owen and she noted his strange look. He spun around and headed up the stairs.

Scotty found herself on her feet and on his tail. She didn't exactly mean to, but her suspicions roared to life.

She followed Owen up the stairs, right into the room he shared with Casper.

Where Owen stood looking at the empty closet. "He took his clothes," he said quietly.

His stripped expression made Scotty step into the room and close the door behind her. "Owen, did Casper . . . ?" She blew out a breath. "I heard you guys talking on Thursday behind the garage—"

"He didn't mean it, Scotty." Owen advanced on her, put his strong hands on her shoulders. "Listen. He didn't mean it. He was upset and scared—who wouldn't be?—and he was talking crazy. And I told him that—"

She pushed his hands off her shoulders. "You also agreed to marry Raina."

He stiffened, his mouth opening as if searching for words.

Silence fell between them. She didn't blink, didn't move away.

Then his Adam's apple dipped. "I don't have to marry her, but . . . yeah, I have a responsibility—"

Scotty held up her hand. "Don't—"

"Raina would be alone with a baby—*my* baby. That means I have to stay. Be a father."

"Stop, please." She fought her voice, managed something calm. "I get it, okay?" But she was blinking hard as she backed away, heading for the door. "I should have gotten it long ago."

Shoot—why hadn't she left this morning? Or better, the day she arrived? Oh, she was a glutton for punishment.

This was why she had rules.

But Owen's hand landed on the door, holding it shut. "No you don't, Scotty! The last thing I want to do is let you go. And I'm not going to because Casper is . . . He's not going to do it."

"Do what, Owen?" She lifted her chin.

He met her with a grim look. "Run. He's not going to *run*. He knows it's stupid and—"

"Selfish? Because if he jumps bail, he'll also forfeit his bond and everything he has left will be used to pay for his defense. And you can bet he won't go to jail for ten years in a plea, but for every minute of those fifteen years!"

"Shh!"

But she was so beyond *shh*. She stalked away from Owen, across the room, half-talking to herself. "I cannot believe I stayed. I should have left that first day. Then I wouldn't be here, knowing something I should not know, watching your family—a family I've come to care about—fall apart because of your and Casper's idiotic decisions."

"Hey—"

"Well, Owen, if Casper is guilty, he should pay for his crime."

Owen's expression darkened. "He's not guilty."

"Then instead of running, he should let us prove it. I told you I wanted to retrace his steps, figure out who might have done it. That's what we should have been doing this weekend instead of dancing and playing board games with your family! I should have figured out that you were going to go along with Casper's stupidity!"

A fire lit in Owen's expression. "He's not being stupid."

"You all are!"

"He's afraid of losing everything! And I get that better than anyone! So yeah, if he has to run, then I've got his back."

He stared at her, a muscle pulling in his jaw. Finally, "So what are you going to do about it?"

She tore her gaze from Owen's, unable to face it. "I don't know. But I do know that if your brother isn't back by morning—"

"What, you're going to call the police? Report him?" He wore such an indignant look, so much disbelief, that it ignited something inside her.

"Yeah. Maybe I am. Because someone has to do their job." She tried to march past him.

But Owen grabbed her arm. "And that's what you're about, isn't it? It doesn't matter if you know in here—" he pointed to her chest—"that Casper's innocent. That he could never kill anyone. It's all about following the law, the rules, with you, isn't it?"

She yanked out of his grip. "Yeah, actually. Because guess what? Following the rules is the only way you don't get hurt. The only way you don't end up falling in love with someone and walking away completely eviscerated."

He swallowed hard, and a beat fell between them. Then he said quietly, "Yeah, I guess it is. You're right, honey. You can't trust anything I say, anything I do. Because I'm trouble. And you can't trust trouble."

She stood watching him breathe. He stared her down, looking so very desperate, very angry.

Very much like the criminal she thought he might have been, not so long ago.

"He'd better be home by morning," she said on a whisper of breath. Then she turned and walked out, heading toward her room.

No, toward *Owen's sisters'* room. *Scotty's* room was back on a ship sitting in dry dock in Dutch Harbor.

Casper stood staring at Layla, her tiny body huddled in the fetal position in her crib, her lips askew, her curly hair wispy against the dim lamplight, and called himself a coward.

Outside, a storm lashed the glass, splattering on the leaf-strewn sidewalk, wetting the pumpkins he'd carved with Raina.

He'd wanted that much—some memory to give them together, before . . .

Raina came up behind him and slid her arms around his waist, her head resting against his back. Her tiny bedroom seemed so crowded with the crib—he hadn't remembered it being that big when he'd assembled it five months ago. Or maybe he'd simply spent too much time dreaming of the house he'd build them on a bluff overlooking Deep Haven, the lake. Dreaming of the life he wanted for his family.

He ran his hands along Raina's arms, feeling her mold her body to his. "I can't miss watching her grow up. She's not even walking yet and I'm supposed to leave? Walk out of her life?" He turned, pulled Raina into his arms. "Out of your life?"

She looked at him, her expression so trusting. "We'll go with you. Sneak away tonight—"

"No!" He didn't mean for his voice to emerge quite so loud. He glanced at Layla, saw she hadn't stirred. Thankfully.

He took Raina's hand and led her to the family room, where he'd built a fire. With her aunt Liza still in Sedona, the house felt like theirs.

Except, of course, that Casper went home every night. Despite the desire to stay, to wake with Raina beside him, he knew he had to wait.

He'd wanted to marry her honestly. After all they'd been through, to give them the right start.

He'd hoped to be married at Christmas. But he'd get married in a Vegas wedding chapel tomorrow if it meant they could start living happily ever after.

They have to forget about me—and you have to do the right thing. He'd hated those words, wrenched from his chest as he'd tried to make Owen see that he couldn't let Casper down. Not again. Not now.

He closed his eyes against the fight inside him, even as Raina settled next to him on the sofa.

You can't leave her.

Do you think I want to? That it doesn't slay me to think of you . . . and her and . . .

He moaned, and Raina lifted her head. "Are you hurt? I should have asked—did they hurt you in prison?"

"No, Raina. Of course not. I was in the county lockup, not Sing Sing."

She offered a wan smile and he winced. "Sorry. No. I was in a cell by myself, most of the time eating my sister's cookies. I was fine. And you were there—I wasn't lonely. Or scared. Or hurt."

Okay, maybe a little scared, but nothing compared to the idea of spending the next decade down in Stillwater prison.

His gaze fell to his duffel sitting next to the door. He'd planned to be gone hours ago, to be at the airport by the time Sunday night football ended, before his family could realize he'd fled.

Except for Layla. He'd read her a book, then made her laugh, sang her a song, too easily prolonging the inevitable.

And now with Raina tucked against him . . . He turned to her, searched her face. "You are so beautiful. How am I supposed to let you go?"

"You're not," she said, lifting her face to his. She smelled of home, and in her kiss was the bittersweet taste of everything he'd wanted for them. He cupped his hand to her cheek, rubbing it as he deepened his kiss. Somehow—he wasn't sure how—he found himself stretched out on the sofa, Raina nestled in his arms.

She sighed, something sweet, contented, and it went through him like fire.

"I should go."

She gripped his shirt, panic in her eyes. "No—Casper. Please." She shook her head. "I tried to be okay with this, but I can't. I don't care what you say. I *won't* marry Owen. I'll pine for you every day for the rest of my life. I'd rather live with you on the run than—"

Oh, Raina. He kissed her again, a heat igniting inside him that only she could quench. Raina. The woman who believed he could save her. He felt her surrender, clinging to him, tangling her legs with his.

Her hand went to his chest, found its way inside his shirt, smoothing along his skin.

Casper jerked back, breathing hard, his heartbeat filling his ears. "I really should go."

"Please stay. Please—Casper, we only have this night together. Can't we be married? . . . I mean, I'm already married to you in my heart. I want to be . . ."

He read the rest in her eyes. And it left him weak. He bent his forehead to hers. "You have no idea how much I'd like that to happen. To be your husband, right now, tonight."

He looked up, saw the *yes* in her expression.

The tongues of temptation licked through him.

No. Oh no. All this time he'd thought himself better than Owen. Not the prodigal. Not the villain. Falsely accused. Even persecuted.

But if anyone knew the thoughts lurking in his heart, glazing his mind as his eyes roamed Raina's face, her lips, as longing filled his body . . . Yeah, he was every bit the sinner he'd labeled his brother.

Maybe more because Owen had barely known Raina. But Casper had pledged to love her, to honor her, to be the man she could trust.

"I can't—" He took a breath and extricated himself from her arms, even as she sat up.

He climbed off the sofa and strode away, breathing out as he braced his hand on the fireplace, staring into the flames.

"Please, Casper."

Her tone could break him in half.

"Don't leave me. I'll wait for you—as long as it takes. Ten years—no problem. Every day, I'll wait."

He closed his eyes to her words.

"Unless . . . unless you don't want me."

He turned and knelt before her, her face caught in his hands. "Are you kidding me? I want everything about you—your smile, your laughter, your kisses—but most of all, your trust. Raina, you are my heart, and being without you will . . . I love you so much, I can't breathe without you." He leaned back, caught her hands, searching for words. "I had a lot of time to think while sitting in jail. I was so angry. For two days, just filled with fury. Here I was, the one who went to find Owen, and when I get back, he's the hero, and I'm thrown in jail."

"It's not fair—"

"But then I went to court. I stood there listening to the prosecutor listing all the evidence against me, and I realized . . . I sounded like a criminal. Owen knew he'd made a mess of things and came home asking for forgiveness. I stood there looking at myself and said, *It's not my fault*. But what if it is?"

"What do you mean?"

"I didn't kill Monte Riggs and dump his body in a ravine. But maybe something I did caused it. And right now all I know is that I'm just as much in need of saving as Owen was. I'm overboard. I'm drowning, and I need help."

"Casper."

"I can't leave you. But I'm so afraid to stay. And not just

because of . . . of how much I want to stay the night with you. I'm afraid of staying and seeing our lives dismantled. Everything we've waited for, everything we dream of, gone. Yeah, I'm afraid of prison; I'll admit it. But I'm more afraid of watching your life be ruined."

As he spoke, something dawned in her eyes, something still tender and growing when he'd left to find Owen.

"Then we'll have to trust God that He will save us. Like your dad said, 'The Lord keeps you from all harm and watches over your life.' We have to believe that, Casper."

They did? Then, to add to his shock, she bent her forehead to his and prayed.

His Raina, the woman who, six months ago, believed God didn't love her. The woman he'd prayed for, hoped in, believed God's redemption for.

She prayed. For him and Layla and Owen and even Scotty. Prayed for their future and Casper's freedom and for faith.

Lots of faith.

He opened his eyes at her *amen.* "Who are you?"

"Your future wife." She touched his face with her cool, soft hand. "Or at least I hope to be someday."

So he didn't wait; why should he when the perfect moment was right now? "Raina, will you marry me? Not in a year or ten years, but tomorrow morning? First thing—we'll get a marriage certificate, find a judge, get married before the hearing."

She was in his arms, nodding. "Of course I'll marry you."

She knocked him over, and he fell back with her onto the carpet, cradling her fall, rolling over to trap her in his embrace.

When he kissed her, it all dropped away—the fear, the fleeing, even the murky, distant future.

Because he wasn't the villain in the story. Not in her arms. He lifted his head. "Wow, I love you."

"And you're the one I've waited for. The only one I want," she said.

Casper pulled a couple sofa pillows to the floor, tucking them under his head. Then he eased Raina back into his arms, where she nestled against his chest, watching the fire. He added a blanket, tucking them in. Snug.

"So you're sticking around?"

"Mmm-hmm," he said, kissing the top of her head. "Just for a little while."

Casper awoke, stiff and aching, on the hard floor, Raina still curled next to him. Sunlight cascaded into the room, the fire dead in the hearth.

Knocking rattled the front door. "Casper Christiansen, are you in there?"

Raina pushed up from him. "Is there someone at the door?"

Casper sat up, blinking sleep from his eyes.

Raina got to her feet, slinging the blanket over her shoulders like a cape. "I think it's Kyle."

Kyle? Casper found his feet and had advanced to stand beside her when she opened the door.

"Kyle, hey, what's—?"

"I'm here for Casper." Kyle stood in the sunlight of the porch, in uniform. An official visit.

"What?" Casper growled, glancing at the way Kyle rested his hand on his utility belt. He didn't exactly know what Kyle had against him but—

"We got a tip, Casper." Kyle's gaze landed on the packed duffel next to the door. Casper had the strangest urge to kick it out of the way. But he couldn't really lunge at the passport lying on top. Or his wallet full of cash, thanks to a trip to the ATM.

"Tip—"

"It looks like you're planning on jumping bail," Kyle said.

Next to Casper, Raina stiffened.

"No—I, uh—"

Layla started to howl.

Raina had grabbed his hand. He turned to her, kept his voice soft against her stricken expression. "It's okay, honey. Listen, I'll go with Kyle, and we'll straighten this out. Don't worry." He kissed her sweetly, wanting to linger, but Kyle stood there like a bouncer.

Kyle touched his arm as he headed out the door. "Don't," Casper barked, yanking his arm away.

"Keep it cool, Casper. We're just trying to keep you from making a bad decision."

"We?"

And that's when he saw her. Standing by the cruiser, dressed in jeans and a baseball cap, looking like she had the day she'd arrived. His warden.

Scotty.

CHAPTER 13

Owen stared at the words of his fight with Scotty all night, tracing them on the ceiling as rain lashed the windows, stripped trees of leaves, left a wasteland in the north.

Because guess what? Following the rules is the only way you don't get hurt. The only way you don't end up falling in love with someone and walking away completely eviscerated.

Falling in love. Yeah, he'd caught those words, let them ping inside him too.

He finally got up before the sunrise and padded downstairs to brew a cup of coffee while he watched the dawn crest over the trees across the lake, turning the water to gold, then a rich, dark blue, the storm long spent.

He kept glancing up to the girls' room, wishing he could knock on the door, wake Scotty, tell her . . .

What? That he was sorry for being the guy who defended his brother? Who would step in and do what was right, despite the fact that it would break his heart?

He set his coffee on the table, returned to the window, his hands tucked into the pockets of his jeans.

"This is not a locker room," Eden said behind him. "Go put a shirt on."

He glanced over his shoulder, spied her descending the stairs, wearing her pajama pants and an oversize sweatshirt.

"Sorry." He hadn't even noticed, just pulled on the nearest pair of pants and headed downstairs. Now he grabbed a sweatshirt hanging on one of the kitchen chairs, recognizing it as Jace's as he pulled the moose-size garment over his head.

Wow, Jace was a big man, and even Eden saw it, grinning as she walked over to the fridge, pulled out orange juice.

"So what's it feel like, almost being a mom?" Owen said, sliding onto a high-top stool.

"Scary," Eden said, pouring OJ. "But pretty exciting too. You know, I had plenty of practice running after a toddler . . ." She eyed him, winked.

"Hey, I wasn't a toddler."

"Belligerent, wanting your own way, moody . . ."

"Fine." He grinned. "I'm all grown up now, trust me."

"Mmm-hmm." She leaned a hip against the counter, cradling her orange juice. "I heard you and Scotty fighting last night, and when she came in, she . . ." Eden made a face. "I'm not sure, but I think she might have even been crying."

And didn't *that* make him feel like a jerk?

"Do you love her, or don't you?"

It was just like Eden to drill in, a hard point right to his heart.

He stared at his coffee, testing the word, knowing the only answer. "Yeah. I love her. She's . . . easy, you know? To talk to. And laugh with. And yeah, she can be a stickler for rules, but she doesn't see me like . . . like everyone else does."

Eden raised an eyebrow. "Oh, I think she does. She just loves you in spite of it. Or because of it. Or maybe she just loves you, period." She took a sip of her juice. "I like her. A lot. It's too bad her dad is selling his boat. Seems to me she'd make a great captain."

"She's an *amazing* captain. Works harder than anyone and manages to keep everyone safe too."

Eden finished off her juice. "I think you should tell her that."

"I will. Do you know where she is?"

"I heard her get up this morning and assumed she was coming downstairs. Are you sure she's not outside by the dock?"

Owen's head snapped up. "Is her duffel still here?"

Eden's face slacked. "I . . . uh, I dunno."

Owen had jumped off his stool, was already halfway up the stairs.

He stopped himself, however, at the bedroom door. Knocked. "Grace, are you in there?"

"Right behind you."

He turned and spied Grace in the bathroom, sitting on the edge of the tub, braiding Yulia's hair.

Owen didn't wait, just barged into the bedroom. Scanned it for Scotty's black duffel bag.

Maybe she left it in the laundry room?

He took the stairs two at a time, headed to the basement. Found the laundry room clean, quiet, empty.

Upstairs, the phone rang. He shut off the light, his chest constricting. No, she couldn't have . . .

But what did he expect? He wanted to wince as his words flooded back. *You can't trust anything I say, anything I do. Because I'm trouble. And you can't trust trouble.*

He'd all but packed her bag for her, shoved her out of the house. Shoot—why did his mouth seem to have its own impulsive mind?

When he returned to the kitchen, Eden stood at the counter, talking on the phone, one hand braced on the granite island, her expression horrified. "Just calm down, Casper. It'll be okay."

Oh no. Owen stalked across the room, practically grabbed the phone from her. "Where are you?" he ground out through clenched teeth.

"Owen? Yeah, maybe you should ask your girlfriend that question. Because she ambushed me this morning. Fetched Kyle and showed up on Raina's doorstep, accusing me of jumping bail. Which I haven't . . . yet."

Owen turned away from Eden, wincing. "Sorry, Casper. I didn't think she'd actually—"

"You *told* her? Nice, real nice, Owen."

"Hey, listen, you didn't come home, and your closet was empty—what did you expect me to say?"

"I expected you to cover for me!"

"It didn't take a genius to figure out what you were up to. She put it together. She's a cop. And she's only trying to do what's best for you."

He could barely believe the words issuing from his mouth. But—"If you jump bail, you're all but admitting guilt. That's going to destroy your defense—and any hope you have of returning to Raina. So just stay calm."

"Calm? Scotty is making a statement right now, apparently

testifying to the fact that she heard me say I was planning on leaving—"

"You were!"

"But then I wasn't. I decided last night . . . I'm not leaving."

"You spent the night at Raina's?"

"Oh, that's rich, coming from you."

"That's not what I mean. I'm just saying, you didn't come home. What was Scotty supposed to think?"

"She's supposed to mind her own business!"

"She was trying to protect you!" Owen hadn't realized how he'd raised his voice, how it had drawn Jace and Max down the stairs and his parents from their room, his mother now wrapping a robe around herself. They came to huddle around the island as he paced the floor of the kitchen. "She's part of the family—she wouldn't betray you."

Casper's voice dropped to a growl. "No, Owen, she's *not* part of the family. She's just another one of your flings. Let's be honest here. Scotty isn't sticking around; she told me on the plane that she was going to get you home and leave. Wake up, buddy—"

"Things have changed." But Casper's words hit like a blow to his gut.

"I doubt that because she *looks* like she's leaving. I saw the rental; I saw her bag in the car—she's not coming back to you."

In that moment, Owen really wanted to hate Casper. To tell him that he was every bit as deserving of a happy ending as Casper was, and that just because he'd made mistakes didn't mean he couldn't be redeemed. *Hadn't* been redeemed.

"Sit tight, Casper—I'll be right there."

"You've caused enough trouble, thanks. Just leave it."

"No, I won't leave it. This isn't over. Have a little faith—"

"In who? You? I trusted you, and you ran to Scotty."

"She *guessed*! She is a detective, after all."

Casper's voice dropped. "Listen, I'm trying to understand; I am. And I am trying to have faith. But it's over, Owen. If the judge decides to hold me for trial today, I'm going to take the plea. Maybe this is the way it's supposed to be. I'm tired of running and trying so hard to fix things. If God doesn't fix it, then it's over."

"There's still time—"

"Not unless a miracle shows up and confesses to the murder of Monte Riggs. I gotta go. Kyle's fixed me up a nice little suite over here."

"Casper—hang tight."

But the phone clicked in his ear. Owen closed his eyes. He didn't want to turn. Didn't want to face his family.

Silence fell behind him. He drew in a breath and turned.

Jace, in a T-shirt and sweatpants, had come to stand behind Eden. He'd settled his hands on her shoulders. Grace had her jacket on, was zipping up Yulia's in the foyer, but shot Owen a pained look. Max leaned against the wall, alternately glancing at Grace, then back to Owen, his arms folded across his chest.

His mother had her hand over her mouth, his father's set in a grim line.

"Casper's back in jail," Owen said, setting the phone on the counter. "He . . ."

"We know," Jace said. "We heard. He was going to jump bail."

"And Scotty turned him in." This from Eden, her eyes sharp.

And there he was again . . . standing on the outside, feeling like he didn't belong.

Not unlike Scotty, probably.

"Dad, I need to borrow your truck." Owen stopped in the

entryway for his boots. He shoved his bare feet into them, grabbed a work jacket and the keys from the hook.

"We're right behind you, Son," he heard as he headed out the door.

Somehow that didn't make him feel any better.

With every word she uttered, Scotty wanted to rewind, to erase the jottings the deputy scrawled on the page.

She pressed her hand against her roiling stomach, which threatened to empty into one of those tin wastebaskets beside the deputy's desk.

Too many eyes and ears fell on her this morning as a handful of deputies coming on shift filled out paperwork and received updates. She wanted to duck below a desk, put her hands over her ears. Make it all go away.

"So then what did you hear?"

"Casper said that he couldn't stay." Her own betrayal could suffocate her. She couldn't look at Casper—sitting across the open room of desks, waiting to be processed back into the system. Not handcuffed, thankfully, because that would only make it worse. She still couldn't believe the calm with which he'd surrendered to Kyle, striding out to the cruiser, getting into the backseat. Sitting in silence as they drove him to the station.

Right then she realized what a mistake she'd made.

It only solidified when they brought Casper in and he sat down in the interrogation room, folded his hands on the table, and looked at her through the one-way glass as if he knew she stood there, watching, scrutinizing. "I wasn't going to run," he'd told Kyle. "I mean, I was, but I changed my mind."

And like before, she wanted to knock on the glass, tell him to shut up. But maybe that was simply Casper, wearing his heart on his sleeve. So painfully honest, wanting to do what was right, to save the day.

Not unlike Owen. No, he didn't exactly wear his heart on the outside of his body, but he certainly took it out of his chest on impulse.

The entire family, it seemed, operated on an emotional code—relationships before rules. Grace without guidelines.

Except perhaps they drew a line at giving grace for betrayal.

No, Owen, she's not part of the family. She's just another one of your flings. Let's be honest here. Scotty isn't sticking around.

Casper probably didn't realize how his voice had traveled across the open, empty room, but she'd kept her head down, despite the words scooping her out.

Not part of the family.

"When did you discover he'd made good on his statement?" the deputy asked.

"When . . . Well, maybe I overreacted." She attempted an expression of chagrin. "He was still in town—he didn't actually leave."

"It's too late for that. They've already decided to detain him until today's hearing. Like you said—this way, he doesn't forfeit his bail."

She had said that as Casper stood in the hallway, waiting for his phone call. She'd kept her voice low, but apparently everything carried here. *Casper, I was just trying to help.*

And he'd turned his back on her.

They all had probably, after the phone call home.

"I saw his clothes gone from the closet. And Owen confessed that Casper planned to leave."

She saw Casper eyeing her across the open room then and followed with, "But even Owen said that he'd changed his mind. He seemed adamant that Casper wasn't going to leave."

"Except for the empty closet. And the packed bag. And the passport and money we found at his girlfriend's house."

She closed her mouth, looked away.

"I think we're done. Sign here, and I'll get this typed up and faxed over to the courthouse."

"Can't you just hold Casper without charging him? You have forty-eight hours to file charges."

By then she'd be back in Alaska, shaking off the memory of her week in Deep Haven.

As if she'd ever forget.

"Scotty!"

The voice made her jerk her head up, and she stiffened at the sight of Owen, his hand on the glass of the reception area. "Let me in!"

The deputy got to his feet. "Owen, sit down. We're nearly done here."

And that's when she did it. Saw her opportunity to . . . what? Set things right? Fix the mess she'd made?

Break the rules.

She grabbed the statement and, with two quick movements, ripped it in half, then again.

The deputy turned at the sound, his eyes wide. "Nice. Now we have to start over."

"No, we don't. I'm done. I take it back. Let him go—Casper's not going anywhere." She glanced at Casper, offering a tentative, please-forgive-me smile.

He frowned.

She wanted to add an *I'm sorry*, but more pounding on the window made her turn.

"Owen, sit down!"

Clearly this deputy didn't realize that Owen didn't have a sit-down in him. Ever. And it broke her heart a little, because being on the receiving end of all that emotion had left her . . .

Loved.

The realization could knock her back into her chair. Loved. So fully, wildly, completely loved.

In fact, Owen Christiansen and his impulsive, overzealous passion had set her free from the fear that she would always be alone, the dark, cold Alaska winter abiding in her heart.

Her heart tore a little more as she glanced at him, his work jacket open over an oversize sweatshirt, his curly blond hair wild under a stocking cap, his beard scruffy, desperation all over his face as he continued to pound on the window.

Then his family filed in behind him.

Scotty stared at them, seeing them all, just the way Owen had described them to her.

Eden and overbearing enforcer Jace, who wore such a dark look it made her realize why Owen had confessed to being a little afraid of him once upon a time. Max was with them, confusion in his eyes—Max, the guy who had pursued the sister of the man he'd hurt because he had to follow his heart. And Darek, the big brother, worry more than anger on his face. Next to Darek was his petite redheaded wife, Ivy, who pushed through the crowd, spoke to the clerk.

And finally, Ingrid and John, his hands on her shoulders, maybe as much for himself as for her.

Everyone showing up en masse, Clan Christiansen to the rescue.

Scotty heard a buzz and saw Ivy turn to the group. She seemed to be talking to Ingrid, the way she grabbed her hand. Then to John, who had found Casper's gaze, meeting it with something solid, unbroken.

It occurred to Scotty that even though she stood at the wrong end of the firing squad, she'd miss them. Their crazy humor and propensity to believe a little lunch would solve all their problems. John's resolute belief that God watched over them, and Ingrid's ability to soothe the day with a plate of cookies. Darek's ironhanded big brother protection, and Grace and Eden's attempts to teach her how to flirt. She'd miss Jace and Max's solidarity and Raina's sweet efforts to make Scotty feel like Owen belonged to her.

And she'd miss the fact that, for a day or two, yeah, she had been part of the family.

Ivy came in, walking across the room toward Casper. But she stopped at Scotty, giving her a grim, sad smile. "I would have done the same thing."

She would have?

Then Ivy touched her arm and headed over to Casper.

The strange, kind gesture from someone she barely knew shook her.

Oh, she had to get out of here. But to do so, she'd have to walk right through the brute squad.

She'd managed a crew of foulmouthed fishermen on the deadly Bering Sea. She could handle a mostly well-mannered group of Minnesotans. She moved toward the door, her head down.

Owen met her there. Like a wall blocking her path. "Are you okay?"

Not at all what she'd expected. "Please, Owen, I have to go."

"What? No, Scotty. Let's talk about this—"

"Owen, let her go." This from Ingrid.

And that did it. Because she'd sort of hoped Ingrid, out of everyone, might be on her side. Might understand. But it wasn't like Ingrid was her mother. She'd never had one, never needed one, and she wasn't going to start now.

"What she said," Scotty said to Owen, and to her great relief, he just stood there, the obedient son he was, and let her push past him.

The group parted for her, like the Red Sea rolling up the tide, as she escaped Deep Haven and the magnetic hold of the Christiansen family.

Owen could only stand there, his emotions locked in his chest, as the woman he loved, the woman he'd just betrayed, walked out of his life.

What was he thinking? He'd seen Scotty's stripped look as he pounded on the glass, calling her name. He'd seen her rip up whatever form the deputy had been filling out. He'd seen the sad, broken smile she'd flashed in Casper's direction as if apologizing. Most of all, he'd seen the way she looked at him, at his family.

In that blinding, breathtaking second, he realized how much she'd wanted—no, *needed*—not just Owen, but his entire loud, overwhelming, too-invasive family.

So now he rounded on them. "It took a lot of guts for her to go after Casper. She did something none of us were willing to do—stand up for what's not only right but *best*, even if it hurt her. And believe me, arresting Casper was about the last thing she wanted to do. But she did it because she cares about this family, which is more of a miracle than any of you realize. More importantly, if anyone is paying attention, Scotty is *right*. If Casper ran, we all know where that would end—him being arrested on the border or maybe even gunned down as a wanted murder suspect."

He saw the effect of those words in his mother's eyes, the jolt, and probably that's what she needed—what they all needed—to wake up here. "Worse, if he succeeded in running, we'd *never* see him again. If you think it was hard on you guys with me being gone, then imagine how gut-wrenching it would be to know that Casper could never come home. Nor contact us. We'd never know how he was, if he was okay."

His dad settled his hand on his mother's shoulder, steadying her.

"Prison might be horrible and unfair, but at least he won't be alone. He'll have us standing by him, standing by Raina. Helping raise Layla. And for the record, I wouldn't—am *not*—marrying Raina. Because she doesn't belong to me. Her heart belongs to Casper, and while I would pledge to provide for her the best I could and show up every minute she needed me and be some kind of awesome *uncle*, I wouldn't ever let Layla forget that Casper is her daddy."

He took a breath even as he saw Grace's eyes fill, saw Eden begin to smile.

"And Scotty knew all that. Because Scotty knows me. Not the guy who left a trail of mistakes, not even the guy who on impulse dove into an ocean or asked her—and Raina, for that matter—to marry him. But the guy God is still working on. The guy who knows there is something amazing out there for him. For all of us. While Scotty might have given up on faith, I haven't. You shouldn't either. Because Casper needs that from us right now. And frankly, Scotty does too. So, Mom, I'm going after her, and you're going to support us, and we're going to believe the impossible from God. Right, Dad?"

He looked at his father, who met his gaze, a spark of something—pride?—in his eyes. "I couldn't have said it better."

Well then.

Owen pushed through them, and Max held the door open, saying, "Go get her, bro."

Owen climbed into the truck. Please let her not be so far gone that he couldn't find her, reel her back to him.

He floored it out of the parking lot, not caring that he passed two gassing-up cruisers on his way.

Stopping at the intersection, he peered down the road, searching for the rented blue Ford Escape.

Nothing.

Please.

He gunned it, tapping his brakes as he hit the 30 mph zone, then stepping hard on the gas as he climbed the hill.

Please, God.

He topped the hill at sixty, was just about to break the law when he spotted the Escape pulled over to the side of the road, right before the *Come Visit Us Again* sign.

He pulled in behind her. Put the car in park.

Creeping along the passenger side, he saw her hunched over. Scotty?

Oh, Scotty. She had her head down, clinging hard to the steering wheel, sobbing.

Sobbing?

He didn't bother knocking, just reached for the handle.

Locked.

His effort to open the door made her raise her head. She stared at him with such horror on her face, he thought she might put the car into drive.

She *did* put the car into drive.

"Scotty!" Owen dashed around to the front of the car, a defender blocking the goal, hugging the bumper even as she tried to maneuver around him.

Now they were just sticking out into traffic. Scotty tried to straighten the car out, but Owen grabbed the hood. "You'll have to run me over!" he shouted. "I'm not leaving."

She sat back, her reddened eyes like daggers, her skin blotchy.

"Let me in." He wanted to move over to the driver's side door but feared she'd just gun it.

Then she broke, her face crumpling. She shook her head, put the car in park.

Attagirl. He leaped on the opportunity, grabbing the driver's door handle and banging on the window. "Unlock it and scoot over."

She looked up at him, and he raised an eyebrow. "If I have to, I'll climb on and ride all the way to Duluth."

The door unlocked, and Scotty pulled the emergency brake as she climbed over the middle into the passenger seat.

Owen got in. Shut the door behind him.

Silence. She folded her arms over her chest, stared out the opposite window. "Go away." Her breath hiccuped, and she seemed to be tamping down what he had no doubt she'd categorize as a reckless display of emotion.

Which, at the moment, she didn't need from him. So he went straight for the facts.

"Thank you for stopping Casper."

She glanced at him, frowning.

"Yeah. We know what you did, and it was right, even if it was painful."

She looked away.

"And more than that, clearly none of us is thinking straight here, so . . . we need you, Scotty."

That got a response. A trembling swipe of her hand across her cheek, a shake of her head. "No, you don't. Casper was right—I'm not a part of your family. I'm not sure why I thought—"

"You are a part of our family."

She looked up, tears carving trails down her cheeks. He wanted to reach out, to touch her cheek, to pull her into his arms.

Except the last thing she needed was more impulsiveness.

Although he could admit having to fight the urge to scream when she said, "No, Casper was right. This was just a fling."

Owen centered himself, like he would before a shot on goal. Breathing in, slowing his careening heartbeat. He kept his voice low, gentle. "A fling is something impulsive. Fast. Driven by emotion. What I feel for you is . . . logical."

She frowned.

"Scotty, if I have a hope to be anything like the man I want to be, I need someone who isn't going to freak out every time an old teammate, headline, or past romance walks into my life. Someone who can logically look at the man I am now and see the truth. That, trouble or not, I'm also changed, a little more every day. And I'm going forward, not backward."

"You want me because I have faith in the person you're going to be? Isn't that based on emotion?"

"Nope. It's based on what you know." He took her hand. "What do you know, Scotty?"

She seemed to be sorting that through her head. "That . . . you're not afraid of facing your past and doing the right thing."

"Mmm-hmm."

"And that you're more than a little loyal to the people you . . ."

"Love? Yep, that too."

"And that if you could, you'd go to jail in Casper's place."

Huh, he hadn't expected that one. But that proved she did know him. He nodded. "See, not emotional. Facts. Are they enough for you to believe me when I tell you that I am absolutely not letting you leave Deep Haven? That you are not a fling? And by the way, I told my family exactly that."

"You . . . did?" Her voice filled with something he'd call . . . hope?

"Yep. Right after I told them that I'd never marry Raina and that this dog wasn't out of the hunt for Casper's innocence. Not yet. It's not over until it's over."

"That sounds a little like 'We're not dead till we're dead.'" A tentative smile broke through her expression.

So much for holding back his emotions. "Wow, I love you. You're the one—the only one—I want. Please don't run away. Because I'll only have to chase after you."

She tucked her hair behind her ear, looked down at her lap as if embarrassed.

And because he'd already gone this far, already taken his heart from his chest and handed it over . . . "Do you love me?"

She swallowed, her breath shaky.

Please, Scotty, don't be afraid.

She looked up and the words filled her beautiful eyes. "I love you so much it terrifies me. I was driving away and . . . I couldn't. I got to this sign and my brain said to keep going . . ."

"But your heart said stop," he said softly. "Aw, Scotty, look at that, breaking the rules for love."

"Stop it."

Not on her life. Because as he traced the vulnerability in her expression, it ignited that hot ball of emotion he'd wadded in his chest.

He reached for her, curled his hand around her neck, and pulled her close. He let his touch be sweet, despite the fact that he wanted to crush her to himself, never let her go. But perhaps showing her that he could be slow, gentle, not so passionate as to scare her away—

Scotty grabbed his lapels and kissed him back, her touch so overflowing with emotion that he lost himself in the rush of wanting her, loving her.

By the time he lifted his head, she was over the center console, in his lap—he'd pushed back the lever on the seat, giving her room to put her arms around his neck, his around her waist.

A car drove by, honked.

Owen pulled away, his heart pounding, keenly aware of the taste of her on his lips, the smell of her filling his brain.

Her face reddened.

He laughed. "Oh, Scotty. Just when I needed you to put the brakes on . . ."

And there was her beautiful smile.

"Don't get ahead of yourself there, Eye Patch." She climbed back to her side of the car. "It's your own fault for being so irresistible."

"Irresistible, huh?"

Suddenly her smile dimmed.

"What?" He fought a spurt of panic. "Did I say something wrong?"

She shook her head, her eyes alight. "Not this time. Because I think I know who killed Monte Riggs."

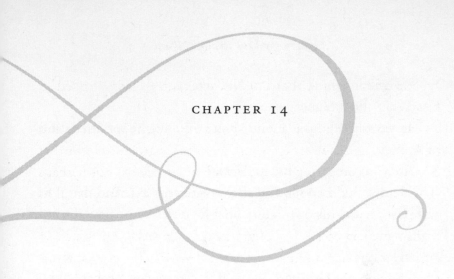

CHAPTER 14

"I THINK WE NEED TO TAKE ANOTHER LOOK at Signe Netterlund."

Scotty's words seemed to jerk through Owen, who simply stared at her. Cars whizzed by them on the way out of town, the morning bright, the sunshine drying the wet highway and turning the leaves to gold and copper along the ditch.

Poor man. She had been almost inhaling him moments earlier, losing herself completely in his words.

You're the one—the only one—I want. Please don't run away. Because I'll only have to chase after you.

Wouldn't that be a kick—Owen Christiansen chasing her? Back to Anchorage?

Because hello—so what if he loved her? What now? Did she give up her job in Alaska? Become a small-town cop in Deep Haven?

She couldn't think about it. Not yet.

"What about Signe?"

"It was what she said about Monte thinking he was irresistible to women."

"Are you comparing me to *Monte*?"

"Hardly. But then she said she wasn't surprised. And that if he was dead, it was his own fault. That he never knew how to treat a girl right."

"He didn't."

"Did you not hear her? She said that someone 'probably beat him up and left him for dead in the woods.' According to the coroner's report, he had broken ribs, consistent with the reports of the fight, and a fractured skull—as if someone hit him on the head. But the first report said he died of exposure. That conversation has been itching at me. This town is small. How could she not know about Monte's death?"

"Unless she did and was trying to pretend she didn't."

"And if they printed his cause of death as exposure in the paper, then Signe's 'guess' seems a little too close to the truth."

He frowned at her. "You think something happened between Signe and Monte?"

"She was very vague about how she lost that necklace. I think we need to have another chat with her."

Owen already had the car in drive, turning a U-ie. They headed back to town, stopped in front of the VFW.

"It looks closed," Scotty said.

"Your point?" He got out, came around, and reached for her hand.

She debated a moment, then slid it into his.

Apparently he meant his words about not letting her go.

He pulled her around to the back of the building. "Dugan Schmitt is head cook, and his kid played hockey, just a couple years older than me. We'd go to practice early in the morning, and when we were finished, we'd come down here and Schmitty would fix us up with flapjacks." He found the back door, buttressed with cardboard boxes and a Dumpster, and pulled it open.

The smells of burgers, french fries, and beer that embedded the walls could make a girl's empty stomach roar to life.

"Schmitty?" Owen called.

It was like old home week again as the cook came out of an office. A blond Swede, lean but for a pouch where he kept his extra burgers, his narrow face pocked with a lifetime in front of a grill. He extended his hand. "Anders would be glad to know you're back. He's coming home for Thanksgiving."

"Tell him to give me a call. If I'm in town, we'll slap the puck around."

If he was in town?

"You looking for some breakfast?" Schmitty reached for an apron, but Owen shook his head.

Shoot. She might not argue with breakfast.

And the thought made her smile—when did she turn into a Christiansen?

"I'm looking for Signe Netterlund. I need to talk to her."

Schmitty walked over to the schedule posted on the wall. "She starts her shift at one."

Owen pulled a cell phone from his sweatshirt pocket. "Signe gave me her number, but I don't have it with me—this is my brother-in-law's phone. Do you have a number for her?"

Schmitty rattled it off but added, "She doesn't always answer—doesn't get reception out at her place."

"She doesn't live in town?" Scotty asked, wishing she'd taken the time to pick up a new phone.

Owen dialed, put the phone to his ear.

"She's staying at her parents' place."

Owen hung up. "Voice mail. Thanks, Schmitty." He pulled Scotty out to the parking lot.

"What—?"

He pointed at her, grinning. "You're so smart." Then he took off in a jog for the car.

She jogged after him. "I thought you were still wounded!"

"Feeling much better!"

She got in as he fired up the car. "I don't get it."

"You will."

He drove them out of town toward Evergreen Resort.

Scotty braced herself. She didn't want to see his family again, not yet. Because how would she possibly apologize for sending Casper back to jail?

Thankfully, Owen didn't stop at the resort but kept driving down the road past their entrance. "It's just a ways up here."

"What is?"

"The scene of the crime."

Owen pulled into a gravel lot, littered with branches and leaves but otherwise empty. His expression fell. "Shoot, I thought we'd find Signe's car here."

She frowned.

"Get out; I'll show you."

The scent of evergreen filled the air along the loamy path they took into the woods. They'd gone maybe fifty yards when it split. "Signe's parents' cabin is one of the grandfathered properties overlooking Twin Pine Lake. If you follow this path, there is a cluster of them—everyone knows about it because the government wanted to buy them out and tear the cabins down to keep the BWCA pristine, but the residents banded together and won."

"So you're saying Signe lives down this path."

"And this one leads to . . ." He took her hand again and walked her another twenty or so yards to where the forest opened into a large clearing.

"A blueberry patch."

A gorgeous swath of land, tangled with blueberry bushes and downed trees, but overlooking a glorious blue lake, foamy with whitecaps as the October wind raked it.

"Twin Pine Lake. Where Monte Riggs died . . . and just a stone's throw from Signe's cabin," Scotty said quietly.

He didn't let go of her hand as he started weaving through the clearing. "My mother loves to pick blueberries here. But there are rules about where we can pick because . . ." He stopped short and tightened his grip on her hand. "Careful."

A crack in the earth opened to a chasm before them. It widened toward the end of the overlook. "If I understand my dad's explanation of where they found Monte's body, it was right around here."

She turned, gauging the distance to the cutoff. "If someone was coming up this path at night, it wouldn't be hard to miss that cutoff, end up in the clearing."

"And if you don't know about the ravine, then—"

"No wonder your mother had rules."

"I hear rules keep you alive."

She wanted to stop right there and kiss him again under the arch of the blue sky.

Instead, she let go of his hand, walked out into the clearing, stared at the lake. "Let's say Monte got here on his own. Working with the connection of Signe's family's cabin, the necklace, and the fact that Monte had it on him in the ravine, maybe he came up here to see Signe."

She heard Owen behind her, crunching through the brush, then quiet as he sat on a boulder. "Do you think he and Signe were dating?"

"What I think is that there's a lot more to her story. She sounded almost . . . angry, even hurt." Or how Scotty might have sounded a week from now, had she gone back to Alaska, her heart in pieces.

Owen who? Oh, he didn't mean his proposal. Just wanted a quick fling. The charmer he is, he can't be trusted with a woman's heart. Words to mask the deep well of hurt she'd carry if she left. And really, how could she leave the guy sitting on the rock, one leg propped up as he surveyed the lake? With his beard, his work jacket, his hiking boots, he looked like he belonged on an "Alaskan Men" calendar.

Then he smiled at her, full wattage, so warm she might turn into a puddle.

"What?"

"I'm just thinking of you standing at the helm of your own boat."

He got up, came over to her, and it felt a little like watching a grizzly move in his own environment. Big. Graceful. Then his hands landed on her shoulders, his gaze latching on to her. "I have money. What if we bought your dad's boat? What if we . . . became partners?"

His words swept through her, engulfing her. "I . . . Owen. What about your life here? You can't leave again. And you have Layla." She shook her head, breaking free of the delicious, glorious possibility, and stepped out of his embrace. "Let's just . . . figure out how to get Casper free. Then we can—"

"Plan for the future? Get married?"

"Oh no—not this again."

"Don't make me get on one knee."

"Owen! Stop it."

"Why? Because the idea of living happily ever after is too big? Too amazing? And yeah, there is Layla, but we can figure that out too."

His mouth closed, and shoot, the wind in her eyes made them burn. "No. We just don't have room for your crazy future in our lives—not right now." She breathed out, then brushed past him on the way back to the road.

He caught up with her, cut in front of her, his hands on her shoulders again. "Stop—"

"No. Owen, you're way too far out into never-never land here. Let's just stick to today's task—clearing Casper. We don't know if we can prove any of this, and if we can't and Casper goes to jail, then Raina will need you—"

"I have faith, Scotty. This is going to work out."

"Yeah, a wild, too-hopeful faith."

He'd stepped close, wrapped his arms around her waist, pulled her against him. "You need to get used to the fact that you're in this now. A part of the messy, loud, overcaring bunch of us. And we believe in the happy ending."

Oh—

His kiss was short, sweet. "Listen," he said softly, his voice sending tenderness through her. "I know you're not ready for anything impulsive, but there *is* a proposal in your future. We will live happily ever after. Believe it."

He took her hand, headed back to the car, and oh, she wanted to just fall into step.

To have faith.

They got into the car, and he pulled out the phone. "Eden texted me—she must have figured out I had Jace's phone—and reminded me the hearing is starting in a half hour. I gotta get to the courthouse."

"I'll drop you off at the resort. I'm going to track down Signe."

He put the car into drive. "I should go with you."

"No, you should go with your family. Besides, if Signe is going to talk to me, she has to do it without trying to flirt with you."

"She's not—"

"Have a little faith, Owen."

He glanced at her; then the smidgen of a wry smile appeared. "Yes, sir."

Scotty laughed, but his response lingered even after she dropped him off at the resort.

We will live happily ever after. Believe it.

Maybe.

She headed down to the VFW.

The Open sign had been flipped over, the bar already hosting a few flannel-shirted regulars. Scotty walked in casually and spied Signe tying on her apron, her blonde hair up in a messy bun. Skinny, shapely, and yet something in her eyes . . .

Sadness?

Signe broadcast a smile for the patrons as she entered the bar area, touching one of them on the shoulder, laughing with another. But her smile was . . . wary, maybe?

Especially when her gaze landed on Scotty.

"Hi, Signe. I was wondering if you had a second to chat."

Her friendly demeanor vanished. "About what?"

Scotty had debated the entire drive over about how to frame her conversation, how she might start with the facts of the case, then move on to Signe's cabin, the scenario she'd cooked up with Owen. Maybe end with a question about her whereabouts that night.

But a cool wall of suspicion in Signe's eyes had her regrouping. Maybe it was time to chuck the rules and have a woman-to-woman chat. To tap into Signe's emotions by confessing her own.

"It's not easy living way up here, is it? It reminds me of where I grew up in Alaska, a tiny town called Homer. Everyone knows everyone, but sometimes that's not a great thing, huh?"

Signe frowned. "Can I get you some water?"

For Scotty's suddenly parched throat? "Yes."

Signe took a glass from the shelf, scooped in ice, filled it with water, and set the glass on a napkin.

"In Homer, there's maybe a handful of guys to date. And once you've sort of ruled them out, then . . . there's no one else."

Signe glanced at the fellas at the bar, most of them retired, a couple who might be trying to forget their mistakes in a beer. "You probably nabbed the last eligible bachelor in Deep Haven." She looked back at Scotty. "Not that I'm trying to edge in."

"No. Of course not. But the truth is, it's better to have no man than the wrong man, right?"

Signe shrugged. "Depends."

"I get that too. I know what it's like to go home alone, night after night. To watch other people get the romance, the long walks on the beach, someone to actually care about you and deal with the messy and ugly mistakes . . ."

Scotty took a sip of her water. "I know what it's like to have no one to turn to, to talk to when life feels overwhelming and alone."

"Do you have a point?"

"I'm just saying that if someone did come along who cared, it would be hard to ignore him."

"Do you want a burger or something?" Signe said, pulling out her order book.

"Cheeseburger. Owen says that you know how to doctor them?"

"He always liked them with mayonnaise and lettuce, pickle, onion, no tomato."

"Perfect."

Signe walked away and Scotty wanted to bury her face in her hands. Okay, she couldn't pinpoint exactly where all that had come from but . . .

She wasn't so different from Signe. Alone, wary. So lonely that she had fallen for a guy she barely knew. And if Owen hadn't turned out to be the opposite of the criminal he looked like, then . . . she might be way too deep into a mess she couldn't escape.

Signe came back. "I forgot to ask. Fries or onion rings?"

"Signe, I keep thinking back to what you said about Monte." She gentled her voice. "Did he ever hurt anyone you knew?"

A flash of pain on her face. Bingo.

"Signe, did Monte hurt *you*?"

She swallowed. "People didn't understand him like I did. He . . . he wasn't always mean. He could be a charmer when he wasn't drinking."

"And when he was drinking?"

She reached up, flicked her finger across her cheek as if wiping a quick tear. "I take back what I said. He *didn't* deserve to die in a hole in the ground."

All Scotty's instincts flared to ask her how she knew *that* tidbit of information. But she slowed down. "You know something about how Monte died, don't you?"

Signe yanked her arm away, headed to the kitchen. Scotty hopped off the stool, running after her. "You don't live that far from where he died. In fact, you're about the only one who lives up there—"

"Leave me alone." Signe disappeared into the kitchen.

Scotty noticed one of the patrons look her way, start to slide off his stool. She ignored him and pushed into the kitchen. The smells of sizzling burgers, the fry bins, onions, and fresh tomato assaulted her. She needed food, and soon.

"You can't be in here." Signe was reading one of the tickets. Or pretending to, because tears ran down her cheeks. "Go away."

If Scotty were back home, she'd simply order Signe to come to the station, and there, put the screws to her. Because Signe definitely had information about Monte's disappearance and . . .

But Scotty wasn't at home. Here she had no jurisdiction. No rules to fall back on.

Just . . . her gut. Instincts. Even impulses.

"Signe. Casper Christiansen is going to be indicted for a crime we all know he didn't commit."

"How do we know that? Monte hated him for taking Raina away."

"How did that make *you* feel? Because you loved Monte, didn't you?"

Signe's mouth tightened to a bud of anger.

"And the fact that Monte pined for Raina must have killed you."

"I just didn't get it. Raina was a tease and had Casper's baby. Why would Monte want her?"

Scotty didn't correct her. "So after the fight that night, you decided to remind him of that, didn't you? You probably saw how drunk he was and got worried about him. Maybe you even saw Casper and Monte talking in the parking lot. It was late that night. Maybe you were just getting off work?"

She wiped her cheek. Shrugged.

"And with Casper threatening him, you knew he needed someone."

She grabbed a napkin. "He was really upset and yeah, drunk, and I was worried about him. So I told him I'd take him to my place . . ."

When she looked at Scotty with such sadness in her eyes, Scotty saw herself. Alone. Sad. And while Signe filled her world with flirting and empty hookups, Scotty filled hers with . . . danger. Work. Anything she could to get her mind off how lonely she felt all the time.

Until now. Until her life had suddenly gotten messy and big and . . . happy.

Really happy.

"What happened, Signe? You said he was only mean when he drank." Then she got it. "Did he see Casper's necklace around your neck and lose it?"

Her voice turned low, broken. "I forgot it was there. I remember talking about it, but I didn't know he knew who it belonged to. And he just grabbed it. It was leather—it wasn't going to come off, not easily." She pressed a hand to her mouth. "He was choking me. I don't know how I got away. I remember the thong breaking off my neck. But it was dark, and I just ran and hid. . . . I headed up to Twin Pine Point. I knew he would think I went to the cabin but . . ."

Signe gave a quick, broken shake of her head. "I was so scared. I heard him come up the path, and suddenly he was there, standing over me. He grabbed my arm, so much anger in his eyes—I don't even remember thinking, just reacting. I hit him—I had grabbed a rock, and I just . . . hit him. He fell back and I ran. I heard him yelling for me. And then . . . he screamed. It was terrible, but I was so afraid that I took off and went back to the VFW, slept in Schmitty's office. I figured Monte would hike back to town. And when he never came back in, I thought he'd left town. I had no idea that he'd . . ." She started crying again. "I should have gone back for him! I keep thinking of him there in the ravine, dying in the darkness. Alone. Cold. Scared."

For a second, Scotty was there too, imagining him broken, hurt. No one to rescue him.

She found her arms around Signe, awkwardly hugging her, her words soft. Kind. "Shh, it'll be okay."

She spotted Schmitty, spatula in hand, looking over at them. Scotty offered him a wan smile.

Then she found the cop inside. "Signe, you have to give a statement to the court."

Signe pushed her away. "Are you kidding me? They'll accuse me of murder, just like they did Casper. And I don't have a family like the Christiansens to stand beside me, tell the world I'm innocent. I'll go to jail—"

"No, you won't."

"Why not?"

"Because I'm going with you. You're not in this alone."

Not in this alone.

She completely understood the way Signe stared at her. Disbelieving.

"Have a little faith, Signe."

Have a little faith, Owen.

Crazy how those five words could light so much hope inside him. And not just that Scotty's theory would somehow materialize into a miraculous answer that exonerated Casper, but also . . .

That she might actually have . . . faith.

Wouldn't that be something? God using a guy who'd given up on life, on faith, to ignite it in someone else?

Owen looked at his father, seated in the gallery behind Casper at the defense table, and his words rushed back to him. *God is constantly using broken, messy people to restore the world and bring Him glory.*

Oh, he longed for that. To be someone God could actually use, a guy with purpose again. A guy with a long-term contract with the winning team.

"All rise," the bailiff said, and Owen found his feet next to the rest of his family. He glanced at the clock on the wall. *Please, Scotty.*

He sat down as instructed, wiping his suddenly sweaty hands on his pants. Down the row, his mother had his father's hand in a tight grip.

Casper had showered, shaved, and wore the suit his mother brought him. He sat next to Bryce, his jaw clenched.

"This is simply an evidentiary hearing," the judge was saying. "Mr. Christiansen, after it is determined whether to hold you over for trial, then you may consider your plea." The judge looked at the papers on his desk. "We will also, at that time, take into consideration, if necessary, the complaint and request to revoke your current bail."

Raina bounced Layla on her lap, the little girl sucking on her fist and playing with her stuffed bunny. She leaned over and grabbed at her shoes, the bunny falling to the floor.

Owen picked it up, handed it back to Raina. She smiled at him, her expression strained.

He should offer to hold Layla, maybe.

The prosecutor stood and began to outline the charges against Casper. "We're asking for a charge of voluntary manslaughter. We will show that although Casper Christiansen had no prior intent to kill, he acted in the heat of passion in such a way as to leave Monte Riggs fatally wounded."

Owen checked the clock again.

"The state will show that Mr. Christiansen had motive, means, and opportunity by exploring his violent history, his relationship with the deceased's former girlfriend—"

Yeah, even Owen felt the prick of those words.

"—a previous assault charge, and witnesses to an altercation on the night in question. We will also show the familiarity of Casper Christiansen with the location of Mr. Riggs's body. Finally, we'll produce physical evidence that puts Mr. Christiansen at the crime scene, as well as show his attempt to flee the crime."

"Your Honor—" This from Bryce, who'd driven up from Minneapolis that morning. "This evidence is at best circumstantial. It's not a crime to have an argument with someone. More, Monte Riggs had a history of threatening the accused's girlfriend, and we are on record with a restraining order taken out—"

"Two days after the deceased went missing," the judge said. He put on his glasses as he considered the documents the prosecution delivered. Silence fell over the courtroom, Owen's heartbeat in his ears.

"Mr. Christiansen, do you have an alibi for the time period in question?" The judge looked up, and Owen wanted to bounce to his feet, say something—anything.

Even confess to a crime he couldn't have committed. Because Scotty was exactly right—Owen would go in Casper's place if he could.

Now Owen sank his head into his hands as Casper quietly answered, "No, Your Honor. I went for a drive to cool off."

The judge nodded. "Very well."

And Owen knew, just knew, what would come next.

"This case is weak at best, but it is—"

"Please!" Owen was on his feet, holding on to the railing in front of him. "Please don't do this. He's innocent, I swear it. But he's got this little girl, and he can't go to jail and—if anyone goes to jail, let it be me. I'm the one who screwed up. If it weren't for me, Raina wouldn't have gotten pregnant and Casper wouldn't have . . . we wouldn't have . . ." Oh, he had the sense that he was making it worse because the judge stared at him, his eyes dark. But as usual, Owen's mouth couldn't stop. "Casper and Raina would have never been apart and Monte wouldn't even have been in the picture—"

"Sit down. Or I'll remove you." The gavel banged and Owen felt a hand on his arm. Eden, tugging him down.

But—"Your Honor, please!"

"Bailiff—"

Owen held up his hands. "C'mon, don't do this."

His father stood. "Your Honor, just listen. He doesn't mean any harm—he just cares about his brother."

And then Darek moved to stand in front of Owen. "Don't you touch him."

"Everybody calm down." Jace loomed over them all.

"C'mon, Judge, are you serious?" Max, behind him, having his back.

Casper, now standing too, turned. "Owen, let it go!"

Layla started crying.

"Leave my brothers alone!"

The voice, high, sharp—and new—echoed from the back of the room.

Everyone froze.

Except of course, the bailiff because he had no idea that Amelia Christiansen had suddenly appeared, from Africa, in the Deep Haven courtroom.

"Amelia—what are you doing here?" Ingrid scooted out from the bench, pulling her daughter into a quick embrace.

Owen just stood there, breathing hard, his gaze darting between the bailiff, who now had him by the arm, and Amelia. Wow, had she really grown that much? Beautiful, with her long auburn hair, a tan, and a new confidence about her.

And behind her, what, her chaperone? Because he looked about five years older, dark hair, lean, tall, and wearing a solemn look as he put his hand on Amelia's shoulder.

"Who's that?" he said to Raina.

"That's Roark, remember?"

"I don't remember." During their Skype call, Amelia had seemed more interested in hearing about his return and Casper's arrest. "Someone left him out of the picture."

"Oh, he's definitely in the picture now. Especially after he chased her across the ocean and apparently back," Raina said, trying to soothe Layla.

As he watched, Roark shook John's hand.

"Order!" This from the judge as the bailiff wrestled Owen out of the row, turned him around.

Handcuffs? He glanced over his shoulder. Casper gave him a sad smile, an inexplicable warmth in his eyes.

"Your Honor, can I say something?" Amelia stepped forward to join Casper at the table.

Owen tried to shrug out of the bailiff's grip. "Wait; will you—?"

"Who are you?" This from the judge.

"My name is Amelia Christiansen, and I have something—well, Roark actually has something to say about the case." She flashed a smile at Roark—and clearly she'd grown up because it was the kind of smile that said, *You are my whole world.*

Owen knew just what that kind of smile felt like.

"Roark lived here this summer, above the Java Cup, overlooking the municipal parking lot," Amelia said, turning back to the judge.

"I'm listening."

Roark stepped up beside Amelia. Nodded to Casper. "Your Honor, when I heard about Casper's case from Amelia, I realized that I had information pertinent to the court's findings." His voice came out in sharpened, aristocratic syllables.

"He's rich," Raina said to Owen. "And from Brussels."

Of course he was.

"Go on," the judge instructed.

"On the night in question, as Amelia has pointed out, I lived above the coffee shop, which overlooks the municipal parking lot. I heard the row between Mr. Christiansen and Mr. Riggs."

Oh no. Owen wanted to kill His Highness.

"I saw them push one another."

Perfect.

"And I saw Mr. Christiansen leave."

Owen shot a look at Casper, whose mouth hung open.

"That doesn't account for the time during which Mr. Riggs disappeared." This from the prosecutor.

"Except Mr. Riggs didn't leave alone, Your Honor. Shortly after Mr. Christiansen left, I saw Mr. Riggs with a woman. He seemed intoxicated, and she put him in her car. They left together."

Owen scrambled to untangle the testimony, to fit it into Scotty's suppositions.

What if that woman was—?

"I appreciate your testimony, Mr. . . ."

"St. John. Roark St. John."

"Mr. St. John, I'm sure the defense will add your statement into evidence, but we still have no alibi for Mr. Christiansen. And barring testimony from said woman, I am afraid I'm finding—"

"I have that testimony, Your Honor."

And hallelujah, Owen had just known his faith would be rewarded because Scotty came in the side door, beckoning Signe Netterlund in beside her.

The judge appeared ready to throw them all in cuffs, especially when Owen finally broke free of the bailiff, started toward Scotty. "What took you so long?"

She patted his cheek as she walked by, winking.

Winking?

Then the bailiff had Owen by the arm again. "Come with me—"

"Not on your life!"

But Scotty was right there, edging in between him and the bailiff. "Easy there. He's still nursing an injury." She turned to Owen and said, "Go with the man." But when he shook his head, she put her hands on his face. "Don't worry. We'll come and get you when it's over."

We. As in Scotty and his family, who now looked at him, the lot of them, nodding.

They'd come and get him.

So he took a breath and let the bailiff lead him away, into the anteroom, then out to a cruiser, where he climbed into the backseat and soon after found himself taking up residence in Casper's cell.

Which actually felt about right.

Casper stood frozen as the judge's words echoed in his head.

Free to go.

Free. To. Go.

He turned, and his eyes landed first on Raina, tears cutting down her cheeks as she rocked Layla. Then on Amelia, who launched herself at him, flinging her arms around his neck. He returned her hug.

"I can't believe you came back!"

She practically glowed as she smiled at him, then glanced at Roark. "He's the one who insisted. When I told him about our conversation, he remembered that night exactly."

"Roark. Thank you." Casper held out his hand, still amazed that the guy who'd once broken Amelia's heart had landed on the happy end of the story. But maybe the same thing could be said for him as he embraced the members of his family, one after another, working his way to Raina.

Finally, Raina. Her eyes shone. He held her face in his hands, kissed her. "I love you."

"I love you too," she said. "But I think you're going to have to bail Owen out of jail."

Owen. He still couldn't believe how his brother had freaked, the words issuing from him turning Casper inside out.

Owen was the hero of the story. Yeah, Casper had trekked across the country to find him, to bring him home to face his mistakes, but Owen, in his too-passionate, impulsive, die-hard way, had saved him by believing in him and convincing Scotty to help, and by his stubborn determination to find the truth and never give up.

Or maybe they'd saved each other. Both prodigals. Both villains. Both heroes.

Signe. Casper searched for her, found her, surprisingly, standing next to Scotty, being embraced by Ingrid.

As usual, his mother's overlove of everyone had Signe rattled, her face wrecked with tears. "Thank you, Signe," Casper overheard his mother as he came up to them.

"Yeah. Thank you." He didn't know what to do. Hug her? Shake her hand?

"I should have come forward, but I was too afraid and . . . I'm so sorry, Casper."

He drew her into a quick hug. "No, I'm the one who's sorry. I know you cared about Monte."

She held on a little longer, arms around his neck. When she let go, Scotty led her over to the prosecutor to give a proper statement.

"I suppose Owen will have to spend the night in jail?" Max shoved his hands in his pockets.

"I already talked to the judge. He's going to levy a fine, and Owen can be released," Bryce said, walking into their conversation. "Stop by the court offices and pay it, and then go get your crazy brother."

"Hey!" Casper said. "He's not crazy. He's just—"

"Very passionate about what he believes in," Scotty said, returning. She looked at Casper. "I don't suppose you'd spring my boyfriend out of jail?" She wore a half smile, hope in her voice.

"I'll meet you there." Casper's smile lingered, and in it, he hoped she saw forgiveness.

He returned to Raina, lifted Layla from her arms. "How about while I'm at the county clerk's office paying my brother's fine, I pick up a marriage license?"

"You're so romantic, Casper Christiansen," Raina said, grinning.

He wiped a tear from her cheek. "Oh, honey, you haven't seen anything yet."

He hooked his arm around her waist, headed for the door. His mother caught him with a hand on his arm. "I'm making a little celebration lunch," she said, her eyes still misty. "Go get your brother and bring him home, will you?"

"It's what I do."

Here he was, the outcast once again. Owen sat in the cell, his back to the cold wall, wanting to wince as he sorted through his behavior in court.

He should count himself fortunate that they hadn't thrown him to the floor, opened his stitches, and dragged him out in chains.

Clearly he needed to learn to curb his emotions.

In fact, if he'd learned to do that from the beginning . . . to curb his passion for hockey, which had led him away from home . . . Maybe that passion wouldn't have been so terrible if hockey hadn't become his entire life.

If being someone, proving himself, becoming the best, hadn't turned into an obsession. Which led to his trying to prove himself off the ice.

And losing everything.

But he hadn't learned, not even then, still hell-bent on proving that he wasn't a failure, channeling his grief into dangerous and heartbreaking decisions.

Which only left a trail of disaster.

Owen got up, paced the cell. Wow, how he wanted to be different, wanted to have faith. . . .

Except . . . all this time, every impulse had been about . . . him. His hurts, his wounds, his fears, his hopes.

Until now. Until he'd wanted to step in, take Casper's punishment. Because he loved Casper more than himself.

Finally.

For us, Jesus stood in front of death and said, "No. You may not have them. They are what I came for, who I want."

Owen searched for the voice in his memory, found Pastor Dan's sermon.

He proved this by gathering all us wretched prodigals behind Him and spreading out His hands in our defense and paying for our sins.

Owen sank down on the bench.

God hadn't just brought Owen home. He'd forced him to take his focus off his wretched self and see a God who hadn't forsaken him, even when he deserved it.

Even when he'd wanted Him to.

A God who stepped between him and death and said, *No.*

Welcome to grace.

Owen sank his head into his hands. *God, I'm so sorry for the wreck I made of my talent, my life. I ask Your forgiveness. Your redemption. Your wholeness. I ask for a future, being Your returned, redeemed son.*

He closed his eyes, waited, hearing his heartbeat.

Seeing his mistakes.

Except in the dark quiet of the jail, he felt suddenly as if a hand reached in and pulled from his chest a weight he hadn't even realized existed.

He leaned his head back on the cement wall. Breathed. Just breathed.

But I warn you, once you embrace Christ, you too become a rule breaker. Because a life committed to God requires us to live uncomfortably. Inconveniently. Accountably. Bravely. Transparently. Vulnerably.

Whatever You ask, God.

Footsteps. Then Kyle opened the door to the cell. "You're free to go." He stood back. "By the way, welcome home."

Owen got up, met his outstretched hand. "Thanks."

He turned and neatly intercepted Scotty as she ran into his arms, hers going around his neck. "Easy, girl, I'm still—"

"Oh, shut up," she said, pulled his head down, and kissed him.

A full-on, impulsive, passionate, no-holds-barred, emotional kiss.

He wrapped his arms around her waist, dove into her exuberance, and no, didn't feel a smidgen of pain.

When she leaned back, her eyes shone. "We did it. Signe confessed everything."

"Everything? I don't—"

"The short of it is, Monte attacked her and found himself in the ravine of his own devices. He wasn't murdered—he was the author of his own demise."

Her words landed painfully close to his own mistakes.

Thank You, God. Owen pulled Scotty close, just held on.

"You okay?"

"Very," he said into her neck, smelling her amazingly smooth skin. He leaned back. "Thank you for not giving up."

"For having faith?" She winked. "I think . . . I might be starting to, well . . ." She lifted a shoulder. "I used to think faith was for the weak. But I agree it takes strength to have faith, to believe the crazy thought that God would step in, choose us, want us. That He's on our side."

Owen ran his gaze over her face, her smile, trying to catch up to her words. "Yeah, actually, it does."

She pressed her hands to his chest. "So I think I'm ready to start believing in a happy ending."

"Really?"

"Mmm-hmm." She caught his hands, wearing an expectancy on her face.

"What?"

"I'm waiting for you to propose."

"Uh—" He looked around, not sure. "Right here?"

"And now he turns shy."

"I'm not shy! Sheesh—"

"Calm down, Eye Patch. I'm just kidding." She grinned. "C'mon. Your mom's making lunch. Our family is waiting."

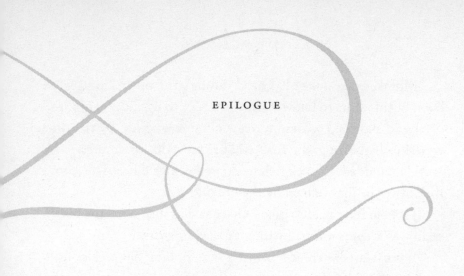

EPILOGUE

INGRID COULDN'T IMAGINE A MORE PERFECT DAY to start a new life.

The late-afternoon sun hung just over the tree line, sending a honey-colored glaze across the deck of the Evergreen lodge. A slight wind reaped the piney scent from the trees, stirred the rich loam embedded in the forest across the lake. Water lapped the shoreline in quiet rhythm, and the fragrance of hamburgers on the grill seasoned the Indian summer air.

The perfect wedding reception for Casper and Raina. Small, intimate. The family celebrating today's after-Sunday-service nuptials.

The timer on the oven beeped, and Ingrid reached for the hot pads, opened the door to retrieve a fresh batch of chocolate chip cookies.

"Mom!" Eden poked her head through the open sliding-glass door. "Dad wants to know if you want him to light the campfire."

Ingrid slid the cookies onto a cooling rack. "Yes. By the time we're finished eating, the coals will be just right for s'mores."

Eden nodded, then closed the door, but Ingrid heard her shout the answer to John, down by the fire pit.

"I should have made a cake," Grace said as she stirred the potato salad. "Who gets married without a wedding cake?"

"It was Casper's choice," Amelia said, pulling dill pickles from a tall jar. "He said that s'mores with Mom's cookies were all Owen talked about in the hospital—well, s'mores and pizza. I think it's his way of saying thank you to Owen."

Ingrid dropped the cookie sheet into the sink and turned on the water. Steam rose and she stood a moment, letting it hide the moisture in her eyes at the memory of Owen standing up with Casper as his best man, Darek beside them, his hand in Tiger's.

And on Raina's side, Grace, Eden, Amelia, and Liza, Raina's aunt, home in time for the long-awaited wedding.

A simple, just-family wedding, the perfect kind, filled with fulfilled promises, the breath of joy, and the rich expectation of happily ever after. All of it written in the look on Casper's face as he watched his bride walk down the aisle. It had made Ingrid slide her hand into John's, give it a squeeze. She'd seen that same deeply overjoyed expression thirty years ago, in the very same church.

Indeed, it seemed as if time might be rewinding with Raina glowing in Ingrid's hand-me-down wedding dress, holding a bouquet of fresh-picked red and orange chrysanthemums, garnished with mountain ash berries, her hair down, barefoot as she approached her groom. Ingrid found herself holding her breath, knowing just how much they had waiting for them. All of them.

Darek and Ivy, Tiger and Joy, moving into their new house at the resort in a matter of weeks.

Jace and Eden, expecting their first child.

Grace and Max, embracing each precious day with their daughter.

Roark, his eyes only for Amelia as he stood beside John and Ingrid in the pew. And why not, after his closed-door conversation with John last night, where he asked for his blessing on his engagement to Amelia.

And Owen and Scotty. Ingrid could hardly believe that God had not only brought her prodigal back to her arms, but also given her another beautiful daughter. Because she knew exactly what was on her youngest son's mind when he'd asked for his grandmother's ring.

Of course he wanted to gift the woman he loved with a family heirloom, entwine her into the legacy of the Christiansens even as they built a life in Alaska. Ingrid couldn't escape the sense that, with the purchase of Scotty's fishing boat, God had plans to turn her son not only into a fisherman, but a fisher of men.

"Mrs. Christiansen?"

A hand slid over her shoulder, and Ingrid grabbed a towel, touched it to her face as she turned. Raina stood there, flowers still pinned to her hair, Layla on her hip. "Casper said to put Layla in your room to nap while we're out on the deck. I hope that's okay?"

And Ingrid couldn't help it. She reached out, pulled Raina into her arms. "*Mom*, Raina. You must call me Mom."

Raina still showed the slightest hesitation to return her hugs. But she'd catch on. Because once you became a Christiansen, you had to get used to being loved large. To belonging to a family that didn't have it all figured out but weathered life, as Owen said, by holding on to faith.

Ingrid leaned back and kissed Layla's cherub cheek. "Sweet dreams."

Grace grabbed the potato salad. "Amelia, bring the paper plates with you, please."

"I can help," Roark said from where he leaned against the doorjamb to the den. In the next room, her boys erupted as someone scored in the current football game. Thankfully the Vikings didn't come on until Monday night or she'd have lost the lot of them to hours of NFL.

"I still don't understand how you can call this *football*." Roark lifted the plate of pickles, grabbed the ketchup. He glanced at Amelia and winked as he carried them outside.

Amelia glowed.

Ingrid knew exactly how that felt.

The front door opened, and Tiger flew through. "Nana! We're here!"

Ivy followed him in, grabbing the door before it could bash another hole in the wall.

"Sorry we're late. I wanted to pick up the fruit salad." Ivy put a bowl on the counter. "I suppose Darek and Joy are watching the game?"

"He fed her and put her down in the boys' room upstairs," Ingrid said, trying not to let the nostalgia overwhelm her. The next generation, napping all over the house. "Could you tell them dinner is about ready?" She glanced outside to where Owen and Scotty manned the grill, just to confirm.

Oops. Scotty sat on the rail of the deck, her feet on the bench of the table, Owen's arms around her, neither of them paying a lick of attention to the smoking grill.

"Avert your eyes, Mom," Grace said. "I'll attempt a rescue of the burgers." She slid the screen door open, and Ingrid hid a smile as she watched Owen jump.

Then John appeared on the deck, raising the lid to the grill, saving the burgers from a charbroil.

Ingrid retrieved the cookies, utensils, and cups and followed Grace outside to finish setting the picnic table. John scooped hamburgers onto a platter. Ivy added her salad to the table, and the boys tromped out from the den. Jace, Max, Darek, Casper, plus little Yulia.

"Sorry, Mom. It's the Packers-Lions game. We got carried away," Casper said.

Ingrid held up a hand. "And now it's time to celebrate."

Casper slipped his hand into Raina's.

Eden leaned against Jace, who wrapped his arms around her belly.

Max took his place between Grace and Yulia, holding their hands.

Roark stood behind Amelia, his hands on her shoulders.

Darek's arm encircled Ivy, the other catching Tiger in a football hold.

And Owen sidled up next to Scotty.

John stood beside Ingrid. "We're going to pray for dinner. But first . . ."

At his elongated pause, Ingrid looked up. He was staring at her, smiling.

"What?"

"We have a little something for you," John said. He glanced at Darek. "You ready?"

Darek released Tiger, who ran off the deck, around the house.

"Where's he going?"

"Just wait, Mom," Casper said. "You're always telling us to be patient. Now it's your turn."

"Believe me, Son, I know all about patience," Ingrid said.

Casper grinned, as did Darek. Ingrid found Owen's gaze on her, something so sweetly vulnerable, sweetly warm in his expression that she pocketed it in her heart.

Patience. Yes, every hour of prayer had come to fruition. Faith answered. Promises kept. Hope fulfilled. At last.

As if reading her thoughts, John leaned down, gave her a kiss on the cheek.

Barking—the high-pitched yips of a puppy.

She turned as Tiger reappeared, running down the walk and onto the porch holding a floppy, wiggly, long-eared, tail-wagging, golden-haired puppy.

"How adorable!" Ingrid knelt down to pet the animal, who was lunging for her now with its puppy tongue. Slobbery kisses landed on her chin, and she laughed. "Tiger, is this your puppy?" She reached up to grab the baby paws and rub its glorious velvety ears. "He's gotten so big!"

"No, Nana. It's yours!"

She stilled. "I . . . don't understand."

John retrieved the dog, chuckling. "The kids got you a puppy."

Got her . . . She stood. "What?"

Eden wore a wide smile. Amelia clasped her hands together, her eyes aglow. Grace waggled her eyebrows. The boys all looked at each other, smug. She half expected a round of high fives.

"For me?"

"It's a sister to Tiger's puppy. Yulia helped pick her out."

Ingrid smiled at her newest granddaughter, who caught her lip in her teeth. "She's beautiful, Yulia."

Grace kissed the top of her daughter's head.

"When we picked up Tiger's puppy, this one was left. No one adopted her, so when the breeder called and asked if we wanted her, I knew she needed a home." Darek walked over, ran his strong hand over the puppy's head. "*This* home."

"I can't believe you got me a puppy," Ingrid said, her eyes watering.

"You still have plenty of good mother in you," Owen said. "And with us out of the house—"

"But not very far away," Casper interjected.

"At least in spirit," Owen said, casting a frown at Casper. "We thought you needed a Butterscotch 2.0."

Oh. Ingrid cupped the puppy's face in her hands, stared into her chocolate eyes, bright, inquisitive. Exuberant with the joy wriggling through her body.

Exactly how Ingrid felt as she stood on the deck, surrounded by so much.

She pulled the puppy into her arms. The puppy climbed Ingrid, putting floppy paws on her shoulders, her cold nose bumping Ingrid's chin. "Oh, my, you are friendly," she said. The puppy slathered her lips and nose with a kiss.

"She loves you already, Mom," Amelia said, coming over to scratch behind the dog's ears. "What's her name?"

"I don't know. Maybe . . . Sunshine?"

"Sunny!" Tiger said. "I like it. Hello, Sunny." He put his face near the puppy's and earned a lick.

Ingrid pressed her nose into the animal's fur. Inhaled. "Thank you." She smiled at her people, the autumn breeze warm on her skin. The watercolor-blue heavens arched overhead, the wind like a song in the trees.

"Let's pray," John said. "The burgers are getting cold." He tucked his arm around Ingrid.

Thank You, indeed.

The ranks closed in, joined hands, and Ingrid breathed in the aroma of home. Puppy breath, hamburgers, the smell of pine in the air, and her entire family chorusing, at the end of John's quick prayer . . .

Amen.

COME HOME TO

the Christiansens,

WHERE FAITH AND FAMILY MEET REAL LIFE.

TURN THE PAGE FOR A PREVIEW OF BOOK 2 IN THE SERIES,
WHERE OWEN'S JOURNEY BEGINS . . .

CHAPTER I

THIS WAS A BAD IDEA—the last person Owen would want to see was his big sister.

It didn't matter. Apparently tonight someone had to watch his back, and that's what sisters did. Eden Christiansen turned up her collar and marched across the street.

Sammy's Bar and Grill hosted one of the largest collections of hockey paraphernalia in Minnesota. The pub had been an old shipping warehouse, its grand windows now lit up with neon beer signs. Inside the brick-and-mortar interior, promo posters, signed pictures, goalie equipment, and framed team sweaters plastered the walls. Flat screens hung from the ceiling and were tucked into every nook, televising games from around the nation.

The owner, Sam Newton, had played eight seasons as a Minnesota

Wild defenseman before being sidelined by a hip injury. Now he lived out the action from behind the long oak bar.

As Eden entered, the sweaty heat and raucous noise flooded over her. The odors of too much cologne, fried foods, and chaos tightened her stomach. Bodies pushed against each other, and she heard the chanting even as she stood at the entrance and looked over the crowd.

"Fight! Fight!"

Perfect. She plowed through the onlookers, ignoring the protests, dreading what she heard—the familiar sounds of men hitting each other, laughing, huffing as they tumbled onto the floor.

She reached the edge of the brawl and there he was. Owen, power forward for the St. Paul Blue Ox, with a button ripped off his shirt, his long hair over his face, his nose bleeding, writhing as right wing Maxwell Sharpe caught him in a headlock.

"Tap out!" Max yelled.

Oh no. Eden watched as Owen flipped him over, broke free, and found his feet, his eyes too bright.

"Eden!" Kalen caught her arm. "We have to get him out of here." He wore a black Blue Ox T-shirt, a plastic lei around his neck. And he had cut his hair into what looked like a Mohawk. Nice.

"Where are his keys?"

"Jace took them. He's at the bar. I'll get Owen's coat."

She turned and found the hulking form of Jace "J-Hammer" Jacobsen sitting at the bar.

Someone, probably the Blue Ox PR department, had tamed the beast, at least for tonight, dressing him up like a gentleman in a pair of black wool pants and a silver dress shirt with the sleeves rolled up over his strong, sculpted forearms. Up close, she could admit that—for others—he possessed a raw-edged, almost-dangerous allure that might have the ability to steal a girl's breath. Maybe *Hockey Today* magazine hadn't been completely wrong about putting him in its lineup. His dark, curly hair fell in tangles behind his ears, as if groomed by a fierce wind, and he'd close-trimmed his dark beard. His fitted dress shirt only accentuated all his cut muscle and brawn, but she knew he had the finesse of a skater, smooth and liquid on blades. And his eyes—blue as ice—yes, they could look right through a gal, send a shiver through her.

But Eden was immune to Mr. J-Trouble and his apparently lethal smile. Because she wasn't a rink bunny, wasn't a crazed fan. Wasn't dazzled by the star power of one of hockey's top enforcers. She was family, thank you, here for one reason only.

Owen.

Yes, Eden was made of ice, and Trouble hadn't a prayer of thawing her anger. She marched up to Jace. "Nice birthday bash. If Owen gets in trouble and kicked back down to the AHL, it's on you."

"Hey!" Jace turned, looking backhanded.

But she didn't plan on listening to his lame excuses. "You're the team captain. Who else is supposed to watch Owen's back?"

He rebounded fast. "Are you kidding me? You're not his mother or his trainer. He's just blowing off steam. Trust me. Your brother can watch his own back."

"Really? This is watching his own back?" She gestured at Owen, who had grabbed an eager girl, begun to slow dance. If that's what she could call it. "Who gave him alcohol, anyway?"

"Seriously?"

"He's underage. He doesn't turn twenty-one for three months." Jace raised a brow at that.

"Yeah, that's right. And if he makes the papers—"

But Jace's eyes tracked past her, to the door.

Eden followed his gaze. And the terrible roaring of anger inside stopped on the burly image of Ramsey Butler, Blue Ox manager, sliding into a booth.

Kalen appeared with Owen's coat. "You distract Butler, Eden, and we'll get Owen out the back."

She gaped at him. "*Distract* him? How?"

Jace slid off the stool, towering nearly a foot over her. "Flirt with him or something."

Flirt—oh, for crying out loud. "Fine. Get Owen to his car, but don't let him drive." She shrugged out of her coat and draped it over the chair. Flirt. Right . . . But what choice did she have? As long as this was the one and only time. Besides, truth was, she would do anything to protect Owen's future.

She looked like a mortician in her black pants and white blouse, but maybe Butler wouldn't notice. She still had game, right? After all, tonight she'd had a date.

Maybe she was hotter than she thought. Eden put a little sashay into her walk, feeling stupid, but making her way to the booth. "Hello there, Mr. Butler. Nice to see you tonight."

In his midforties, Butler had his own reputation to manage—the kind that traded players midseason and fired those who embarrassed the newborn franchise. Eden managed not to look behind her as she stood at the booth, blocking his view of Owen. She added a smile, propped a hand on her hip. Tried to look . . . flirty.

He looked up from where he perused the menu. "I'll take an appetizer basket of curly fries and a Guinness on tap."

She stilled. "Huh?"

"And what are your specials?"

So much for flirting. She glanced at the chalkboard over the bar. "Uh, fish-and-chips and a cheddar bratwurst?"

"I'll just have the bacon cheeseburger."

"Good choice. How do you want that done?" Now she glanced back and saw Kalen with his arm over Owen, directing him through the kitchen entrance.

"Rare. And bring out some of Sam's special mayo sauce."

"You got it."

She quick-walked to the bar, grabbed her parka, and stepped out into the frigid cold.

Jace stood over Owen, barring him from opening his car door. Owen put up a meager fight, then let Kalen maneuver him to the passenger seat and buckle him in.

Eden shook her head and held out her hand. Jace set the keys in it.

She closed her hand around them. "I know I should say thanks, but frankly, you should do better. You're some *captain*. Is this how you take care of your players? Or maybe this is what you want— for them to all turn out like *you*." Then she opened the door and climbed in, ignoring Jace's glare. "Owen, what were you—?"

Owen turned to her, wearing a green expression. And then his double-mushroom-and-Swiss cheeseburger, curly fries, and about a fifth of whiskey mixed with the sweet syrup of Coke landed on her lap.

"Thanks for coming to get me, Sis."

HAVE YOU EVER MADE A TERRIBLE MISTAKE? Or worse, sinned big, deliberately or not? I have. There are moments in my life that I look back on with a terrific shudder and think . . . *Who was I, and how could I have done that?*

Our first response—at least mine—is to run. Maybe not physically, like Owen, but definitely to flee from the pain of our failures. Of disappointing those we love. Of seeing ourselves in the mirror and wondering who we are.

We run from the guilt. From the truth. From God . . . and especially from forgiveness. Because we look at ourselves honestly and, like Peter in Luke 5:8, say, "Oh, Lord, please leave me—I'm too much of a sinner to be around you."

Faced with such truth, we see only that. A sinner. Unredeemable. Unable to accept anything but condemnation.

But God will not allow us to stay in that place. He is a pursuer, and even as we push Him away, He says, *"You are not alone. If you will allow Me, I will fix this."*

The words are beautiful—and yet brutal because even the touch of grace is a living ember, and we are reluctant to grasp hold, to bring it to ourselves, to bear the fiery cleansing. Easier to endure is the self-flogging, the shame, the guilt. Because that, we know we deserve.

It was from this place that I launched out on Owen's journey. From the first, Owen knows he is wretched. He is fully aware of his sins and the destruction in his wake but is unable to face it or fix it. Even after he realizes his folly and begins the crawl back to faith, it is more words and hope than reality.

Owen sees grace but hasn't accepted it.

In his estimation, he owed God everything. And yes,
he could agree that in the face of his sins, grace felt a bit
too overwhelming. It almost seemed easier to live like
Scotty—alone, unbeholden to God.

Because a God who dispensed grace was a God a
person couldn't bargain with.

Except perhaps that was the point. God didn't want
to bargain.

See, grace is free, but without our ability to bargain for our freedom, we are left wondering exactly what we have to give. More, even when we step under the mantle of grace, it feels too heavy upon our shoulders.

Like Owen, it could be that we've been prodigals so long, we can't see any other visage in the mirror. The question becomes *Who am I beyond the prodigal?*

We are the redeemed. The forgiven. The sons and daughters of the King.

Suddenly we can rise, look forward into a new dawn, glorious and rose gold, full of promise. And it is this view that changes everything. Because what are we to do with the unblemished future? As Pastor Dan says:

> "I warn you, once you embrace Christ, you too become
> a rule breaker. Because a life committed to God requires
> us to live uncomfortably. Inconveniently. Accountably.
> Bravely. Transparently. Vulnerably."

We are the bold, the fishermen, the warriors of Christ, going forth to tell the world the truth of grace. Of redemption. Of second chances and fresh starts and happy endings.

As John Christiansen would say, "Some of God's best players were His imperfect, broken prodigals."

When I conceived this series, I wanted a story about real people dealing with real issues of faith and family. I didn't want to shy away from the mistakes but to tell a story about a family that faces its share of darkness . . . and discovers a God who is standing at the doorway—even more, launching out in relentless pursuit with the goal of bringing us home.

Thank you for reading the Christiansen Family series. I pray that you, too, have heard the call of grace, let it into your heart, and found your way home.

Grace to you!
Susan May Warren

SUSAN MAY WARREN is the bestselling, Christy and RITA Award–winning author of more than forty novels whose compelling plots and unforgettable characters have won acclaim with readers and reviewers alike. She served with her husband and four children as a missionary in Russia for eight years before she and her family returned home to the States. She now writes full-time as her husband runs a resort on Lake Superior in northern Minnesota, where many of her books are set.

Susan holds a BA in mass communications from the University of Minnesota. Several of her critically acclaimed novels have been ECPA and CBA bestsellers, were chosen as Top Picks by *Romantic Times*, and have won the RWA's Inspirational Reader's Choice contest and the American Christian Fiction Writers' prestigious Carol Award. Her novels *You Don't Know Me* and *Take a Chance on Me* were Christy Award winners, and six of her other books have also been finalists. In addition to her writing, Susan loves to teach and speak at women's events about God's amazing grace in our lives.

For exciting updates on her new releases, previous books, and more, visit her website at www.susanmaywarren.com.

DISCUSSION QUESTIONS

1. Ingrid's letter details Owen's strengths but also cautions him about his weaknesses. How do you see the traits she highlights play out in Owen's story? Is there someone in your life who has similar insight into your character—the good and the bad? How has that person's wisdom affected you?

2. In her letter, Ingrid tells Owen, "God has a special place in His heart for messy, passionate, live-out-loud people. The young. The inexperienced. The blindly brave. The ones who dive in, not looking back, believing they can slay giants with a stone." Do you think this is true? Later, John lists a few people from the Bible who fit this description: "Rahab, the prostitute; Samson, the playboy; Paul, the terrorist; and Peter . . . the impulsive." Can you think of other examples, from Scripture or from your own experience?

3. After nearly two years of running from his mistakes, Owen wishes he could go home, that he could repair the damage he's done, but thinks it's impossible. Have you ever felt the same way—stuck between a longing to make things right and a belief that it's too late? What was the outcome?

What parallels do you see between Owen's story—and Casper's—and the biblical parable of the Prodigal Son? (See Luke 15:11-32 for the story.)

4. Scotty distrusts emotion, adopting a "no crying" rule for her life. This has affected not only her relationships with other people, but her perception of faith. She tells Owen, "Being a Christian makes you weak. Makes you . . . emotional." Do you tend to equate emotion with weakness? How would you respond to Scotty?

5. As he and Scotty drift at sea, uncertain whether they'll be rescued, Owen makes an impulsive proposal . . . and Scotty impulsively accepts. What consequences does this have once they're rescued? Have you ever made a rash promise in the heat of a moment? When that moment passed, did you follow through or look for a way out?

6. Scotty has convinced herself that she's not "marriage material." What does she mean by that? How do other characters respond to her pronouncement? What, in your opinion, makes someone marriage material?

7. Watching how Casper and Owen interact, Scotty observes, "People who loved each other that much knew how to wound the deepest." Do you agree? How do Casper and Owen bring out the best and worst in each other? Have you seen similar dynamics with your own siblings or between siblings you know?

8. Several characters struggle to advise Owen, Casper, and Raina on the right thing to do in their complicated situation. Some believe Owen and Raina, as Layla's parents, should get

married; others, that Raina and Casper should marry since they love each other and want to raise Layla together. How would you have advised them in these circumstances? What did you think of the decision they ultimately make?

9. Owen was forced, by consequences of his own bad choices, to give up the life he'd dreamed of, and in this story he really grieves that loss for the first time. What do you think his life would've been like if he'd never been injured? What parts of his life might have been better . . . or worse?

10. As he sits in a jail cell, Casper angrily thinks that he has "come home, swept up Owen's mess, fixed everything. And this is how life—how God—repaid him." Is he justified in feeling this way? Have you ever felt similar bitterness at your circumstances, or even at God for those circumstances? Looking back at that time, do you still feel the same way, or has your perspective changed?

11. In his sermon, Pastor Dan says, "A life committed to God requires us to live uncomfortably. Inconveniently. Accountably. Bravely. Transparently. Vulnerably. It requires us to love without rules. Welcome to grace." Is this an accurate picture of the Christian life? What does it mean to "love without rules"? What characters in this story embody this kind of love?

12. Which Christiansen sibling do you identify with most? Who would you turn to in time of need? What about for a laugh and encouragement? Picture the Christiansen family five or ten years down the road. What do you think their future holds?

MORE GREAT FICTION

· FROM ·

SUSAN MAY WARREN